Book Two of Magick

THE GOD-KING'S FALL

Derry Wadham

Copyright © 2019 by Mr Derry Wadham.
All rights reserved.
This book or any portion thereof may not be reproduced or used in any manner whatsoever without express written permission by the author, except for the use of brief quotations in a book review.

This is a work of fiction.
Names, characters, places and incidents are either the products of the author's imagination or are used fictitiously. Any resemblance to actual persons, living or dead, businesses, companies, events or locales is entirely coincidental.

Chapter One

Clomping angrily down the stairs, Kristina shivered and cursed herself repeatedly for leaving the heating down too low the night before.

Glaring at the thermostat, her breath fogged from her mouth as she flipped the dial to twenty before stalking into the living room.

Looking at the pre-prepared fireplace, she focused on the logs that were set securely on top of the kindling in readiness for what she was about to do.

'*Ambustum*,' she growled, visualising the fire roaring into life a moment before it did so.

Staring into the flames, she suddenly noticed how the logs had been arranged and tried to recall preparing them the night before.

'They are placed *his* way,' she thought, studying the way in which they had been positioned.

She always laid the logs across the grate and not from back to front in the way he had shown her. Looking at their positioning now, 'his way' was better, she knew, seeing that the logs would not slip or roll from the fire when the kindling began to shift. But that was *his* way, not hers, and this was *her* house, regardless of how 'it' felt about that.

Shaking her head, she put it down to her rather tipsy condition the night before and shrugged it off as she did with most things.

Picking up the empty bottle of wine, she entered the kitchen to brew herself some tea. The house was still cold and she fumed at herself for turning the heating off, wondering why on earth she kept doing these annoying little things.

Reaching for the bread, she put four slices into the toaster and pushed the lever down. Yawning loudly, she made her tea and buttered a piece of toast with Marmite before taking a large bite. Sighing with pleasure, her taste buds exploded with the tantalising flavour. Washing it down with a mouthful of tea, she headed back into the living room.

Setting the toast down upon the coffee table, she turned to the sofa and froze, her eyes widening in disbelieving dread.

'Kristina!' a deep voice growled, sounding low and terrible in the morning silence. 'You've been a very, very naughty little girl,' it continued, speaking the words in a very impressive Lastat accent which would normally have made her laugh but for the one who had spoken them.

She could only stare back at that moment, seeing the fire dancing in his eyes as it had done before he had left. She could sense his dark aura still, knowing absolutely that he was still the monster who terrified her.

He was not the wild-eyed creature she had seen the year before, however. She realised with rising dread that he had now grown into whatever it was he was turning into.

'At least he looks human,' she thought, even though her instincts screamed for her to run.

'Oh my god! You're alive!' she squeaked at last, the colour in her face draining to white.

The smile on his face faltered at her reaction and his eyes narrowed as he took a step towards her.

Still frozen to the spot, she felt like a child with her hand caught in a cookie jar, and try as she might, she could not escape the feeling that something awful was going to happen.

'You don't seem happy to see me,' he observed, looking at her coldly. 'Why is that, I wonder?' he asked, causing her to freeze like a rabbit in the headlights.

She needed to speak and was about to when she heard the front door open and her friend's voice ring out.

'Hey! It opened the first time!' Janet laughed, closing the door behind her.

Walking from the hallway, she stopped suddenly with her mouth open to say more and dropped the small box she was carrying in alarm.

Turning in her direction, Daire whispered at her, but there was no mistaking the cold authority in his tone.

'This is not a good time for you, Janet. You had better leave,' he advised, though it sounded more like a threat than a request.

Kristina was surprised at how human he appeared all of a sudden and felt confused as to the reason behind it.

Thinking her friend to be vulnerable, Janet seized the opportunity and lifted her chin in defiance.

'I will stay if you don't mind. Kristina and the kids need me,' she replied, walking further into the room.

Daire's dark eyes twinkled mischievously as a slow smile played across his lips.

'Oh, but I do mind, for it is I who decides who and what my children need. Now, leave, or I will *make* you leave,' he replied, the threat now unmistakable in his voice.

Kristina looked on in silence, her head felt fuzzy. It was all happening too quickly for her. All she could think of was how human he appeared and she felt as though she were being blocked from speaking about it out loud.

'Why does he look so human?' she thought dizzyingly, trying to make sense of the change in him. Her mind simply refused to process the information.

'They have a loving family around them and are far better protected now that our circle is complete. They don't need the *legendary* Dark Wolf,' Janet retorted, her pale face reddening as she spoke.

Daire's eyes widened in shock at the mention of the circle and stared at her in silence before finally turning to Kristina.

'What?' he asked, looking at her with pain in his eyes. 'You didn't?' he gasped, his face seeming to crease with the signs of betrayal.

Kristina's response was quick and precise, with her tone rising the longer she spoke.

'You were not here, Daire! I thought you to be dead and there have been vampires here… Bloods!' she cried, puffing out the last words as her breath gave way.

Picking up where her friend left off, Janet continued relentlessly.

'We are more powerful now, and you are no longer required,' she sneered, standing before him with a confident smirk.

'You dare to tell me that *my* children don't need me?' he growled, although lacking the customary boom of thunder.

Kristina heard a door closing quietly upstairs and knew immediately that it was the house protecting the children from what it knew must surely come.

'Please! Both of you, just calm down. Jan! Stop it, please!' she cried, desperately trying to dissolve the situation.

Ignoring her, Janet's face was now a crimson mask of rage as she spread her arms wide.

'My power comes from my coven, your children included!' she spat, sweeping her arms forward suddenly in his direction. 'I will defeat you with your children's power,' she crowed, whispering a spell of binding and wrapping it about him.

'What are you doing?' he gasped, feeling the binding take hold of him as he looked to Kristina with concern. 'You would allow her to do this to me?' he asked, straining in the effort to break the invisible bonds.

Kristina looked from his accusing eyes to her friend's elated, power-hungry glare and began to struggle with the indecision of what she wanted to do.

'You see, Kris? He's not so powerful,' Janet gloated, madness flashing in her pale blue eyes. 'I've conquered him easily,' she scoffed, feeling a flush of pleasure at having him at her mercy.

Daire closed his eyes in concentration, seemingly attempting to break the hold upon him before opening them again in what looked like defeat.

'I don't deserve this, Kris! All I want is to protect them, as you do,' he whispered, staring at her with pleading eyes.

Janet clapped her hands together ecstatically.

'He can't break my binding!' she squealed, overwhelmed by her mastery over the previously forbidden art. 'His power lies in the summoning of others to do his dirty work, he has no true power of his own,' she screamed, binding him tighter with a gesture of her hand.

Shaking her head in warning, Kristina stepped forward in alarm.

'He has, Jan! I've seen it!' she cried, looking back at him suspiciously. But Janet seemed not to hear, for she was so caught up in her dominance over him.

'Are you going to allow her to hurt me?' Daire asked, causing Janet to scream in fury and cast yet more spells to silence him.

Not liking the look on her friend's face, Kristina shook her head and took another step forward.

'Is our circle so powerful?' she thought, nervously excited by the prospect but fearful of a trap.

Daire lowered his head and closed his eyes, seemingly to succumb to the witch's will at last.

'I can cast him away from here, Kris. He need never bother us again. Or, maybe, we should just kill him?' Janet asked, the mad look growing stronger in her eyes.

Shaking her head, Kristina knew then that this had gone far enough and immediately made her decision.

'Janet, stop! Stop it right now!' she demanded, taking another step forward.

Anger flared anew in her friend's eyes, but it was no longer directed at Daire as she turned to Kristina.

'You would let him take them away from us? You are no longer able to make that decision, Kiki!' she snarled, speaking the words through her gritted teeth, causing spittle to gather at the corners of her mouth. 'They are ours now and the goddess allowed it. We are more powerful now than we could ever have dreamed and it's all because of the kids,' she growled, glancing briefly to the vanquished man.

Kristina's face paled at her friend's confession and her voice cracked like a whip in response.

'They are mine!' she snapped, raising her hands to cast a shield about herself. 'And they are his!' she added, taking a protective stance between them.

Janet looked at her childhood friend and shook her head slowly.

'You don't know how wrong you are, Kris! You gave them to us,' she sneered, slowly raising her hands.

Kristina opened her mouth to speak, but the shock of what she was hearing rocked her to the core. She found herself wondering why the house had not acted in Daire's defence but found that she could not process all of what was happening at once.

'You've come here to take them?' she asked, speaking with a note of panic in her voice.

Janet smiled coldly and nodded her head once.

'You can come too, of course, but I will not be leaving without them. You can be replaced if need be, but not them. Do you even know the magick they possess?' she asked as power-hungry lust contorted her features.

Tears came to Kristina's eyes, but not from weakness as her friend now thought. She was about to speak when her friend continued.

'You didn't even feel the disturbance last night, did you?' Janet asked, disgust creasing her mouth as she shook her head in answer. 'We did, and knew that something was up,' she continued, stabbing a finger in Daire's direction.

Kristina looked at him and whispered in a self-loathing voice.

'I've been drinking in the nights,' she confessed, feeling a flush of guilt reddening her cheeks.

At her words, his head raised and he gave her a reassuring smile but she shook her head, refusing his forgiveness.

'I am so sorry,' she whispered, raising her hands against her friend in his defence.

Still looking at her, Daire shrugged and then smiled wryly with a shake of his head.

'Better late than never, I suppose,' he admonished her as his smile grew wider. 'I forgive you,' he rumbled in his thunderous tone, the illusion of humanity washing from him in an instant.

Screaming in rage, Janet threw more bindings at him in an attempt to keep him subdued.

'How can you speak? I've bound you!' she screamed, looking as though she were about to attack him physically.

Turning his head towards her, he saw her anger turn to dread as his eyes took hold of her, the power of his gaze sending her to her knees.

'Game over,' he rumbled, his voice deeper and more sinister than ever it had been. He began to swell before her, his true devilish appearance coming suddenly to the fore. 'Your coven is broken,' he announced, bringing his previously hidden might to the fore with a deafening clap of thunder from above.

Kristina threw her hands to her mouth, the truth of the situation finally dawning upon her.

'No! Please, Daire!' she cried, dread for her friend sweeping through her. 'She's lost control of the magick! This isn't her!' she cried, knowing absolutely what his wrath would demand.

Ignoring her plea, he turned his reflective, hellish glare upon Janet.

'In attacking me with all the power from your precious little coven, I have seen all those connected to it and have now added myself into the mix,' he informed as he smiled an evil smile through his clenched teeth.

Spreading his arms, he showed then that he was unbound from her magick, or, more likely, that he never was.

'My turn!' he announced as the vicious smile faded from his face. 'Now for the reckoning!' he roared, closing his hand slowly into a fist as the sound of ripping rent the air.

Dread filled Kristina in the understanding that the circle was not so much being broken as it was being crushed, and done so in the most brutal way imaginable.

A wave of dizziness hit her suddenly, forcing her to reach out to steady herself against the wall.

Feeling none of the agony that was clearly inflicted upon her friend, she watched through blurred vision as Janet's hair began to whiten and her skin dry into a shrivelled-looking leather.

Horrified beyond reason, she bore witness to her friend's silent agony as the circle was broken in one brutal attack, and she understood that what was happening now was what the goddess had hinted at after its creation.

The dizziness began to recede suddenly, giving her some sense of clarity as she looked from her friend to Daire, wishing immediately that she had not.

Believing that she had already seen a glimpse of what he was hiding within him, she knew at that moment that she had not even scratched the surface.

His appearance shifted suddenly, turning into a nightmarish creature that stood towering over them. She took in the blackness of his flesh and the reflective catlike eyes that caused her own to widen in fear.

Within the blink of an eye, he was himself again, but she had seen the truth in that dreadful moment and knew that what she had seen was his true form, his true nature.

Gasping suddenly, she felt her connection to the circle break and felt immediately and surprisingly lighter after the separation.

She understood that some witches may die in time and knew that a circle, though weaker without all thirteen, would, nevertheless, remain powerfully unbroken without them.

'Yet, he has destroyed it! Crushing it in his hand like a dried leaf,' she thought, desperately trying to get to grips with what had just happened but still not trusting herself to believe it.

'What have you done?' she gasped, even though she already knew the answer.

'I have undone your sin,' he growled, still speaking in his thunderous tone, the dark, unrestrained power finally getting the better of him.

She could almost feel the rage emanating off him and saw him try to fight it, struggling in the attempt to contain the desire that seemed to shine ominously in his eyes.

Breathing out a deep, venting breath of air, Daire closed his eyes in the attempt to cool the wanton violence he envisioned in his mind.

'The house told me of what you did, and of what you allowed to happen!' he seethed, causing her to flinch back a step. 'If not for my sweet little girl...' he continued, seeming to calm a little at the mere mention of his daughter.

Kristina flicked her eyes nervously to her friend who lay motionless upon the floor and then back to him in absolute horror.

'How?' she thought, unable to comprehend how he had achieved the impossible. How had he crushed the coven and destroyed their circle?

He seemed to read the question in her eyes and nodded at her with a glower.

'Until Daddy comes home,' he answered, the wild, untameable light flashing again in his eyes and looking like that of lightning in the blackness of night. 'That was the deal you made with our daughter, was it not?' he asked, more in control of himself at last.

Kristina looked up with a flush of guilt reddening her cheeks and nodded silently, having not the words to defend herself.

Looking up at him, she could see that his once dark-brown hair was now black as pitch, as was the visible flesh of his face, that even now in the early-morning light seemed to be cast in shadow. But it was those reflective eyes that she feared the most.

Somewhere in the back of her mind, she took in his strange attire and noted the loose-knit top that seemed to be made from some unknown black fabric that absorbed the light as he did. She saw that it had an abnormally large neckline that stopped halfway across his trapezius muscles and saw those muscles flex suddenly before disappearing beneath the weave of the clothing.

Her eyes did not wander out of attraction, for those days had long since passed, she looked now out of fear, like seeing the stripes of a tiger before its attack.

'Did it need to be so painful?' she sobbed, looking again at her fallen friend.

Following her line of sight, he shrugged uncaringly as he shook his head.

'No,' he replied with a sinister widening of his mouth. 'I caused the pain for my own gratification,' he admitted, causing her head to turn back in horror.

Appalled by his confession, her hand flew to her mouth and she began to cry pitifully.

'I kill those that would harm my children,' he seethed, turning his attention back to her.

Swallowing hard, the colour drained from her face as she raised her hands defensively before her.

'Don't you know me, woman?' he asked, his voice deepening to roll from him like thunder. 'I have zero tolerance for those that would abuse my children, and give no second chances to those that would kill them,' he continued, the words growling from deep within his chest. He stopped then, his eyes reflecting the light coldly back at her. 'Except in regard to you, it would seem,' he added, shaking his head in disappointment.

Pausing, he closed his eyes and fought for the calm that seemed so elusive to him.

'After being attacked in my own house by that stupid cow!' he continued, glaring down at her friend, 'I chose to destroy rather than to break,' he finished, with every exhale of breath sounding like a rumbling growl.

Appalled, she involuntarily backed away from him, shaking her head in denial.

'You caused her that pain, intentionally?' she asked, unable to hide her judgemental tone.

His eyes took on a feral look and his human appearance began dissolving as he replied.

'Indeed I did!' he hissed, his eyes beginning to shine like some hellish hound from hell itself.

She stared back in dread as he fully transformed right in front of her.

'Had you not stepped up in my defence at the last, you might very well have joined her,' he growled with venom, his black head now almost touching the ceiling.

Kristina backed away from his wrath, keeping her hands fearfully out before her.

'Please, Daire, don't hurt me,' she cried, backing up towards the doorway, but then stopped suddenly, unwilling to retreat any further. 'You will not hurt them,' she declared, staring up fiercely as she closed the door from behind her, sealing both of them in.

'Daire?' he asked, shaking his head in confusion. 'Daire is dead!' he growled, towering over her without a trace of humanity. 'You saw to that!' he hissed, spreading his arms wide as he showed her at last what he truly was.

Casting her shield, she cried out for help in the hope that her home would protect her.

'House? Help me, please?' she wailed, and sent out a blast of lightning that struck him in the chest. 'I will die before I let you hurt them!' she screamed, anger suddenly replacing her fear.

Daire grimaced and looked at her in amazement before brushing absently at his undamaged clothing.

'It is *you* that keeps hurting them,' he snarled, incensed by her attack.

Kristina's eyes widened imperceptibly as a thought suddenly struck her. Lowering her hands, she dropped her shield and simply stood there, causing him to tilt his head suspiciously.

'Cesca and Lucian are in my bed,' she said, staring up into his cold, reflective eyes. 'They are sleeping now, but will be waking at any minute,' she continued, studying his face as she spoke.

Daire peered up suddenly to stare at the ceiling and closed his eyes as he sniffed at the air.

'Lucian is in your bed, but Cesca is in mine,' he replied softly, shaking his monstrous head. 'What you saw of her was an illusion, for it was she who called me back last night,' he informed her proudly, smiling at his daughter's guile.

The unnatural depthless quality of his flesh began to recede suddenly and she saw again the shadow of the man she had known. After a time, the darkness gave way to more human-coloured tones and the white eyes darkened once again.

'Is that likely to happen again?' she asked on his return, her back still pressed up tightly against the door.

Surprising her, he smiled, far warmer than she had anticipated, and shrugged at her defensively.

'You stop putting my children in harm's way and I will stop hulking out, agreed?' he asked, frowning at her once again. 'You got off lightly. Nothing like a witch-hunt to stir my blood, obviously I was going to be a bit testy after what she tried to pull,' he continued, glancing at her friend with a look of distaste.

'Bloody *testy*?' she challenged, putting her hands to her hips in her trademark show of irritation.

'I was attacked and lost control. Sue me!' he grumbled, folding his arms defensively across his chest. 'I have always reacted in that way when attacked,' he explained, looking at her as though she knew this already.

Kristina's eyes widened and her face flushed a deep red before she stared at him incredulously.

'You were going to kill me, you bugger!' she exploded, looking as though she was about to hit him.

Pulling a doubtful expression, he grimaced at her as he shook his head.

'You are being overdramatic!' he replied, rolling his eyes at her. 'And you were defending that hag anyway, so who could blame me if I was!' he accused, gesturing towards the defeated witch that still lay sprawled upon the floor.

Kristina was dumbfounded by his manner and looked back at him in astonishment.

'So that's grounds for ending my life?' she demanded, her eyes full of hurt.

'You have put the children in continuous danger! *You* first let them into my room to practise magick even though I told you of the dangers. *You* forcefully bound them into your pathetic coven, even though I expressly forbid it, and *you* took them into the forest even though I warned you not to,' he stormed, spreading his arms in exasperation. 'I mean, why shouldn't I kill you?' he asked, but smiled when her eyes widened further. 'Look, after she attacked me, my blood was up and I just hulked out for a second,' he explained at last, shrugging his shoulders apologetically. 'What's a man to do?' he asked, spreading his arms helplessly.

Kristina's reply was sharp, precise and to the point.

'Not bloody kill me, you sod!' she stormed, just as a moan from the floor caused them both to look down.

Immediately crouching down, Kristina instinctively reached out to help her friend rise as Daire stood where he was, watching with a look of disbelief.

Looking to have aged many decades in those painful few seconds, Janet appeared old and bent as she fearfully looked up towards him.

'What have you done to me?' she shrilled, leaning heavily against Kristina for support.

With his hands clasped behind him and his legs spread apart, Daire replied to her in an uncaring tone of voice.

'My guess would be that I've broken the unbreakable and destroyed that which was blessed,' he replied, smiling down without humour.

Kristina could see the shadow of the monster in him again and gave him a 'you dare' look that caused him to check himself.

After a moment, he nodded to her reassuringly and smiled a little awkwardly.

'I ripped my family away first, of course,' he continued offhandedly, his smile widening at the old woman's expression.

Janet glared at him with pure hatred, before glancing down at her liver-spotted hands.

'What else?' she spat, incensed by his cavalier attitude.

Shrugging mockingly, he appeared to ponder the question.

'Hmm, let me see… I stripped you of your power, which was not yours to begin with…' he answered, and then as though almost forgetting something, he added the final admission, 'oh, and aged you to the point of death,' he sighed, winking at her mischievously.

Her grey-blue eyes filled with tears at that and she began to cry pitifully in her friend's consoling arms.

'Why? I don't deserve this!' she wailed, looking up at Kristina beseechingly.

'Because I don't leave enemies alive, Jan, and you have become my enemy. You will not be given a second chance at my children,' he replied with the soft rumbling of distant thunder in his tone. 'You were on borrowed time after deserting my son anyway, be thankful of the time you had,' he remarked, all amusement fading from him at that last comment.

Janet cackled madly and shook her head wildly as the mad glint returned to her eyes.

'My sisters will find a way to undo this, and then we will take our sweet revenge on you!' she replied bitterly, her breath beginning to rattle in her chest.

Sticking his bottom lip out in mock sympathy, he shook his head with a sad expression.

'I'm afraid that your sisters have fared no better than yourself,' he assured her as his malicious smile spread across his face.

She stared hard at him, trying to read the truth in his eyes.

'You didn't?' she gasped, falling back again into Kristina's supportive arms.

Continuing his mockingly sad nod, he pouted his lip again.

'Oh, I'm afraid that I did,' he admitted, seeming to enjoy the moment. 'I don't leave enemies alive,' he repeated, nodding at her seriously this time.

Kristina looked up at him sternly, stroking the old woman's head in an attempt to soothe her.

'You have overreacted again! Why did you have to go this far?' she wept, distraught at the plight of her friend.

He shrugged again, infuriating her further, but his darkening expression stilled her reactive tongue.

'I don't believe that I did overreact! I was attacked, albeit foolishly, but attacked nonetheless, and in doing so, she gave me free rein to do as I pleased!' he replied, turning to her with an unrepentant glare.

Kristina was about to respond when a thought occurred to her and her eyes widened again.

'You intended for this to happen!' she cried, gesturing to her friend. 'You wanted her to attack you, didn't you, you fiend? And don't bloody shrug again,' she warned, throwing caution to the wind.

A slow, mischievous smile spread across his face and she knew then that she was right.

'Indeed, I did,' he confessed, smiling more coldly this time. 'My power allows me to witness things that would otherwise go unseen, and after sensing their awareness touch the house last night, I rode it back to its source. Cesca refused to go to bed after summoning me, and so slept in my arms for most of the night. I used that time to commune with the house and learn all there was to know. When I eventually put her in my bed, I sought the knowledge of your beloved coven's intentions,' he continued, pointing down at Janet.

'Daire truly is dead,' Kristina thought tragically, seeing only a fraction of the man standing before her.

'How did you know?' Janet asked, causing Kristina to look down at her in confusion.

Daire turned and put two fingers to his temple and then twisted them as though unlocking a door inside his head.

'*Unagi*,' he replied with a solemn expression and then smiled again in amusement.

'This is not the time for humour!' Kristina exploded, causing him to smile all the more.

Janet's breath shallowed and she slumped back to the floor, causing Kristina to look up at him beseechingly.

'Please don't kill her! She was seduced by the magick but it won't happen again. Please, Daire, please?' she cried, clearly afraid of losing her one and only friend.

Staring back at her at that moment, all the good-humour faded from his eyes.

'You are right about one thing, Kris. It will not happen again,' he confirmed, looking down again suggestively.

Her eyes followed his instinctively and she sobbed at seeing the still form of her lifelong friend.

'No!' she wailed, clutching at Janet in desperation, shaking her softly as though to wake her.

'She died for what she was going to do to you, and the abuse intended on our children,' he whispered, saddened a little by her apparent pain. 'Everything I do is for a good reason,' he added coldly, turning his back on her show of emotion.

Running from the room, Kristina wept at her feeling of loss. Believing that she was now all alone in the world, she began to cry out her heartache. Feeling unable to be in the same room as him and what was left of her friend, she felt a desperate need to escape.

The back door seemed to beckon to her but it was a path that she could never take, she realised, knowing that she was anchored to this place as he was.

'The children,' she moaned, knowing that she could never leave them. 'He's killed Janet,' she sobbed, the shock of what he had done slowly sinking in.

Looking up, she heard the front door open and felt a vacuum of cold air lift the hair from her shoulders. Peering into the hallway, she could see him close the door again and walk back in her direction.

Not knowing what else to do, she turned back to the window and saw the wind pick up suddenly, blowing discoloured leaves past the glass in front of her.

'Bloody hell,' she cried, pressing her face up against the windowpane before jumping back in fright. 'Good god!' she gasped, seeing what could only be a tornado forming just outside the house. 'What's happening?' she asked without looking at him, pointing outside at the turbulent weather.

'Pay no heed,' he replied, waving away the question with a dismissive gesture of his hand.

Moving tentatively back to see what was happening, she saw that the wind had already begun to die, the fierceness abating almost as quickly as it had started. Only the gold and copper leaves could be seen now, swirling around aimlessly as they were carried upon a gentler breeze that lessened by the second.

Daire approached her and she backed away from him, fearful of his intentions towards her.

'Why?' she whispered, referring to the death of her friend. 'Why did you do that, Daire?' she asked in a whisper, completely unravelled by what he had done.

'I did what was necessary to protect my family,' he answered, standing his ground against her judgemental tone.

The silence between them grew and she could see him purse his lips in his tell-tale way when chewing over something in his mind.

Suddenly, she lost control, shaking with a mixture of anger and anxiety at the death of her friend.

'You killed Jan! I grew up with her... and now... now she's gone! Totally gone! Because of you!' she wailed, beginning to shiver uncontrollably.

A light breeze lifted her hair again but instead of the chill from outside, this air was warm like a summer breeze. A voice began whispering, growing clearer as the wind increased.

'I'll convince her to come back to us, I swear it! Honestly, she trusts me again,' a voice said, causing her to close her eyes in recognition.

'Janet!' she thought, crestfallen for what she guessed would come and what had prompted his ruthless response.

'And what if you fail? Have you the strength to do what is necessary?' Jacky asked, her voice unmistakable, though uncharacteristically cold.

Kristina gripped the worktop for support as her tears moved across the surface of her eyes. A watery vision appeared before her, of her friend nodding in determination.

'Coven first,' Janet stated, her face alive with lusty passion. 'I will remove her from play, if necessary,' she added, holding her chin high as she had done to Daire.

Jacky's response was as sharp as a razor, her teeth flashing as she snarled her reply.

'You will kill her? Yes or no?' she barked, showing little tolerance for the inept witch, causing Janet's expression to harden as she nodded once again.

'How?' Jacky snapped, looking almost ready to kill the woman.

'I have cursed and poisoned a box of tea. I'll simply brew her a cup,' she replied, shrugging with an ugly expression on her face. 'Just one sip should do it,' she added smugly, confidence shining in her magnified eyes.

A hideous cackle of laughter caused Kristina to flinch, the sound of it echoing outside of her field of vision as the unseen others began applauding from the darkness.

'I do so hope that is the way of it, Jan,' Jacky replied, a motherly expression fixing on her face. 'She has too much influence over them, and it's time for that to end. You of all people should understand this! You who have no natural gift of your own,' she rasped, the caring facade slipping again from her features.

Janet's eyes shone with the mad light that Kristina had seen earlier, causing her to finally understand. The magick had not been meant for her to wield and had consumed her utterly.

The image faded and Daire let her digest what she had witnessed, knowing that it must be a bitter pill to swallow after everything else that had happened.

Watching her in silence, he let her come to terms with it in her own way, waiting silently for her reaction.

On finally opening her eyes, she stared at him in defeat and shook her head sadly.

'It was the magick that caused it, you know? I should never have taught her,' she whispered as fresh tears welled in her eyes.

Daire felt an instant surge of pity for her, sensing then how alone she felt, and made to move to her but she backed away instinctively, unsure of his intent.

'When will you get it into your thick head that I...' he said softly, thumbing his chest, '... mean you...' he continued, pointing his finger at her, '... no harm!' he finished, his tone softening with each pause and gesture. 'I am truly sorry for hulking out on you earlier,' he continued, holding her eyes with his. 'I honestly believe that even in that state I would never have caused you harm. I would not have hurt you,' he assured her, willing her to believe him.

Kristina said nothing and wrapped her arms about herself comfortingly, crying silently into her chest.

He glided closer and made to touch her but held his hand back at the last moment.

'They were not your friends, and I see now that you deserve better. From me also,' he added, feeling her loneliness like a dagger in the heart.

Realising that he was holding something in his hand, her eyes lowered to the poisoned box of tea.

'What should I do now?' she asked, speaking as though in a daze and unable to tear her eyes from the poison that had been intended for her.

A small, reassuring smile touched his lips and he finally reached out to squeeze her shoulder affectionately.

'You make friends of my friends,' he answered, raising his eyebrows at her expressively. 'My friends are much better!' he assured her, lifting his head slightly to the ceiling before a sound was actually heard.

The sound of crying caused Kristina to flinch and then rush out into the hallway in a panicked state.

'Oh my god! What now?' she cried, thinking immediately that they were fighting again.

Flying down the stairs, Francesca flew into her mother's arms and began sobbing uncontrollably.

'What is it, baby?' Kristina asked softly, stroking her hair tenderly and feeling silently thankful for the interruption.

Lucian appeared at the top of the stairs and sat himself down on the uppermost step.

'She had a bad dream, Mammy,' he said sadly, wrapping his arms around his drawn-up knees.

With her mother stroking her head, Francesca sobbed out her distress.

'I dreamed that I called Daddy and he came home, right out of the fire. I thought he was a monster at first, but it was him!' she wailed, emotion racking her little body. 'He cuddled me all night, saying that he would never leave me again,' she added, struggling to get the words past her heaving chest.

Looking up from her daughter, Kristina was surprised to see Daire standing in the doorway, still out of sight of his son on the stairs.

Slowly, the child's tears subsided, leaving her breathing in shaky gulps of air.

'It was so real, Mammy! He promised he would stay!' she cried, her breathing now nearly under control.

Looking up as though sensing something amiss, Francesca frowned at the nervous smile on her mother's lips.

'And I meant it, baby girl,' came the deep, powerful voice that she had missed so much.

Spinning around, Francesca looked up at her father and immediately ran to him with her arms outstretched.

'Daddy!' she screamed, throwing her arms tightly around him.

With adoration shining in his eyes, he scooped her up and held her tightly to him as fast footsteps came racing down the stairs.

'Daddy!' Lucian yelled, latching himself onto his father's leg.

Laughing with joy, Daire lowered himself to one knee so that he could hug them both.

'Daddy,' they sighed together, happy at last to be where they were.

Kristina, suddenly in a panic, began searching the floor for signs of what had happened and moved past them to close the living room door.

'I got rid of it,' Daire whispered without looking up, causing her to frown, not entirely sure if he was talking of her friend or the poisoned box of tea.

Groaning with exaggeration as he sat with his children on one of the sofas, Daire looked to the heavens and closed his eyes as though in pain.

'Of course, I'll be leaving again, Cesca, but not for as long, a couple of days at most. Okay? We can't spend every minute of every day together, can we?' he asked, looking back down into her wilful blue eyes.

'Why not?' she demanded, frowning up at him in defiance.

Pretending to cry in exasperation, he caused both children to laugh automatically.

'Daddy!' Lucian said in a knowing tone. 'You're not really crying,' he announced, looking up from his father's side.

Looking down at his children, he squeezed them to him and smiled reassuringly.

'No Luc, I'm not,' he confessed, but his face grew serious as his brows began to furrow. 'Do you know who missed you even more than I did?' he asked, glaring down at them. 'And neither of you have even once asked after him…' he growled, shifting his weight slightly to better his position.

Looking around at each other, the children shrugged quizzically at one another.

'He is *very* angry with you,' Daire continued, a fierce look now entering his eyes.

Francesca straightened and frowned with confusion, totally at a loss to whom he was referring to.

'Who?' she demanded, trying to think of somebody who would miss them more than him.

Arching his eyebrows menacingly, Daire held them close before finally enlightening them.

'Elmo!' he roared, causing Lucian to scream through his laughter and fight frantically to get away.

Daire's hands flexed and then turned into snakelike hand puppets as they turned to face each of the children.

'You didn't miss me!' Elmo roared, low and guttural before attacking their ribs in a tickling frenzy.

***

Kristina smiled as she lay upon her bed, enjoying the sounds of joy coming from her children. On hearing the screaming and then the laughter, she chuckled softly, knowing that it could only mean one thing, 'Elmo' had arrived.

Chuckling at the memory, she remembered when Daire had first created the angry thing all those years ago.

'A different time, in a different world,' she thought sadly, as her mind crashed back to the present.

Getting up from the bed, she straightened her dress and made her way back downstairs.

'Call Elmo again, Daddy?' Lucian whined, hitting the now-prone hand.

'No, he's gone to sleep now,' Daire moaned, drained from the unrelenting attention.

'Please?' they asked together, pleading with him unblinkingly.

'No!' he roared, but his fingers flattened together with his thumb dropping down for Elmo's mouth, causing the children to cower apprehensively, eyes as wide as the smiles on their faces.

Appearing in the doorway with her hands on her hips, Kristina stood silently and everyone knew that playtime was over.

'We need to talk,' she announced with a sorry expression on her face for the children's sake. 'So much has happened,' she continued before suddenly realising where she was standing and quickly moving away with a shudder, looking back to where her friend had died.

Reading her unasked question, he frowned and rolled his eyes in her direction.

'I told you already, I took care of it,' he answered, shaking his head at what else she could be wondering about.

She stood staring at him for a moment, clearly struggling with what he had done and unable to accept his unbothered reaction about it. It was as though the act of killing meant nothing to him, but Janet had been her friend and she would have her say over the matter.

'The wind?' she asked, remembering the whirlwind outside of the house.

He nodded, knowing that it was still a very fresh and delicate subject.

'How did you know for sure that they were all in on it?' she asked, talking of her entire coven and his confession of what he had done to them.

Holding her stare, he shrugged without regret and lifted his arm off his children as he spread his hands wide.

'I didn't,' he replied, unwilling to show her what she wanted from him. 'If your bestie had been turned to the dark side, then why would any of the others refuse? Now drop it,' he demanded, his voice deepening several octaves below what was natural.

She looked at him as her mouth began to curl into a snarl, her anger igniting from his uncaring attitude.

'Later,' he added in a softer voice, looking pointedly at the children in his arms.

Nodding slowly, she held his eyes fiercely.

'Later,' she reluctantly agreed, but felt determined to have it out with him sooner rather than later.

Seating herself cross-legged on the opposite sofa, she placed her hands leisurely on top of her knees.

Looking pointedly at the children's vacant expressions, she indicated that they were oblivious for the moment as they watched the same YouTube channel on their iPads.

Sighing tiredly and knowing that this conversation simply had to happen, Daire looked down once again before spreading his hands.

'What do you want to know?' he asked, sighing in resignation.

'How much has the house actually told you?' she asked, raising her eyebrows seriously.

Pursing his lips, he considered the question before answering.

'I knew that she was the enemy,' he began, referring to her now-dead friend. 'I know of the attack in the damned forest!' he continued, a note of thunder rumbling from his chest, sounding far off for the moment.

Kristina looked nonplussed, holding his gaze with wide eyes.

'Don't even go there!' she replied evenly, glancing meaningfully to the floor where her friend had died.

'She was the enemy, it's that simple to me. It doesn't matter that she was corrupted by magick or whatever the reasons were. I wouldn't care if she was controlled by another or did it in her sleep! If you come here to cause harm, you die, as will those who stand with you. It is that simple!' he whispered, incensed by her continuing judgemental attitude.

Glaring at one another, he shrugged suddenly and let his anger go.

'You only have yourself to blame anyway, for introducing her to it in the first place. One of the many mistakes you have made that I expressly pointed out for you not to make!' he replied, frustrated that she continued to go against him at every turn.

Believing that she did it simply to go against him, he knew that to protect his children she would have to change.

'Knowing you as I do, I put my mind, my "will" if you like, into the house and made its sole reason for being to protect them. If you hadn't already noticed, it has a mind of its own and will make the tough choices when you are unable or unwilling to. Just in case you have yet another lapse in judgement and invite a Blood to tea or something just as ridiculous,' he said, raising his hands in a gesture of 'that's it' before returning them to the children.

Both children sat obliviously unaware at either side of him, still engrossed by the antics of a father called Duddy and his children playing games on their consoles. A high-pitched scream from the father caused Daire to look down and smile, totally distracted as a granny swiped a club at the iPad's screen.

Kristina cleared her throat loudly, clearly angered at how easily distracted he was from their 'important' conversation.

'I am so glad you possessed the house,' she replied sarcastically, dragging his attention back to her. 'I wonder, did you do that before or after you changed into whatever you are?' she asked, failing to keep the sneer from her tone. 'I'm willing to bet that it was after,' she added, her ever-present sarcasm thick in her tone.

Daire raised his eyebrows and pulled the corners of his mouth down drastically.

'It might have been after,' he pondered, still pulling the comical expression.

'Oh, I can assure you it was!' she hissed, her eyes blazing with righteous anger.

Ignoring her tone, he smiled and shook his head.

'It was before,' he reassured her confidently, smirking at her. 'You'd be dead now, if it was after,' he whispered, amusement washing from his face.

Lowering her tone and leaning forward in her seat, Kristina glared at him accusingly.

'This house plagued me for ages!' she rasped, saying each word slowly for emphasis. 'And I'm sure it keeps turning the heating off!'

Daire smiled again, tickled by the news of the house punishing her.

'Well you had been a very, very naughty little girl,' he replied, chuckling again at his choice of words. 'It didn't hurt you though, did it? No! Job done, as far as I'm concerned,' he sighed, breathing out contentedly. 'Job very well done,' he added, shrugging to himself and unable to stop himself from smiling.

She looked at him incredulously as her cheeks began to redden.

'This house is possessed and it overreacts! Just like you!' she accused, lowering her tone again so as not to disturb the children.

'I have a question for you,' he informed, changing the subject to one that suited him. 'How did the Bloods get past the elements?' he asked, the problem of not being able to sense them weighing heavily on his mind.

Kristina let out her breath loudly and rolled her eyes at him.

'Maybe it's because they need their bloody beauty sleep!' she answered, sarcasm still present in her tone.

Daire's face paled at this and all the humour faded from his face.

'What?' he gasped, his eyes narrowing in anger. 'How do you know this?' he asked, light suddenly flashing in his eyes like a gathering storm.

Kristina merely shrugged, feeling exhausted by the whole palaver.

'It's more that they've been *put* to sleep,' she sighed, realising that he had to know. 'A web has been placed over us that has put them to sleep. Jack and Cristian are in the forest trying to break it, but I think it's beyond them,' she said, shaking her head. '*The thing about webs is that they're so damned easy to break*,' she added, imitating the wizard's tone perfectly. 'That was a month ago,' she sighed and rolled her eyes again.

His silence made her pause and in that instant, she knew what she had done.

'Cristian?' he asked, his voice sounding dangerously low, causing her to study him in silence, looking for signs of his darkness.

'I'm not the bloody Hulk!' he snapped, irritated by her scrutiny of him.

'Just checking,' she answered lightly, gesturing for him to remain calm.

He smiled despite himself and waved for her to continue.

'He saved us. He killed a vampire lord that was about to kill Cesca,' she continued, mouthing the words for her daughter's sake.

Pursing his lips again, Daire did not seem convinced as his scowl began to deepen.

She saw him purse his lips and continued before he could form some sort of an overreaction.

'He's left the Egni and wants to help protect them, *for you*,' she stressed, looking at the children.

'Could it be a trap?' he asked, a slight reflective cast entering to his eyes suddenly.

'Definitely not!' she answered, speaking in a tone of absolute certainty. 'He could've killed us all and taken the kids many times over if he had wanted to. He thought you long dead and feels guilt for whatever it was he did to you. He wants only to make amends, Daire,' she said, nodding in emphasis of her own words.

Continuing to purse his lips, he threw the problem around in his mind.

'He's here, and there just happens to be a web over the land?' he asked, looking at her expressionlessly.

Sighing audibly, she leaned forward to make her point clear.

'For the love of god, listen to me! He is sincere, even your "Dark House" has accepted him in,' she replied, waving her arms in the air to indicate the walls around them.

His eyebrows rose at that and his expression relaxed somewhat as he pondered his next move.

'I wonder why it chose to withhold this from me,' he said, narrowing his eyes as he looked around the room.

'Probably because it knew how you'd react,' she replied, giving him a look that clearly meant that he would overreact.

His eyes narrowed suddenly and he looked at her in confusion.

'Don't you pray to a goddess, you frivolous witch?' he asked and then burst out laughing at the look on her face.

'Oh my god!' she exclaimed again and then put her hands over her mouth.

'Wow. You really are a harlot,' he remarked, shaking his head in amusement. 'Your goddess will not be pleased with you invoking another's name so frequently,' he continued, but his smile faltered then and she saw sadness reach his eyes.

Chapter Two

The sun shone through the gaps in the trees, casting beams of blindingly bright light down upon the gloomy forest floor, giving the whole area underneath an enchanted feel.

The two men stood in the shade of these trees, looking bleakly out across the clearing.

'It's no good, my vampiric friend, it can't be broken,' Jack pronounced, shaking his head defeatedly. 'This is beyond me,' he grumbled, kicking at the earth in defeat.

Cristian felt the power of the web as he could all the energy that pulsed around him, but what was more, he could actually see it without having his eyes unfocused.

Kristina had somehow opened him up to such things, changing him beyond measure. She had enhanced him, and he doubted that even she knew the extent of what she had done to him. He felt different, alive for the first time since his vampirism, and silently thanked her for it.

Casting his eyes down, he looked upon the earth and could feel the power beneath it vibrating, almost thrumming, under his feet. He had missed this sensation most of all, and seeing the wizard tap into it constantly filled him with an ache that he had long thought forgotten.

'But I can feel it now,' he thought, feeling it rise at the wizard's call, and tentatively began to reach for it himself.

Expecting the power to withdraw from him, his eyes watered when he finally felt its touch and began to cry when it instantly began to nourish him.

'Gods bless you, Kristina,' he thought, fighting hard to hide the emotion.

Turning his back to the wizard, he looked up at the web again and saw it billowing gently like some gigantic sail, stretching from one edge of the trees to the other.

'I wish I'd had more of an interest in this kind of thing when I was human,' he whispered, dreaming of what he would be able to do by now had he remained so.

They had tried everything he knew, even attacking the web head-on, but it simply absorbed their might before rendering them unconscious.

Both greatly feared being left vulnerable and incapacitated for their enemies to find, they had agreed not to combine their power in an attack.

Jack threw up his arms in frustration, breaking the vampire out of his brooding. The wizard began pacing around the glade like a spoilt child, his feeling of impudence finally getting the better of him.

'We've tried everything, damn it!' he cried in frustration. 'There has to be a way!'

Cristian watched him silently and shook his head.

'All that wasted effort,' he thought, mildly curious as to what it had achieved.

They had found the glade easily enough from Kristina's directions and had buried the charred remains of his brother soon afterwards.

Closing his eyes, Cristian felt the heartache of seeing his brother in such a way and wiped at a solitary tear that trickled down his cheek. Looking down, he gazed at the grave at his feet and shook his head in misery.

Crouching, he placed his palm upon the freshly-dug earth and closed his eyes again.

'I miss you so much, little brother,' he whispered, his voice breaking at the confession. 'I am so sorry,' he wept, his bitter tears beginning to strike the earth.

'Well, this is awkward,' a deep voice sounded at his back, causing the vampire to freeze in his grief and look up at Jack, who stared back with his mouth agape.

The wizard's eyes flicked to Cristian suddenly and he shook his head, whether in disbelief or in warning he could not tell.

'Who the hell could come up behind me undetected?' Cristian thought, feeling totally vulnerable in that dreadful moment.

Slowly rising to his feet with his eyes never leaving those of the wizard's, he noted the old man's wide eyes and gaping mouth and knew instantly that he alone was to face whoever was behind him.

'I forgive you, Cris,' the voice whispered, a moment before a firm hand gripped his shoulder. A sob escaped him and he turned slowly to see his long-dead brother standing before him, smiling sadly at his show of emotion.

Daire had always stood a little shorter than his eldest brother but that was no longer the case as the vampire looked up slightly to meet the eyes of the legend.

'Daire,' he whispered, stepping into his brother's embrace.

Jack saw the two embrace and felt a lump in his throat as he slowly exhaled in relief. He could not believe what he was seeing, so suddenly had his friend appeared. One second, Cristian had been bent over the grave, the next, the one who had caused him to come on this quest in the first place had materialised behind him as though out of thin air.

Feeling rooted to the spot, Jack held back for a moment and consciously closed his mouth before finally walking forward.

'Well, you took your damn time!' he growled as he got closer, causing the two men to separate.

Locking eyes with the wizard, the legend paused before a knowing smile touched his lips.

'Blue,' he greeted, seeing through the disguise immediately.

Jack shrugged and spread his arms wide.

'It's Jack now, if you don't mind,' he replied, causing his friend to shrug, seemingly unbothered by the wizard's many guises.

'Whatever floats your boat, Jack,' he replied, hugging his old friend close. 'Thank you,' he said sincerely, giving the wizard a genuine shake of the shoulders. 'Thank you both,' he added, turning back to his brother. 'My children are alive because of you,' he continued, smiling broadly at their still-shocked expressions.

'I thought you were dead… again,' Cristian replied, gesturing down to the earth at his feet.

Daire followed his gaze and then sighed regrettably.

'You thought right… but I come to you now at the turn of the tide,' he replied, narrowing his eyes in an attempt to look wizened.

Jack immediately burst into hysterics, throwing his head back in uncontrolled mirth.

Cristian shook his head and laughed softly at the statement.

After a few moments, Jack stood back and held his stomach with both hands.

'I bet you've been waiting to say that for ages,' he guffawed, wiping tears from his eyes as he started to laugh again.

Smiling at having the desired effect on his old friend, Daire brushed off the imaginary dust on his shoulder.

'Mine are always the best,' he replied, enjoying the game they played.

'That's going to keep me awake tonight,' Jack gasped, trying but failing to regain control.

Casting his gaze over the glade, Daire noted again the timeless quality about the place that he loved so much and though he thought it much the same as he had left it he could, however, sense the remains of Bloods nearby.

The huge stone still sat near the centre, looking odd and out of place as he scanned the area.

'As it should,' he thought, not knowing exactly where it had come from. 'So, that's the web,' he said, eventually looking skyward.

'We can't break it!' Jack sighed, dabbing at his eyes, finally overcoming his hilarity. 'We've tried everything, believe you me,' he grumbled, looking at Cristian for support.

Daire looked at him sadly, pouting out his bottom lip in mock sympathy.

'Oh, of course you have,' he replied condescendingly, causing a chuckle to bubble from his brother. 'It's fine, honestly,' he continued, causing Jack to scowl.

Cristian laughed again and shook his head at the wizard.

'He's goading you, Jack, stop being so easy,' he advised, looking to his brother and gesturing him forward to overcome what they could not.

Striding forward a few paces, Daire put his fists on his waist and looked up at the sky for a moment.

'My appearance may change,' he warned without turning back.

Cristian looked at Jack, who silently began miming to him, imitating a monster with big teeth by placing his fingers where the fangs would be.

Mouthing for him to shut up, Cristian turned again to study his brother who stared up for a minute longer, tracing the intricate details of the web in his mind.

Turning back, he looked Cristian in the eye, his face suddenly livid with rage.

'He did this,' he hissed coldly, causing Cristian to nod in response, knowing his father's work only too well.

Growling in rage, Daire raised his arms and stretched out his fingers in a grasping motion. The web pulsed brightly and Cristian felt a shiver run up his length at seeing the shadow of his brother's true form beginning to appear.

His dark-brown hair turned suddenly to black and the visible skin of his shoulders became a depthless shadow, seemingly untouched by the light of the high midday sun.

Cristian felt relieved that he could not see his brother's face at that moment, for the monster who stood now with his back to him was at least a foot taller than the man had appeared.

The web pulsed again, more violently this time, and on turning again to the wizard, Cristian saw him shake his head in shock.

A deep rumble of thunder sounded as the web pulsed for a third time, more vibrant and less stable than it had appeared at first.

With a roar of anger, Daire took hold of the shameful binding and lightning instantly streaked across the sky, smashing with deadly effect into the stubbornly resistant web. From his hands came an arc of magick that clove a way through the strands, leaving them to fade in tattered disarray.

Jack's mouth fell open at seeing the web disintegrate so quickly and knew in his heart that no mere man could have summoned such a force.

Finally, the unnatural being lowered his arms and stood breathing heavily, intentionally keeping his back to them.

Cristian saw him turn his head a little and caught a glimpse of his white eyes as they peered back at him peripherally.

'You need to see me as I am now, Cris,' his voice boomed, shocking the vampire with its raw, unfiltered base before he turned his eyes onto those of his brother.

A cold shiver passed through Cristian as soon as the alien eyes touched his own. He felt a compulsion to raise his shield but steeled himself against the reaction.

'I am corrupted Cris, even beyond what the Bloods are,' Daire said, thunder seeming to rumble through his words.

Looking like nothing he had ever seen in life, Cristian was reminded suddenly of an artist's impression of a hellish creature that he had seen in a fantasy book.

Untouched by the world around him, his legendary brother appeared alien in every possible way and appeared not to belong in this world of the living.

Cristian had only one name that screamed in his mind for such a thing and as he studied his brother, he hoped with all his heart that he was wrong, more wrong than he had ever been before.

***

Francesca stood by the kitchen sink and scowled at the dirty dishes. She hated doing chores, especially the dishes, but used the time to stare out the window in front of her. It would be dark soon, and she wanted her father home.

'Where are you?' she stressed, desperately looking for signs of movement within the trees.

Sighing, she looked at the stack of saucepans and wished, just for a second, that she could clean them using magick.

'*Fy enwyllys arnoch chi,*' she thought instinctively, knowing which words to use from one of her father's books.

Deciding right from the off to follow in her father's footsteps, she had learned the ancient language and found it surprisingly easy on the tongue.

No sooner had she thought of the words, the nearest pan flew into the water, dousing her with suds and lemon-scented water.

Jumping back, she could only stare as the pan was scrubbed clean with the brush she had only just been holding.

Suddenly, all the remaining dishes turned to her expectantly, causing her eyes to widen and a thrill of excitement to prickle over her skin.

Calming herself, she realised what was required of her and a mischievous smile spread across her face.

'She'll never know,' she thought, knowing that her mother would freak out if she used her magick for something so trivial.

Raising her hands before her like an orchestral conductor, she directed her art at the remaining cookware.

Gesturing gracefully with her right hand, the pots, pans and crockery all stood to attention and lined up in an orderly fashion. With a flick of her left hand, the clean pan hopped out to dry on the drainer.

Smiling broadly and feeling unable to contain herself further, Francesca threw caution to the wind and began to conduct her masterpiece.

One by one the crockery hopped along, matching their movements to the motion of her fingers. The magick flowed through her, unlocking doors within her mind that she had not known to have existed.

'Let's do this!' she whispered to herself, letting her breath out slowly before rising up on her tiptoes.

Launching herself into the air and dancing to the tune in her head, Francesca gracefully began flapping her arms in a near-perfect imitation of the 'Dance of the Little Swans' from her favourite ballet.

Seeing the drainer filling to capacity, she split her fingers, pointing her middle finger to the towels on the radiator. Instantly, they flew into the air, circling the room once before descending upon the soaking dishes in a drying frenzy. Gesturing to the cupboard with her little finger, the doors flew open suddenly as the pots and pans danced inside to the tune in her head.

Winking at the cutlery drawer to open, she spun and gestured for the silverware to do the same with a delicate nod of her head.

Coming to the end of her performance, she threw out her arms and splayed her fingers wide as she approached her triumphant conclusion.

The cupboard doors and the cutlery draw slammed closed as the last plate danced inside and the silence that came after seemed deafening to her ears.

Curtsying to an unseen audience, Francesca basked in the silent applause and threw her head back with her eyes tightly closed. Standing there, panting hard, she felt a thrill of exhilaration at her completed task.

'Thank you!' she whispered to her would-be crowd and then brushed imaginary dust from her shoulder as her father was known to do.

Watching from just inside the hallway, Kristina looked on with astonishment at the miraculous control of magick her daughter clearly had. Completely awed by the show of power, she knew absolutely that this kind of magick was totally beyond what she could achieve.

Clearing her throat, she placed her hands on her hips and stared at her daughter sternly.

'And what do you think you are doing, young lady?' she asked, causing her daughter to spin in surprise.

'Multitasking, by the look of it,' Daire answered, somehow managing to get inside without being noticed.

Raised his hands, he clapped slowly in appreciation of his daughter's talent and shook his head at her natural gift.

'Absolutely brilliant,' he approved, opening his arms invitingly to her. 'One can only imagine what you will be capable of in the years to come,' he continued, clapping his hands together quickly for her to come to him.

Francesca beamed and skipped forward to meet him.

'Did you see what I did? Did you see?' she gasped, still breathless from her routine.

'I did indeed, baby girl, and it was bloody awesome!' he replied, hugging her to him and spinning her around.

Francesca gave him a stern look of disapproval and pushed against him as she frowned her disappointment.

'You said the "Buh" word!' she scolded, shaking her head at him. 'And where *have* you been?' she asked, placing her hands to her hips as he held her.

***

Laying sprawled on one of the sofas with his daughter virtually on top of him, Daire began to doze contentedly as she snored softly in his arms.

On the opposite sofa, Kristina and Lucian were in much the same position, awaiting the arrival of their guests.

With his breathing beginning to deepen, Daire's fingers began to slow in the massaging of his daughter's soft hair.

Opening his eyes suddenly, he sighed tiredly before the front door unlocked and opened of its own accord.

'I wish it would stop doing that!' Cristian whispered, as both he and Jack entered the living room with the sound of the door closing again behind them.

Smiling at the house's good graces, Daire shifted himself up a little.

'The house likes you, Cris, be thankful,' he replied, looking up tiredly.

Cristian nodded apologetically, remembering what his brother's home could do to those it disliked.

'It didn't like me at first,' he replied, glancing about the room more warily.

'That's because *I* didn't like you,' Daire replied, arching an eyebrow up at him. 'Things change,' he added, closing his eyes again.

Seating himself beside his brother, Cristian was careful not to disturb the sleeping child. Jack took the seat next to Kristina, placing his hands upon his knees and then patting them awkwardly.

'They still sleep,' he stated, talking of the elements, and then looked at his friend with concern.

Daire merely grunted before finally responding to the words.

'I know,' he answered, opening his eyes once again. 'I can't get through to them in my current... state,' he added, frowning in annoyance.

Staring at him expectantly, Kristina waited for him to begin his tale of where he had been and what had happened to him during his disappearance.

'I'll tell my story tomorrow, Kris. I'm knackered,' he answered, knowing her unasked question. 'We need to talk strategy if we are to survive this fiasco,' he added, seeing her scowl sullenly at his response.

Jack looked at him incredulously and shook his head in refusal, wanting to hear the tale for himself.

'If you think for one minute that…'

Daire groaned loudly, cutting him off before he could finish, realising that he was outnumbered.

'Okay! Okay, but it's a long story so no interruptions,' he warned, looking pointedly at Kristina before kissing his daughter's forehead softly.

Forcing himself more awake, he shifted his weight in his seat and stretched out both arms.

'As you all know, I was having difficulties with my…' he paused, searching for the right word, '… duality,' he finished, nodding satisfactorily at his choice of word. 'I would lose myself for hours and sometimes even miss days at a time before finally snapping out of it,' he began, recalling the images in his mind.

Sighing heavily, he felt the weight of the words to come.

'It was actually by the grace of another that I was able to return at all,' he continued, looking at Kristina for the longest moment. 'I met someone,' he announced, his meaning clear.

Kristina merely shrugged, clearly unperturbed by his admission.

'Meh,' she replied, causing him to shrug in response.

'Okay…' he continued, drawing out the word awkwardly.

'Wait!' she cut in, frowning at him sternly. 'You're skirting over the story and I want to hear it all, every juicy titbit of it,' she added, daring him to deny her this small request.

Daire shook his head before looking to the children, but they were both asleep and he groaned in resignation.

'Very well,' he conceded, rolling his eyes at her, 'here it is.'

Getting himself even more comfy, he kissed Francesca on the head again.

'After leaving here, I thought I was done. I could literally feel myself slipping away,' he began again, taking a deep breath and remembering that night of slaughter.

'After I left David, AKA Jack,' he continued, looking over at his friend with a smile, 'I gave myself over to the wildness and attacked the Bloods head-on. I ripped them limb from limb and it was so easy. Can you believe that?' he asked, looking across to his brother.

Cristian shook his head, knowing only too well the power needed to achieve such a feat.

'There were more than sixty of them, or so I heard, and you took them on physically, hand to hand?' he asked, looking at his brother in disbelief, but then remembered what Daire had turned into in the glade.

Daire nodded and shrugged, weighing up what had happened in his mind.

'Well, I did have the elements with me, I suppose, but it would've been the same result in the end I think. There weren't any lords among them, but they were Bloods all the same and you know as well as I what they are capable of. They seemed only to be pale imitations of what I am now and I cut through them like butter,' he replied, catching Kristina's expression as her mouth curled up. 'I'm not a bloody vampire!' he growled, reading her expression.

She gave him an insincere nod as her lip continued into its sneer.

'Of course you're not,' she replied sarcastically, before lowering her voice into a hiss. 'You're their bloody Daddy!' she accused, widened her eyes at him.

He held her glare for a moment but bit back his angry retort.

'Anyway...' he said, moving on, 'I knew that I was lost after that and couldn't trust myself to return, in case I was the one who turned hostile,' he continued, catching Kristina's eye again as she gave him a look that said,

'You hostile? Never!'

But she did not interrupt him again.

Amused by her expression, he looked away from her as he continued.

'I lived deep within the forest, hunting all the Bloods that I could find, and when I couldn't find any more, I returned to the place where I was changed...'

Kristina broke in, unable to control herself.

'Changed into what exactly?' she demanded, her eyes wide and daring.

Pursing his lips in thought, Daire relayed the story of what had happened that dreadful morning in the glade.

'You're an element? The spirit element?' she asked, staring at him and waiting for him to laugh. 'So they enhanced your body?' she asked, flabbergasted by his tale.

Daire shook his head irritably, annoyed at having to explain himself further.

'No! My body *died*, woman! You found my damned corpse! I created this from the old one,' he finished, raising his arms expressively to see if she now understood.

Cristian gave him a look that suggested he was following the story easily enough.

Jack simply shrugged before shaking his head and rolling his eyes at Kristina.

'Anyway, we can talk about that later,' Daire continued, annoyed at yet another interruption. 'Now, shut up!' he snapped, daring her to speak one more time.

Breathing out slowly, he calmed himself before continuing.

'One night when I was feeling pretty low, I lit a fire and sat staring into it, as one does when trying to seek wisdom. I was tired of communing with the elements, for they could tell me nothing of what I needed to know. So as I stared into the flames, I reopened the part of my mind that I had stored my personality in... my identity...' he corrected, closing his eyes to relive that night by the fire.

Chapter Three

Sitting cross-legged before the fire, Daire stared into the flames and cried in desperation.

'I'm losing this fight,' he knew, feeling the darkness inside rising once again.

Having exhausted every idea, every magickal enchantment that he could possibly place upon himself, he found that nothing could undo what he had done and so turned his senses inward. He missed his snowflake, and seeing what had replaced it made him dread that he was now his children's greatest threat.

The last time he had become aware of himself after one of his blackouts he had awakened just outside his house and had known instantly that even in his darkened state, his children were still his only fixation.

He knew that he had gone there solely for them and had felt the fading desire to corrupt them as he now was, wanting them to be like him so that on some base level, they could remain together.

Staring into the fire, he contemplated unbinding his body rather than to hurt them or worse. As the thought grew in his mind, a log slipped within the fire, dropping an inch to send fresh sparks up into the cold night air. On a whim, he pushed his mind into the fire and blanched at seeing energy not unlike his own.

'From water to fire?' he mused aloud, still staring into the flickering flames.

Taking a deep rumbling breath, he could feel himself slipping back into the darkness again and knew then that he had to act.

'Help me!' he cried, desperately trying to hold on to who he was. 'Someone please help me!' he screamed, placing his head into his hands.

The thought struck him suddenly that he needed to speak to the element of fire, but knew that he was now out of time.

Reaching inside himself, he opened the box in his head and felt the resulting emotions flush though him.

'I am Daire!' he thought, willing himself to remain.

'Will I do?' a soft feminine voice purred, cutting off his desperate thoughts.

The voice had sounded from beyond the fire's circle of light and outside his field of vision, causing him to rise in an instant, his awareness reaching out instinctively.

Almost lost within the gloom, a shadowed form lounged regally nearby with one arm draped majestically over a low-hanging branch.

'Who are you?' he demanded, drawing power from the earth as he did so.

A throaty laugh escaped from her as the shadowed woman chuckled in amusement.

'So direct and so impatient, Dark,' she replied, tilting her head mischievously to one side.

'I have not the luxury of patience, my lady, for my mind may be gone at any moment,' he replied respectfully, guessing correctly at what she was.

Disentangling herself from the limbs of the tree, Daire took in her regal form and graceful manner as she walked slowly towards him. Her hair, he saw, hung straight to her shoulders but he could see no human tones of flesh as she neared the glow of the fire.

'While you are in my company you will remain as you are,' she assured him, the outline of her cheekbones rising with amusement. 'I am the Queen of Air,' she proclaimed and curtsied deliciously before him. 'What would you have of me, Dark Wolf?' she asked, stepping a little closer to him.

Daire was stunned, clearly not expecting one of the deities from another world to come at his call, let alone this one.

'The Fae Goddess, herself,' he thought in shock, not knowing why she, of all gods, would come to him. There were those of her ilk in this world, he knew, that would surely have heard his plea before her.

Having heard of the Queen of Air, he knew her to be a goddess not of this world. She was a deity to the Fae and not known to appear without a price.

Worshipped in this world by many a witches' coven, she allegedly came only to bless them in their circles, but to what end he was yet to learn.

'Is it possible for me to remain, me?' he asked quickly, guessing that she would understand his meaning.

Stepping in closer and yet remaining in shadow, the goddess smiled at him.

'Yes,' she replied, but offered him no further explanation than this.

'How can I achieve this, please?' he asked, desperation edging his tone.

Ignoring the question, she moaned in pleasure at his respectful request.

'So polite,' she purred, the whites of her eyes brightening suddenly as she blinked at him slowly, like a cat does to its much-loved owner.

'First, you must answer me this, Dark Wolf, hunter and killer of all mankind. Why do you wish to stay as you are?' she asked, staring at him openly.

For a long time, they stared at each other before he finally answered.

'I need to be "me" to protect my children, for they are in danger and need me as I am now, not as the monster I'm turning into,' he answered, whispering the words passionately.

Moving in closer still, she stood before him now, remaining draped in shadow.

'Why?' she coaxed, her glowing white eyes lighting up as though from the power within.

Taking a deep breath, he tried to see if she was genuine in her interest or just teasing him as the Fae were known to do.

'They are powerful, and will be used or killed by one faction or another,' he answered honestly, not knowing what else to say.

The goddess was now face-to-face with him, close enough for him to see the starlight shining in her eyes.

'A worthy reason, but what you ask will take time and so you must be removed from it, at least in the way you know. You must surely know that you have ascended by now, yet you resist it, and in fighting against what has been given, you are losing yourself, being neither one or the other,' she enlightened him before pausing to lean in a little closer. 'You must accept what you are,' she whispered in his ear and then stepped to the side, circling him as though he were her prey.

'What am I?' he asked in desperation, his voice shaking with emotion.

Stepping behind him, she answered into his other ear as she passed.

'You are a creature of light, though I am sure you would disagree at this stage,' she answered, pausing for a moment before continuing. 'You have, however, corrupted what was done to you,' she whispered, completing the circle to stand before him again.

'I am truly an element, then?' he asked, spreading his arms in confusion.

The goddess laughed and shook her head in amusement.

'That was their intention, no doubt, but you are unmanageable, wild even, and had other ideas, it would seem. You are a spirit-being enhanced by them, and in creating you anew, they have bound themselves to this realm, becoming a part of the way things work and so are "accepted" by the world, for want of a better term. This was their intent, to be sure, but you rebelled and changed yourself further, becoming something different, something more or maybe even something less,' she said playfully, smiling as he raised his eyebrows.

Growing serious again, she reached out to touch him on the shoulder.

'You were not meant to dwell in this physical world and as with all things, a price will need to be paid,' she continued, looking at him sternly.

'Will you help me, my lady?' he asked, bowing his head humbly.

A moment passed before she finally lifted his head with a pointed finger under his chin.

'No,' she answered, causing his eyes to close. 'But I will instruct, for you will need to be your own master in this and in all things to come,' she continued with a determined tone in her voice. 'I will take you from this place so that you have the time you require to master yourself and then we will see about protecting your children,' she said, a smile tugging at the corners of her mouth.

His face flushed as a swell of relief washed up through him.

'Why?' he asked before he could think to stop himself.

She laughed at that, long and musical, her velvet voice filling the hallow with the song of her speech.

'I will take something from you, Dark, as you will, I'm sure, take something from me,' she replied cryptically, smiling at his discomfort. 'But fear not, for what we lose will be freely given,' she added, smiling at him mischievously.

Willing to pay almost any price at this stage, Daire nodded his agreement and smiled at her nervously.

'What do I call you?' he asked, surprising her by the frankness of the question.

Her eyebrow arched sternly in reply, causing him to continue swiftly.

'What I mean is that it's going to be a bit long-winded calling you "Queen of Air" all the time, or Goddess?' he suggested, raising his eyebrows at her again.

She seemed to think it through for a moment before finally responding.

'You may call me, Mistress!' she replied and laughed at his open-mouthed gape. 'You may call me Olivia, but only when we're alone. When in company, you will address me accordingly,' she purred, linking her arm through his and walking him towards the shadow of the trees, away from the firelight.

'What is it that drives you to remain shackled to who you are now, Dark?' she asked, the question catching him off guard.

'The need to protect my children. And please, call me Daire,' he replied, shrugging his shoulders.

Olivia's eyes flashed with irritation for an instant, seemingly annoyed by his mannerism.

'Daire,' she breathed after a time, looking at him passionately before shrugging her own shoulders, mimicking him as she answered her question for him. 'It is the wants of your mortal coil that drive you. You want this and you want that, but…'

she said, pausing for emphasis, 'you are no longer mortal,' she finished, stopping then to look at him.

He stared back at her, his eyes widening at the enlightenment.

'Surely you have suspected this?' she asked, frowning as though speaking to a child.

Daire pulled the corners of his mouth down as he shrugged his response.

'Shrug again and I'm going to hurt you, Daire,' she warned, causing him to smile.

'I suspected maybe that was the case, but it's not like I've had the time to find out for sure,' he replied, staring deep into her eyes.

Olivia's eyes sparkled with delight, having missed the feeling of being with someone who did not appear to be cowed in her presence. She was just another 'person' to him and it made her feel alive again.

'What holds you to who you are now? What is the anchor?' she asked, turning to watch his reaction.

'My children,' he replied immediately, speaking the words without hesitation.

She nodded slowly, seemingly happy with his answer.

'Yes! Your children! Now pretend, if you will, that there are two of you. The "now you" that wants nothing more than to protect them and the "subconscious you" that understands that all things end in one way or another,' she paused, looking at him sideways to see if he understood.

Wondering why she had stopped, he raised his eyebrows curiously and waited for her to continue.

Smiling at his response, Olivia fought the sudden urge to pinch him to see if he was real.

'When one ascends, there is to be only one mind. You can't fight it, only accept the change in you and let it run its course. You have been fighting yourself all this time and it's time for you to stop,' she continued, nodding at him slowly.

He frowned at her and shook his head, knowing what had been his intent when he had awakened in front of the house.

'I am a danger to them,' he stated, unwilling to take the risk.

'Embrace it!' she replied, looking at him sternly. 'And once you've completed this mental metamorphosis I will help you in prioritising your priorities, as it were, for you to be as close to how you are now when all is said and done,' she continued, leading him on through the darkness.

Daire cocked an eyebrow at her, remembering her earlier statement.

'I thought you weren't going to help me?' he asked, narrowing his eyes suspiciously.

She shrugged then and smiled at his instant chuckle.

'A lady's prerogative,' she purred, pulling him in closer with her linked arm.

The darkness washed away suddenly and she let him see her for the very first time.

Daire breathed in and held it, looking at her in silence as he took in the details of her face. He noted the high cheekbones and the slightly slanting eyes that rose up somewhat at the ends. She looked caring and wild at the same time, he thought, and felt as though he knew her suddenly, had known her for a very long time.

'So beautiful,' he almost whispered, continuing his stare, but there was something more to her that struck a chord in him. 'What am I not seeing?' he thought, lost for a moment in her eyes.

'Are we to be friends, then?' he whispered, inching his face closer.

She looked back with a look of passion previously unseen, and he thought for a moment to have offended her.

'I think that between us, it will be all or nothing!' she replied, her eyes showing just a hint of concern over the matter.

Moonlight shone down on them suddenly, casting a light so bright that it lit up the land around them.

Distracted by the sudden change, Daire looked up instinctively to see a moon several times the size of the one he was used to.

'Where are we?' he asked, looking around like a child at a fairground as they stepped from the trees.

His voice was hushed, almost reverent, as his eyes darted this way and that, taking in the enchanting scenery.

The goddess smiled, following his line of sight, and breathed in deeply as one only can on returning home.

'This is but one dimension apart from your own. It is still Earth, just not as you know it,' she replied, smiling again at his awed expression. 'All the dimensions belong to each other and so are all Earth, in one way or another, except that here it is magick that holds sway instead of the science of your world,' she answered, looking at him again with that fierceness in her eyes. 'Welcome to Fairyland!' she bid him, spreading her arms wide with a grand proclamation. 'Land of the Fae.'

Without another word, she took his arm in hers again and walked him from the opening in the trees, moving onwards into the vast forest beyond.

He could sense magick in everything and felt that the air itself was alive with its touch. Taking it all in silently, he looked at the forest through the moon's silvery glow and felt that somehow he had been here before, but the memory was obscured, as though it was a long-forgotten dream resurfacing yet again.

Olivia let him absorb it all in silence, watching him intently from the corner of her eye and smiling on occasion at his wowed expressions.

Feeling content to simply walk beside him, the goddess fought hard to hide the joy she felt at having him return from almost certain death.

'How can this be?' she thought, unable to take her eyes from him.

'Why is the moon so big here?' he asked suddenly, looking up through the trees and snapping her out of her thoughts.

Regarding him with a slight smile, she stopped suddenly and turned to face him.

'Many things are different here, Daire. Do you not prefer it as it is now?' she asked, holding his eyes with her own.

Daire nodded, matching her smile.

'I do, very much,' he replied honestly, pulling on her arm to keep them moving.

Her smile spread wider at that and she hugged his arm a little tighter.

'As do I,' she whispered huskily, breathing the words into his ear.

He drank in the forest, mesmerised by each and every leaf as they passed beneath them.

'I feel like I recognise this place,' he whispered, shaking his head at the foolishness of the statement.

Olivia tensed for a moment, taken off guard by his remark, and stood staring as though waiting for more.

'Maybe you should,' she replied after a moment, her eyes fearfully searching his.

'I know this place,' he announced, more confident this time, and pursed his lips as he pondered the problem.

Surprising him, she stepped in close, causing him to suck in air and hold it.

'Maybe it was a dream,' she breathed, her mouth close to his own now.

He felt a longing for her, as though he had missed her greatly.

'Maybe it was,' he replied, holding her gaze.

On impulse, he closed the distance between them and felt her mouth so hot against his that he thought for a moment she might burn him.

Breaking the kiss, she stepped back to glare at him with a wild look of anger.

He shook his head suddenly, looking as shocked as she was.

'I'm sorry,' he apologised, fearing that he had offended her.

She held his gaze intently for a moment and he had to stifle the urge to kiss her again.

'At this time, we are forbidden to each other,' she whispered, desperately trying to control her tone.

Closing her eyes, she sought her centre in a desperate attempt to regain that control.

'I am, however, willing to forgive your...' he kissed her again, cutting off her words. Long and deep this kiss was, the hotness of her like fire in his mouth. It felt to him that she burned so much hotter than he did, like fire itself against his softer warmth. He was lost in her and was happy to be so, feeling her return the kiss this second time.

'You have enchanted me, Liv,' he whispered after they finally parted, and he felt suddenly childlike in her presence.

Her eyes widened in surprise at that and she stepped back in anger again.

'I have not, nor do I need to enchant anyone to want to kiss me!' she stormed and then smiled at his widened eyes. 'Liv,' she purred, half-closing her eyes. 'I like that,' she whispered, pulling him to her and kissing him again.

He felt light-headed as their lips parted and she smiled again at his reaction.

'You must know that I am a jealous goddess and will allow no one else to have you after me. You will be mine and will rue this day if you ever betray me,' she promised, staring at him with that wild, untameable look in her eyes. 'I will, however, give you one last chance to stop this,' she added, holding her breath as she awaited his response.

He drank in every detail of her, enjoying every elegant curve of her face.

'Would you betray me?' he asked, turning the question around on her.

Her eyes widened a little, the unmitigated promise now shining in her eyes.

'I will never betray you,' she promised, raising her chin in challenge.

Mirroring her passion, he nodded with the same fierce expression.

'Then know this, Liv. I will be lost to you if you do. No matter how hard you search or what power you bring to bear. I will become a memory to you, and disappear like a thief in the night,' he swore, laying himself open for her to claim or reject.

She stared hard at him and then nodded once to the terms in which they were to be bound together.

'Well, that was romantic,' he remarked, kissing her again to seal the deal.

***

In the early hours of the morning, when the stars above began fading into the blue, the couple rose together, grinning like schoolchildren. They marvelled at each other, unable to look at anything else, they simply stared, lost in the moment.

The mantle of the Queen had dropped from her, allowing him to see her as she truly was. She was simply a girl, opening her heart to a boy who did likewise.

Gone was the image of the all-knowing goddess, an armour she wore well, he thought, seeing her now with the veil lifted.

'I do believe that I am yours, Olivia,' he whispered, causing her to return his smile, not seductively or mischievously, but a broad joyous smile that made her shine to him.

'You *are* mine,' she replied, stating the fact without a trace of humour. 'My Daire, and my Dark,' she announced, cupping his face between her hands. 'At last,' she wanted to scream, but kept this thought to herself.

She walked them through the forest until the sound of flowing water filled the air, and it was not long before a river could be seen. The water flowed steadily, twisting and turning through a sloping ravine. The dense forest thinned a little here, stopping short at the water's edge and though still cast in shadow, there was light now that shone down between the leaves. The shafts of moonlight beamed down through the far-reaching branches, causing the water below to glisten enchantingly in its silvery light.

Sitting cross-legged with his hands resting gently on his knees, Daire meditated with his palms facing up. Olivia sat opposite him, adopting a similar posture, but after a short time, the goddess opened her eyes sharply and glared her frustration, annoyed by her failure to link with him.

Tilting her head to one side, she smiled suddenly, letting the image of him dissolve her anger.

'My Daire,' she thought, her smile growing wider at the thought of their union. She wanted more, however, feeling desperate to connect with him on a spiritual level.

Staring longingly at him, she remembered his anguished plea into the fire. She had felt the overwhelming need to respond, not believing at first that it was actually him she had heard. On finally seeing him there with his head in his hands, she had nearly wept, feeling emotions stir that she had not felt since the last time she had seen him.

Looking at him now, she experienced the same tightening of her insides and nervousness in her blood. He did not know her of course, 'How could he?' she thought, for she had been as different then as the sun was to the moon. She wondered then if he had ever truly loved her before now, wishing on some base level that he had always loved her.

Bringing her gaze out of focus, she looked at him with her magickal sight and saw the illusion for the first time.

'No, not an illusion, a dampening, like he's smothering something,' she thought, feeling a coldness seep through her.

'How could I miss this?' she admonished herself and then tried desperately to break through to him again. But try as she might, he was forbidden to her. 'Why is he so closed to me?' she thought, knowing that he had not been so in the past.

Feeling the prickling of fear, she knew that there was but one being, one foe that was hidden from her kind, and pictured the long-forgotten enemy in her mind.

Shaking her head at the ludicrous idea, she looked at him again and saw his dark eyes staring back at her. A frown creased his brow as he narrowed his eyes in thought while reading something amiss in her own.

'Problem?' he asked, searching her face for the answer.

'Maybe,' she answered, frowning back with concern. 'You have hidden something from me,' she accused, feeling stung by the deceit. 'Why would you do that?' she asked, finding it difficult to keep the hurt from her tone.

Closing his eyes, he lowered his head in resignation.

'I did not hide myself from you,' he whispered, keeping his eyes closed. 'This is my true form, I have just suppressed the darkness in me that I foolishly enhanced,' he continued, finally looking up. 'I did not intend to deceive you,' he assured her, regret thickening his words.

'Yet you did,' she whispered, adopting again her queenly persona.

He shook his head, willing her to understand.

'I assumed you knew. I didn't do it to deceive you, Liv! I hid the darkness initially so as not to scare my children!' he stressed, looking at his hands before holding them up. 'I look better this way,' he mumbled, lowering them again. 'I hate what I've become… or what I'm becoming,' he whispered, looking up at her sadly.

She sighed, understanding his reasoning, but felt betrayed all the same.

'Show me!' she demanded, holding his eyes coldly.

Daire shook his head resolutely, feeling his shame flushing his cheeks.

'Absolutely not!' he shot back, determination setting his features into stone.

Her eyes blazed then and she leaned forward to enforce her words.

'Show me!' she hissed, her tone now low and dangerous.

He felt the weight of her words, felt her will like a mountain pressing down upon him, making him want to show her what she wanted to see. But he clamped the compulsion down, defiance in his eyes.

'I will not!' he growled, his eyes becoming reflective for only an instant before he pulled them back. But she had seen it, and knew that her worst fear was being realised.

'I thought that gods and goddesses knew everything,' he whispered miserably, saddened by the sudden tears in her eyes.

'Do *you* know everything?' she spat, wiping at her eyes. 'As you have risen, so it is with us! We see more than most when living outside of the "now", seeing life unfold from that ageless perspective rather than to live in it alongside you, and it's for reasons like this that I now understand why!' she vented, as her anger began to boil.

She stared at him long and hard, shaking her head imperceptibly.

'We prefer to look at life as a whole rather than to live in the moment, closing off our foresight, never truly knowing what will happen, as I have done for you!' she shouted, though her voice broke at the end.

'You said that I would remain myself while in your presence! What did you mean if not this?' He asked in a raised voice before letting his true form come to the fore. He felt himself swell instantly, felt his otherworldly power unleash and take presidency over him.

Opening his eyes, he looked down onto her grief-stricken face and saw fresh tears fall to her cheeks.

Seeing the pain in her, he willed himself once more into his human appearance and reached out tenderly to wipe the tears away. He felt like crying himself when she did not flinch, seeing her simply sit there with that sad look in her eyes.

Staring deeply at her, he leaned a little closer and was relieved when she did not back away.

'Nothing has changed,' he whispered, tears of his own welling suddenly in his eyes. 'I am still me, underneath,' he stressed, taking her hands in his. But she shook her head and finally pulled away.

'You are a daemon. You are a damned daemon!' she cried, shaking her head in disbelief. 'How can you be?' she sobbed, lowering her head to weep into her hands.

Shaking his head in bewilderment, he failed to understand her meaning. She moaned in frustration and slapped his hands away as they moved to her again. She glared at him, shaking her head again.

'Do you know the cause of your old world's end?' she asked suddenly, causing his expression to darken instantly.

'I always thought that it was the earth's retaliation against us. Kill or be killed,' he replied, dreading her response.

Her eyes creased with sadness again and the words she intended stuck in her throat.

'What?' he coaxed, seeing her anguish and not knowing the reason why.

After a long moment, she finally replied, choosing her words carefully.

'You are right, of course,' she replied in a shaky whisper. 'The world was going to die, what with your weapons being what they were. If allowed to continue, your kind would have caused all the worlds to perish alongside your own,' she continued, speaking the words with a note of finality.

He fixed her with a penetrating glare and pursed his lips in thought before finally replying.

'It was you who caused it,' it was not a question.

She shook her head, but then nodded and took a trembling breath before speaking.

'In a way, I did, because I allowed her to rule in my stead. She was a darker Queen than I, and someone I should have replaced a long time before I did,' she confessed, swallowing hard against her emotion. 'Instead of fighting, I merely watched and tried to influence from the shadows, but this goddess was impatient, refusing to wait and see if peace would finally win out. War in your world was imminent and it was going to be a war to end all wars in all worlds,' she continued, looked down as he began to speak.

'I remember. I thought it was the war at first, especially when the fire came,' he replied, remembering the nightmare of that first night.

Tears brimmed in his eyes suddenly as he remembered his loss anew and felt all of his buried emotions come flooding forth.

'Was there no other way?' he asked, almost sobbing out the words.

She shook her head, unwilling to meet his eyes.

'I don't know,' she whispered, closing her eyes.

Sitting back, he stared at her and shook his head sadly.

'You will never know what was taken from me that first night,' he whispered, feeling the unequivocal pain anew.

Looking up, she knew in that terrible moment why he had sacrificed so much and why he would continue to do so in defence of his children. Understanding flowed through her of the devastation dealt upon him and on the billions of others that had died that night, and she felt it now like nothing before.

Daire shook his head and cast the feelings aside, intent on moving past his heartache.

'She has, after all, brought this topic up for a reason,' he thought, needing to get to the bottom of it.

Pursing his lips again, Daire believed that he knew why she had brought up this painful topic.

'Why did we change?' he asked, feeling a tightness in his stomach as he awaited her answer.

She stared at him hollowly and silently wished that she had not spoken of this at all.

'Something forbidden was done that night, an evil deed that was carried out without the consent of your world's gods. The goddess opened all of the gateways to your world, letting in magick and much more besides,' she replied, seeming to wrench the words out. 'She commanded the elements to defend against what you would destroy, causing the sea to rise and the land to move. She unleashed fire across the land and fuelled it with the very air that had been so polluted, almost beyond repair,' she added, speaking the words now in a monotone, as though voicing the words from behind an emotionless mask.

Daire's eyes closed and he tried desperately to fight the return of his heartbreak.

'Almost,' he agreed, letting her know that there had been at least a little hope. 'But that does not explain the change in me,' he whispered, determined to move on.

Staring at him in silence, Olivia eventually nodded and moved on for his sake.

'She opened the gateways to all dimensions, allowing their magick to enter for the very first time,' she revealed, her emotion finally getting the better of her.

He let her cry, guessing that it was something she had needed to do for a very long time. At last, she sobered a little and looked at him again.

'The daemons in the underworld sent their darkness through, but instead of destroying as she had intended, they chose to pervert and to corrupt those that might survive. You see, they had been kept apart for too long and silently planned for their return,' she announced before clearing her throat. 'She had not foreseen this, in her anger, and did not find out until much later,' she added, shaking her head miserably.

'You speak of the Queen of Shadows,' he stated, referring to the dark goddess, which drew a small, teary smile from her in response.

'Whenever you do that with your lips, I just know that you're going to say something… unexpected,' she sobbed, pursing her lips in imitation.

'How did you finally defeat her?' he asked, ignoring her distraction, for so intent was he on knowing it all.

Her face hardened for a moment as she remembered her past.

'I know that you had dealings with her in the past and that you were nearly killed several times,' she replied, looking at him knowingly. 'It was my influence that kept that from happening for I too had had my head turned by the Dark Wolf,' she whispered, holding his eyes for a moment. 'But to answer your question, she perished by her own hand just before your vampire war ended,' she continued, swallowing again as she stared at him and then smiling at the pursing of his lips.

'She took everything from me that night. I hope my hate follows her into the afterlife,' he said coldly, shaking his head in anger. 'I thought for a long time that she wanted me dead, or maybe to punish me for some past transgression,' he continued, shaking his head at the memory. 'Though I had no idea it was you who was my guardian angel... I thought she was just playing a game with me or something, wanting to see how close she could get me to death before jumping in to save me,' he continued, picturing the raven-haired goddess with her ebony-coloured horns.

'That is not what you were thinking of when you pursed your lips,' she replied awkwardly, looking flushed by his words. 'I know this because whenever you do that pout, you are reasoning something out and not reminiscing over the past,' she added, arching an eyebrow at him.

He looked at her and smiled, seeing that he was fighting the urge to purse again.

'I was just thinking about vampires,' he replied, chuckling at her insightfulness before gesturing for her to continue with his line of thought.

She smiled tightly in response and then nodded her head slowly.

'What those first wizards did to themselves in becoming those vile creatures was to become the most affected by the daemons taint. But their essence is in you all, every wizard, witch and every creature that has an affinity with magick,' she answered, with an apologetic look on her face.

Daire put his face into his hands and sighed softly.

'So that's why I look like this!' he moaned, allowing his true form to appear again.

Staring at his black depthless hands, he let his breath out slowly.

'I'm a bloody demon!' he groaned, gripping his now black hair in his hands.

Olivia reached out and put her arms around him comfortingly.

'I'm sorry, Daire, but at least you're not a true daemon, for your origins lie on Earth and not in the darkness of the underworld. Yes, you have been tainted, but your body was born from a human and so at your core, you are human,' she replied, seeking to give him hope. 'Are you not made of light, as I am?' she asked, stroking her fingers through his thick mane of hair as he shook his head in disagreement.

'That body died,' he moaned, sagging against her. 'I created this out of the old one… and on a whim, a damned whim! I enhanced the darkness and let it run free,' he cried, burying his head into her neck.

She continued to run her fingers through his hair, massaging his head underneath.

'Your appearance notes you as a daemon and you were wise to hide it, Daire, for my people will struggle with the knowing of it, but you are at your core made of light. You have seen this for yourself,' she assured him, secretly not entirely sure if daemons were the same or not.

She lifted his head by the chin and cupped his face affectionately between her hands.

'Those of the underworld are not so bright, my Daire,' she whispered, staring hard into his eyes and willing him to believe it. 'You are beautiful to me,' she whispered, kissing him deeply for a moment. 'I love you,' she announced, looking past his demonic appearance.

He held her gaze, his terrifying face set now in resignation.

'My body died when the elements took me, Liv. I died. This body?' he replied, holding up his black forearm between them, 'Was made anew. I am no longer born of a human. Don't you get that? I am a full daemon,' he stressed, using her pronunciation.

The goddess stared as though pondering on the problem, before finally seeming to register his words.

'Yes, but you have never been there, so how can you be?' she asked, shaking her head. But then her eyes grew wide, causing his eyebrows to lift.

'Tell me!' he demanded, the feeling of dread he felt making his words snap.

'You are hidden from me,' she answered, taking a deep breath of acceptance. 'As are all from the underworld,' she added, closing her eyes again.

A cold chill ran up his back and he shivered nervously at finally finding out the truth.

'What does this mean for me?' he asked, fear draining his face of colour.

'This changes nothing! You are not the same as they,' she said fiercely, glaring into his eyes.

He stared back, his eyes searching hers for the answer. At last, he sat back again and seemed to accept what was happening to him.

'Okay,' he said reassuringly, forcing a half-smile. 'This may sound crazy, but I feel like we've known each other forever. I think that I've always loved you,' he announced, meaning every word.

'I've loved you longer,' she replied, smiling through her tears.

With a shake of his head, he decided to make a game of it to lighten the mood.

'I love you a googol,' he continued, his smile widening in an attempt to diffuse the tension.

The goddess raised her eyebrows at him in mild surprise but was determined not to be outdone by his clever wording.

'I love you a googolplex,' she replied, appreciating his understanding of how she felt.

'You just added to what I said,' he remarked, frowning disappointedly.

She arched her eyebrow again. 'It was there to be exploited,' she replied, though was unable to hide the pain of his condition. 'Thank you for not judging my lack of action in the fall of your world,' she whispered, looking at him sadly.

'There's nothing to judge, Liv. You didn't do it. There is no shame inherited from another's actions and you should feel no guilt for the lives she took,' he replied, kissing her softly. 'There was a bond between us, she and I. I can't explain it, but in the end, there was something there. I can't believe she killed… so many,' he whispered, unable to speak of the ones he meant.

Laying down together, they held each other close and listened to the water flowing off to the side.

Closing her eyes, she felt fear for when the underworld would call to him and dread for when he would want to answer.

***

Somewhere in the deepest reaches of the forest, he heard a plea for help and sat up in shock to scan the surrounding area. The moon hung low in the sky, hidden behind the tall reaching trees causing long deep shadows to stretch all about him.

'Liv?' he whispered, casting his awareness out before realising that she was hidden from him as he was from her.

He was alone, he realised, as the terrified scream sounded again, causing him to direct his senses in that direction.

'There!' he thought, sensing something dark and calculating in that direction.

Rising smoothly to his feet, he took off through the trees in a near blur of motion.

Though the moon was low and the forest dark, he found that he could see everything in perfect clarity. He saw that everything had a bluish hue to it which appeared to be free of corruption, and he suddenly realised that he was running with his eyes closed, his elemental magick seeming to work for him on instinct alone.

The all-seeing sight came from his spirit, he knew, as it was with the understanding of things that simply popped into his head when the need arose. Having traversed the astral plane often enough to recognise its appearance at night, he began to smile, feeling intrigued at what else he was to discover about himself.

Becoming excited, he had never been able to achieve the feat before, not whilst in motion anyway.

'Handy!' he thought, elated with this new ability.

After a minute or two, he passed a break in the trees and exploded from the tree line like some bloodthirsty creature from hell itself. Deeper than even the darkest shadow, he focused his reflective eyes on the scene before him.

A whimper sounded from within the foliage and he narrowed his eyes, seeing nothing at first.

'Please, help me!' a girlish voice pleaded, a voice that could easily have been a child's but for the music in it.

Crouching low, he realised suddenly that he was in his true form and immediately cast his camouflage about himself.

Walking forward in his human guise, he raised his hands peacefully as he began to speak softly.

'I am not here to hurt you, but to help if I can,' he answered, spreading his arms wide to show that he meant no harm.

Looking down, he saw what could only be a fairy and thought it beautiful as it glowed upon the ground.

Sprawled on its back, it was clearly in pain and so he dropped to one knee, speaking again in hushed, soothing tones.

'Do you need assistance, little one?' he asked, squatting down beside her.

The fairy looked young and badly damaged, as though she had been snatched out of the air and crushed within a hand.

He saw that her legs were bent painfully at odd angles and that her shimmering wings seemed to have been fractured around her small frame.

All in all, she looked broken, he thought, and felt an immediate flush of protectiveness for her.

Regarding him with distrustful blue eyes, she shimmered slightly into a deeper shade of purple.

'You are truly here to help me?' she asked, speaking in a pitifully weak voice.

Tenderly, he picked her up and smiled reassuringly at her. 'I am indeed, little one. I am a friend to the Queen of Air and do not prey on those so fair,' he announced, casting his gaze about wearily. 'I seem to have lost her though, for the moment at least,' he added, frowning a little.

Nodding her head, the fairy girl enlightened him quietly. 'She has left the forest for a time, summoned yet again by the witches and their circles. She warned us not to go into the secret wood beforehand, under any circumstances,' she replied, hanging her head rather guiltily.

'But you did anyway,' he replied, arching an eyebrow at her judgementally and smiling with amusement.

The fairy nodded with exaggerated regret.

'I am one of the Sidhi,' she whispered covertly, whispering the words past her hand before casting her eyes skyward. 'We need to get out of here, for he looks down upon us even as we speak,' she warned, searching the heavens nervously.

The hairs on the back of his neck stood suddenly on end and he raised his shield on instinct as his senses screamed at him of danger.

A ground-shattering impact from above took him by surprise and dropped him to his knees as his protective sphere of magick was driven down into the ground.

Looking up, he stared directly into a face of death and cried out involuntarily at the suddenness of the strike.

A head the size of a car glared down at him in a seething, hateful mask of rage as fiery-yellow slitted eyes burned brightly, seemingly on fire themselves as they promised a painful death. Huge pointed teeth, the length of his arm, lined up evilly before his face as the beast hissed its hatred at him. Flames gathered deep within its throat and as it took in a deep sucking breath its scaly nostrils flared suddenly, causing hot air to steam up into the night.

'Bloody hell!' Daire cried, raising his hands above him instinctively.

'Who are you, little man?' the creature hissed through clenched teeth, the sound of it as evil as Daire had ever heard.

Gigantic reddish-black wings the height of a house unfolded from behind it, adding to its intimidating size as its reptilian body stretched up impressively before him.

Daire slowly got to his feet and used the time to gather himself mentally. He took a slow, deep breath and, letting it out even more slowly, he used all of his long-life skills to recover from the initial shock.

The vast experience he had gained over the years allowed him to recover more quickly from this dreadful attack, but still, his adrenaline threatened to undo him.

'My shield holds,' he kept telling himself, forcing the fear down and taking control of the sensation before speaking his response.

'No one of consequence, but no one to be trifled with,' he finally replied, smiling a little at his choice of words. 'Blue would've loved that one,' he thought, thinking of his old friend suddenly.

He had always wanted to say that line but knew that the quote would be lost on this creature, as it would be to all that lived in this dimension.

'Why do you attack me, dragon?' he demanded, trying with all his might to sound more confident than he felt. 'You have attacked me without warning and are therefore without honour,' he continued, shaking his head in disapproval.

The dragon roared at him, the glow of fire deepening in its throat.

'Balls!' Daire cursed, regretting the words immediately.

'Honour?' the dragon raged, clearly insulted by his scolding tone. 'What do you know of my honour?' it spat, the blazing eyes now round and livid. 'You are food, nothing more!' the creature growled as its forked tongue dripping acid to the earth, scalding it with a noisy hiss. 'Does a wolf announce its presence to a sheep?' it asked, baring its teeth at him suggestively.

Daire seemed to think about that for a moment and then finally shrugged his agreement.

'That makes sense,' he answered, putting his hands to his waist with a look of reflection.

The dragon paused and blinked several times before closing its mouth, clearly taken aback as it pulled its great head back to study him.

The scaly brow furrowed with indecision and the vicious eyes underneath simply stared for the longest of moments. The huge mouth opened again as if to speak but then slowly closed, seemingly stumped by his meal's change of opinion.

'So you do not think me dishonourable?' it asked after a while, obviously confused by his admission.

Daire pursed his lips as though considering the question and then spread his arms in apology.

'Not anymore,' he answered, shrugging slightly. 'I see you now for what you are,' he continued amiably, dipping his head to the mythical creature.

The dragon's eyes turned suddenly to slits again as it leaned into him.

'And what is that exactly?' it asked, its deadly-looking claws digging up the earth as it clenched them in anger.

Folding his arms across his chest, Daire tapped his foot rhythmically and though appearing casual, was, in fact, nothing of the sort.

He had learned long ago, that this simple movement would stop his leg from trembling when the adrenaline hit as it had a moment ago, and instead of looking petrified, he would appear unbothered by what had spooked him.

The shaking was caused by the release of adrenaline he knew, that now flowed unchecked throughout his system. Released to enhance his physical prowess in times of need, he had won many a fight with it coursing through his veins. If unused, however, the adrenaline would cause the muscles to tremble, which in turn caused his body to shake. Daire was at this stage, very afraid and full of adrenaline.

'You are a hunter,' he stated admiringly, looking over the deadly monster approvingly. 'I thought wrongly of you and apologise for my error. You are magnificent, now that I truly see you,' he continued, seeing the dragon's eyes widen again.

Slowly, the creature leaned back and rested on its huge hind legs as it straightened up to tower over him.

'I see,' it rumbled, watching him carefully.

Daire's mind was racing, though outwardly he appeared calm and almost carefree under the dragon's scrutiny. Lowering himself, he sat cross-legged upon the floor in an attempt to hide the continuing shake.

Looking up at the creature, he noticed that he in turn was being studied and felt something pass between them at that moment.

'You are not food,' the dragon announced at last, nodding once as though to insure its decision.

Daire dipped his head in acknowledgement and smiled in relief.

'I am not food,' he confirmed, breathing out slowly.

The sides of the dragon's head pulled back suddenly, revealing the deadly fangs again, and it took Daire a moment to realise that it was smiling at him. Relief flooded through him and a broad smile split his face.

'Bloody hell!' he thought, looking up at this fantastic creature as they smiled at one another in the darkness.

Suddenly, the dragon started making huffing noises through its nose and then burst into a deafening roar of laughter that caused Daire's mouth to open stupidly.

The dragon roared again and was forced to turn its head to the side as fire bubbled from its mouth.

Unable to comprehend what was happening, Daire began to smile and couldn't suppress a chuckle. So caught up was he with the infectious laughter, the release of tension fuelled his mirth.

Both bellowed their amusement out into the night, though only the dragon could be heard, and it was some time before both settled down again, breathing hard while looking at each other differently.

Raising a hand to his face, Daire wiped the tears from his eyes and sighed tiredly, the spontaneous hysterics having taken a toll on him.

Glancing down, he saw an incredulous expression on the face of the fairy and instantly steeled himself as he looked again to the dragon.

'Where does this leave us?' he asked, silently praying that the danger had passed.

The dragon regarded him coolly for a moment, amusement still flickering in its fiery eyes.

'You are free to be about your business, but I will be having my bait back,' it replied, eyeing the fairy coldly.

Looking down at what quailed in his hands, Daire frowned before looking back to the dragon.

'Bait?' he asked, at which the dragon nodded sinisterly.

'What are you hunting?' Daire asked, looking around for what the creature was trying to trap.

Turning its huge head towards the trees, the dragon smiled more wickedly.

'More fairies!' it grinned, showing those arm-length teeth again.

Glancing to his left, Daire squinted and then saw that the trees were full of the creatures, tiny glowing lights that flickered delicately within the branches.

'They will come for her and would have by now if not for your untimely interruption,' the dragon grumbled, shaking its head in annoyance. 'I have not had fairy for many a year, and so would have many,' it said, flicking its tongue out to lick its lips.

Closing his eyes, Daire groaned at the dragon's admission.

'Oh, bugger!' he thought, not wanting to fight this beast for many reasons. But he knew in his heart that he could not allow this terrible deed to take place.

'Would you allow me to leave with this one and make a friend of me in the process?' he asked, wincing as the dragon's eyes grew into slits again.

'You would take my food for yourself?' it growled, although lacking its previous hostility.

Daire shook his head, grimacing at the thought of eating such beauty.

'I do not wish to eat her,' he replied, spreading his arms regrettably. 'I have spoken with her and promised my aid... before I knew of you,' he added quickly, wincing again at what was to come.

The dragon roared expectedly, throwing its head back to light up the sky.

'You would choose this conniving thing over me?' it bellowed, looking hurt at the mere suggestion of it. 'You would choose to fight me even after our souls have touched?' it asked, clearly upset by the notion. 'Has *that* ever made you laugh?' it hissed, pointing a long claw at the cowering fairy.

Feeling a pang of sorrow for the upset dragon, Daire could see that its feelings were indeed hurt, and raised his arms placatingly before it.

'I have given my word and am now bound by it, as you would be,' he replied, hoping to strike a chord with the beast. 'Honour demands that I save her,' he added, rising slowly to his feet.

The dragon watched him and though its eyes looked fierce, it did not strike.

'I do not wish to fight you, my friend,' Daire whispered with a slight shake of his head. 'As you said, our souls have touched and it would grieve me greatly if we did not benefit from it. I am truly sorry, but I am honour-bound. Please forgive me,' he babbled, before bowing his head and taking a single step back.

He saw the dragon tense suddenly, causing him to do likewise in anticipation.

'It is my absolute honour and pleasure to have met you, dragon. I am called Daire, and I offer you my friendship from this day forth,' he continued, realising that he was doing all the talking. 'I will now simply walk away, in the hope that our new friendship is worth more to you than a mouthful of fairies,' he finished, walking stiffly away and grimacing with each step.

The magick of the land came immediately to his call and he put it all into his shield as he almost goose-stepped away. Wincing expectantly, he silently prayed that he was not going to be attacked.

'Please, please, please,' he mouthed repeatedly as the distance between them gradually began to lengthen.

The dragon watched him leave, its glowing eyes now wide and round.

'Why did you have to say mouthful!' it grumbled sullenly, looking forlorn as its food was taken away.

On Daire walked, feeling the dragon's eyes on him the whole way. He stiffened at the loud intake of breath, which caused him to involuntarily hold his own. 'Please!' he prayed again, screwing up his face in fear.

'We are indeed friends now, me and thee!' shouted the dragon, causing Daire to let out his breath in a whoosh of relief. 'You may call me *Ddraig*! For that is my name,' it continued, puffing itself out proudly.

'As have you, Ddraig! I hope to see you again soon,' Daire called back, overjoyed by the experience and his narrow escape.

The dragon's teeth glinted again and Daire smiled back before bowing his head in respect.

Suddenly the great wings spread out as Ddraig launched himself into the air, causing the ground beneath it to tremble from its lift.

Feeling the gust of wind against his face from the continuous beat of the colossal wings, Daire leaned his head back to enjoy the sensation of it against his skin.

'Why did you have to say mouthful!' the dragon cried again, the words fading quickly into the distance as it was swallowed by the night.

Looking down at his hands again, he smiled his relief at the fairy.

'You okay, or what?' he asked, puzzled by her expression.

Staring up with wide, searching eyes, the fairy looked first amazed at what had transpired but then scowled suddenly, letting him know what she thought of his friendship with the dragon.

'What?' he asked, feeling a little paranoid under her reproving stare.

'You are a dragon friend,' she stated, speaking the words in an annoyed whisper.

Swallowing his irritation, he remembered what Ddraig had done to her and forgave her judgemental tone.

'I am sorry, little one, but it just kind of happened, don't judge!' he reprimanded lightly with a shake of his head. 'You're alive, aren't you?' he asked, speaking the words defensively.

She nodded and then shook her head at his misunderstanding.

'You didn't hear me, Daire. You have befriended a dragon,' she replied, still whispering, but now with a note of awe in her tone. 'No one has ever done that before, not ever! For they are hateful creatures and eat my kind,' she continued, looking down at her body as though proof of her words.

He studied her face to see if she was serious or not before shrugging offhandedly.

'Why not?' he asked, having found Ddraig fascinating, but then he had not wanted to eat him, he supposed.

She frowned up at him and spoke slowly as though he were somewhat slow of mind.

'Because... they... are... hateful... creatures,' she repeated slowly, narrowing her eyes thoughtfully. 'Will you also be my friend?' she asked, glancing up innocently with a shy smile.

He returned the smile, amused by the question.

'I think that was decided when I saved your life,' he answered, feeling amused suddenly by what the dragon's reaction to this might be.

The darkness around them began to brighten suddenly, as the previously hidden fairies descended from the trees.

At the wondrous sight, Daire threw his head back and laughed out loud, causing the lights to be drawn to him instantly. Hearing a sound like music, he realised that it was their singing, though sung in such a tone as to make him want to weep.

Tilting his head to the side, he strained to listen but could not quite make out the words as they swirled around him.

Kneeling on his outstretched hands, the fairy tried to open her wings experimentally but found that they were too broken and refused her attempts at movement.

Closing his eyes, he sent his mind into her but instead of seeing the light he had expected, he saw only the darkness and understood that this must have been what the goddess had seen in him.

'So it was the dragon I sensed on awakening,' he thought, thinking back to when he had first heard the fairy's cry for help.

The Fae were closed to him as he was to them, he realised, and began to wonder if both species were doomed to be natural enemies.

Determined that this would not be the case with him, he cast a circle of healing around her and willed the earth's energy up into it. The magick of the land rose immediately at his summons and his visualised circle began to glow with its power.

Yelping in surprise, she saw her legs begin to straighten and then heal into their correct position. The wings were next, popping into place like an inflated plastic bottle as they opened beautifully behind her with gold and copper shades that shimmered in the starlight.

At seeing the healing of one of their own, the fairies slowed in their circling and came finally to a stop at the gift he had given her.

After flapping her butterfly-like wings experimentally, she lifted off his hand with an expression of love.

'Thank you, Daire! You have given me such a gift that a song shall be sung about it,' she cried, causing him to wave off the compliment awkwardly.

'You were injured and now are healed, it's that simple, and isn't that what friends do for each other?' he asked, looking at her more nervously.

Her smile widened and she flew to him adoringly.

'You are a true fairy friend,' she announced, looking up at him expectantly.

Relieved beyond reason, he felt glad that she did not think it any more than that.

'Happy to be so,' he replied, as all sounds around them stopped suddenly.

'You are a fairy friend, yes?' she asked again, her little head nodding for him.

He was about to agree when something stopped him, a feeling not unlike the premonition of the dragon just before it had attacked.

Recognising that it was his instinct warning him, he narrowed his eyes as he pursed his lips in thought.

A cold light reflected in his eyes and he could feel the darkness in him reacting to her fiercely.

'What does that entail exactly, to be a fairy's friend?' he asked, his eyes now reflecting more than they should.

'It is an honour to be a friend to us,' she replied cautiously, backing away from this sudden change in him.

His expression darkened further as his demon-self began to rise at the sensed trap.

'I think that it should be you declaring your friendship to me,' he reasoned, feeling the growing tension like ice against his skin.

'Fairy friend is a status in our land and I would bestow it upon you,' she replied, trying to force a smile.

Stretching his arms out wide as though loosening up before a fight, Daire spread his legs a little and shifted his weight onto the balls of his feet.

'I would first like you to call yourself Daire friend and let it carry all of the same commitments and responsibilities as that of fairy friend,' he replied, smiling with his mouth only.

The fairy stared at him without expression, appraising him silently before continuing.

'To refuse such an invitation from us could be deemed an insult,' she retorted, the subtle threat unmistakable and clearly used to coerce him into submission.

Anger lit up his eyes suddenly and he knew that they were the cold reflective white that had frightened Kristina. He narrowed them in an attempt to hide it from her but could see from her expression that it had not gone unnoticed.

'Do you think, perhaps, that *I* should be insulted by *your* refusal?' he countered, desperately trying to quell the urge to snatch her out of the air and crush her as the dragon had.

All the love and warmth evaporated from her face immediately, replaced now with a much colder expression.

'Daire friend is something you just made up,' she replied evenly, trying unsuccessfully to hide her annoyance. 'To be a fairy friend is to be accepted by us. It is a contract set in place long ago and a tradition that was created when the first of your kind were brought here to us... And you refuse?' she asked, shaking her head in disbelief.

Standing stock-still and fighting off the dark desire growing in his mind, Daire took a deep breath in an attempt to control himself.

'I am Daire,' he thought, willing himself to remain as he was, but the goddess was gone now and his demon was rising.

Try as he might to stop the images from coming, Daire pictured them burning and dying in his mind, envisioning a firestorm that would render these manipulative bugs to ash.

'I am Daire,' he willed again, forcing himself to remain.

Sighing heavily, he dismissed the idea with a shake of his head and then drew power into his voice as he had with the elements.

'I would have been a good friend to you, Sidhi, but if you don't wish to be...' he said, shrugging his shoulders a little, 'then this conversation is over,' he added, a low rumble of thunder emanating from his chest.

He subtly cast his shield but instead of the usual sphere, he created it just under his first layer of skin and bound it there so completely, that when he moved, it would move with him. Harmless to himself, undetectable to them.

With his eyes unfocused, he looked to better see what she was up to and as expected, saw her magick extending out towards him, as it was from all the fairies that were gathered around him.

Cold fury drained his face of colour and he had to control his breathing as the darkness took hold.

'After placing my life in danger for her, she would enslave me? Bind me to her will?' he seethed silently, picturing again the life being crushed from her fragile form.

There was no doubting the change in him this time and she backed away fearfully, seeing the creature within coming for her.

'I see your magick around me, Sidhi,' Daire remarked, the thunder in it almost drowning out his words. 'Do you seek to bind me, little one?' he asked, seeing that he was surrounded now by a wall of light.

'I mean you no harm, Daire, and am simply ensuring that you will do likewise with us,' she answered, glaring back with a cold look of her own.

He glanced at the wall of light around them and saw it begin to close as though to hem him in.

'You seek to enslave me, and that is why you cannot be my friend,' he challenged, thinking again of ending the debate with violence. 'If your intentions were pure, you would not ask me to be this "fairy friend",' he continued, his face beginning to darken as his eyes took on a more reflective sheen.

She saw that he was almost black now and felt sure that he was as dangerous to her as the dragon had been. They stared at each other for a long moment, neither one backing down.

'I suggest,' he said at last, giving her one final out, 'that we are to be "friendly" with one another. No pact or contracts, just friendly as it should be,' he offered, already picturing his hand snaking out.

The fairy's head tilted to the side and he knew that she was thinking of another angle to manipulate the situation.

'If I agree to this, granting you this favour, then you shall owe me a favour in return,' she replied, smiling at him slyly.

He smiled wider in return, but it was more like the leer of a wolf that had finally cornered its prey.

She saw the hint of fanged teeth as his lips curled back and was reminded once again of that dreadful dragon.

'Your time is up, little one,' he whispered, his tolerance finally at an end. 'I'm done with this tiresome debate,' he snarled, tensing suddenly to spring.

'Friendly!' she cried, blurting out the word that caused the now white eyes to narrow in response.

After a brief pause, he nodded once before turning to leave.

'Time I was gone,' he announced, feeling his control at its end, but her held-up hand signalled him to wait.

'You owe me a favour for allowing this,' she barked, the authority back in her tone.

White light suddenly flashed behind his eyes, the light of Spirit interceding before the demon was finally set loose. Annoyed by her continuous attempts to bind him, he rounded on her with a cold and calculated frame of mind.

'It is you that owes me, my friendly little fairy,' he replied, snarling out the words. 'For I have not only saved your life but healed you also,' he growled, flexing his hands involuntarily.

The fairy's head snapped up, her face growing fierce.

'I did not ask for your help, and could have healed myself!' she replied, her fury plain to see, and he began to revel in it.

Tutting mischievously, he raised a finger and began wagging it at her slowly.

'You called out for help and were non-specific in whom it was you called for. I came and the deed was done. Also, you thanked me, which if I am not mistaken is a life-debt!' he continued, knowing now that he had her exactly where he wanted her. 'If you didn't need me to heal you, then you should not have thanked me for it and in doing so accept the gift that I bestowed upon you,' his voice rumbled as the sky flashed suddenly as though to mark his words for emphasis.

The fairies flew into the air suddenly, looking like a fiery tornado as they swirled up faster and faster, their anger at being outdone apparent.

They would have fought him then, or fled, he was sure, if not for the fact that they had agreed to be friendly.

She stared at him hard, spite twisting her features into an ugly grimace.

'My agreeing to be friendly cancels them out,' she replied testily, pouting up at him like a scorned little girl.

He shook his head and smiled his disagreement.

'Not so! Agreeing to become friends is simply an amiable thing to do, nothing more. My labour on your behalf was before this and requires a debt owed,' he hissed, looking to her now more fiercely than any dragon she had ever seen.

A high-pitched wail issued from the tornado of lights and Daire smiled as though it were music to his ears.

'Were I your true friend, however, then no debt would have been incurred at all, but...' he added, pausing for effect, 'you refused!'

She screamed then, low and guttural, causing him to laugh aloud that one so fair could utter such a sound.

Without a word of parting, she flew from him and merged into the mass of fairies that hid her instantly within its light.

A long time passed and he looked back across the clearing to the point where he had entered, seeing it clearly now in the light of the swirling storm of fairies.

Thinking it well past time to leave, he turned back suddenly when a light detached itself from the rest and came flying back towards him. It was her again and she was chuckling in resignation.

'You have bested me Daire, bested me, *bested me*!' she repeated and flew a little closer to him, although not too close as to put herself in danger. 'We have all agreed that we would rather be friends with you than to owe such debt,' she continued, shaking her head incredulously. 'Will you allow us to be your friends, and in so doing, cancel all favours owed? For friends do such things freely, do they not?' she asked, regarding him with what looked like respect.

He looked at her suspiciously, but could not see how she could manipulate the situation any further and so finally nodded his agreement.

She laughed with genuine amusement at his wary expression.

'Fear not "friend", for you have bested me, earning yourself our respect and our true friendship. I name you "Friend to the

Fae" with no contract binding you in any way,' she announced, bowing low in apology. 'Forgive me Daire, it is simply our way,' she added, smiling at him a little sadly.

Glowing ever-brighter, she threw her head back and made her oath.

'We fairies are friends of this one called Daire, having from this day forth his best interests and that of his kin in our hearts. We also decree that all Fae acknowledge him as a creature of magick and accept him as thus from this day forth,' she announced, smiling mischievously at his uncomprehending stare. 'We leave you now, friend, to do what thou wilt,' she finished, and like a mass of giant fireflies, the fairies swarmed back up through the trees.

Standing alone in the gathering darkness, he felt its black touch a welcome companion, for there was no longer a moon to illuminate the area and the stars that shimmered gave off little of their light.

'Did this just happen?' he asked himself, looking up at the lightening sky. 'Bloody fairies,' he thought, pleased that he had not killed them in the end.

'Where the bloody hell is she?' he whispered, thinking again of Olivia before turning back the way he had come.

On returning to where she had left him, he laid down and closed his eyes, falling instantly to sleep. His wariness from the long night's toil sent him into a deep slumber and his last thoughts were of two small children calling his name.

***

Just before dawn, the shadows darkened suddenly, chasing away the blue haze of morning when it should have been getting lighter.

A shadow detached itself from the darkness and crept up to him slowly before settling down behind him.

'Forgive me for what I have allowed tonight, my Daire,' she whispered, softly kissing the back of his neck.

He opened his eyes at her touch but kept his breathing regular, unwilling to announce his wakefulness in that moment.

'What have you allowed?' he thought fearfully and prayed that his children were safe.

***

They made their way through the enchanting forest, all the way to its eventual end, and saw at last a palace of white rising mysteriously out of the mist-shrouded lake that surrounded it.

Five tall spires reached hundreds of feet into the air. But for its elegant beauty, the structure seemed in itself impenetrable. The sheer, glasslike walls glistened as though cut from diamond, and what looked to be a massive moat was, in fact, a lake that spread out a mile or so in all directions.

Within the outer walls was a vast city of a graceful people, fair-haired and pointy-eared.

Daire knew that these were the mythical elves that were once believed in back in his world and could not help but stare at them as he passed them by.

He frowned suddenly, seeing fairies fly past like fiery bees or the glowing embers from a fire.

Standing at the water's edge, he paused a moment with a question in his mind.

'Do you think that we've been seen together?' he asked, gesturing back into the forest.

She looked to see if he was serious, clearly taken aback by his concern over the matter.

'What do you think?' she asked, raising her eyebrows at him questioningly.

His shrug caused her eyes to flare, and his mischievous smile disappeared when she punched him on the arm. The contact was perfect as both leading knuckles struck him, pinpointed to the lower end of his bicep.

'Bloody hell!' he exclaimed, instinctively holding his hand over the pain.

'I told you that I would hurt you!' she raved, glaring at him fiercely.

Seeing that her point was made, she took a deep breath and began to smile as she spoke. 'No one saw us, but that is not to say that they do not know. All will know that we are bound together,' she answered, rolling her eyes at his look of pain.

Rubbing at his arm, Daire smiled wryly.

'Well, not awkward at all then,' he replied, causing her to laugh at his distress.

'As awkward as you choose it to be,' she responded, her tone turning lofty as she once again became the Queen of Air.

On entering the gates to the city, three guards in glowing silver armour stepped to the side and bowed before them deeply, their bright blue eyes twinkling in barely-contained amusement.

The same expression seemed to be on all of the faces that passed them, and after bowing low to their goddess, they all looked up at them in the same way.

'My Queen. My Lord,' they would say. Daire was almost positive that one elf winked at him as he turned to leave.

Stealing a glance at Olivia, he smiled sheepishly at her deeply crimson face.

'Not awkward at all,' he said sarcastically, chuckling to himself.

'Shut up!' she snapped, turning an even deeper shade.

'You're positively glowing,' he continued, attempting to see how red she could go.

The Queen shot him a scathing glare, her embarrassment making her bite at his provocation.

'Shut up!' she demanded, eyeing his arm in a threatening manner at which he shrugged over-dramatically and shook his head.

Her eyes widened at his teasing and she leaned into him swiftly.

'Shut up!' she hissed, daring him with her eyes to continue.

'That's a negative,' he replied, causing her to chuckle involuntarily.

'Stop distracting me!' she said through her giggling, before fanning her face with her hand.

As they walked on, several fairies flew down before them to bow before their Queen.

'Greetings to you, Goddess, and to you our beloved friend, Daire,' they said as one, laughing mischievously as they flew away, leaving their goddess at a loss for words.

Olivia shot him an incredulous look and searched his eyes for what she had missed.

'You have some explaining to do, I think,' she remarked, believing that she had not been gone that long the night before.

Taking her hand, he winked at her confidently.

'I'm a nice guy, everyone wants to be my friend,' he bragged, chuckling again at her reaction.

Turning to him before the palace gates, she took his hands in hers.

'I need you to control yourself at all times, Daire,' she said seriously, holding his eyes with hers. 'You cannot ever let them see your true form. They will not understand,' she warned, feeling guilty for asking him to do this.

Daire simply nodded, having other issues on his mind.

'Are my children safe?' he asked, causing her eyebrows to lift in surprise.

'I will not lie to you Daire, they are not safe and won't be until you learn to control yourself,' she answered, then tilted her head at a sudden thought. 'Unless you bring them here?' she asked, nodding at his unasked question. 'I would for you,' she whispered, squeezing his hands tightly.

Daire looked at her and smiled tightly.

'They would not come alone,' he replied and then frowned as she shrugged her reply.

***

The fire crackled back into life after Kristina had plonked two new logs on top of it. The sap pockets within the wood exploded suddenly, causing burning embers to spit out one after the other, sounding like a cracking whip as they were spat into the air, before finally diminishing upon the hardwood floor.

'You've met someone?' she asked sarcastically, throwing her arms up in exasperation. 'The bloody Queen of Air?!' she blurted, but instantly took back the comment and whispered a silent prayer of forgiveness. 'I pray to her!' she rasped harshly, keeping her tone low.

'Don't put your faith in that one,' he advised bitterly, but she saw that there was a note of regret in his voice. 'She blessed your circle knowing that it would hurt me,' he added, struggling to hold his voice in check.

Kristina's brow furrowed and she shook her head in disagreement.

'The goddess did not bless the circle, Daire. She allowed it, yes, but refused the blessing,' she replied, waiting for him to understand.

It was his turn to frown and he looked to Kristina to translate.

'Huh?' he grunted, causing her to roll her eyes and sigh tiredly.

'Not as all-knowing as you thought, are you?' she sneered, staring at him brazenly while shaking her head. 'A blessed coven has the god's or goddess's protection, it has her strength and is, therefore, damn near impossible to break. You would not have been able to crush our circle if it had been blessed,' she informed, looking at him with a little resentment.

'But she allowed it,' he replied, annoyed by her manner.

She nodded patiently as though to a small child.

'Yes! She allowed it, but you clearly don't understand the rules of witchcraft. If she had not allowed it, she would have killed all thirteen of us!' she replied, driving the words home with her glare.

Closing his eyes, Daire appeared to deflate at the news and rest his head back in misery.

'It matters not,' he whispered finally and Kristina saw the pain in him again. 'It's done with now anyway,' he added, sighing sadly.

Jack slapped his hands down hard upon his knees, drawing attention to himself.

'Can we get back to the story?' he asked, giving Kristina an irritated glare.

Cristian held up a hand, causing Jack to huff with impatience.

'So what are you, Daire?' he asked, looking across at his brother. 'I mean are you a demon? An element? God or what?' he asked, causing the old wizard to grunt his approval.

'I was created as a spiritual being, ripped as I was from my mortality, and then, in my great wisdom, I was corrupted by demonising myself,' he replied, grimacing as he spoke. 'I can't even begin to tell you how happy I am to have done that,' he continued sarcastically before groaning to himself. 'I'm not even sure if my corruption is just skin-deep, or whether I have polluted my spirit too,' he added, shrugging his shoulders at whatever the outcome would be. 'Que sera,' he whispered, closing his eyes again and running his fingers through his daughter's hair, remembering what followed after entering the palace of light.

Chapter Four

The goddess stood before him, staring at him sternly with one hand placed femininely upon her hip.

'You are thrice born,' she began, speaking in the commanding voice of the Queen of Air. 'Born of man, spirit and daemon. This is who you are and you need to accept it. Become one with it and have no regrets,' she continued, striding towards him purposefully.

Daire shook his head, a look of disagreement crossing his features.

'My body was killed, surely that makes me just spirit and daemon?' he asked, but she continued as though he had not spoken.

'You must, therefore, combine all three personas into one mind, as I have said before!' she said, widening her eyes slightly. 'You have a "now" mind or "conscious" mind and a "subconscious" mind. I have said also that you are to become of one mind,' she continued and then stopped, raising an eyebrow at him.

'I understand,' he intoned, sounding like a robot, which caused her to laugh.

'Well, now you also have to incorporate your daemon-self into the mix and use the benefits of all three. Can you name them?' she asked, raising both eyebrows this time.

Daire looked ahead vacantly and almost raised his shoulders but stopped himself at the last moment.

'I have no clue,' he replied, forcing himself not to shrug.

Her eyes narrowed warningly after sensing his urge and she shook her head at him in warning.

'Firstly, from the man in you comes free will and imagination. Secondly, the spirit gives you strength of will and would have given you purity, but you cocked that part up, didn't you?' she asked, admonishing him with a scowl. 'Thirdly, with the daemon comes immense power, near invulnerability and a natural hatred for life,' she announced and waited for his reaction.

'I don't hate life!' he retorted, annoyed by the remark.

'Really? Is that so?' she asked, saying each word slowly. 'So tell me then, o man of peace, when was the last time you thought of killing someone, or anything, for that matter?' she asked, fluttering her eyelids at him prettily.

Instantly thinking of the fairies, he began to scowl at remembering that it even crossed his mind to off Kristina, thinking her too much of a risk to the children. There were the Bloods and the Egni, not to mention the entire world, if he failed to protect his children.

'Okay, let's move on,' he sighed, folding his arms grumpily before him. 'I didn't act on it,' he mumbled as he looked to the floor.

Olivia laughed then, amused by his childlike manner.

'I'm glad to hear it!' she replied, still chuckling. 'Just know that they are the daemon's urges within you, which are now your own, I suppose,' she added, frowning at him again.

'Anyway!' he snapped, spreading his arms in frustration. 'Where do I start?' he asked, eager to get on with it.

Nodding her approval, she thought it best to start at the beginning.

'Let's deal with what the elements did to you, first. What is it you believe they did to you?' she asked, needing him to understand before he could control it.

Daire half-shrugged but stopped himself again, feeling irritated suddenly by her dislike of it.

'They killed me,' he answered, frowning at the memory.

'No!' she snapped, but then sighed more patiently. 'That was incidental. The elements are spiritual beings with an affinity to their respective element. They took your spirit and reshaped it, moulding it, if you will, into something different. They enhanced you, making you more than what you were,' she paused, waiting for him to acknowledge her words.

'I understand,' he intoned, drawing yet another smile from her. 'Sounds great on paper,' he added sarcastically, then waited for her to proceed.

Satisfied that he understood, she continued more swiftly. 'They basically made you one of them, or as close to them as they could, and in creating you anew in your world they thought to tie themselves there, which they did, for now they have a connection to it, a right to be there as all others have,' she said, pausing again for him to answer.

Daire breathed out dramatically, feeling as though they had already discussed this at length.

'I understand!' he growled, drawing an annoyed look from her this time.

'Good!' she snapped, glaring at him venomously. 'What they actually did was cause you to ascend, to become a higher form of life and not the element that they had intended. It's why you fought it from the very beginning. You fought it because you have free will, a quality the elements lack and, therefore, don't understand,' she stopped again, looking at him in an odd sort of way, causing him to raise his head in question.

'So, what am I then?' he asked tensely, frustration getting the better of him.

Olivia shrugged and pursed her lips, imitating him exactly.

'You are something new, not a man or an element, and not a daemon,' she answered, seeing him relax a little at this.

His eyebrows rose hopefully as an answer came to his mind.

'A demigod?' he inquired, smiling a little as he nodded his head.

'No,' she replied bluntly, but pondered on the question further. 'Though that is in the realm of where you belong,' she replied, looking at him thoughtfully. 'I think that you're probably more of a Titan than anything else, simply for the fact that you have corrupted yourself so completely,' she finished, shaking her head as though to a foolish child.

Daire looked skyward and groaned loudly, annoyed now by her continued rebukes.

'Yes, yes! Get over it, will you?' he moaned, running his hands through his hair in irritation.

'Well!' she grumbled, scowling at him in frustration. 'This would be so much easier if you hadn't, you fool!' she added, annoyed by his whimsical ways. 'You're almost there already but for the daemon in you, and it needs to be addressed sooner rather than later,' she continued, looking at him with concern. 'I fear what merging with it will do to you. However, if you don't try then you'll simply lose control whenever you get angry,' she warned, lifting her chin decidedly. 'You must surrender to the daemon,' she announced, knowing exactly when and where he would have to do it.

***

Waiting for the time of Samhain, when she believed the darkness in him would be at its strongest, the goddess took him deep into the bowels of her palace where a hidden door opened at her touch.

The cold stone blocks receded from her, folding in upon themselves to reveal a dark and ominous-looking passageway.

Stepping forward, Olivia gestured towards the mounted torches set all along the walls. Fire flickered instantly into life, revealing a circular chamber that filled him instantly with dread.

Looking around apprehensively, Daire eyed the large iron-linked chains that lay upon the floor and then turned to her with a scowl.

'What the hell is this place?' he asked, wrinkling his nose in distaste.

'This is where we imprisoned the daemons before they were defeated,' she replied coldly, remembering the last demon to be shackled here.

Daire instantly felt trapped and looked at her with his hackles rising.

'You would bind me here?' he asked, his face draining of colour.

She looked hard at him and slowly shook her head.

'This is where *you* bind yourself,' she replied and held up a hand before he could respond. 'We need to find out how strong your daemonic self is and if your other aspects have the strength to control it. You need to win this fight and you need to do it now, for them,' she added, meaning his children.

He stared at her and nodded, believing that she must know what she was doing.

'I trust you,' he whispered, walking to the centre of the chamber. 'For them,' he repeated, closing the clasps around his wrists.

'Now, drop your mask,' she ordered, speaking again in her queenly tone.

He closed his eyes and released his control, causing her eyes to widen at the immediate transformation. It was quicker than usual, the time of year making the darkness in him stronger, as she had predicted, and she began to worry that it was too much for him to master.

Where the man had been, stood now a demon, taller by a foot or more, and as deadly as any she had ever seen. His only definition was his eyes, shining reflectively as they absorbed the light of the torches.

Feeling a cold shiver of remembrance, Olivia saw again the last demon to be shackled here. It was one of the most powerful she had ever encountered, and there was no telling them apart now as the darkness cloaked him.

Taking in a deep breath, she strode forward to confront him.

'The chamber is circular so that there are no corners for evil to hide in,' she began, gesturing around the room with a sweep of her arm. 'I have brought you down here because I have something to say, something that I dared not tell beforehand,' she continued, waiting for his reaction, but the demon, her demon, merely stood there waiting, or biding its time, she was not entirely sure.

Taking in another deep breath, she placed a barrier around him for good measure.

'There has been an attack on the house, and upon your children,' she declared quickly, bracing herself for his reaction.

A low rumble of thunder shook the chamber, causing her to look up before realising that the noise had come from him.

'The vampires attacked your children in the forest after their mother foolishly took them there,' she continued, holding back the outcome.

The demonic eyes narrowed and she could see his teeth glint evilly in the torchlight.

'So you chain me here, fearing my reaction,' he replied, the power in his voice causing the walls to tremble around them.

'I dreamed of such a thing last night. I heard my daughter calling for my help and that I helped them through it,' he continued in a tone that was deepening by the second. 'I am with you,' he whispered, remembering the dream.

The goddess nodded and poured more of her power into the barrier. 'The reality was, sadly, so much worse,' she answered coldly, folding her arms before her.

With impossible speed, he smashed the iron clasps together, sending the shattered pieces to scatter across the floor.

'Iron will not hold me,' he growled and then hissed at her through his teeth.

'I will bind you here until you control yourself,' she replied defiantly, internally shaken at the ease in which he had escaped the enchanted chains meant to hold him.

'You think me some mindless beast?' he seethed, glowering at her with what looked like hatred. 'I should thank you, however, for finally unleashing my full potential,' he growled, taking a step towards the entrance. 'I see now that I was foolishly locking this part of myself away, even after having tasted its power so sweetly before,' he confessed, breathing in deeply and stretching as though waking from a deep slumber.

She studied him silently, seeing nothing of the man she knew. She watched as he paced towards the exit, stopping just before her magickal containment.

Surprised that he could sense exactly where her barrier was, she swallowed hard as he began to angle back towards her, following the curve of his containment. He touched a finger to it as he approached, causing a long golden line of reactive magick to trail in its wake.

She rose her chin challengingly, daring him to test his might against her own.

'Tell me how they died,' he demanded, speaking in a low and thunderous tone of voice.

She watched him closely and started to doubt this tactic, wishing desperately that he was more susceptible to her influence.

'Kristina took them into the forest after sensing the remains of your previous body and they were attacked there. They managed to fight their way back to the house but there was another attack there, and this time there was a Blood Lord,' she replied, hating herself for doing this to him.

A low growl erupted from his chest, mixed now with true thunder which reverberated around the stone chamber, causing dust to fall from the high ceiling above.

The torches along the walls began spluttering out one by one until none but two torches burned.

She stood her ground, though was baffled as to how his influence could extend beyond her own.

On reaching her, his baleful eyes bore into her own and she believed then that she had lost him forever. The evil face creased then and the pain she saw made her sob suddenly.

'I ask now that you kill me,' he growled, surprising her to the core.

She wept then quite unexpectedly and desperately wanted to go him.

'I can't,' she sobbed, emotion causing her voice to tremble.

Surprising her further, he lowered himself to the cold stone floor and knelt before her.

'I must depart this life,' he replied, no longer wishing to continue his existence.

Looking down upon him in horror, she realised what he was about to do.

'Oh, my Daire. No!' she cried, weeping loudly.

'I will kill if I am allowed to continue,' he replied, tears glistening in his catlike eyes. 'How badly I want to kill. I would not stop at the Bloods. I would kill them all,' he whispered, raising his hands to look at them.

All the torches roared into life simultaneously, illuminating the chamber as though having never gone out at all.

Crouching down before him, she dropped the barrier and took his hands in hers.

'Your children live, they survived,' she sobbed, pulling him to her.

'What?' he rasped, tensing suddenly against her embrace.

'You have friends that have joined the fight. They slew the vampires, the Blood Lord among them,' she replied, nodding at him in earnest.

He closed his eyes and fought the demonic urge to strike her down, understanding finally that the desire was not his own, or that it was, but not what it should be.

'They are safe?' he asked, almost choking on the words.

She nodded, letting his hands go at last.

'They're safe, I sent many elven knights to watch over them. They slew most of the vampires but couldn't fight them all. The lord sent most of his force to engage mine and then proceeded to hunt your children,' she sighed, regretting not sending more of her army. 'If not for your friends...' she stopped, letting the rest go unanswered.

Rising to his feet, his eyes never left her as he towered over her.

'Well, I believe that I'm as one minded as I can get after this little ruse,' he said, his reflective eyes seeming to darken a little. 'I need to go back to them, now,' he added, intent on leaving immediately.

Reaching out, she touched his arm to stop him.

'We have barely scratched the surface of your abilities. We need to continue the training,' she stressed worriedly, but he shook his head resolutely.

'That's not why we're here,' he replied, leaving little room for further discussion on the matter. 'I need to be with them and only when they are safe will I return to you,' he said, feeling an instant ache at having to leave her. 'Unless you come with me?' he asked, his eyes pleading with her silently.

She looked down to the floor and felt saddened by her inability to accept.

'I can't, Daire, I am forbidden from taking direct action in your world after what was done in the past. It would anger those that rule there if I stayed too long,' she replied, wishing with all her heart that she could accept.

Daire was about to say more when a shocked expression crossed her face.

'What?' he demanded as a shiver crept up his back.

She shook her head with a look of disbelief crossing her features.

'There's a daemon in the forest,' she answered, her voice a deadly whisper.

Before he could respond, she took him by the arm and the chamber fell away, leaving them standing suddenly in the throne room.

Focusing his mind on his appearance, he visualised himself human once again as the assembled crowd turned to face them.

Armed elven warriors were gathering in a hurry, as were the knights that led them, and all seemed to have gathered around a small central figure.

'The Queen is here,' a guard shouted, after seeing her stride purposefully towards them. 'Make way for the Queen!'

The crowd parted and Daire was surprised to see so many different types of Fae gathered together in one place. From the long-legged elves to the short squat forms of what could only be dwarfs. Fairies hung in the air high above as they too neared the object of scrutiny.

Upon the floor rested a small, spindly creature with large disproportionate features and a thin cruel-looking mouth. After a moment's thought, Daire realised what he was looking at.

A pixie, standing no more than two feet tall, came slowly to his feet.

'My Queen,' he greeted, bowing low while in her presence. 'There be a daemon in the forest,' he announced, his tone grave as he peered up.

'To arms!' their Queen cried, needing no further incentive.

'We are ready,' a lightly-toned voice answered as a tall elven knight stepped forward immediately.

The Queen raised her arms into the air and spoke with the air of a goddess. 'Elimon, eradicate this foul creature from our lands,' she commanded, giving her knight a nod of approval.

'My Queen,' he responded, bowing his head to her will.

'I'll go with you,' Daire declared, stepping forward before she could object. A roar of approval resounded around the room, stopping any attempt she might have made to keep him there, and left her staring at him worriedly.

Elimon stepped forward and clasped Daire's forearm in a warriors grip, his large blue eyes shining bright with determination.

'You are most welcome,' he approved, before turning for the door with his men in tow.

As all the elven warriors followed, Daire glanced back to her briefly and as their eyes met for that singular moment, he read the worry in hers.

She understood, of course, knowing that this was something he had to do. He had to see this creature that he was now akin to and know also if he could overcome it. She closed her eyes to hide the tears and began to wish futilely that she was not bound by an ancient promise to her people. She knew that her safety was paramount to them, the risk of the Shadow Queen's return simply too great to ignore.

He was gone when she finally opened her eyes, and she stood there for a moment as a solitary tear fell to her cheek.

'Please,' she whispered, dreading what he would find out there.

***

Deep within the forest, the elven warriors stalked silently through the trees like ghostly spectres hidden within the green.

Elimon was pleased to find that this 'Daire' was just as silent as the rest of them, if not more so, and found that he had to quicken his pace just to keep up with this strange new man.

After refusing a sword to arm himself, his Queen's consort had raced on ahead and they had been forced to follow, having no ability to sense the evil creature themselves. Intrigued when he had apparently picked up the scent, they had been hard-pressed to keep up with this mysterious stranger.

The knight found himself wondering what manner of being this 'Daire' truly was, for clearly he was no mere human. His speed and silence marked him as Fae, but he could sense no such kinship from this young-looking man.

Elimon crouched down low and scanned the area ahead for any sign of the one who led them, seeing Daire simply vanish into the trees ahead of him, dissolving into the underbrush without so much as a sound.

'Where are you?' he pondered, squinting his elven-blue eyes a little.

Edging forward, he froze suddenly when a hand clamped over his mouth and pulled him back a step into the shadows.

Paralysed with the shock at what had just happened, Elimon knew that he was at the mercy of the one who held him.

'Only a daemon can get the drop on an elf,' he thought, waiting for the demon to finally kill him.

Slowly a hand came into view, pointing off through the trees and on into the distance.

'Shhh!' a voice whispered, causing the elf's eyes to follow where he was directed. 'I see you,' the voice hissed, still pointing ahead.

Through the foliage, Elimon saw what he was shown, seeing a deeper shadow easily missed as the demon bent over its kill. Only its movement allowed the elf to track it. One by one the fingers lifted off his mouth and then the hand relaxed as it slowly lifted clear. Glancing back, he saw Daire with his strange eyes still fixed on his target.

Nodding to the knight, Daire rose fluidly to his feet and strode purposefully toward the alien-looking creature.

At his approach the daemon's head snapped up, sensing his presence at last, and it turned to receive him.

'You are not welcome here, demon!' Daire announced, pointing at the creature without breaking stride. 'Go back to the shadow!' he growled, instantly thinking of his old friend again.

Rising to its full height, the demon waited for him with a gnash of its teeth.

Realising that the demon had only been kneeling, Daire took in a deep breath as it now stood towering over him. Standing a good twelve feet off the ground, its eyes, that were surprisingly different from his own, glinted a hateful red. Huge leathery wings as black as the rest of it unfolded from behind it, adding to its size.

'You shall not pass!' Daire shouted, but then froze at what lay at its feet. 'No!' he cried, seeing the broken body of a little child and the blonde hair that lay strewn across her face, almost covering her sightless blue eyes.

'No!' he screamed again, seeing his own little girl where the other now lay. Without pause or deliberation, he sent his wrath at the creature, lifting it off its feet to crash through the trees.

Caught off guard by the sudden attack, it rose again amongst the many felled trees and roared back at him, throwing out its clawed hand in a crushing gesture.

Daire's shield took the blow and began to glow white in his defence before his counter-attack blinded those who witnessed as silvery lightning shot forth from his hands, smashing into the damned thing with terrifying force.

The huge wings ripped back as the raw energy struck at the creature, punching into its chest and then continuing along its torso.

Hissing in pain, the demon sent its power again, intent on destroying this little man that had hurt it so badly. Its red lightning hit his shield with sickening force, causing the trees around them to burst into flame as it ricocheted off the sphere of white.

Seeing his protection weakening, Daire triggered his ring by kissing it and the might of the land responded to its need, replenishing the weakening sphere immediately. Looking up, he saw the vile creature fall upon him with a ferocious disregard for its own safety, intent only on ending his life swiftly.

With a wave of his arm, Daire called the fire from the trees and sent it roaring into the thing, engulfing it within a torrent of flame, but the demon seemed hardly to notice its touch, even after it was sent into its eyes and down its cavernous mouth.

Arrows thumped into the demon's chest several times in succession, causing the creature to grunt in pain and take a step back, but they seemed unable to penetrate deep enough into the thick, leathery hide and so, after a growl of rage, it came at him once again.

The demon's claws punched through his shield suddenly with a sound like gunshots, causing him to quickly glance about for anything that would help vanquish this terrible monster.

On seeing the blonde hair again, he froze, his instant emotion ripping the breath from him with a scream of loss. In his anguish, he hurled his hatred out, holding nothing back as he poured his very soul into the attack.

The victorious gleam in the demon's eyes turned instantly to fear, for the little man was man no longer, transforming now into something far more deadly.

It backed away immediately at the transformation, shaking its terrifying head in shocked recognition at what now stood before him.

The hateful dark power held the demon fast, wrapping itself around its wings and crushing them in a vice-like grip. Loud cracking sounds erupted, the bones of this murderous creature now beginning to break, and in its desperate attempts to break free, it began ripping itself from them.

Elimon stood aghast at seeing the change in the man, knowing now that there were two demons standing before him. He wondered briefly as to why this child-killer was so afraid of the other, taking in its size and overall viciousness as he stared in muted horror at what, if not who, this Daire truly was.

He saw the two demons clash again, but could see now that one was pitifully afraid of the other and desperately trying to escape. He saw the giant creature fall back from this other, blacker one and saw a look of pleading in its eyes as it fought to stay alive.

'Forgive me!' it cried as black blood began frothing from its mouth, but the plea fell on deaf ears as the ceaseless attack continued.

Finally, the snapping sounds were replaced with that of crunching, and Elimon realised that this killer of children was being crushed from the inside. This was no longer a fight, he thought, looking on with widening eyes, this was torture, pure and simple.

The white reflective eyes looked up suddenly, straight into the blue of Elimon's, causing him to inhale sharply and hold the gaze as he was rooted to the spot.

Without blinking, Daire stood slowly to tower over the elven warriors and with a monstrous clap of his hands, the defeated demon turned instantly to ash.

A deathly silence descended as the elves looked to one another in uncertainty. Should they attack their mortal enemy? But he had killed the other and was now bound to their goddess!

Spellbound by what had occurred, Elimon stared at the demonic form as it began to slowly move away. Stopping before the child, it seated itself beside her and slowly reached out to stroke the young girl's hair. Frowning at the scene, he saw the black shoulders begin to shudder suddenly and frowned at his warriors in confusion, before realising that the creature was weeping.

Sharing a look of sadness, the Fae moved forward to sit likewise around the little girl and extended their hands to touch them both. It was a gesture of sharing, sharing the loss of one so young.

Time passed and the sun began its descent towards the distant horizon, lowering itself to sit upon the treetops before finally succumbing to the darkness. Not one of them had moved in all that time, each mourning the tragedy that lay sprawled within their circle.

Finally, Daire lifted the still form and cradled her to him, rocking her back and forth as he continued the stroking of her hair. He whispered to her gently as though she were still alive and kissed her upon the brow, wetting it with tears.

Closing his eyes, he visualised the power of the land rising through him and into her, knitting her broken bones and healing her savage wounds. A part of him knew that he should not be able to heal her in this way but in his grief, he had not the inclination to ponder it further.

Finally, Daire stood, lifting her effortlessly in his now human-looking arms and turned in the direction of the palace.

'She could be sleeping,' he sobbed, looking to Elimon as a fresh wave of emotion threatened to unhinge him.

He looked into each of the elves' eyes and saw his own pain in theirs, the evil committed too vile to accept but must be endured.

'The fairies rightly call you friend,' a tall, muscular warrior whispered, tears coursing freely down his face.

'We care not for your origins or your heritage,' said another, still with his hand placed upon his own.

Elimon looked at him, his tear-stained face a mask of agony.

'You are Fae,' he said simply, finding no greater compliment to give in that moment.

'Not all will see me as such,' Daire replied, his voice strained and full of despair. 'But I thank you all the same,' he added, nodding in response to the knight's gesture, and together they made their way back through the forest, bonded now in more ways than one.

***

She stood waiting as the warriors finally emerged from the forest, seeing them appear like wraiths to stand at the water's edge.

She had seen the fight that had been fought, witnessing it in detail from the sense of the trees, and had felt from the resulting fear that the change had come over him, fear of him becoming the demon that her kind hated.

Even from this distance she could see the child and knew that this had been the cause of his torment.

'Oh, my Daire,' she wept, seeing that it was Daire himself who held the small child, holding her tightly in his arms as though she was his own little girl.

Blinking away the tears, she saw her elves touching him, sharing in the pain and anguish they felt.

'Oh, my Daire!' she cried again, unable to contain herself further. 'What grief you must have shown them,' she whispered, crying suddenly into her hands.

A wail went up at the sight of them and the mass of waiting Fae rushed forward to meet them. The warriors continued and the gathered crowd parted before them, reaching out their hands to join in the sharing.

Tears coursed down Daire's face and the anguish in his eyes would never be forgotten, for none but the Fae could feel so deeply for one of their own.

A fresh cry erupted as a couple of elves stood waiting in his path and Daire stopped then before them, reading the worst kind of a pain in their eyes.

Lowering his head, he kissed the girl upon the head and then tentatively passed the child over to her father, who stepped forward to take his burden tenderly in his arms.

A great wracking sob escaped the elf and he buried his head in the child's neck, crying pitifully as her mother rushed forward with a high-pitched wail.

Daire shook his head, not having the words to console them and turned to hug a warrior closest to him, unable to contain himself any longer.

***

Three days later the body of the child was laid upon a large stone platform at the centre of the courtyard, with the Queen herself standing regally on top of it.

The entire area around them was packed with Fae of all kinds, come now to say goodbye to one that should never have been allowed to leave.

'She goes now to the light, for light she is and always shall be,' the goddess intoned, her emotion causing her voice to tremble. 'Her body has been healed and cleansed from the touch of darkness and for that, we give you thanks, Daire,' she said with feeling, but avoided his eyes so that she could continue.

He closed his eyes at her words, seeing his own daughter in his mind as he lowered his head in silence.

'Her spirit departs now to the afterlife,' she continued, looking down at the child's parents.

Standing apart, he watched from a distance, fearing that he would pollute what came next with his dark essence.

Slowly, the gathered masses touched one another on the shoulder, as the warriors had done with him, their combining magick caused them all to glow subtly, until both grief-stricken parents pulsed with the energy of it.

Gesturing for both parents to touch their child, the goddess bent down to kiss her upon the brow as the body received the light, causing it to glow like the morning star itself.

In his anguish, Daire was unable to differentiate between this child and his own, causing him to double over from the agony of the emotion. Looking up suddenly, the breath caught in his chest at the sight of the child sitting up and then standing for a moment upon the dais. He was unable to hear what was said, if indeed anything was, but the goddess glanced at him briefly before returning to her task.

Finally, the essence of the girl became transparent and floated up as it faded from this world, moving on to another.

In his grief, Daire was unaware of what his heartbreak had caused in the Fae, for they believed that his agony was solely for the death of their own, and as one they opened their hearts to him.

Something out of the corner of his eye caused him to flinch instinctively, before seeing that in an attempt to console him, several of the elves had sent their blessings to him.

Glimmering like golden sand upon the air, a glowing butterfly dissolved instantly into his chest as it made contact. Concerned, he thought for a moment to shield himself, but a head shake from the goddess warned him against it.

Closing his eyes, he let them come, bracing himself against the rush of magickal wishes. He felt a warmth begin to spread through his body and a swell of love wash over him as the magick seeped in.

Opening his eyes, he bowed low and placed his hand over his heart in appreciation. Smiling in response, the Fae returned the gesture with a bow of their own.

***

Standing in her bedchamber, Daire looked out of the high-arching window and on towards the forest beyond, feeling a deep need to be from this place though not from any desire in his heart.

'How did it cross over? There has not been a crossing since the old ways were barred,' the goddess pondered, glancing at him briefly. 'I just don't understand how, after so long,' she continued, narrowing her eyes at his silence.

Sensing her displeasure, he turned and saw her staring at his vacant expression.

'Penny for your thoughts?' she asked, causing him to snap out of his contemplations.

He shook his head, dismissing his worries. 'Nothing, I just feel vexed,' he replied at last, holding his arms out to her.

Sliding smoothly from the bed, she stepped into his embrace and kissed him tenderly before they stared at each other, forehead to forehead.

'Funny,' she thought, thinking that this simple gesture was now their trademark move.

'I must leave,' he whispered, kissing the tip of her nose.

'I know,' she replied, silently wishing for him to stay.

'What will you do if another demon comes through?' he asked, fearing for the elven warriors.

Olivia smiled and arched an eyebrow at him. 'We are not without magick,' she chided lightly, shaking her head at his concern.

'Your elves are not up to the task,' he said flatly, picturing the demon in his mind.

'Elimon and his warriors are the first line of defence, and it's a tradition to send them in first. I was forbidden to act, but no longer!' she replied, her eyes widening fiercely. 'My people's magick is strong and after putting the realm in a state of alert, I am now allowed to act after the nature of the threat has been identified,' she continued, her expression saddening. 'Will you walk with me, my Daire, one last time?' she whispered, feeling tears well in her eyes. 'You need to say farewell to them and accept the gifts that they give to you,' she advised, looking as though she was about to cry. 'You have won their hearts as you have mine,' she added, wrapping her arms around him.

Puzzled by her words, he pursed his lips in thought.

'How do they know that I'm leaving?' he asked, kissing her earlobe softly.

'They know,' she whispered, unwilling to say any more.

***

Elimon stood waiting with a look of regret masking his features, and was the first to present him with gifts.

'For the battles that lie ahead,' he whispered, holding out a black spell-woven tunic that seemed to absorb the light, as he had appeared when fighting the demon.

'A most befitting gift that has clearly been given much thought,' the goddess remarked, eyeing the clothing appreciatively.

Elimon had insisted that he change immediately, forcing a black pair of leggings and boots of the same depthless quality into his encumbered arms.

'Very impressive,' she approved after he had changed, eyeing him up and down admiringly.

'I do like them,' he confessed rather self-consciously before smoothing himself down and smiling at her boyishly.

'You look fantastic!' she assured him, amused by his unease before stepping behind him. 'This is from me,' she whispered, kissing the back of his neck tenderly.

About his shoulders, she draped a cloak of majestic beauty that was as black as the rest but made by her hand. It was long but only in places, hanging to his calves in uneven strips.

His mouth opened in awe as a light shimmered across the surface of the black fabric, causing him to appear translucent suddenly, and just before he vanished completely, he saw the faintest hint of starlight.

'May it protect you and see you safely wherever you wish to go,' she whispered, stepping back once more.

'I love you,' he admitted, knowing that she had given this gift so that he could return with his children. But he would not dare until the demon threat had been taken care of.

The city streets were packed with the Fae, all bowing low as they walked amongst them. On being seen from across the street, a few elven men approached with heads bowed to their Queen.

Interpreting their intent to do the same to him, Daire stepped forward to stop them and after taking each by the shoulders, he hugged them in turn.

'I am your friend, nothing more,' he assured, dipping his head to them. 'May we always be so,' he added, bringing smiles to their faces.

A hug from an elf, he was to find, was like that of a child and he laughed with joy at their tight embraces.

'You will regret that before this day is over,' Olivia remarked, her face flushing with humour.

She was right of course, for now, every few yards, after first greeting their goddess appropriately, he was then stopped by all manner of the creature to be hugged in farewell. Young and old, elves, pixies and dwarfs all came to hug their friend goodbye.

A heavy thump of impact sounded somewhere up ahead, causing them to feel the vibration of it through their feet. A deafening roar from that same direction caused fairies to scatter in all directions, true fear etched onto their faces.

Seeing Daire brace at the sound, she placed a calming hand on his arm and smiled reassuringly.

'When I summon, all come,' she said smugly, leading him through the gathering crowd as they approached the cause of the disturbance.

Daire noticed that the elves showed none of the concern that the fairies had and began to smile to himself. Hearing another roar at their approach, he could think of only one creature that could make that terrifying sound and began to chuckle in recognition.

The massive form of a heavily-scaled blood-red dragon crouched low before them, but even hunched as he was, Ddraig could not conceal his impressive mass for long.

Rows of vicious-looking teeth glinted suddenly in the sunlight, bared now into a smile of greeting. Rising to his impressive full height, the dragon spread his huge wings high in a display of grandeur.

'Greetings to you, Goddess,' Ddraig began in a deep and terrifying tone. 'I have come as requested to aid and counsel in your time of need. Be assured that the daemon did not pass using the old ways,' his voice boomed, echoing loudly through the full city square. 'I am the first, but more will come,' he added, dipping his head to her respectfully.

Positively glowing with pleasure, Olivia knew only too well that dragons were a law unto themselves and not known to answer a call to arms even when summoned by the goddess herself.

Feeling a flush of relief at the dragon's words, she felt thankful that these unpredictable creatures were ignorant of the crossing and seemingly eager to help in putting it right.

Being the self-proclaimed guardians of the dimensional gateways, the dragons had a natural gift to traverse the worlds, and the underworld was of no exception. Due to this ability, they were unable to be locked away as the demons had been, and the gods had been forced to call peace with them, rather than to seek their utter annihilation. However, the dragons knew that they too would have been cast down into the darkness had it been achievable, and so the truce between them was fragile at best.

Having the dragons here to fight alongside them meant a great deal to Olivia. Their added might would ensure her people's safety.

Smiling outwardly, she wondered what the reasons were for answering her call now, at this time, knowing also of another of their gifts.

'What's changed?' she thought behind her smile.

'Daire!' the dragon roared and lowered its head down to his eye level.

The huge yellow eyes glowed brightly at spying him and he smiled even wider than before.

'It is good to see you, my friend,' Ddraig greeted, winking at him conspiringly. 'I was wondering when we might meet again,' he continued, speaking in a wicked-sounding tone.

Suddenly, Ddraig pulled its head back and opened its front legs invitingly.

'I've been watching for quite some time actually,' he added, inching his massive head forward.

Laughing finally in understanding, Daire stepped forward to hug the beast as he had the Fae for most of the morning.

'Careful now, not so tight!' the dragon mocked, grimacing as though in pain.

On a whim, Daire spontaneously drew up the earth's energy and sent it up into the dragon, renewing the creature to its peak condition and then some.

Daire found the correction easier than expected, seeing a similar quality in the dragon as he had in himself, and after mastering the manipulation of water, fire, he found, was of little difference.

Erupting in a thunderous growl of pleasure, Ddraig seemed to glow momentarily before settling back down, the blood-red of his scales now almost black.

Revitalised, the magick burned brighter in Ddraig's fiery eyes, which now looked down on him with surprise and maybe a touch of sadness.

'You have given me such a gift!' it roared, looking down to the man with wide appreciative eyes.

'No!' the goddess screamed, but she was too late to stop the exchange as something else passed between the two, a gift that was great and terrible at the same time.

Stumbling back, Daire buckled to his knees with a taste of copper in his mouth and the acrid stench of metal up his nose.

'He has too much in him already!' the goddess cried, admonishing the dragon with an angry glare.

'Then a little more won't matter!' Ddraig retorted, placing a claw around the falling man to steady him.

After a moment the dizziness passed and Daire shook his head as though to clear it. He was dimly aware of the heated exchange and raised his hands to signify peace.

'Whatever was done, was done in friendship,' he mumbled, breathing in deeply to right himself. 'Let it go, what's done is done,' he stressed, desperately trying not to vomit.

The goddess glared at him and shook her head at the ridiculousness of what had just happened.

'I started it anyway,' Daire added, looking up at the dragon dazedly. 'What exactly did you give me, Ddraig?' he asked, still holding onto the claw for support.

Slowly turning its attention from the goddess, Ddraig lowered his head conspiringly.

'I gave you what all secretly desire, my friend,' the dragon replied, before inching forward more secretively, 'I made you a dragon,' it whispered, winking a flaming eye at him.

A gasp swept through the crowd at the admission, for a dragon's whisper is not a whisper at all but more of a hoarse bellow.

'Well, he did start it!' Ddraig growled defensively, gently pushing the man towards the waiting goddess.

She shook her head in exasperation as she took him in her arms and held him to her tightly for a moment.

'What else are you to have thrust upon you?' she asked, holding onto him as though in fear of losing him.

Glancing back to the dragon, Olivia sighed suddenly in resignation.

'Forgive me, Ddraig, I tend to overreact when it comes to this one,' she apologised, dipping her head a little in the creature's direction.

Ddraig seemed to swell at the apology and then smiled, taking the high ground.

'As do we all,' he replied, suddenly launching himself into the air, ending their conversation with a huge beat of his wings.

Feeling more himself, Daire stepped back with a look of concern.

'What does this mean?' he asked, concern making his voice sound tight.

She regarded him contemptuously and shook her head with a look of frustration.

'You've taken on yet another aspect to overcome, you fool!' she barked, before finally controlling her tone. 'Ddraig has bonded with you and given you his essence, it will grow in you, changing you yet again!' she clarified, chuckling nervously. 'What else is there for you? Fancy some unicorn shit?' she asked sarcastically, glaring at him again.

'What will that do?' he asked, lifting his eyebrows and quirking his mouth down at the sides.

She stared at him for a moment before finally realising that he was shrugging at her with his face! Her eyes widened wildly and then narrowed in annoyance, for now was not the time to test her patience.

'So, I'll be some kind of Dragon Lord?' he asked, making the expression again.

'No!' she snapped wrathfully, incensed that he had been pulling that expression ever since she had struck him for shrugging. 'You will be some kind of dragon!' she snarled, angered further by his incomprehension. 'At least that's what would have happened… but you have so much in you already, so who knows what the outcome will be,' she continued, and then laughed again, somewhat hysterically. 'Oh, my Daire, is there no end to your self-harm?' she asked, thinking it better to laugh than cry.

He shrugged then with his face and shoulders and smiled slyly at the look in her eyes.

'You annoying, pain in my arse!' she growled, raising her fist threateningly.

'Took you long enough,' he laughed, holding up his arms defensively. 'I've been pulling that face for ages, ever since you took issue with me shrugging,' he replied, laughing at her livid expression. 'Like, who has an issue with shrugging?' he asked, raising his shoulders again. Her eyes narrowed, causing him to pull 'the face' again in defiance.

The elves nearest them began to giggle but turned their heads quickly as she glared in their direction.

Shaking her head slowly, she stepped forward and held him close.

'You are the bane of my existence,' she whispered wearily.

'You have no idea,' he replied, kissing her gently on the nose.

She stiffened suddenly and stepped away from him before turning back in the direction of the palace.

Puzzled by her reaction, he felt a coldness creep into his blood as she distanced herself from him further. Seeing the cause of her separation, he bit his tongue and turned to the man who approached them.

Studying the newcomer's movements, Daire knew immediately that he was a warrior born, and noted the self-confident manner in which he was draped.

The muscles in Daire's jaw pulsed rhythmically as he clenched his teeth in anger, and on glancing back to Olivia he saw her cheeks flush as though she were caught red-handed.

The warrior's fair hair was tied back and the loose top he wore showed much of his muscle, 'Designed for exactly that purpose,' Daire thought, hating the man on sight.

'Diar,' she gasped, as the fighter approached with a confident swagger.

Dressed in many shades of grey, the man reeked of wealth and clearly set himself above the gathered Fae. Simply by the way he looked down upon them as he passed, Daire knew that his first opinion was not going to change. Coming to a stop before them, he nodded to the Queen with an affronted expression.

Across the warrior's back hung a great sword of iron and another smaller blade was sheathed at his waist. Two long spears were held loosely in one large hand, but what was most noticeable about the warrior was the red spot on his forehead that seemed out of place and somewhat unintentional.

After a moment of silence, he bowed before the goddess and spoke in a smooth Irish lilt.

'My Queen, you have called and I have come,' he greeted, ignoring Daire completely.

She smiled at the newcomer and replied to him in kind.

'Greetings Diarmuid, it is good to see you also,' she responded, stepping into his embrace for longer than was needed.

'Come, dismiss this servant so that we may speak more freely,' he said, almost daring her to refuse with his penetrating stare.

Glancing at Daire briefly, she saw his white face and collected herself immediately.

'You are mistaken Diar, this is no servant. Daire, this is Diarmuid, demigod to the Irish people of your home world,' she replied, keeping her tone carefree and her face composed.

Smiling wider at this, Diarmuid showed her his very white teeth as he voiced his reply.

'I wonder,' he inquired, ignoring her words and angling her away with a guiding arm. 'If we might spend some time together, just the two of us,' he added, slyly glancing over his shoulder.

She shook her head apologetically and spread her arms a little.

'I'm afraid that I cannot,' she replied, appearing nervous in his company.

Daire began to boil at seeing her act in such a way, believing her almost coy in this man's presence, like a love-struck teenager. Jealousy rose in him and he desperately needed her to put this stranger straight. He needed her to claim him, to say that he was hers and that she was his.

'Why aren't you telling him!' he silently raged, feeling the pain like a dagger in his heart. 'I am going to kill you, Diarmuid!' he seethed, though spoke only with his eyes.

Glancing at Daire nervously, she seemed to read his expression and shrugged off the warrior's restraining arm.

'I am with Daire now,' she replied, moving back to him immediately and linking her arm through his. 'My Daire,' she added, finally acting like herself again.

The colour drained from Diarmuid's face, causing Daire to smile at the sign of danger.

'So it's true, you have chosen,' the warrior replied, his voice shaking now with fury. 'How long have you known each other? You think that I…'

Her eyes flashed in anger at his tone and she cut him off abruptly.

'Be warned, Diar, for such questions are not yours to ask. Know only that I have chosen and you can either rejoice as others do, or leave. I am glad that you have come to assist against the daemon threat, but that is where it ends. That is all,' she said, feeling her face flush.

Expecting him to back off after the threat in her voice, Daire was surprised to see the warrior enraged by her words.

'Rejoice? For what? Being rejected? Rejoice that you have chosen a weak, pathetic little human over me?' he sneered, looking in disgust at Daire once again. 'You chose before I had a right to challenge him!' he shouted, gripping the spears in his hand more tightly.

Without hesitation, she stepped in front of Daire protectively, barring Diarmuid's path as he moved to step forward.

'As you have done so gallantly in the past?' she asked, her weak persona dropping like a stone. 'You challenged any who showed interest in me and killed them, for what?' she asked, speaking now in her queenly tone. 'For nothing!' she answered, reaching back to subdue Daire's desire to fight.

The goddess was taken aback as she touched his arm, feeling his restrained power somehow rippling under the skin and she knew that he would not be able to contain his nature for long.

'Now leave us, for I tire of your unwarranted jealousy,' she continued, dismissing him with a wave of her hand.

Diarmuid's face twitched and Daire knew that the conversation was over. The darkness inside him responded to the threat, rising from within him like a volcano and he closed his eyes in an attempt to contain it.

'Is he so weak that you need to protect him so? Is this what your people need in one who is to become their king? A coward!' he hissed, as froth began to gather at the edges of his mouth.

Feeling the demon just under the skin, Daire sought desperately for the clarity of Spirit and became dimly aware of Elimon and his warriors spreading out around them, held at bay by the eyes of their Queen.

Knowledge and understanding came to Daire suddenly, enlightening him from the spiritual light but spoken from a mind of darkness.

'*Diarmuid Ua Duibhne*,' Daire's voice rumbled, booming from him like the sudden thunder above. 'Fury will not avail you against my might,' he continued, his dark eyes beginning to lighten as the darkness began leaching into his skin.

Olivia looked at him in horror, seemingly frozen with indecision. She had given her word to a god, promising that his son would be safe in her land, and sought for a way to end this foolishness without breaking any of her oaths.

Thunder boomed again as a sheet of lightning blanketed the sky above them and she knew without looking, that the same light now pulsed in her Daire's eyes.

'Decide, or I will decide for you,' Daire thundered, stepping towards the waiting demigod.

Diarmuid Ua Duibhne, son of Donn the god of the dead, crouched low in defence, facing off against the Titan who possessed the might of the underworld and that of the elements, and whose veins now flowed with the blood of dragons.

Diarmuid hefted his spears in both hands now and stepped to the side to stalk his would-be prey.

'This is no man,' he thought desperately, seeing something tremendous darkening the once mortal-looking flesh. He realised then that the man had been an illusion and that what he now faced was just a hint of what was underneath. Deciding to keep a cautious distance between them, Diarmuid kept sidestepping to keep his enemy off-balance.

Watching the slowly circling demigod, Daire raised his darkening hand before him and shattered the spears that were clutched in the other's hands.

With a cry of alarm, the fragments cut Diarmuid all about the arms and torso, sending blood into the air with a blinding flash of light. The previous confidence leached from the wounded warrior as his blood began to flow, turning his expensive grey clothing black.

Staggering back, Diarmuid looked down in alarm in the knowledge that his blood would not stop flowing from the contact with the enchanted wood.

Desperate to end the fight quickly, the so-named Fury Blades appeared in his hands and he launched himself forward with fear-fuelled rage.

'Enough!' the goddess commanded, the sight of so much blood forcing her into action.

Diarmuid fell to the stones and gasped in pain as she finally intervened, stopping them both by the suddenness of her attack.

Buckling to one knee, Daire felt her numbing control take hold of him and looked back in surprise, unable to believe that she had turned her power against him. The last thought he had was of her, who he had given his heart to and who had now ripped it from him.

His expression was not missed by Olivia and her stomach tightened at the judgement in his eyes.

***

His awareness returned to him suddenly, causing him to sit up and look around wildly. He saw that he was back in her bedchamber and felt the white silk sheets cool against his skin.

He looked into the large hazel eyes that were there to greet him but held her back with the look in his eyes. They regarded each other in silence for a time, realising that this was a pivotal moment for them both.

'Why did you attack me?' he asked, his eyes shining at her betrayal.

She took a deep breath and let it out patiently, the air of the Queen wrapping about her.

'I didn't attack you. I stopped you, there's a difference,' she replied, causing his expression to turn cold.

'Not to me!' he hissed, causing her to recoil from him.

'I will not be spoken to like that, not by you or any other,' she admonished him, still carrying the mantle of the goddess.

Biting back another wrathful retort, he closed his eyes and continued in a more measured tone.

'You did to me, what was done so very long ago. I didn't forgive it then and I won't forgive it now,' he assured her, nodding his head with sincerity.

Her eyes grew wide at his promise and she sensed the change in him, feeling his dreaded withdrawal from her.

'You're overreacting, I did what I had to do. Please believe me!' she whispered, casting aside her regality.

He shook his head, unwilling to hear her reasons, and she felt the loneliness in him, the overwhelming sense of betrayal.

'Please, Daire, you don't understand. I love you. Please understand, I have sworn to his father that no harm shall come to him,' she cried, her status now long forgotten.

Ignoring her, he rose from the bed and began to dress swiftly.

'Where are you going?' she asked, placing her hands over her stomach.

Pulling on his boots, he glared at her and replied with a note of conviction.

'My time here is at an end,' he announced, rising again to his feet.

Dressed in his black garments, he reached for the cloak but then glanced at her and shook his head imperceptibly.

'Daire, please? You were turning daemonic right there in front of everyone,' she pleaded and made as though to reach for him but stopped at his fierce expression.

His eyes looked into hers with an expression that said more to her now than his words ever could.

'I would never have turned on you, Liv. Not ever! So what if your people saw? They would have found out about your embarrassing little secret sooner or later. The warriors know and you know and I suspect that the fairies know also, so why not the rest?' he vented, causing the walls to crack behind him. 'So what if I had killed that scum? You said yourself that he'd killed many in the past. Why did *you* attack me?' he roared, unable to accept her apology.

Stalking towards the doorway, he growled back over his shoulder.

'I was attacked like that before, by my father! He struck me while my back was turned, as you did,' he seethed, throwing her betrayal back in her face.

There was nothing Olivia could say and she knew that now, for his hurt from his previous betrayal was far too deep. She sat back on the bed, their bed, feeling tears sting her eyes and a sickness settle in her stomach.

'I love you,' she whispered, lowering her head with regret. Without looking up, she knew that he was gone and began to cry at the hole that was forming in her heart.

***

The glade looked very much like his own, he thought, staring across the wide expanse of grass in the middle of the forest. Except there was no large stone, he noted, and no sign of the fight he had fought.

Looking up at the night sky, he bathed in the rays of the oversized moon and closed his eyes sadly. 'Why did I return at all?' he whispered, remembering himself creating this new body.

He had thought of destroying this corrupted body many times, thinking that maybe he could make a new one.

'But what if I can't?' he thought, daunted by the prospect of being unable to return. 'What if the corruption is more than just skin deep? I am more a danger to them than even the Bloods are!' he thought, knowing more from the knowledge of Spirit than he had told the goddess. 'Maybe I could help them better as a spirit,' he mused, not knowing which way to turn. He wept at the thought of his children, picturing again the murdered elven child.

'Time to die,' he whispered, deciding to end it there and then, but for the low moan of anguish from behind him.

'All or nothing,' Olivia sobbed, feeling dread that it might now be the latter. 'I can't survive again without you, Daire,' she whispered, pleading with him to forgive her with her eyes.

In a fit of despair, he looked inward to see how he could unbind this tainted version of himself and fly free once again into the realm of Spirit.

Looking up at her, he smiled sadly and accepted his fate.

'Goodbye,' he whispered, falling to his knees in the moment of decision.

Olivia screamed at realising his intent and ran to him in desperation.

'Don't leave me!' she cried, hauling him back to his feet. 'You need to protect them!' she screamed, knowing the trigger that would ignite him, and she saw his eyes blaze as she knew they would.

'I am betrayed! My family, Kristina, and now you!' he answered, choking on the words. 'If I stay, I will be the betrayer! Don't you see? I am more a danger to them than all the others put together! If I can see this, then why can't you?' he cried, dropping again to his knees.

Looking lost and forlorn, she lifted him again in her crushing embrace, willing him to forgive her.

'I'm sorry, Daire. I am so sorry,' she wept, cupping his face in her hands. 'I love you and will prove it to you given the time. But you must exist for me to do that!' she cried and held him close.

He sagged against her, shaking his head in defeat.

'When you see as I have seen, you will regret this moment and the chance you had to stop me,' he whispered, causing her to stiffen.

'You come before all others. To me, you come first,' she replied fiercely, meaning every word.

Pulling back, he stared at her long and hard.

'If I am to stay, then you must promise me that no matter what, you will put my children first. Their lives before mine,' he said, staring at her unblinkingly.

Knowing him as she did, she nodded her agreement and voiced her oath.

'Their lives before yours,' she swore, knowing that nothing short would suffice.

Light blazed suddenly off to one side, close enough for them to feel the heat of it. Turning to investigate, he narrowed his eyes to study it further.

He saw fairies come from the trees, drawn to the fire like moths to a flame, but without the expected finality. He watched them dreamily, resting his head on her shoulder and wondered tiredly as to its meaning.

'Please?' a voice cried, causing his eyes to widen.

Chapter Five

The room was dark by the time he had finished, with only a low flame flickering over the now decimated logs.

'A Titan!' Jack announced, clearly impressed by what his friend was.

'Dragons are real,' Cristian whispered and whistled low as he shook his head.

Kristina said nothing, but her thumbs tapped furiously upon her mobile phone and only after the information was supplied, did she sit back with an indifferent shrug.

'So you *are* their daddy!' she remarked, speaking of the Bloods and grimacing coldly.

'Titans are real bad-asses,' Cristian informed her, looking at his brother as though he were about to sprout wings.

'So, who was this Queen of Shadows character? Sounds a bit dramatic and fanciful if you ask me,' Kristina cut in, looking around the room for answers.

'That must have been that witch that took a liking to you after you first managed to raise the earth element,' Jack guessed, looking at Daire for confirmation.

'I think she took an interest in me a long time before that, mate,' Daire replied darkly, remembering all the times that he had encountered one malevolent witch or another. 'Though I didn't know her to be a goddess at the time, which was my main reason for disliking witches in the first place,' he continued, looking at Kristina pointedly.

'So, what do we do now?' she asked, changing the subject immediately.

'Right now? I'm going to Bedfordshire,' he announced, lifting Francesca gently in his arms.

The child moaned but did not stir and without further ado, he silently left the room. 'Goodnight,' he whispered, leaving them to it.

After putting his daughter to bed, Daire slumped behind his desk and peered down at the half-read book that lay discarded upon it. Turning it over irritably, he glanced at the title and read the words aloud.

'Practical Magick - for the truly gifted.' Intrigued, he flipped it over again and read the chapter's title. 'Seeking,' he read aloud, smiling at his daughter's intuitive mind. 'You're too intelligent for your own good,' he thought, picturing her searching through his shelves.

Snapping it closed with one hand, he looked again at the cover and wondered how many of the tomes she had searched through before finally stumbling upon this one. 'You never lost hope,' he whispered, looking at the mountainous volumes on the arcane.

The attic was spacious and looked more like a library than the storage space it had been intended for. He had fitted the large bookshelves seamlessly along its borders and had built large skylights into the roof to allow in all the light he needed.

Taking in a deep breath, he took in the smell of old paper and musty books, breathing the scent in warmly before placing his head in his hands.

'I miss you,' he whispered, thinking suddenly of another and feeling incomplete for the very first time.

Gesturing lazily to a stack of shelves opposite him, the wall of books slid forward suddenly and then parted smoothly to reveal a double bed with shiny white sheets.

'Like hers,' he thought glumly, remembering her sitting there crying.

Rising to his feet with a sigh, he walked around the table and frowned, seeing something dark placed upon the white. Stopping at the foot of the bed, he swallowed hard and picked up the gift that she herself had made for him.

'The Cloak of Shadows,' he announced, naming it there and then.

Laying down, he wrapped it about himself and closed his eyes to dream of her.

'Goodnight, Liv,' he mumbled, before finally falling into darkness.

***

From within the shadows at the far end of the room, slanted white eyes regarded him coolly until his breathing deepened into the rhythmic sounds of slumber.

'Goodnight, my Daire,' she replied softly, tilting her head a little as she watched him sleep.

***

'So, what's the bloody plan?' Kristina asked again as the four settled themselves back onto the sofas.

'For you to listen, understand and follow my bloody instructions!' Daire growled in reply, barely able to contain his irritation.

Jack cleared his throat irritably, intent only on getting down to business.

'I think we should seek an alliance with the MD,' he advised, annoyed at their constant bickering.

Cristian shot him a condescending look and shook his head mockingly at the old man's choice of words.

'Could you be more of a dork?' he asked, grimacing over at his brother.

'Meet the King of the Dorks,' Daire announced dryly, gesturing grandly in the wizard's direction.

'Mankind's Magical Defence Department,' Kristina piped in innocently, her eyes opening wide.

'Meet the Queen of the Dorks,' Daire added, using the same tone of voice as before.

Cristian laughed, seeing the same wide-eyed expression on both of the proclaimed royals.

Giving the brothers a vulgar gesture, Jack continued unfazed.

'All the factions have united again since your father's attack...' Jack began, drawing a gasp from Kristina that stopped him dead.

Daire scowled at her and sighed in irritation, causing her to flush suddenly with embarrassment.

'How can you know about the MD and not know about the attack?' he asked, looking at her impatiently.

Sitting a little straighter in her seat, she placed her hands awkwardly on her lap before answering. 'It's not that, it's just that... I only now realised that Colin is your father,' she replied lamely, feeling her face growing hotter.

Frowning quizzically at her, Cristian narrowed his eyes.

'You knew that he was *my* father, though, and that Daire is my brother?' he asked, squinting his eyes further as though struggling to understand.

'Yes! I just didn't make the connection until now. Okay?' she snapped, warning him not to continue with a glare.

'Okay...' he breathed, raising his hands before him and smiling at her a little too awkwardly.

Shaking his head, Daire sighed tiredly.

'Shall we continue?' he asked in a tone that sounded like boredom.

Staring at her out of the corner of his eye, Jack began again but kept his focus on her as he spoke.

'The council was attacked by Colin,' he began again, slowly taking his eyes off her. 'The druids sent him packing, though, and unified the factions,' he continued, clapping his hands together at that last announcement.

Daire cut in, having already heard the tale.

'I agree, David, Jack, whatever! We should go and invite them here. It might be good for the children to see others with magick, not just those rancid witches,' he growled, giving Kristina another look of disapproval.

'Get over it,' she sighed and rolled her eyes tiredly, causing him to glare at her all the more.

'If you put them in danger again, it will be the last time you do,' he promised, his voice deepening with the threat.

Cristian spoke up to break the renewing tension.

'I have a card to play that may even "up the playing field", so to speak,' he offered, glancing across at his brother.

Grimacing at the Egni vampire, Jack covered his ears with his hands.

'How many game analogies can you put into one sentence?' he scoffed, giving another vulgar gesture.

'Daddy! Jack's being rude,' Francesca said, entering the room from the darkened hallway.

'That he is, baby girl,' her father agreed, frowning over at the wizard. 'Should I smack his bum?' he asked, arching an eyebrow at the old man menacingly.

'Silly, Daddy,' she giggled, and then laughed at his expression. 'I have a question,' she blurted, sitting herself down on his lap.

'Okay,' he replied with a smirk, patiently waiting for her to continue.

'Why do people with magick have different strengths?' she asked, tilting her head back to look at him.

Daire smiled at her inquisitiveness.

'I think maybe because there are two types of people. Those that have the gift, where the magick is inside you,' he began, pointing at her heart. 'Those with the gift, like you and Lucian, can do stronger magick than those that have learned it,' he finished, kissing her on the head.

'So, why are there people with different strengths who have the gift or have learned the magick?' she asked, struggling to verbalise her question.

'Hmm,' he mused, pursing his lips as he pondered the question. 'Some simply study harder, while others have the ability to visualise more clearly,' he answered and continued before her mouth could open again. 'Visualisation and imagination,' he bellowed in a booming, over-dramatised tone of voice.

Francesca screamed as he tickled her ribs and she squirmed frantically to get away.

'Elmo... stop!' she laughed, before jumping off his lap not the least bit distracted.

'So, why is mine and Lucian's magick different?' she asked, keeping her distance from him this time.

'Well, you are going to be a sorceress, that is clear,' he said, the smile slipping from his face. 'A sorceress is someone who has magick in their bones, someone who finds using magick as easy as breathing,' he continued, struggling to find the right words that she could understand. 'Lucian however, lacks the excitement you have for rudimentary magick and only seems interested in... battle mage, maybe,' he mused, as though talking to himself and staring off into space for a moment.

Francesca closed her eyes and repeated the names in a whisper.

'Thanks, Daddy,' she said, running from the room and racing back up the stairs.

'Why did she run off like that?' Jack asked, still looking out into the hallway.

'She's gone to research the names I gave her,' Daire replied, smiling satisfactorily on hearing the attic door close. 'My girl,' he announced proudly and closed his eyes with a smile. 'She takes to magick like a duck to water,' he added, shaking his head ruefully. 'So!' he barked, keeping his eyes closed. 'Jack and I will contact the wizards. Cristian will play his card... and Kris?' he said, opening his eyes to look at her. 'Don't cock-up!' he warned, receiving her finger in response.

***

Maps lay spread over the large wizard's table as John, Chloe and Charlie peered over them meticulously, drawing up plans for the continuing war. The wizards' head office was abuzz with activity, with satellite imagery and thermal scans showing on many of the computer monitors.

Battle mages were filed all along the outer walls, weaving untold magick in defence against another attack.

Not taking any chances, Charlie thought that another attack was more probable than not and that it was better to be prepared than to be caught off guard.

Truth be told, he was not really worried about the Bloods at all, his primary concern was Colin, the once high wizard of the ancient world, and his deadly faction.

'It's no use!' a wizard reported from the hearth at the end of the room, causing Charlie to look up as those next to the scry nodded their agreement. 'The house, the two new powers, everything! Gone as though never there at all,' he announced, slumping back onto the stone floor.

John looked from the scry to Charlie and was surprised to see the mage smile.

'He's back!' Charlie growled, thumping his hand down hard upon the mapped-out table.

'But how do we make contact?' John asked, seating himself tiredly as Chloe's head shot up, an enlightened expression on her face.

'Why not send a letter?' she asked, shrugging her shoulders.

John laughed at the simplicity of the notion and was about to nod his agreement when her glare silenced him abruptly.

'Quiet!' Charlie shouted, turning towards the large glass doors as the room silenced immediately.

A low growl came from beyond the entrance and as they strained to listen, the growling grew louder as more of the wolves joined in.

'Bloods!' Charlie bellowed, spurring his mages into action as he began weaving protective spells around them.

'How did they get in?' Chloe asked, her face now fear-stricken.

Ignoring the pointless question, Charlie placed his ear to the cold glass door and heard the sound of a vampire's hiss mixing in with the wolves' aggression.

Flinching back, he touched the doors and strengthened them just as they vibrated from the momentous battle erupting on the other side.

A scream from behind caused him to turn as black forms began dropping through the ceiling.

'How the hell did they get up there unnoticed?' he thought briefly, before cursing himself for the useless, time-wasting thought.

***

Crouching low, Daire glanced over at the setting sun and assessed the situation with mild detachment.

On approach to the headquarters, he had pulled Jack aside and held a finger to his lips before pointing down a side alley.

Jack stood paralysed, seeing shadows mass in preparation for an attack and move as one into the building.

People on the street screamed and ran for cover as the creatures of the night moved among them, a first and last for many of them.

It was rare indeed to see Bloods in daylight but not for the reasons the humans would believe, if they had known of their existence in the first place. The sun was only as harmful to them as it was to everyone else, but within its natural light, these creatures of myth were highlighted for the killers they were, shown to be different and something to be feared.

In this growing age of technology where mankind could possibly devise a way to defeat them, the Bloods chose to go unseen by the masses and hunt as they always had throughout the ages, safely from within the darkness. Their pale, bloodless complexion and the unnatural way in which they moved, caused them to look too demonic for humankind to ignore.

Standing on the roof of the opposing building, the legend watched the assault unfolding and knew immediately that the wizards could never survive these odds. He knew that this was not a strike to cripple its enemy, this was an attack to annihilate them.

'Time to stretch my legs,' Daire rumbled, causing the wizard to flinch by his side. 'Do you feel lucky, Punk?' he asked, jumping off the building.

Jack ran to the edge and peered over, seeing the black cloak flap about him like that of some giant vampiric bat.

'Is he gliding?' he gasped, stepping back nervously from the edge. 'To hell with that!' he cried and ran for the door.

Crashing through a window halfway up the building, Daire scattered office cubicles as though they were the pins of a bowling alley. Rolling to his feet, he immediately crouched low to scan the area.

Office workers lay sprawled and unmoving on the carpeted floor, black-looking blood still oozing from their throats.

The vampires that were still in the vicinity backed away from him and spread out cautiously to assess this new threat.

Raising his depthless black hand before him, a blanketed flash of light illuminated the area, turning those closest to him to ash. The remaining Bloods hissed in pain and backed away from this terrible magick.

Stamping his foot down hard, Daire felt the whole floor shudder beneath him and then, roaring his presence, he stomped heavily towards the retreating Bloods.

***

'What the hell was that?' John asked, shouting above the din of his arcing green light. His lightning tore into his attackers, striking them hard and scorching their flesh but slowing them very little.

Glancing behind him after hearing a scream, he saw that Chloe's shield had cracked in several places, the Bloods around her intent, it seemed, on clawing their way through to her.

Catching her eye, he shared a silent look of defeat with her and then raised his hands in her defence.

Standing in the centre of the room, Charlie wove his magick into a fiery serpent, turning it one way and then another to wreathe the surrounding vampires in flame. Sweat shone on his forehead, a clear sign of his exertion as he sought the magick of the earth.

'No!' he whispered, seeing the motionless bodies of his fallen mages. 'There are too many!' he shouted, still cursing himself for his stupidity.

He had not thought for one moment that the vampires would come through the ceiling.

'Why had the building's shield failed?' he thought, but no sooner had he thought the question, he knew the answer. 'Colin!' he seethed, casting his serpent into the teeming undead. 'There are too many,' he thought again, believing absolutely that they were now undone.

***

Climbing up the final stairwell, Daire sighed with relief when he entered the marbled hallway. The lights were out as they had been on the previous floors, and one would have thought that the power had been cut but for the random lights that shone from overturned computer monitors.

The sound of howling reached his ears, causing him to cock is head familiarly before dismissing his thought and moving on.

He had thought that after fighting a true demon these poor reflections of it would have been so much easier, but he had been wrong. The younger ones died easily enough but the elders took a great deal more effort and he thought with growing concern that the older these creatures were, the stronger they became.

'Why have headquarters this high up?' he thought, shaking his head at their folly. 'So far away from the magick of the land,' shaking his head in disbelief, he walked on more silently than he had at first.

Blue lightning lanced into him suddenly, causing his shield to glow white in an instant and then crack right up the middle. Spinning on his heel, he sent his power out in defence and a shield in the distance flashed as it shattered on impact.

A recognisable cry caused him to halt his counter-attack and peer through the darkness at the old man in the distance.

'Jack! You dick!' he hissed, throwing up his arms in exasperation. 'You cracked my shield, you numpty!' he added hoarsely, pointing at the large jagged line before him.

Standing up, Jack threw his arms out wider still, jumping up and down in his excitement.

'Look at what you did to mine!' he hissed back, waving his arms about expressively.

Chuckling at the reaction, the legend loped towards his friend but knew from the look on the old man's face that something was wrong.

Two dark shadows detached themselves from behind him and fell on him like rabid dogs, but his shield reacted instinctively, turning immediately offensive at the creatures' touch.

Clearly not expecting this, both vampires hissed in pain as the lightning torched their bodies, and backed off immediately before attacking again.

With a gesture of his hand, Daire almost severed one of their arms completely, the unseen attack crippling the thing as it spun away in silence.

Startled as he ran to aid his friend, Jack backed up as a huge wolfish beast the size of a pony crept from around a corner.

'Gilga's balls!' he cried, seeing another slightly larger wolf slink into view.

Unaccustomed as he was to seeing the wolves fully transformed, he swallowed nervously at the hungry look in their eyes.

'Bloody hell!' he gasped, as both sets of eyes turned in his direction.

Looking at him with their different coloured eyes, he saw that one set was an almost luminous blue, while the other was a bright golden-brown.

As though smelling his fear, both appeared to huff in amusement before turning back to the fight.

Leaping into the air, the wolves launched themselves with such speed that the remnants of their shredded suits fell from their rippling fur. Closing their huge maws around the necks of the vampires, they began shaking their heads ferociously, causing the Bloods to grunt in pain.

Jack picked up his pace, only to falter again with his face draining in fearful recognition, remembering again where he had seen this type of vampire before.

'Blood Lords,' he gasped, recalling Cristian's fight with one such creature. 'But now there are two of them!' he quailed, remembering the unrelenting power of the Blood Lord, Bael.

Looking as impressive as the legend himself, they towered over the wizard as they sought to free themselves from the jaws of the wolves.

The white shield finally exploded into what looked like a thousand stars bursting forth and fading into fragments as they floated to the floor.

Without pause, the lords reached for Daire, screeching their hate of him with the wolves still attached.

'Wake up!' Daire roared, before sending his hate at the striking vampires as he had done only once before.

The vampires were cast from him, their blood spraying the area black within the darkness.

Feeling the explosion of emotion, Jack dropped to his knees, retching onto the marble corridor, and though the attack was massively reduced, he still felt as though he was dying inside.

Looking up through watering eyes, Jack saw the legend's demonic form roar in fury and then stalk forward like death himself.

'Die!' Daire growled, causing the walls to tremble from the sheer power in it.

Swallowing hard, Jack knew that he was of little use without the earth's magick and so decided that this was what he would put his mind to.

'Back!' Daire growled, pointing at the wolves, causing the pair to groan but withdraw without hesitation.

Fire immediately engulfed the lords, causing them to hiss and screech as they backed away.

A voice deep inside his subconscious screamed for him to take back control, but the demon was out and fought to remain free.

Though bloodied and burned from the demon's attack, the vampires recovered quickly and advanced yet again.

'Impossible!' Daire gasped, before forcing himself to listen to the voice in his mind. 'They do grow stronger!' he realised, the final confirmation of his fear now standing before him.

The realisation hit him hard, knowing that these vile creatures had indeed evolved with the passing of time, having killed countless numbers of them in the past without this hardship.

What power did he possess besides hate, which could destroy these damned vampires? He thought, believing that to delve further into darkness would be to lose himself utterly.

'Free will,' he thought suddenly, focusing instead on what he would have done had he still been human.

Clearing his mind, he fought for calm and the silence within him.

'Emotion is the mind-killer,' he thought, thinking the words through Spirit.

The beast in him simmered down, leaving the spiritual element to come to the fore. Raising his hands with his palms facing upwards, he lifted both lords from their feet.

'You will die, one way or another,' he promised them, sounding more human now that the demon was controlled.

The vampires flailed in the air, trying to find purchase on the walls and ceiling as they glared at him with undiluted hate.

Calming his mind further, he banished the darkness and sought the light he knew was there. With the flame of hate extinguished, he found it, could feel it, untapped and, up to now, forbidden to him.

He realised then that while the demon held sway, he could never become what he truly wanted to be. The light of what the elements had intended danced at the edges of his consciousness and the more he quashed the darkness, the brighter that light appeared in his mind.

He was reminded suddenly of the white glow of his snowflake and decided on a whim to seek what he had lost. Putting all his considerable might into changing himself back, he cried out and sank to his knees with crippling pain.

Beginning their return to the marbled corridor, the vampires lashed out at him frantically, hissing in their excitement.

Jack, feeling rather impotent, cast his arms out in fear, halting their slow descent.

'Damn!' he cursed, seeing that his friend was fallen, but the magick of the land was around him now and he split his mind to hold it in place.

With a scream of pain, Daire tried visualising his snowflake, but he was of water no longer and could not change back.

Staggering back to his feet, he knew then that he was lost to what had been done to him and that the dream of returning to what he had been, had been exactly that, only a dream.

'You must accept what you have become,' he heard her words again, thinking of the goddess, and with a feeling of resentment at what had been done to him, he did just that.

The magick was sent from him again, not the arcing glare of lightning but the pure light of the elements. The Bloods began to glow suddenly with a dull white light that seemed to render them immobile as they hung in the air.

Convulsing in the purest of agonies, their death screams echoed throughout the corridor, causing Jack to cover his ears from the pain of it.

The dull white aura began to intensify, building gradually into a blinding light that cut off the screams as ash fell to the floor.

For the first time since his rebirth, Daire truly understood that he was indeed corrupted, finally realising that the demon was his weakness, not the strength he had previously believed.

'You were right, Liv,' he whispered, finally understanding what she had said to him.

Lowering his arms, he turned again to his friend with a look of determination.

'Job done,' he whispered with a nod of his head.

Jack nodded back at him and turned as the wolves came creeping back into view.

'Let's finish this,' he whispered, at which the howling began.

***

John fought desperately to get to her but he was badly battered and had little strength left.

In her terror, Chloe had put her life force into her shield and the signs of age were beginning to show as a lock of white hair hung down the left side of her face.

Anger raged through the druid at seeing her plight and he sent fire raging into her attackers, binding it to the very essence of them.

Two of the vampires turned instantly to ash, the fire making short work of their undead flesh, and in surprise at his handiwork, he sent the flames out again to scatter the remnants like flies from a carcass.

Seeing an opening, Charlie sent balls of his fire smashing into their confused ranks, giving him a little reprieve to scan the area.

A swell of sorrow rose within him then, seeing his valiant mages lying dead or dying on the cold stone floor. In the far corner, he saw a mage staring helplessly back at him, a vampire drinking greedily from his exposed jugular. Understanding the plea in the fallen man's eyes, he sent a ball of fire at the pair and with one last agonising look, he saw a nervous smile flicker across the fallen man's face.

Wrenching his eyes away, Charlie screamed in agony at having allowed this to happen and threw his anguished might into the rest of their attackers.

Turning again, he saw the burning forms of the older and more powerful Bloods rising from the ashes of the fallen. His heart sank in defeat at this, realising that these burning demons were not the same as before, noting them to be worse than those that had already crushed them.

These new vampires were Blood Lords, he knew, and the true power behind the might of the Blood Vampire Faction.

How he had dreamed of this battle, to be face-to-face with these evil creatures and to kill them, ending their sickening reign of terror. He shook his head. He had never thought that they would be so strong, realising now with dread in his heart that the ages had given them a strength he had not dared dream of.

'Dark,' he whispered, looking bitterly towards his end. 'I see now that you were right,' he confessed, closing his eyes at defeat's last sting. 'May the gods of this world forgive me for what I allowed to endure,' he whispered, feeling tears of regret welling in his eyes.

Above the sounds of screams and the hisses of hate, a mournful howl rose up, causing his eyes to snap back open.

'The wolves!' he gasped, feeling a flush of excitement rising on his skin. 'They're alive!' he whispered, drawing on magickal reserves he thought not there, rekindled now from long-lost hope.

The ancient alliance with the wolves had been mutually beneficial, coming together in the aftermath of that first war when collaborations were needed in order to survive.

Ancients from the old world themselves, they were those that had been gifted physically after surviving the Shadow Queen's judgement day.

Resilient to all manner of attack, they had been sport for those with magick and had been hunted almost to extinction in those dark times.

On hearing their call now, Charlie could barely believe his ears, until he felt the earth's magick around him as though gifted to him by some benevolent force.

Bringing forth his shield, new and undamaged, he cried out in desperation for the survivors to do the same.

The four lords and something else that stood with them turned to the mournful sound and braced themselves for what was inevitably to follow.

Charlie could see that this fifth creature appeared different somehow, a little larger and clearly in control.

'Azazel,' he dared to guess, believing that it could be none other than the source of all vampires.

Glancing at those still alive, he saw Chloe crouching down with wild, fearful eyes and then John, who stood protectively over her. He saw Michael, his second in command, a heavily-muscled man, his shaved head glistening with sweat. To his left, he saw Kevyn, a mage of quick reflexes and an uncanny ability to win, who stood near, sharing his look of doom.

Almost out of sight, he took note of Kim, recognising her by her long brown hair and the destructive power she wielded, striking down the Bloods even now. As he watched, she threw her magick at two advancing vampires and took their heads off with a wide sweep of her arm.

There were a scattering of others out there in the darkness, unrecognisable, for most of the lights had long since gone out.

Bloodied and scarred in more ways than one, all now stared in the direction of the eerie howling that came echoing down the marble corridor.

Having turned to the new threat, the black-clad Bloods came together as one, appearing as though from the shadows themselves to surround their elders in a ring of death.

'Still so many,' he thought, seeing them come to defence against this new threat, and he hoped desperately that the wolves had the numbers to defeat them.

Squinting his eyes through the ash-filled gloom, Charlie saw a blue-robed wizard striding purposefully down the corridor towards them.

Raising his arms, the wizard unleashed a devastating arc of violet light that struck the shield of vampires, turned many of them to ash before continuing ceaselessly to cut more down as it passed through them.

The wolves appeared then, racing past him on either side with deafening ferocity, tearing into the undead with a savagery that was finally unleashed.

Suddenly, one of the lords broke away from the rest and rushed towards the new threat with an impossible blurring of speed.

Taken aback by the sudden move, the blue-robed figure faltered and stumbled back as the vampire appeared before him.

'No!' Chloe screamed, having now regained her feet but clutched at the druid's arm for support.

Opening his mouth in a silent scream of dread, the hope in John's eyes turned suddenly to horror at this terrible turn of events. Staring in wide-eyed disbelief, he saw yet another shadow rise from behind their fallen saviour and wanted desperately to turn away in that moment but felt spellbound by the unfolding horrors.

Swallowing at the dryness in his throat, John saw that this new lord's eyes reflected the light in a way unlike the others of its kind.

'Vampire eyes don't do that!' he had time to think before its black arms raised out before it.

He sucked in his breath and heard Chloe do the same as the attacking vampire was lifted off its feet. Blinding white light lit the corridor and the lord, along with all lesser vampires, turned instantly to ash, leaving only the wizard and the monster in the returning darkness.

Walking through the ash cloud of the recently deceased, Daire strode forward, leaving the particles in the air to swirl behind him.

The light struck again, more focused this time as it as it was sent towards the leader, but the three lords protected the fourth and took the brunt of the attack.

Their hideous cries caused the witnesses to grimace at the sound, the white light clearly hurting them like nothing before.

Slipping to the side, the largest of them broke away to bob and weave its way under the blinding attack.

Seeing an avenue of attack, the wolves fell on the three injured lords and tore at them with unnatural savagery. One of the foul creatures was dragged backwards by the neck, the huge blue-eyed wolf ripping off its head with a twist of the neck.

Eight others clamped down hard on the second lord's limbs and shook their heads violently, growling ferociously as they tore into it.

Drawing on the earth's magick, the druid and witch raised their arms to lift the last from its feet as they had seen the monster do.

With the combined might of the wizard, mages, druid and witch, there was a sound of shattering bones as the remaining lord crumpled to the floor.

Within seconds the wolves pounced on it, casting its ash into the air as they ripped and tore into the now decimated remains.

Coughing and spluttering, the survivors choked on the dense remains of the fallen Blood Lords, until Charlie cast it to the side with a wave of his arm.

Seeing John staring over at him, he shared a look of doubt with the druid, neither of them daring to believe that the attack had been foiled.

Chloe opened her mouth to speak but was silenced by a look from the druid, causing her to frown at him sullenly before she too heard the immense struggle being fought just beyond the wall of ash.

Huge dark shadows grappled within the darkness, the gigantic silhouettes clinching in a fight that was now magnified upon the ash from a light behind.

'You cannot defeat me, *Blaidd Tywyll*, not anymore,' the vampire hissed, using the ancient name for its legendary enemy.

John turned abruptly to Charlie at hearing the words but the mage had missed the exchange and looked back with a question in his eyes.

'I am Azazel, little man, the first of my order and the prize you have coveted from the very beginning,' Azazel sneered, taunting the killer of his kind. 'I should have let you catch me sooner,' he mocked, toying with his foe like a cat does with its catch.

'Wake up!' Daire commanded, the words sounding strained from the grip at his throat.

'What?' snarled Azazel, believing that the words were meant for him and not for those that finally heard them.

The building shook suddenly as though hit by some tremendous force from outside, causing ceiling tiles and window-glass to smash upon the floor.

A howl of wind ripped through the upper levels of the building, blasting doors from their hinges as it responded furiously to the summons.

A high-pitched whine was taken up by the watchful wolves and they began backing away from this unseen force.

Charlie gasped in astonishment as the ash before them was sucked from the building, allowing him to see the two combatants locked in their struggle. He realised immediately that the vampire had the edge over the other and felt a dire need to intervene on its behalf, even though the demon looked as evil as Azazel himself. He flinched suddenly when fire spontaneously engulfed the pair, the heat of it burning his skin from several paces away.

'Who did that?' he growled, turning to look at the druid who immediately shook his head in response.

The doorframe between them began to bend as the metal warped from the intense heat, cracking the wall that surrounded it.

Chairs that were tipped over in the carnage spontaneously combusted into flames, the metal legs curling away from the heat of the burning creatures.

Hiding his face from the destruction before him, Charlie raised his arm to shield himself from the heat and the blinding glare.

Believing that none other than an ancient could summon such a thing, Charlie turned to the blue-robed wizard but saw that he was as surprised as the rest of them.

A piercing scream erupted but as it began it was suddenly cut short, leaving only the sound of the roaring fire in its wake before it too winked out of existence.

Grey, smoky ash filled the air once again, drifting lazily over the steadily decreasing glow of those objects that were closest to the fire.

When the dust finally settled, a dark, shadowy figure stood silently in the gloom, black and indistinct but for the fiercely white eyes that, even now, seemed to be narrowed in concentration.

As Charlie watched, the shadowed figure slowly became something else as the darkness of its being softened into more earthly tones.

Feeling a cold chill of recognition, Charlie saw the definition of a deep scowl over darkening eyes that he had not looked into since his fall so many centuries before.

'You!' he gasped, looking at the man with cold remembrance.

Jack came coughing through the gloom and waved his arms about dramatically at the bothersome dust before stopping beside the mage.

'If I inhale any more Bloods, I'm going to turn into one of the damned things!' he growled, nodding to the druid in greeting.

John merely stared through him, unable to look at anything other than the man walking towards them.

Chloe stepped from behind the druid and smiled at the wizard warmly.

'Thank the goddess for your timely arrival, wizard,' she croaked, wafting at the persistent ash.

An awkward silence ensued, with Daire looking at Charlie, Charlie, Chloe and John looking at Daire and the wolves looking back and forth at everyone.

Jack looked up to blow at the ash that now tickled his bald head and looked at the legend with a scowl of irritation.

'Do you mind?' he whined, looking at him pointedly. No sooner had he spoken, a vacuum of air sucked the vampire remains out of the windows. 'Thank you!' he huffed, knowing that the element would do a far better job of it than a mere wizard.

Still locking eyes with Daire, the mage held out his hand in an offer of peace.

'Forgive me for not seeing the light before now,' he said, nodding his head sadly to one he had looked up to as a child.

A moment passed before Daire took it, his dark eyes never leaving those of the mage.

'Peace?' Charlie asked, staring up at him. 'Will you accept my apology, for my part?' he continued with sincerity, the expression on his face beginning to falter.

Daire pursed his lips for a moment and then nodded once, sighing as he did so.

'Peace,' he rumbled in a deep echoing tone of distant thunder. 'Though I would have killed you many times over had I seen you at any other time,' he added, before finally shrugging off the past.

***

The attack had been intended to decimate the headquarters and, more importantly, those within, achieving that which their Egni cousins had not. However, it was the Bloods who had received the fatal blow, losing almost all of their might in one dreadful night.

A mighty victory had been won but not without cost, for many had lost their lives this night in defence of the building.

Silently, the lucky few that remained searched for survivors, reaching down to feel for life, but found that the Bloods were too good at what they did.

John sighed heavily, shaking his head at the losses sustained.

'What happened to you, Chloe? You seemed to lose yourself in the attack,' he asked, expecting more of a fight from her.

She did not look at him when she eventually answered, appearing to carry a hidden burden that weighed her down even now.

'They attacked me first,' she replied, her voice shaking as she relived what had happened.

Frowning down in confusion, John patiently waited for her to continue, feeling that there was more to this than initially met his eye.

'This was not the only attack this night,' she sobbed, finally looking up in pain. 'They've killed many witches tonight, so many covens and their circles have been utterly destroyed,' she whimpered, leaning into him for support. 'I felt them John, every one of them. It felt like a knife twisting in my guts!' she cried, tears falling to her cheeks.

'I'm so sorry, Chlo,' he replied, his large hands rubbing her back softly. 'How can Bloods destroy so many circles? Surely the blessing gods would have intervened or something?' he asked, not knowing exactly how it all worked.

The priestess shrugged miserably, clearly at a loss as to how it was achieved.

'I don't know, they shouldn't have been able to. There's clearly more to this than I can see,' she replied, resting her head against his arm.

After a time, she shook her head and stepped back.

'You saved me!' she said in an accusatory tone and searched his face for the reason. 'More than once! You risked your own life to save me, John!' she challenged, looking up fiercely.

Nodding his head, he inched a little closer to her.

'Get used to it,' he whispered, leaning low but keeping a respectful distance.

Surprising him, her arm came up to encircle his head and pull him even closer. He did not resist.

The headquarters lay in ruin with the tall glass doors laying shattered across the stone floor, glistening eerily from the lights of the fallen monitors that lay flashing upon the floor.

Amid the devastation, Charlie had seen the kiss and began to smile despite himself.

'We may yet survive this,' he whispered, shaking his head at their somewhat disrespectful timing.

'We have taken massive casualties,' Kevyn announced, moving up silently beside him.

'They have suffered worse,' he replied, looking at his mage soberly. 'You fought masterfully tonight, Kev,' he continued, speaking in a tone full of pride. 'Almost as good as myself,' he added, trying to lighten the mood.

Kevyn did not reply and only nodded in greeting to Michael, who was second only to Charlie in his discipline.

'We few, we happy few,' the big man quoted sombrely, looking bleakly at his elder.

'We band of brothers,' Charlie added, slapping the man affectionately on his broad back. 'Okay! Let's tally up,' he sighed, looking at the two mages seriously. 'I killed forty-three,' he announced, raising his eyebrows to Michael.

'Thirty-nine,' Michael sighed, causing Kevyn to smile like a cat.

'Fifty-nine,' the slim man answered, laughing softly as only veterans can in post-battle conditions.

'Seventy-three!' a feminine voice announced, causing all three men to turn at once as Kim came striding over, her long dark hair pulled back into a tight ponytail. Her lithe frame was covered in sweat and more than a little blood, giving her a manic, wild-eyed appearance.

Charlie smiled approvingly at the wily mage and nodded his head to her in respect.

'You can sit the next one out!' he replied, chuckling at her defiant expression.

Turning abruptly, he nodded in Daire's direction.

'I will tell you one thing for nothing,' he announced, looking across at the legendary figure. 'I bet you all the tea in China, he killed more than the lot of us.'

Kim watched as the man of interest walked the room, pausing now and then to inspect the dead.

'What's he doing?' she asked curiously, noting that he was not checking for life.

'He's making sure that none have been turned,' Michael answered, smiling at her shocked reaction. 'The Dark Wolf,' he breathed, thinking the legend looked as evil as the books had depicted, even now in his human form.

Suddenly glancing about, Charlie searched for something he had previously missed.

'Speaking of wolves, where have they gone?' he asked, peering intently into the darkness.

'I saw him speaking to them for a bit earlier when you were checking for survivors, and then they ran off,' Kim answered, gesturing in the direction of the doorway.

'They answer to him now?' Michael asked, sharing a look of concern with Kevyn.

Closing his eyes in regret, Charlie felt the loss of such an asset and then breathed out a sigh of resignation.

'It was bound to happen, I suppose,' he grumbled and then sighed again, rubbing at his temples with his forefingers.

Kim scowled at him, wanting to know it all.

'Why would they do that?' she asked challengingly, knowing that he was holding something back.

Raising his eyebrows at her tone, Charlie felt incensed by her manner and held her glare in silence.

The flush of anger faded from her face and she stepped back, allowing him this small victory.

'Why would the wolves follow Dark after aligning themselves with us for so long?' she asked, speaking the words in a more measured tone of voice.

Holding her stare a moment longer than was necessary, he breathed in deeply before answering her question with one of his own.

'Why do you think that of all the names he could have been called, the Bloods decided on the Dark Wolf?' he growled, still irritated by her attitude.

Before Kim could answer, the rangy druid came striding over with a forced smile upon his face.

'Merry meet,' he greeted in the old way and then stood awkwardly at sensing the tension.

Welcoming the interruption, Charlie appraised the tall man with a mischievous twinkle in his eye, seeing also the druid's hero making his way towards them.

'Ahh, John my friend, may I introduce...' he paused, cringing internally at the look of wonder on the other's face, '...Dark,' he finished, gesturing at the two men with his hands.

'So pleased to meet you, Dark,' John blustered, thrusting his large hand out in greeting.

'Sorry,' Charlie apologised, grimacing slightly. 'This is John, the arch druid, and, apparently, your biggest fan,' he introduced, sighing in disapproval at the grin on the druid's face.

Taking the proffered hand, the once-again living legend shook it firmly and then pulled the druid to him conspiringly.

'Call me Daire,' he advised, speaking in a tone less thunderous than before.

Nodding slightly, John noticed Chloe approaching and held out his long arm invitingly.

'This is Chloe, high priestess of the witches' faction,' Charlie cut in, dragging the introductions on and away from the embarrassing druid.

A scowl set across Daire's features, his dark eyes narrowing at the blonde woman's approach.

'I have had little pleasure in knowing others of your ilk,' he stated, taking her hand in his.

Chloe reddened at the tone and wanted to look at anything other than his dark, penetrating glare but felt held by it, unable to escape.

'I assure you, they acted alone and did not have my blessing,' she whispered, feeling very small suddenly in his presence. 'I'm sorry that your children have been sealed within a circle,' she continued, speaking the words very quickly. 'But I am confident that they will be happy, given the time…' she trailed off lamely and then opened her hand that was still held in his.

Smiling slightly, he seemed to read the truth in her, and it was not what was spoken.

'They're already happy, now that I have returned,' he replied, smiling wider at her doubtful expression. 'For I have removed them from said circle and from the coven itself,' he continued, watching her face intently.

The witch blanched, the colour in her cheeks draining to white.

'Removed?' she whispered, shaking her head in disbelief. 'I would have felt it,' she replied, her eyes rounding like those of a frightened rabbit.

'Removed,' he repeated, knowing only too well of her involvement and resenting it utterly. 'The circle is no more, as is the coven,' he announced, pulling her to him a little to whisper the rest. 'Sadly, there were casualties. I hope you understand,' he confided, before smiling apologetically. 'It would be best for you, I think, to leave my children alone from now on,' he continued, pulling her even closer. 'So that there are no more… casualties,' he added, the threat now evident in his tone.

'Of course not! I mean, of course,' she stammered, swallowing hard and wanting nothing more than to end the conversation. 'Like I said, they acted alone,' she continued, slipping her hand delicately from his. 'I have no designs regarding your children,' she stressed, stepping back from him.

'Let us hope so,' he whispered, shrugging with mock apology. 'I have zero tolerance where my children are concerned and give no second chances. The next time it will be you and your entire faction that will pay the price,' he promised, turning to look for a seat.

Silently watching him from the shadows, Jack observed the altercation and noticed the things that Daire was trying to hide. His friend looked positively battered, the battle with Azazel clearly taking its toll.

'What did the first lords you fought do to you?' he asked, concern creasing his weathered face.

Staring vacantly back with eyes that seemed unfocused, Daire simply stared at his friend as he approached.

'Huh? Pardon me?' he asked in reply, frowning down uncomprehendingly at the older-looking man.

Jack spread his arms in exasperation as frustration grew in his eyes.

'The bloody Blood Lords! The ones you lifted off the ground? The first ones? What did they do to you?' he asked, scowling up in irritation.

Daire shook his head in confusion before realising at last what the old man was talking about.

'Ahh. That was me. I was trying to tap into another kind of magick,' he answered, shrugging his shoulders dismissively.

The wizard's eyes widened and then he threw his head back to look up at the heavens.

'You chose that exact moment to experiment?' he gasped, staring up in bewilderment.

'They were bloody hard to kill, Jack, and I didn't want to completely give in to the darkness in order to defeat them!' Daire growled, anger sharpening his mind. 'Or had you not seen what I was becoming?' he asked, arching an eyebrow at his old friend.

The old man baulked and waved off the comment with his hand, focusing now upon himself.

'Did you see my entrance? The wolves at my side and my Sith Fire?' he asked, nodded for him and answered his own question. 'Bloody brilliance, if I say so myself,' he continued, sighing in self-satisfaction.

'Right up to the point where you cringed like a little girl and fell on your arse,' Daire replied dryly, causing Kim to laugh unexpectedly from behind him. 'Look, Jack, I didn't just think, while in the fight of my life, to sit down and meditate! I was reaching for what I knew was there and just got carried away with it,' he confessed, upending a chair and slumping down into it. 'I thought that I would be able to kill them more easily,' he grumbled, closing his eyes tiredly before leaning back in exhaustion. 'Titan, my arse,' he mumbled, closing his eyes.

'Titan?' Kim asked, frowning down at him and then smiling when he glanced her way. 'Sorry! I'm Kim and these punks with me are Michael and Kevyn,' she introduced, gesturing to the mages at her sides with her thumbs.

Nodding to each in turn, Daire narrowed his eyes at them and then smiled in recognition. 'Battle mages,' he announced, nodding in approval as he turned his attention back at her. 'I could always tell,' he added, dipping his head to her in respect.

Nodding back at him, she curtsied teasingly and smiled in return.

'Titan?' she repeated, raising her eyebrows at him to answer her question.

Tickled by her persistence, Daire found himself liking the woman instantly.

'So I was told,' he answered, comically grimacing up at her. 'You would think that a Titan such as myself, would be able to kill a bloody vampire lord with ease,' he sighed, feeling a little depressed by the final outcome.

Kim shook her head, causing him to arch his eyebrow.

'I would think that they'd be classed as Titans too,' she replied, looking to Charlie for confirmation.

The black man frowned and pondered her question before finally agreeing.

'That sounds about right, definitely in regard to Azazel,' he replied, nodding at her thoughtfully. 'Maybe even more so,' he mused, remembering the terrifying might of the creature.

'She's going to bloody love this!' Daire thought, thinking of Kristina and her accusations.

***

The sky outside began to lighten, turning from black into a deep shade of blue. Down in the street far below, flashing lights of red and blue reflected off the bottom of the buildings, looking cold despite the lightening sky. The emergency services littered the streets and had cordoned off the entire area, allowing none to enter until the final word was given.

John lifted a fallen chair and seated himself beside the seemingly sleeping man, looking at him for a long time in silence.

'The legend, the Dark Wolf!' he thought, having read all there was regarding the ancient man. 'So many questions,' he thought drearily, the secret to becoming younger at the top of his list. Thinking this, he glanced subconsciously over at the much younger priestess and felt the age between them like a weight around his neck.

He was about to speak when he felt something odd, a feeling like he was surrounded by something unseen and yet familiar in a weird sort of way. Closing his eyes to focus more clearly, he almost started in alarm on sensing the elements, attuned as he was to such things, and closed his eyes again to see what else there was.

'Hunt them down and kill them, all of them,' Daire whispered, barely audible from under his breath. 'No, just the blood drinkers for now,' he answered, replying to an unheard question.

When it was clear that the conversation was over, John cleared his throat apologetically.

'You actually converse with them?' he asked, his eyes now wide with longing. 'It's a dream of mine to do as you do,' he added, speaking in a wanton tone, before slumping down in his seat.

Opening his eyes, Daire regarded him sombrely for a moment and shook his head with irritation. 'When they are awake!' he grumbled and shook his head at the private joke. 'I have an offer for you, John,' he continued, causing the druid to sit up straighter.

At hearing the words, Charlie and his mages turned to listen, as did Chloe, but she kept a safe distance from the unpredictable Titan.

'I want you to come with me to my house,' he announced, looking then to them all. 'All of you,' he added, looking directly at the witch.

Chapter Six

The barren mountaintop was a desolate place at the best of times, more so now in the early hours of the morning. Thick grey clouds hung oppressively in the air, seemingly untouched by the wind that whipped all about her slender frame.

Standing atop the highest peak, the goddess seemed oblivious to the harshness of the climate and waited patiently for the one she had called. Looking up, she saw the lightening sky and smiled.

'The time is now,' she whispered, hearing the sound of his approach as if in answer.

Ddraig landed beside her and tucked in his wings quickly to avoid the insistent pull of the wind.

'Queen of Air,' his dark voice growled, his wild eyes focussing on her coldly.

'Ddraig,' she greeted, dipping her head a little in greeting.

The dragon eyed her in silence and waited for her to continue, knowing only too well why she had summoned him here at this time.

'I need your council,' she began, intending to feed the creature's ego before continuing. 'I have fears,' she whispered, her eyes sad and without pretence.

Ddraig bowed his head and a look of understanding flashed briefly in his fiery eyes.

'As well you should,' he rumbled, though more softly than she had anticipated.

A tear ran down her cheek, her voice breaking unintentionally as she continued.

'There have been no more attacks since he left,' she whispered, closing her eyes to hold back the tears.

'Is that not a good thing?' he asked, crouching lower against the wind. 'The daemon he slew was one of the Ars Goetia,' the dragon continued, as though this explained everything she needed to know. 'One of the kings of the underworld who may have had the power to bridge the gap on his own. There will be no other crossings into your realm,' he assured her, nodding his enormous head.

Unable to hide her feelings, the goddess' shoulders jerked rhythmically and she wept pitifully into her hands.

'Please, drop this pretence! I know there is more,' she moaned, almost begging the dragon to comply.

Ddraig shook his great head at her words and his manner became more hostile in an instant.

'We dragons can do nothing, will do nothing!' he growled, looking as though he were about to take flight.

She lowered her hands and looked more lost than he had thought possible.

'Why did you bond with him?' she asked, knowing for sure that it was not an act of whim.

The dragon appeared sad then, if that was indeed possible and heaved a huge sigh of regret.

'That is my business,' he replied, unwilling or unable to share his wisdom.

Her shoulders slumped again in resignation, having assumed that this would have been the way of it.

'I have sworn to protect him and his children. I do so gladly, surly this must make us allies? What have you seen?' she pressed, knowing that dragons had the gift of foresight.

Ddraig shook his head again, a steely expression settling on his features.

'This is beyond you, Goddess, even though your power be great. You look at things as they are and not as they will be. What I did, I did to safeguard the future of my kind. I did not do it to safeguard his. That is all I can say,' he replied, his voice like acid and his eyes ablaze.

Slighted by the creature's secretive way, the goddess flushed with instant anger.

'Not so innocent after all then!' she snapped, remembering their last encounter.

'I gave him what he will need in the time ahead and what I needed for the time after!' Ddraig hissed, rounding on her angrily. 'I make no excuses for the saving of my race!' he seethed, his hackles rising at her judgemental tone. 'He is my friend but his future is set, so why not safeguard my own?' he growled, more to himself than for her benefit.

Knowing that the dragon did not lie, her anger abated at his last admission.

'I love him,' she confessed and swallowed hard at the lump in her throat.

Ddraig regarded her silently for a moment before finally uttering her own fateful words.

'All or nothing,' he whispered, seeing her start in surprise. 'You will fall and the other return if you meddle in this,' he prophesied, voicing the words in the gentlest tone she had ever heard from a dragon. 'Would you see her return for the smallest chance to save him?' the dragon asked, studying her face intently.

She lifted her chin defiantly and then stared in determination.

'All things come to an end,' she announced, her features set.

***

Cristian was furious, his white-knuckled fists digging into the surface of the table as he stood over his new faction.

'You want to stay neutral?' he asked, failing to keep the snarl from his mouth. 'There is no neutrality! There is no side! You will be involved whether you like it or not!' he roared, eyeing the vampire at the far end of the table.

Taking a calming breath, he let it out slowly, but could still feel his anger threatening to unhinge him.

'This is war! A war you shall not escape! You think you will be left alone to multiply as you have been?' he asked, his dark eyes sweeping the room. 'Think again!' he hissed, his face now white with fury.

The lean vampire who stood opposite him was clearly unimpressed by his words and looked back with growing disdain.

'Look Cristian, we just don't see how it benefits us. Nothing personal,' he replied, spreading his arms apologetically.

'If you say that it's just business, I'll rip the life from you,' Cristian warned, his voice now dangerously low.

Those closest to the lean vampire stood at the threat, showing support and more for the challenging vampire.

'We need a new Don,' the vampire announced, his shark-like eyes sweeping the table.

'Now's not the time, Minty!' Warren warned, avoiding Cristian's eyes as he came to his defence.

'Not the time,' Cristian repeated softly, realising that this was not their first meeting on the matter. 'You think you're safe? You think that because you have learned a couple of things from me, that you are now a power to be reckoned with?'

He shook his head again, letting the betrayal sink in.

'Combined, your years don't touch mine!' he continued, his voice shaking in the effort of restraining himself.

The thin vampire gave a dismissive gesture, fuelling Cristian's fire further.

'So what if you're ancient? We have made ourselves strong! We are strong!' he shouted, throwing his arms wide as he played to the crowd. 'We don't need no elder, no king and no lord! We, don't need you,' he sneered, as did those who stood with him.

Cristian let his breath out from between his teeth, trying to clear his mind and calm the rising violence in his heart.

'What would you do if another ancient came calling? Another lord, or gods forbid, Dark himself! What would you do then?' he asked, snarling the words from between his teeth.

Minty rolled his eyes, clearly unimpressed by the perceived fear-mongering.

'Look around you,' he replied, sweeping his arms over the gathered bosses. 'We are many,' he answered, the threat evident in his tone.

Silver lightning flashed forth and continued unabated, striking all those that had stood, driving the screaming bosses to their knees.

A vampire at his side made to stop him but Cristian's shield was already in place, causing the man to howl as he fell to the floor.

Fire erupted around the wrathful lord, sent by one of the more gifted among them, but it was repelled by his defences to rebound across the room.

Seeing that his point was made, Cristian dropped his arms and the blinding assault abruptly ended, leaving the expensive-looking room smoking in the aftermath.

'That is what you have waiting for you. Any one of the ancients can do this to you, some a great deal more,' he hissed, frowning at the carnage he had unwittingly caused.

He had intended to strike only at those who had stood against him, but his defences had returned their fire tenfold, leaving the room in ruin and all the vampires hurt.

He looked upon them then, at this Dark Brotherhood that he had created, and knew at that moment that he would never be one of them.

'So be it,' he conceded, shaking his head.

With a silver blur of motion, the sword of power appeared in his hand, cleaving the large table in two right down its centre.

'You're on your own,' he announced, glaring at them fiercely before striding from the room.

The large, dark form of Geez stood up and spread his arms pleadingly.

'Geez!' he called, but the Egni Lord did not stop. 'Geez!'

***

John was at a complete loss, trying unsuccessfully to get his head around how the legend had done it. One moment they were walking down the dark marble corridor, the next he had suddenly felt the texture of the floor softening beneath his feet.

On looking down, he had seen the soft contours of vegetation and when he had lifted his head in surprise, he found himself surrounded by trees. The darkness of the hallway had given way to the gloom of the forest and the freshness of the air had almost taken his breath away.

They all walked in silence now, each lost within their own thoughts and imaginings of how it was they came to be here.

Without warning, Daire held up a hand to stop them and stalked silently ahead before taking off full tilt through the trees.

'What's that about?' Chloe asked, looking up at John questioningly.

'When you've got to go, you've got to go,' he replied, raising his eyebrows at her in amusement.

Without waiting for permission, the four mages took off after the legend, picking their way through the underbrush with relative ease.

'See?' John asked, shrugging and moving to follow.

Rushing forward, Jack raised a hand and whispered a single word of power, knowing that those left behind would need the light to find their way.

'*Llewyrch,*' he whispered, causing the branches above them to glow suddenly, illuminating the area ahead with a soft green hue.

Impressed by the strange wizard's unusual brand of magick, John nodded his head appreciatively.

'Lead the way, my good man,' he said, gesturing grandly towards the path ahead, but then stiffened with a sharp intake of breath.

Highlighted from the glow of the leaves, John saw the cause of the old man's alarm and the reason the legend had gone on ahead.

'No!' Jack cried before disappearing into the trees, frightened by what was floating in the air before them.

Moving to follow, John sensed that he was alone and stepped back to hold out his hand to his priestess.

'Please!' Chloe whispered, tears forming in her eyes. 'Please, not again!' she cried, the words trembling from her quivering lips.

Bending down, he kissed her forehead tenderly and stroked her face with the back of his fingers.

'I am with you,' he assured her, taking her hand in his.

Shaking with fear, she took a sobbing breath and looked again at the slow-moving ash that lingered heavily in the air.

***

Racing through the forest, Daire was aware that the ash was getting thicker the closer he came to the house. In his dread, he refrained from knowing the truth just yet, feeling too afraid to send his awareness out to see if his children were safe.

Knowing that whatever had occurred here had happened at the same time as the attack on the wizards, he began to curse himself as he blurred towards his home.

He was close to the tree line now and began to quake at what he would find, seeing the entire area as though in the middle of winter.

The forest floor along with the trunks of the trees appeared almost white now, the half-light of the moon casting an eerie spectral glow on the mass of vampire remains.

Closing his eyes, he finally sent out his senses and held his breath at what he might find.

'Fear not, my Daire,' came her soft, familiar tone of voice. 'For I have protected them for you as promised, and have broken all the rules in doing so,' she continued, stepping up silently behind him.

Turning to her voice, he let out a nervous gasp of relief as he took in her beauty through his tear-blurred vision.

Standing there, not two feet from him, was the elegant form of the goddess, appearing in shadow as she had when first they met.

Without saying a word, he stepped in and embraced her, feeling her stiffen at first in response.

Recovering herself from the initial shock, she tightened her arms around him and gripped him more tightly.

'My Daire?' she asked, whispering into his ear before sighing in pleasure at the nod of his head.

***

Creeping silently through the trees, the mages paused at a gesture from their leader and surveyed the scene before them with cold detachment.

Knowing that emotion in the midst of battle was a sure way to die, the years of conflict had hardened them to what they all thought had happened.

There had been a great battle here with many vampire deaths and only the mother and her children to fight them.

Surprised at the amount of ash from what must have been hundreds of deaths, the mages could only guess at the final outcome.

'The children and their mother are dead,' Charlie thought, seeing the moonlight reflect off the ash like glitter upon the air.

Narrowing his eyes suddenly, he saw that within the centre of the rays and amid the shimmering vampire remains, two figures stood entwined together, holding one another amid the desolation.

Charlie found the scene touching and felt guilty for disturbing it, thinking them comforting each other after what had occurred.

'Who's that with him?' Kim whispered, squinting her eyes to sharpen her vision. 'We need to be ready for whatever comes next,' she continued, believing as the others did that his family was dead, and knowing what his response to that would be.

***

The goddess pulled away to better see his face and began to smile joyfully at their reunion.

'Mine!' she whispered, her eyes wide and innocent as they looked into his.

Something in her tone caused him to frown, feeling a sudden sense of 'Deja vu', as though he had heard it said that way before, but he shrugged off the feeling with a shake of his head.

'I was never *not* yours,' he replied after a moment and kissed her deeply.

Her lips parted at the contact and he could feel her hot moisture almost burn his mouth.

'I love you,' she gasped throatily as the kiss finally ended.

'I love you too,' he replied, touching his forehead to hers, losing himself in the moment. 'You have risked much to save them,' he stated, touching his lips to hers again, causing her to smile through the kiss and wrap her arms around him.

'We are no longer alone,' she breathed, breaking the contact between them.

He smiled in acknowledgement, knowing of whom she was referring to.

'That would be the mages,' he replied, looking directly at the quad who still hid in the darkness.

Without looking back to her, he spoke again and held his breath for her response.

'Will you stay?' he asked, his stomach tightening.

'I will,' she answered simply, shrugging her shoulders at him mockingly. 'Where else would I want to be?' she asked, staring at him fiercely.

Relief burst from him and he felt a swell of emotion for her then, with the feeling that he had been waiting for her his entire life.

Smiling at his reaction, she reached around and playfully squeezed his bum.

'My Daire!' she announced mischievously, squeezing it again.

Taking in a deep breath, Charlie realised that their presence had been detected and rose to his feet with his arms spread in apology.

'Forgive our intrusion,' he called, glancing at his rising companions. 'We thought you in need of assistance,' he continued, giving the legend a tight smile before looking dubiously at the shadowed figure beside him.

Daire smiled back, taking the mage off guard.

'I appreciate the sentiment, Charlie. Were all as quick to react as you mages,' he replied easily, the previous tension gone from his manner.

Turning back to the goddess, Daire's voice caught in his throat before he could introduce her.

'Bloody hell!' he gasped, looking not at the Queen of Air but at a very attractive, mortal-looking young woman.

Unable to take his eyes off her, he took in the straight, light-brown hair that stopped at her shoulders and at her eyes that were now a more natural shade of hazel. Still long-limbed, he found his eyes travelling over her very visible curves.

'Wow,' he breathed, taking in her beauty in a completely different way.

Dressed in shades of blue, Olivia wore simple jeans with a light knitted top, making her appear both normal and enchanting at the same time.

With his mouth hanging open, his mind was awhirl at what to say next.

'Hi, I'm Olivia,' she greeted them, shaking hands with the mages one by one.

Charlie nodded at her, convinced by her appearance, and gave his name before introducing the others.

'What happened here?' Kevyn asked in his quietly spoken voice.

Shrugging a little over-dramatically, Olivia smirked at the chuckle from Daire.

'I don't know, I've only just arrived myself,' she answered, drawing a suspicious look from Charlie.

Seeing the expression, Daire stepped in close to his old enemy and whispered into his ear.

'For reasons of my own, I would appreciate it if you would introduce Olivia here, as one of your own. It would make things... easier... when we go inside,' he said quickly, seeing the druid approaching with his witch in tow.

Seeing the ash-covered scene before him, John threw his arms out wide and strode forward in alarm. 'What happened here?' he asked in a raised voice, looking to each of them in turn for the answer.

Everyone shrugged and Daire laughed spontaneously at the annoyed scowl on Olivia's face, causing them all to turn to him with a frown.

'Sorry,' he chuckled, amused by the goddess' faultless deceit. 'Wait a minute, where the hell is Jack?' he asked, scanning the area behind them.

'Here!' the wizard answered, walking out from behind a tree near them.

Narrowing his eyes, Daire pursed his lips in the usual way as he studied the old man suspiciously.

'Sorry, I got turned around in there,' Jack explained lamely, gesturing to the forest rather awkwardly.

'Of course you did,' Daire replied sarcastically, studying the wizard a while longer.

Jack's face reddened under the intense scrutiny and he had a silly little smile playing on his lips.

'Hello, I'm Jack,' he introduced himself awkwardly, holding out his hand to Olivia.

Stepping forward, she took his hand and shook it firmly.

'Nice to meet you, Jack,' she replied, shaking his hand warmly. 'I am called Olivia, one of Charlie's mages,' she continued, giving him the story and smiling at the twinkle in his eyes.

'Pleased to meet you, Olivia,' he acknowledged, bowing slightly lower than was necessary and backing away as he continued to do so.

Rolling his eyes with a shake of his head, Daire grimaced at his old friend.

'Bloody brilliant,' he muttered, glaring at the devious old man with a shake of his head.

***

Kristina awoke with a start, looking around the room frantically for the cause of her alarm before breathing out slowly in relief.

Seeing nothing amiss but feeling that something was definitely wrong, she closed her eyes to visualise herself getting up and going down the stairs.

Blinding golden light erupted in her mind, causing her to click back into her body with a sickening jolt. Something was downstairs, something immense and beyond her understanding.

Untangling herself from the children who must have crept in during the night, she quickly dressed and cast her shield about her.

Glancing back, she cast a protective spell over the children and took a calming breath before finally leaving the room. On the landing, she paused to listen for signs of life.

'House?' she whispered hoarsely and waited nervously for a reply. 'I need you,' she continued, edging herself onto the uppermost step.

The silence of the house added to her anxiety and she cursed under her breath before looking down into the darkness.

'Daire?' she whispered, unable to bring herself to descend any further.

'Yes?' he answered, whispering back in the same hoarse tone that she had used.

'You bloody idiot!' she hissed, still whispering so as not to wake the children.

Muffled thuds sounded as she came down the stairs, causing Daire to shake his head, knowing from experience that she was stepping as quietly as she could.

'You scared the bejesus out of me!' she stormed, marching into the living room and stopping abruptly at the sight of so many people. 'Oh!' she gasped before pulling her dressing gown a little tighter around her as she waited for someone to speak.

No one spoke, however, and the awkward silence continued, causing Daire to smile at her gift of causing such a thing.

She stared at him meaningfully, in a way that told him to speak, but he was clearly having too much fun at the moment. Huffing with embarrassment, she stormed into the kitchen to fill the kettle.

'I could murder a cup of tea, Kris,' Jack called, winking at her knowingly when she glared back in surprise.

'Oh, you could, could you? You cheeky bugger!' she snapped, but was secretly glad that he had spoken at all. 'Anyone else?' she asked, peering back from the sink.

Mumbled acquiesces echoed from the others, with only one of them catching her eye.

'I'll help you,' Olivia offered, rising immediately to her feet.

Something in the young woman's manner calmed Kristina, and she nodded her agreement as she approached.

Nine cups were prepared and the hot water poured by Kristina's shaking hand.

'I'm sorry, you're not catching me at my best,' Kristina apologised without looking up.

'I can see you have your hands full here,' Olivia replied, smiling at her comfortingly. 'He should not have scared you like that. He can be quite wicked at the most inappropriate times,' she said knowingly and squeezed Kristina's arm in a friendly gesture.

Kristina's eyes snapped up to meet hers, trying to read into her words.

'You sound... like you know him well,' she said, choosing her words carefully.

Olivia merely nodded and arched her eyebrow expectantly.

'You *are* close then?' Kristina pressed, digging a little deeper.

Again, Olivia nodded, waiting for her to figure out who she really was. But when no such enlightenment was forthcoming, she smiled, finding herself liking the woman.

'We are together,' Olivia confessed, looking at her apologetically.

Shrugging her shoulders, Kristina smiled at the openness of the girl.

'Thanks for being so honest. He would have hidden it from me,' she replied, rolling her eyes. 'I hope you know what you're letting yourself in for,' she added, chuckling suddenly with genuine amusement.

'I think I have a notion of how much trouble he can be,' Olivia replied, smiling with amusement at Kristina's obliviousness to her identity. 'I just didn't want us to start off with a lie. My name is Olivia,' she continued, causing Kristina to smile and hug her spontaneously.

'Thank you,' she whispered, turning back to the cups, '... and gods help you, Olivia,' she added, beginning to chuckle again.

The awkward silence settled once again after the tea was received and Kristina glared at the one who took delight in it.

'I'm glad to see you again, Jack,' Kristina said forcefully, making polite conversation.

'Glad to be back, thank you very much,' he replied, sitting back contentedly on the sofa.

'I've told her,' Olivia whispered, putting her hand on Daire's arm affectionately.

His eyes widened and immediately went to Kristina's, hoping not to see any pain, but she held his stare with a look of relief and more than a little amusement.

'Thank God, and good riddance,' she blurted, causing Olivia to cough into her tea and chuckle in amusement.

Shaking his head and rolling his eyes, Daire remembered an age-old secret that he should have remembered sooner... women talk.

'Now that "everything" is out in the open,' Kristina sighed, smirking at Olivia knowingly. 'What the hell are you doing in my house?' she demanded, narrowing her eyes at Daire again.

Sitting forward, he placed his hands together before his mouth and pursed his lips behind them.

'They are here to talk to the children,' he replied, breathing into his index fingers. 'For a mock choosing,' he added, waiting for the eruption that he knew would come.

'Absolutely not!' she exploded, standing and putting her hands on her hips. 'Why now? Why after all that we've been through?' she asked, her face flushing with anger.

Looking tired, as though the weight of the world was upon his shoulders, Daire sighed again.

'It's just a contingency plan in case something goes wrong. I don't want them forced into anything again, they deserve better than that,' he replied, closing his eyes for a moment as though praying for guidance. 'I just want you all to talk to them, teach them if you can. I want to see what path they would choose, given the chance. Let me be clear though, this is only to see which way they lean. They are ultimately to remain free,' he continued, looking around the room.

Charlie cleared his throat, a disagreeable expression crossing his features.

'They would still be free, Daire, it's called the "choosing" for a reason. They just "choose" their discipline and continue on that path, ergo freedom of choice,' he replied, looking at the legend with sincerity.

Still pursing his lips behind his fingers, Daire stared at the mage for a long moment.

'Well said, and well-intentioned, I'm sure, but as I said, it's only to see which way they lean. I want them to learn from all of you if that's what they want but without the restrictions and limitations from one train of thought. Please have no illusions about this, even if you think they want to go with you, I will not allow them to be tied to one discipline and will never allow them to join a faction! Do you all understand that?' he asked, leaving no room for a debate on the matter.

It was Chloe that spoke first, unable to contain herself further.

'That doesn't sound much like "free will" to me,' she replied, a pouty expression setting on her face.

'They are children. *My* children. And until such time that they are old enough to decide for themselves, you *will* abide by my rule on the matter,' he replied, with a hint of thunder rumbling in his voice.

Casually placing a hand upon his knee, Olivia calmed him and Kristina's eyes narrowed, noting that he immediately relaxed under her touch, the darkness within him receding as quickly as it had come.

John raised his hands in a gesture of peace, smiling in an attempt to diffuse the tension.

'Shall we just talk to them and maybe teach them a little of our ways? Who knows what might happen?' he asked in his gentle way, smiling warmly at them all.

Daire leaned forward a little with a stony expression.

'After I have your word, John, and not before,' he replied, the thunder in his voice very audible now.

'Why though? Why does it matter?' John asked, spreading his long arms in exasperation.

'Because he will feel less guilty if you were to break your oath,' Olivia answered, staring emotionlessly at the witch at his side.

'Less guilt, after he kills you,' Kristina continued, finally understanding his mind.

White-faced after the colour had drained from his face, Daire spoke again, and the power in it was unmistakable.

'I will not ask again. If I don't receive your word of honour to leave my children alone...' he said, thunder now booming outside the house,

'...this "meeting" will come to an end,' Olivia finished for him, her face now as cold as his.

Kristina smiled sadly, knowing exactly how this 'meeting' would end and pictured again the tornado outside the house.

'Children first,' she thought, realising that this was the ultimate reason he had brought them here. Not necessarily to kill them, she supposed, but to bind them from ever using his children.

'For someone who interjected for the sake of peace, John, you haven't half-escalated the situation, my druidic friend,' Charlie observed, shaking his head at the other's stupidity.

'Who are you to finish his sentences for him anyway, his mother?' Chloe sneered, glaring at Olivia as she came to the druid's defence.

Olivia stared back with a cold smile spreading across her face, knowing already who the true threat in the room was.

Jack sat back, wise enough to keep out of the exchange, watching as Kristina stood with her teeth clenched, staring from one to the other as they debated the future of *her* children.

Charlie glared at the witch, his eyes flashing in anger at this needless debate.

'I give my word,' he announced, nodding to his mages.

Kevyn immediately bowed his head in acknowledgement.

'I also give my word on the matter,' he said solemnly, looking to his left as Michael too nodded his assent, his heavily-muscled frame shifting in his seat.

'My word,' he intoned, glaring at the druid.

Kim stared around the room and shook her head, unable to comprehend what she was hearing.

'Why are you arguing this point? They are *his* children! If anyone touches them after giving their word, I will kill them myself!' she promised, glowering at the high priestess. 'Oh, and I give my word,' she added quickly, nodding to both Daire and Kristina.

'And then there were two,' Daire announced, looking at the pair with deadly intent. 'I realise that you have no designs of your own to go against me on this, druid, and I see that you only argue in support of your priestess, but I will say it again. These are *my* children and you will die if I consider you a threat to them,' he whispered, a shadow of the demon crossing his features.

John froze and nodded reflexively as he shrank back from the glare that suddenly held him, finding that he could do nothing but concede to the will of the ancient.

'I give you my word,' he gasped and was immediately released by the will of the other.

Slowly, Daire turned to the witch and high priestess to her faction, the one that had manipulated his children once before.

'And then there is you,' he whispered, leaning back into his seat. 'I know why you would want to reintegrate my children into a coven and I know also that it was you who instigated that first attempt,' he informed her with a deadpan expression.

Chloe stared back sullenly, flexing her fingers nervously while under his gaze.

'I know that you do this to strengthen yourself and not to intentionally cause them harm. So I'll ask you this simple question. What's more important to you?' he asked, ready to end her life there and then.

Chloe continued to stare and though unwilling to lose such assets as his children, she realised that it was that or her life if she refused. Absorbing the children's might into her faction again or death at the hands of this evil demon, probably in the next few seconds, she thought miserably, shaking her head in defeat.

'My word,' she mumbled, looking down to the floor.

'Swear it!' he roared, making her flinch and cringe in fear.

In her mind's eye, she saw a vision of impenetrable darkness and of teeth gnashing at her from within.

'I swear! I'll not covet them any longer,' she screamed, cowering and gripping John's arm for support.

Olivia reached out and took his hand again, smiling to Kristina in apology as she did so, who shrugged her disinterest immediately.

Daire closed his eyes at the contact and the darkness in him receded at her touch, causing Kristina to frown again, cocking her head to one side.

'What power does she have over him that she can calm him in such a way?' she wondered, looking at the young girl critically for the first time. 'A pretty girl,' she thought, really looking at her now, seeing a deep intelligence that could easily be missed upon the first impression. 'Confident too, especially for one so young,' she thought and was about to shrug it off again when she caught the expression on Jack's face.

His old grey-blue eyes stared as though mesmerised by the couple. No not at them, at *her*! She realised, looking from him back to the girl.

Colour drained from her face and a sickly feeling crept into her stomach. She took in again the long limbs and pictured them black, remembering finally who this girl truly was.

'I've met someone,' he had said.

'You've met someone? The bloody Queen of Air!' she heard herself say again when he had told her of the goddess.

Sensitive to such subtle changes, Olivia looked up at her and there was no denying it, this was indeed the Queen of Air, the goddess that she prayed to.

Seeing the enlightenment that shone in Kristina's eyes, Olivia raised a finger to her lips and shook her head in warning.

'Are you alright?' Kevyn asked, noting the change in their hostess and thinking her unwell.

Daire's eyes snapped to her and saw the look on her face and at whom she was staring. With a sardonic smile tugging at his lips, he shook his head at her lack of understanding.

'I did tell you,' he said defensively, shrugging apologetically.

'Yes, well, I forgot!' she flustered, turning abruptly to walk from the room.

Gathering up the empty cups, Olivia followed in the pretence of tidying up.

John shared a look with the mages, who shook their heads at each other in confusion.

'Women!' he growled, as though that single reference explained everything.

Chloe shot him a dark look, as did Kim, but they said nothing for the moment and just stared out into the kitchen.

Fear twisted Kristina's stomach at the thought of them together and the potential consequences of their incomparable union.

How could she compete with that? She thought, fearing that it was a matter of time before they took her children from her.

'Are you okay?' the question was asked, causing Kristina to stiffen and grip the edge of the sink.

Unable to speak, she took a deep breath as her eyes began to brim.

Without further comment, Olivia stepped forward to hug her from behind and at the comforting contact, Kristina sobbed before pouring everything out in one fell swoop. Fear, dread, guilt and loneliness all came out at the touch of the goddess.

'Let it go,' Olivia whispered, stroking her arms tenderly.

'I have been dreading the day that I would see you again,' Kristina cried, forcing the words through her heaving sobs.

'I'm here for him and him alone,' the goddess assured her, tightening the embrace to instil her words. 'I am not here to take them, nor shall I ever be,' she promised, sensing the cause of the mother's distress.

'What if he wants to take them?' Kristina asked, her eyes fearful as she finally turned.

Olivia shook her head sadly, realising that the mother was oblivious to the will of the father.

'Oh, Kris, he is prepared to kill everyone in that room so that they remain with you,' she replied, wiping away the tears with her thumbs.

Kristina stared back vacantly, causing Olivia to shake her head a little.

'Don't you see? That little ruse in there was just a test to see whom he could trust if he were somehow to fall,' she continued, but her eyes shone defiantly at that line of thought.

'Chloe?' mouthed Kristina, glancing back briefly into the living room.

Olivia nodded and then tilted her head to indicate indecision.

'Maybe. The real test will be when they spend time with the children and see their true potential,' she answered, believing that she knew their father's mind. 'None will make a move while he lives but if he were to…' she stopped, leaving the thought to linger.

'Is that likely?' Kristina asked and then blushed profusely at the hope in her tone.

Olivia stiffened, shocked into silence by the spontaneous reaction.

'I don't want him to die,' Kristina blustered, seeing the goddess's angered reaction. 'I just want him to… leave,' she continued, hating herself for putting a voice to her desire.

'Pray that he never wishes the same of you,' Olivia retorted, her compassionate tone now as cold as ice. 'For you would be dead already if he had,' she continued, unable to contain her anger.

'I know,' Kristina whispered, a flush of shame deepen her cheeks. 'But it's how I feel,' she whispered, feeling bitter tears sting her eyes.

'If the worst comes to pass and he does indeed fall, then call on me when the wolves are at your door. I will come, if only to honour his memory,' the goddess replied, all the previous warmth lost from her tone.

Rocked by her words, Kristina recalled when she had last heard them and remembered that it was Daire himself who had said them.

'Those very same words,' she thought, wondering how bad that time would be. 'When the wolves are at your door,' she thought, knowing that the phrase had some sort of meaning.

'I don't want him to die,' she whispered again, her teary eyes staring back in apology.

'He won't!' Olivia snapped with a steely determination setting on her features.

Chapter Seven

The street was deserted, as was ordinarily the case in the early hours of the morning, the world of the living sleeping through this world of night.

A light fog drifted along the ground like the setting of some long-forgotten horror movie, heralding the approach of the coming dawn.

Looking up, he could see that the sky was yet to lighten and gauged it to be another hour or so before the stars would begin to diminish.

He was being stalked, he knew, but by whom or what he did not know, knowing only that he was being watched and followed from the darkness behind.

Cautiously, he walked up the middle of the road, giving himself plenty of room to manoeuvre when the attack finally came. Not knowing how he knew exactly, he sensed it somehow as he sensed most things since his awakening.

Cristian was aware now of the world around him, the humans in their beds, but then there was a blot amid it all. A something that just did not belong, a shadow that followed him as unnatural to this world as anything could be.

'Ever since she opened me up to the land,' he thought, pondering at what this might mean.

He was changed now, even to the point where he no longer wished to feed. He found that even the thought of leaching life from anything disgusted him.

Feeling the presence on his return to his hotel room earlier, he had cast out his awareness as he lay on the bed.

Visualising the commotion that accompanied the early-evening bustle, he pictured the closing of businesses and the people going home.

A little fascinated by how powerful his senses now were, he had sent out his mind as far as he was able and found something amiss among all the activity.

The unnaturalness of the presence had caused him to pause, but the more he focused on it, the more indistinct it became. Focusing his awareness back on the living, he had picked up the entity again, visible now like a black spot on a photograph.

Deciding to wait until the early hours of the morning, he had finally left to investigate while the world around him slept.

Turning down yet another deserted street, he froze at what lay ahead, sucking in the clammy city air through his teeth.

At the end of this road stood a solitary figure, apparently waiting for him to approach.

Imagining himself gliding forward, he visualised what the man would look like close-up. A flash of pain erupting in his mind and he squinted his eyes against the instant agony.

'A shield,' he realised, admonishing himself for not expecting it.

As he neared, he saw that the man's hair was as black as the sky above him and that his eyes were piercing, even from this distance.

'Colin,' he acknowledged on getting close enough to talk.

'My betraying son,' the master vampire replied, his tone accusing as he snarled out the words. 'What are you doing?' he hissed, running his fingers through his hair in irritation.

Cristian shrugged and made a show of relaxing his stance a little.

'The right thing,' he replied, holding his father's wrathful glare with the calm of his own. 'Maybe you should try it sometime?' he added, causing the piercing eyes to flash.

Colin's eyes pulsed with an inner power, glowing as though lit from behind. He moved forward suddenly, covering the distance quickly.

'You think this a joke? The Bloods are all but wiped out and Azazel himself has been killed, and *he* did it!' he spat, as though the mere reference to his youngest son was like bile in his mouth.

Cristian laughed quietly, enraging his father further.

'Good for him,' he replied, silently raising his shield about him.

Regardless of his stealth, Colin seemed to notice the move and began to smile knowingly.

'I see your true nature, Cris! You seek to surpass me! Did you truly believe that I wouldn't find out about your little army? *I am the master of the Egni. Me!* And that includes your little Dark Brotherhood!' he raged, bits of spittle spraying from his mouth. 'How easy it was to subdue them, though at first they thought to fight. I went myself of course, for maximum effect, giving them a speech as all great leaders do,' he scoffed, seeing the surprise registering on his son's face. 'Ask not what your faction can do for you, but what you can do for your faction,' Colin intoned, laughing wickedly. 'And after a little fear, more fear than you could bring to bear... they decided wisely that there was, in fact, no choice before them,' he continued with a look of distaste curling his mouth.

Cristian berated himself for his short-sightedness and felt angered that he had not seen the truth for himself. With a sinking feeling in his stomach, he regretted his reaction to the doormen's perceived betrayal and closed his eyes in sadness.

'What choice would they have had?' he thought, knowing how deadly his father could be.

Nodding as the realisation sank in, Colin smiled without warmth as he looked upon his firstborn.

'I will crush him and all who stand with him,' he swore, speaking now of his youngest.

Sagging internally, Cristian shook his head.

'Why are you so blinded by hate? Why can't you see as I can?' he moaned. But no sooner had he said it, a thought formed in his mind.

'I see well enough, my deceitful son! I see that he is my enemy and so, now, are you! I have summoned my true sons and they will be here soon,' he sneered, stepping forward again.

Dissolving the shield to allow his father closer, the time had come for Cristian's intention to take fruition.

'You plan to kill two sons then? You'll find it harder than you think, old man,' he scoffed, goading his father even closer.

Colin snarled through his teeth and the light of his eyes flashed even more wildly.

'You're not my sons!' he raged, raising a clenched fist and slowly touching it to his son's jaw.

At the contact, Cristian sent out his awakening, allowing the very essence of what had changed him to pass into the other.

A pulse of unseen power flowed into his father, causing him to reel back, his rage-filled face draining of colour.

'What have you done?' he gasped, shaking his head in confusion.

'I've opened your eyes, as mine have been. Sadly, I think it will take time to fully take hold and that's a luxury I don't have,' he replied, casting his shield about him again. 'Though I eagerly await our next meeting,' he whispered, preparing himself for the inevitable attack.

Recovering from what had been done to him, Colin gathered his strength about him in a crackling flash of light. Arcing between his fingertips, the dazzling white light shone also in his eyes.

Drawing forth the Silver Sword of Power, Cristian backed away slowly, holding it out protectively before him.

'You think that your sword will protect you?' Colin snarled, slowly raising his hands before him. 'Have you forgotten that it was I who made it? One for each of you,' he stammered, his brow furrowing a little in confession.

'Silver for my firstborn, for he is pure and just,' he whispered, looking somewhat pained by the words. 'Black for the second, for his imaginings and silent grace,' his eyes glazed over, seeing a world in a different time.

'Gold for the third, for his hidden glory and the brilliance within,' his eyes watered as tears welled.

'Red for the last, for the wrath of his nature and the love in his heart,' his voice broke at this, the emotion too much after speaking these final words.

Cristian watched through his tear-blurred vision, seeing the man that had once been his father become himself once again.

'Cris?' Colin sobbed, his anguish breaking him as he looked at his son and at the sword held between them. 'In defence against me! My son! I was going to kill my son!' Colin thought, looking down at his hands with loathing. 'Forgive me,' he choked, dropping to his knees in front of him.

Cristian stood stock-still before throwing caution to the wind and lowering himself to hug his father tight, weeping at the miracle of what Kristina had done for them.

'What have I become?' his father cried, shaking his head into his son's chest.

'You have become yourself again,' Cristian answered, gripping him tightly by the shoulders. 'As I have,' he added, holding his father closer.

'Oh, what have I done?' Colin cried, seeing in his mind all his despicable deeds. 'I placed a web on the elements so that the Bloods could take his children!' he wept, pulling at his hair in torment.

Shaking him sternly, Cristian's eyes blazed as he forced his father's head up to look at him.

'It is what you do now that matters! What is it you're going to do?' he asked, his hands like vices upon his father's shoulders.

Colin looked back and nodded imperceptibly.

'I must undo what I did and share this with all the Egni!' he answered, placing his hand over his heart. 'I feel again, Cris! I can feel... *love*!' he cried, overwhelmed by the emotion.

They stayed there like that, kneeling in the street and looking at each other as though they had not seen each other for more than an age.

'What are they like?' he asked suddenly, the question catching Cristian by surprise.

'They look like you,' he replied and smiled at the thought of the children. 'How else could they look, what with Daire looking like your clone,' he added, seeing again the pain in his eyes.

Taking a calming breath, Colin nodded and got to his feet with a sigh.

'You're being stalked,' he announced, causing his son to frown in reply. 'You did not sense me, were you not surprised when you turned down this street?' he asked, arching an eyebrow humorously as he was once known to do.

Cristian had indeed been surprised, for the one who stalked him had always stayed behind and had never once moved ahead of him.

Smiling tightly, Colin nodded at seeing the truth dawn on his son.

'I can go undetected if I wish,' he said, looking back down the street. 'The one that hunts you is a Blood, one of the few to survive thus far. I will help you in dealing with it.'

Shaking his head and smiling confidently, Cristian offered his hand in farewell.

Frowning doubtfully, Colin took it and shared a moment with his son.

'I killed Bael, and now that Azazel is dead, I'm sure that I can deal with whoever is left. You need to act quickly and cure the rest, Dad. Start with Paul,' Cristian advised, believing his brother to be the most affected by the change.

Colin pursed his lips, causing Cristian to smile at the expression.

'He still does that too. The resemblance is uncanny now that I have seen you both so recently,' he said, gripping his father's hand tighter. 'Put our house in order and I will pave the way for your reunion,' he continued, making to turn away.

Nodding, Colin pulled his son into one final embrace and kissed him on the cheek.

'I am so sorry, Cris,' he whispered, kissing him again on the other before stepping back.

Without waiting for a response, he clapped his hands together and ignited his terrifying power. White light erupted, the wildness of it crackling about him with unseen purpose.

Smiling with the old twinkle in his eyes, Colin clapped his hands again and Cristian was left blinking in the aftermath, the bright light dazzling him for a moment.

Standing alone in the deserted street, Cristian shook his head at how secretive his father was and wondered at how long he had been able to do that.

'Well, that was unexpected,' he announced, chuckling to himself.

'So is this!' a voice hissed, catching him completely by surprise.

***

John lay back against an old oak tree, enjoying the sun's warmth upon his face and smiling slightly at the sound of little footsteps thumping nearer.

Amused by the failed attempt at stealth, he opened his eyes to see the little blonde girl creeping towards him.

'Merry meet,' he welcomed warmly, a wide smile spreading across his face.

'What are you doing?' Francesca asked, her brow frowning quizzically at him before looking up at the tree.

'I am drawing energy from the land,' he replied before leaning forward conspiringly. 'I'm trying to make myself young again,' he whispered covertly, bringing a finger to his lips for secrecy.

Francesca laughed at his expression and tilted her head as she studied him further.

'Why do you want to be younger?' she asked, frowning at him again.

He leaned his head back again, sighing heavily.

'I want to be young for someone else,' he answered, glancing briefly at the high priestess who leaned in the open doorway some distance away. 'So I can play,' he continued, chuckling to himself. 'I fear though that I am too old as I am,' he added, feeling his humour beginning to evaporate.

Seating herself on the grass before him, Francesca crossed her legs beneath her.

'I think you're doing it all wrong,' she observed, tilting her head again.

John straightened, amused by her analysis.

'I think you might be right,' he replied, leaning his head back in resignation.

Suddenly feeling sympathy for this sad-looking man, Francesca felt an instinctual desire to help him.

'How do you do that?' she asked, pointing at the tree behind him.

Glad for the distraction, John got to his feet and gestured her in his place.

'You don't need the tree, I just like to think that I take the agelessness of it into myself,' he said, squatting down low beside her. 'Now, close your eyes and visualise the magick of the earth rising into you,' he instructed, spreading his awareness out around him.

Seeking his quiet mind, he sensed immediately the immense power of the land building like a volcano beneath him and instinctively jumped back to see what was happening.

Instead of the trickle of power that he could summon, the area around him now thrummed with the earth's unchecked might.

Looking up, he saw the leaves turn green and the bent old tree begin to straighten as the magick infused it with renewed life.

Gasping in shock as he looked again into her now opened eyes, he saw the green light of the land mixed in with that of her blue.

'Take my hand,' she instructed, their roles reversing as the magick took hold.

Full of trepidation, he nervously accepted and knelt once again before her.

Power of the like he had never felt before coursed through him, renewing what was within him as she had done to the tree.

Arching his back from the sheer force of it, his hair was the first to change as it darkened to a healthier shade of brown. The skin of his face began tightening and the aches of age washed away from him as the torrent of magick returned him to what once he had been.

It was some time before John realised that the magick had withdrawn from him and after slumping back on his elbows, he looked in wonder at the girl who was now smiling back in satisfaction.

'There! That's how you do it,' she said brightly, laughing at his ridiculous expression. 'I think I'm better at this than you are,' she confessed, sighing contentedly.

Putting his hands to his face and feeling the youthful skin that had risen into place, John was unable to speak through his overpowering emotion.

Sitting up, he leaned forward and hugged her tightly.

'You are a goddess!' he gasped, unable to contain himself.

Within the shadow of the doorway, the priestess stood transfixed, staring at the tree that had righted itself seemingly all on its own she saw the green of its leaves glowing now like some burning bush of fable.

'Such a prize!' she murmured, taking her weight off the doorframe in her excitement.

Suddenly, a shiver ran up her spine and the hairs of her neck stood up on end. Something inside her screamed for her to run and she knew then that she should not have spoken aloud.

Turning to look behind her, she saw Daire standing mere inches away from her, having somehow approached without her sensing it, much too close for comfort.

Paling with instant fear and swallowing hard, she nervously flinched away from him.

'I gave my word,' she blurted in defence, feeling the threat of death emanating from him.

'That you have,' he agreed, looking at her as though she were food.

'Why do you treat me this way?' she demanded, angry now.

'Better to fear today than die tomorrow,' he answered, his dark eyes beginning to reflect the light sinisterly.

Chloe paled further at his words and her voice shook when she finally replied.

'I swear to my goddess that I will leave your children be. May she strike me down if I do,' she replied, invoking her most sacred oath.

Daire nodded slowly and pursed his lips in thought.

'She has heard you, Chloe,' he whispered, the unholy light fading back to darkness. 'She will now act on my behalf, should I be unable to perform the deed myself,' he continued, stepping back from her with a shrug. 'Let that be the end of it,' he announced, smiling at her for the very first time. 'I hope that you will be a positive force in their lives and not the negative you have been thus far,' he added, looking out across the garden.

The druid danced about goofily, spinning around in circles, his long legs carrying him from one side of the garden to the other.

Daire smiled at the scene, seeing the branchlike arms extending out with his forearms lowered to swing at either side. As he did so, his legs lifted high to kick out from his sides, causing Francesca to laugh ecstatically as she clapped her hands at the comical scene.

'He has a lot of energy for an older man,' Chloe observed, chuckling as the colour rose once again in her cheeks.

'Not so old anymore, I think,' Daire replied, gesturing with his head for her to go and see for herself.

Looking back in shock, she walked into the sunlight to get a closer look.

Watching her go, the smile faded from his face as he spoke now to another.

'Do you think she's sincere?' he asked, a worried frown creasing his forehead.

'No. But it matters not,' the goddess replied, stepping up behind him and encircling him in her arms. 'She has invoked my name on the matter,' she continued, hugging his broad back tighter. 'They are safe from her,' she assured him, kissing softly at the back of his neck.

***

Staring at the young druid, Chloe laughed with a look of excitement widening her eyes.

'Oh my goddess!' she gasped, unable to take her eyes from the ecstatic, puffing druid as he finally finished his dance.

On seeing her approach, John rushed forward and swept her up in his arms, spinning her around in a dizzying circle.

'Can you believe this? Look! I'm young!' he shouted with wild excitement in his dark brown eyes. 'How young do I look?' he asked, spinning her again.

The repetitiveness of his questions made her laugh aloud and cup his face in her hands affectionately.

'You look maybe mid-twenties? Certainly no older,' she answered and started to laugh as he whooped and started his goofy dance again.

Standing off at a distance, Lucian stared at the scene in silence and then kicked at the grass idly, looking downcast at the show of power.

'Are you okay, Little Wolf?' his father asked, shocking him and causing him to jump.

Amused by the reaction, Daire knelt and pulled him into his embrace. Something out of the corner of the boy's eye caught his attention and he suddenly squirmed to get away.

The hand growled menacingly, the fingers of Elmo's mouth flexing into a snarl.

'Why are you sad?' the hand growled, causing the child to whine and laugh at the same time.

After a moment's play, Daire laid back contentedly on the grass. Lucian, however, unwilling to stop for the moment, pounced on top of him, performing a wrestling elbow move that drove the wind out of his father.

Closing his eyes, Daire hugged his boy who now laid atop him.

'You're sad because you think that you can't do the same things that Cesca can,' he said, making it a statement of fact.

Lucian nodded onto his chest but said nothing.

'Have you considered the possibility that Cesca might not be able to do the things that you can do?' he asked, feeling his son's head raise off his chest.

'Really?' he asked, hope evident in his tone.

Daire nodded and lifted himself onto his elbows.

'Cesca is a Sorceress, the first for a very long time, but you, my little wolf, have a different calling. Your magick is different and, in many ways, more powerful. You feel like you lose concentration or get bored with the little things, right?' he asked, nodding his head for him.

Following the motion, Lucian nodded too as the frown returned to his face.

'You are more suited to direct magick,' he explained and then sighed, knowing he had to reword his explanation.

'There are many different kinds of magick in the world, most of which is what I call, "Subtle Magick". Those that can perform this can influence the world around them subtly but not directly. Kinda like learning something subconsciously,' he continued, looking to see if his son was following and seeing that he definitely was not.

Sitting up further, Daire organised his thoughts in a way that his son would understand.

'Okay, forget what I just said, it doesn't relate to you anyway,' he said, pursing his lips in thought. 'You and Cesca have "Direct Magick". A very strong ability to cast magick. Cesca has a strong gift and a natural ability to work her magick as easily as breathing. Like doing that...' he said, gesturing towards the tree.

Lucian's brow furrowed again as his face began to pout.

'You have that same power, Luc! It's only Cesca's vivid imagination and her interest in all aspects of magick that allows her to do what she does. You are only really different from her because you are not as interested in those things. Here, let me show you,' he said, rising to his feet.

Walking a little way into the forest, Daire gestured for him to sit with his back to a tree as his daughter had done with the druid.

'I want you to draw up the energy of the land but I want you to have a goal. I want you to make the tree your protector, a battle tree that will fight to keep you safe,' he instructed, trying to pique the boy's interest.

As expected, Lucian's eyes widened and his hands clenched into excited fists.

'I can do that?' he asked, jumping to his feet.

Shrugging, Daire stood back with his hands spreading wide.

'Let's find out,' he replied, gesturing him down again.

Closing his eyes, Lucian rested his head against the already impressive-looking oak. Nothing happened at first and Daire frowned, feeling nothing rising from beneath his feet.

The tree groaned suddenly and began to shake violently as the power from the child coursed through it without the added magick from the land.

With a cry of pain, Lucian's back arched as his life force was drawn from him.

Springing forward, Daire drew on the earth's energy and sent it into his son. The magick erupted everywhere, replenishing the spent energy and revitalising the plant life around them.

The pull of the oak's need for more took him by surprise and with a growl of anger, he severed its link to his son as he put his will upon it.

'Enough!' he growled, feeling the tree withdraw its want for what his child had unwittingly given it.

Sitting back, he looked down at his son to see teary eyes staring up at him.

'You have to draw the energy from the land first!' Daire growled, annoyed and panicked at the same time. 'You can't do it without first drawing on the earth. It's the same with lightning, without the earth's magick running through you, it's *your* life that feeds it,' he stressed and then paused, needing to see if the boy understood.

'Do you understand?' he roared when the acknowledging expression was not forthcoming. 'You will die if you don't understand!' he cried, struggling to contain his dread at what nearly happened.

Lucian cowered under his father's anger and Daire hated himself for it, feeling tears of worry fall from his eyes.

'I forgot,' Lucian cried, covering his face with his hands.

Reaching out and hugging his son tightly, Daire began to cry at the dread he felt in his heart.

'What can I do?' he asked, knowing that she was with him.

'Apart from watching him constantly, there is nothing you can do,' she replied softly, her tone full of sorrow at what she had seen. 'His mind should instinctively do this. The problem is that he has too much power and little or no control over it. I have seen this before, as have you, and it's a matter of time before something like this happens again,' she whispered, shaking her head in fear for the boy.

Daire closed his eyes and held his boy close, having indeed seen this happen many times in the past.

He had witnessed many with a similar gift, over the years, perish before they could come into their power, knowing that his instinct should be there to summon up the magick first.

Crying in desperation, he knew in his heart that his son had developed this same self-destructive flaw that had killed so many like him before.

'What can I do?' he pondered, the thought of losing his son to something so stupid, simply not an option to him. 'What to do?' he thought, rocking his son in his arms as he sought the knowledge to protect him.

'No!' Olivia cried, knowing his mind and the terrible risk involved. 'To do it to the house is one thing but to do it on the living could be disastrous for you both!' she warned, shaking her head with a fierce expression.

He looked up at her, the decision already made.

'I will put my mind in his to safeguard against this and more besides. I will not lose him to something as idiotic as this!' he replied, holding her eyes decidedly.

Olivia crouched beside him, her face stern and full of worry.

'No,' she stressed, reaching out to him desperately. 'We can place a block on him from ever accessing his power again and let him live out a normal life,' she begged, pleading with him to agree.

'Absolutely not,' he replied, shaking his head resolutely. 'There is no "normal life" after this!' he growled, knowing that after all the boy had seen and done there could be no taking it away from him. 'I will not have him feel inadequate or inferior and will not weaken him when he needs to be so strong. He was born with the gift and I will be damned to the underworld before I take it from him,' he swore, looking up at the tree. 'What's he done to it?' he asked, looking at the now terrifying oak.

She closed her eyes, wishing that he would not invoke such terrible oaths before reaching out to touch the tree with her hand.

'It is aware for the very first time, aware as we are aware, beyond that I cannot tell,' she answered, placing her hand upon his. 'Let us go inside and discuss our options, there may be another way,' she pleaded, wanting Kristina or one of the others to change his mind.

He looked at her in a way that she had grown accustomed to and she closed her eyes in resignation.

'You fool,' she whispered, knowing that he had already begun what he had intended.

Pain lanced through his mind like a knife wound to his very soul and he opened his mouth in a silent scream, a pain too great to be voiced. Light flashed behind his eyes and he was thrown back as a mirror of himself was ripped away into his son's mind.

'No!' Olivia screamed, putting her hands upon his writhing form. 'You overreacting fool!' she screamed, feeling the child's aura becoming closed to her. 'You will dominate him!' she shouted, glaring at him in anger.

A familiar frown began to settle on the child's features and she knew then that he was now something different.

'Those with his power develop this defect as a way of protecting the rest of you,' she whispered, slumping her shoulders in defeat. 'It's like the world knows that they will be too strong and weeds them out early,' she continued, looking down at the still form of the one she loved, had always loved.

Slowly the pain receded and his pallid complexion began to colour once more.

'Damn the consequences and damn this world,' he vented, looking at her without an ounce of regret. 'He will live and learn to do it for himself,' he continued defiantly. 'Your way would make him even more complacent! He needs it drummed into him and to this end I have placed myself within his subconscious. He won't know I'm there! It will appear to be his instinct at work, there will be no fight for dominance,' he assured her, drawing up magick to heal himself.

Kristina rushed into view and came to a stop with her hands upon her hips.

'As you did to the damned house?' she stormed, her face white and twitching with rage.

Looking at the goddess, his eyes accused her of allowing Kristina to approach undetected in his weakened state.

'This is not the way, Daire,' Olivia whispered, looking from him to Lucian.

***

Watching the scene unfolding before him, Lucian felt better than he ever had and much clearer-minded. He felt embarrassed for not calling up the magick first, wanting only to show his father what he could do. Feeling ashamed that his father had to help him, a new determination took hold from within.

'I will do things properly from now on,' he promised himself as a new confidence took hold of him like a vice.

'Yes,' a voice whispered in his mind, comforting him with its reassurance and causing him to smile as he rose confidently to his feet.

Walking several paces away, he turned to face them with a presence previously unseen.

'Lucian! No!' Kristina ordered, not knowing what he was about but taking no chances.

Lucian beamed his open-mouthed smile and his teeth flashed white in the sunlight.

'It's okay, Mammy,' he replied, closing his eyes on her.

Instantly the magick came up at his call, the ground around them vibrating slightly with the sudden power of it. Spreading his arms out wide, he turned and sent his magick out into the forest.

The trees around them groaned and shook at his direction, growing taller and stronger as had the first. The pulsing magick travelled in waves from his hands, the light of it shining like a rainbow in the rain as it washed out through the changing forest.

The earth could be heard moving in the distance and the sound of stone on stone echoed back to them with ground-shaking finality.

When he finally opened his eyes, Lucian saw the entire household standing there, watching what he had done with more than just concern.

Daire clapped his hands together slowly, beaming proudly at his son and then at the forest.

'My little wolf!' he praised in an awed whisper, still weakened but unable to hide the pride and relief from his face.

Kristina glared at him, her eyes still accusing.

'That was all him,' he announced defensively, looking to the goddess for support.

Olivia looked from him to Kristina and nodded her agreement.

'It was him, but with the confidence of another,' she answered, arching an eyebrow back at the father. 'If he can do all that and be okay, then I think he'll be safe for the time being,' she continued, nodding reassuringly at Kristina.

Bowing her head in respect, Kristina did not look happy and kept her hands where they were as she glared back at her son's father.

'It's this or death!' he growled, incensed by her expression. 'Tell her!' he snapped, glaring at, Olivia.

'Mind your tone!' she snapped back before controlling herself. 'He does speak the truth, however, those with the child's gift have never survived for long,' she confirmed, smiling sadly.

Swallowing hard, Kristina's eyes brimmed as she finally nodded her agreement.

'Okay, then you did right,' she murmured, staring tearfully down in apology.

'He will be fine, trust me,' Daire replied weakly, trying to lay her fears to rest. 'The house reacted the exact way I intended it to. The same it will be in this. I will not allow my children to perish, not ever!' he promised, nodding to Kristina assuredly.

The now youthful John walked forward and raised his arms out in wonder and exasperation.

'This is so unfair!' he cried, shaking his head in flabbergasted misery. 'Why can't I do this kind of magick?' he asked, envious at the abilities of the children.

'The difference between one with the gift and one without,' the goddess replied, smiling tightly at the man.

'But magick is in my blood, my parents were druids! Surely, I must have the gift!' he whined, causing Daire to smile.

Olivia put a reassuring hand on John's shoulder, squeezing it tenderly.

'These children are the direct offspring of one of the ancients, but more than that, Lucian is more like what the daemons had intended all along, and Francesca is only a single step behind. What I'm saying is that their gift is strong, stronger than even the ancients. You, however, have been born from the descendants of such beings and so your gift is, for want of a better word, "watered down",' she replied, squeezing his shoulder again supportively.

John looked at Daire, his eyes wide with astonishment. 'Demons? What are you talking about?' he asked, looking around questioningly. 'Ignore that! You can fill me in later. You mean to tell me that Dark can do more than this?' he asked, gesturing to the now scary-looking trees.

'My name is not Dark,' Daire growled, glancing pointedly at his children.

'Not as he was, but as he is he can do much more than this,' the goddess answered, moving back to Daire's side and taking his hand in hers.

'What the demons intended? What exactly does that mean?' Kim asked, intrigue widening her eyes as she sat on the grass to listen.

Olivia looked at the mage and acknowledged her inquisitiveness with a smile.

'The ancients and their magick come directly from the daemons of the underworld. They had intended for each corresponding generation to be more powerful so that the family lines would eventually have so much daemon essence in them they would create a link between themselves and this dimension. A doorway, so to speak,' she answered, waiting for what she knew would come.

'Why didn't the offspring get stronger?' Kim asked, absorbing the knowledge like ink on blotting paper.

The goddess smiled again, intrigued by the woman's line of questioning.

'Some did, but developed this "flaw" and died as this child would have, had *he* not intervened,' she answered, glancing briefly at Daire. 'Most, however, were born weaker for reasons I am yet to understand. Whether influenced from an outside source or a miscalculation on the daemons part, the offspring simply got weaker, mostly,' she continued, looking suddenly at Lucian.

'How do you know all this?' Kim asked, believing the words but not understanding how she could know of such things.

Looking through the trees, Charlie's eyes grew vacant for a moment.

'He's armed the forest!' he interrupted, drawing an annoyed look from Kim. 'He's a natural battle mage,' he continued, smiling appreciatively at the boy.

Daire tutted and shook a finger at the man.

'Close, but no cigar,' he replied, smiling wider at Charlie's dawning expression.

'You can't be serious!' Charlie stammered, looking reverently down at the boy.

Daire rose to walk behind his son, placing his hands upon his shoulders proudly.

'Serious indeed. My little wolf is a war wizard.'

***

The room was dark with the smell of damp hanging heavy in the air, like a mildewy blanket of decay that tasted of corruption when ingested.

Discoloured floral wallpaper hung in strips down the walls, suggesting the room's long disuse.

Groggy from the blow that had sent him into unconsciousness, Cristian took in the blurred scene with a dreamy detachment. Confused as to the reason someone had bothered to tie him to the bed, he took a deep intoxicating breath and readied himself to rip free.

A shadow flickered past his field of vision, causing him to jerk his head in that direction. A dark form sprang on top of him, pinning him down at the elbows.

'Ahh, Criiistian,' a voice whispered as strong hands held him down, stronger hands than his, he realised, feeling the unyielding pressure bearing down on him. 'I told you we were going to have some fun,' Lore whispered, licking her flattened tongue across his cheek.

He felt vulnerable under her pressure and knew that for the moment at least, she had him pegged.

'You are too weak for me, Cristian,' she purred, lowering her face to his. 'I have fed off you,' she announced and licked her lips suggestively. 'And will continue to do so,' she breathed huskily, inching down towards him. 'So that Dark's damned fire can't find me,' she continued, smiling like a cat that had just got the cream and kissing him passionately.

Struggling, he turned his head away and unwittingly allowed her access to his neck.

'Mmm,' she purred as her feeding began again.

Lore drank deeply until his vision began to darken and the room spun sickeningly around him.

It was some time before she pulled slowly, almost regrettably, away and licked the wound before kissing it.

'Get used to this, Cristian, for this is how it ends for you, baby,' she breathed, wiggling her bum on him like a cat before its pounce. 'We will be here for some time, I think, at least until it's safe for me to leave again. With your blood inside me, the fire will leave me alone, maybe,' she continued, kissing him again.

This time, he did not turn his head, causing her to kiss him more passionately than before.

'This is going to be more fun than I could have ever imagined,' she breathed lustily before lowering herself once more.

Time passed in a haze of lips and teeth with him falling in and out of consciousness as he steadily became weaker. He could feel himself dying inside, feeling his life's energy being leached from him by this insatiable woman.

She did not lie about how close they would be, never leaving him for more than a moment at a time as though he was a drug to her, her fix.

His dreams now were of her lips and of the fangs that entered him, of her kissing and biting, kissing and biting, feeding upon him until there was nothing left.

Her moans and laughter were all he could hear now and all he could feel was her draining him, his last moments, as his life was slowly being sucked from him.

Intolerable heat awoke him and he could see her drearily through a haze of fire.

She tore into him then, drinking more than was normal until it subsided, leaving him lost and weak in the darkness.

He was not sure if it was an illusion or some sick delusion that he had created in his mind, but she had laughed afterwards, patting his head like a good little boy.

'See, Crisss? I told you it would work,' she whispered, before finding his mouth again.

He cried then which only added to her enjoyment.

With all the blood that she had consumed, she no longer needed to pin him down, for she now had some perverse control over him, holding him there with her will alone.

'I do believe that I am the last of my kind,' she said, nuzzling into his neck. 'Soon I shall be leaving,' she purred, lifting herself to look at him. 'But not before I have drawn every ounce of liquid from you,' she promised, rubbing her nose against his in an affectionate manner.

'Please...' he whispered hoarsely but he was unable to further his plea.

Her thighs squeezed against him as she stared down lustily into his eyes.

'I love it when you beg,' she whispered, lowering herself once again. But the kiss never came and on opening his eyes, he saw fear in her for the very first time.

'Up!' a menacing voice commanded, causing him to look up to the right.

She backed up, scooting away from the black line at her throat.

At first, it appeared to be a choker of some kind, an indistinct piece of clothing that had previously been missed.

Blinking away the haze of exhaustion, Cristian realised suddenly that it was a blade, a black blade that he had seen before.

Lore backed away, her chin forced upwards by the pressure of the sword's tip.

'Back!' the voice ordered, forcing her to retreat until her back was to the wall.

Very cautiously, a darkly-clad swordsman stepped into view, positioning himself between her and her victim with the sword's tip resting at the hollow of her throat.

'Please,' she whispered, holding her hands up in surrender as she beseeched with her eyes.

'Unlike yourself, begging does nothing for me,' the man sneered, putting pressure on the blade so that it drew blood.

Without warning the swordsman was buffeted back against the wall, the air blurring suddenly as it condensed around him.

'Bloods have no magick!' Cristian fretted, frantically looking back to Lore, but she had not moved and her image too was distorted by the same thickening of the air.

'Damn you, Dark!' Lore screamed, knowing exactly what had returned for her.

A spark of light blinked suddenly into existence. A glowing ember that rose gracefully from the floor, flickering dully before the vampire's eyes, causing her to scream in her terror.

Knowing that there was no bargaining with the thing, she desperately reached inside herself and unleashed that which had been previously been denied her.

A thunderous explosion of brick and mortar blasted the wall out behind her, leaving a gaping hole that led to her freedom.

The fire roared in fury, enlarging into the size of a football before driving after her through the ruined wall.

Blinking slowly, Cristian stared at where she had stood but saw only darkness now that the fire had gone.

Struggling against his bonds, Cristian found that in his weakened state, he was not up to the task and laid back in defeat.

'Of all the ways to go, brother, that has to be up there with the best of them,' the swordsman remarked, his low tone full of dark humour. 'One might even think that you did not fight hard enough,' he continued, chuckling wickedly.

Despite himself, Cristian laughed weakly, recognising the Blade Master's voice.

'Shut up and cut me free,' he replied, shaking his bound wrists for emphasis.

The black blade flashed through the air in a figure of eight, severing the cords instantly.

Sitting up, Cristian had to reach out to steady himself as his vision began spinning from loss of blood.

'What was that she said at the end? Shamyu shark or something?' Paul asked, sheathing his sword behind his back.

Looking up at his brother, he shook his head and regretted the motion immediately.

'Damn you, Dark,' he clarified, saying each word slowly.

Silence greeted his words, the naming of their brother sitting heavy with the swordsman.

'I have made peace with him and it's time for you to do the same. I will not turn on him again,' Cristian whispered, finally staring up at his brother.

Paul nodded, looking down to the floor.

'How do I even start breaking bread with him?' he asked, his normally confident manner lost for the moment.

Shrugging, Cristian closed his eyes and pictured the demonic creature that was now his youngest brother.

'He has not changed much on the inside,' he replied, causing Paul to frown.

'What does that mean? Is he old and decrepit or something?' he asked, raising his eyebrows questioningly.

'Or something,' Cristian replied, with a sardonic smile touching his lips. 'He's literally gone through hell to keep his children safe. Let's just say that the Bloods have nothing on him now,' he continued cryptically before taking a deep steadying breath.

Paul huffed judgementally, his trademark scowl setting back upon his pale face.

'So he's too high and mighty to become one of us but had an epiphany or something?' he asked, unable to keep the contempt from his tone.

Cristian shook his head, breathing in a few times to steady himself.

'The change in him is new and not of his choosing,' he whispered, standing up unsteadily. 'Let's not carry on where we left off, brother! Stop with your bloody judgements,' he growled, leaning heavily on his arm for support.

'You need to feed,' Paul observed, ignoring his brother's rebuke.

'Just get me out of here,' Cristian croaked, repulsed by the very thought.

Chapter Eight

Amid the solitude that darkness brings, a low groaning that sent all nocturnal creatures scurrying from the area suddenly rent the air.

High above, an owl had just begun its descent with its eyes fixed firmly on the prize when it banked sharply to disappear above the treetops.

The sound seemingly came from everywhere and nowhere at once, as though issuing from the world itself. It sounded as though the land itself moaned in misery as the grass atop it began to wither and die, turning black with the earth beneath it.

As the sound grew in volume, a black line sliced down through the air, causing a vacuum of air to be sucked into it.

The line parted like a curtain, pulled apart by the long black fingers that passed through it.

Large-knuckled black hands pushed through to grip at the edges of nothingness and then closed themselves around these edges with cold efficiency.

The howl of wind intensified as the hands began to part, clenching more tightly so as not to be sucked back into the void from whence it came.

At the creature's passing, the dimensional tear closed, leaving a black scar in the darkness of the glade.

Standing over eight feet tall and as silent as the grave, the towering form of the Reaper surveyed the land around it. Its deeply-cowled head turned instinctively to that which had drawn it and remaining statue-still, it waited.

***

Lucian's scream tore from him, his terror absolute as he screamed for his mother.

Francesca was the first to arrive, beginning to cry herself at the look of terror in his eyes. Looking up, her father appeared and hugged them both tightly, asking what the matter was.

'What is it?' he asked softly, running his hand up through his brown hair. 'I am here, you are safe,' he soothed, concerned by his son's terrified expression.

Eyes wide with terror, Lucian began to shiver uncontrollably and was unable to tear his eyes from the window.

Kristina came in, and at the sight of her, the boy scrambled in desperation to get to her.

'Oh, my baby boy,' she soothed, taking him in her arms. 'What did you dream about?' she asked, stroking the back of his head with her fingers.

Turning again to the window, he peered past her, still trembling with fear.

'Daemon!' he screamed, burying his head into her neck.

With a cold shiver of dread, Daire felt goosebumps ripple over his body at the pronunciation and instantly rose to his feet, the house coming alive with him.

All around them the doors and windows could be heard slamming shut as the house fortified its defences, the walls throbbing with an intense energy as a shield of white spread out to surround it.

An eerie, mournful howl rose up outside that was immediately answered by many more in the distance. Something was wrong, and the wolves knew it.

Kristina turned with a cold feeling in her stomach but she saw only her daughter staring back at her with eyes wide and fearful.

'When the wolves are at the door,' Francesca whispered, clutching at her father's ring and kissing it.

'Daemon!' Daire thought, hearing the correct pronunciation from one who should never have known. 'He said, daemon!' he panicked, knowing as his house knew, that this was no mere dream.

In the living room, he was pleased to see that the mages had taken up defensive positions around the house and nodded to them as he entered.

Chloe sat cross-legged upon the floor, summoning the strength of her remaining covens and adding it to the building's defences.

John glanced at him from the kitchen and nodded in greeting.

'Bloods?' he asked, his face white with adrenaline.

'Something else,' Daire replied, causing the mages to glance at each other with concern. 'Where's Olivia?' he asked, catching Charlie's eye.

'Outside with Kim,' he answered, turning back to the window.

John flinched as the legend walked past him to the back door, seeing the Dark Wolf in his true form for the very first time.

Now towering over the tall druid, the legend was terrible to behold up close.

On leaving the house, Olivia had picked up a tail and nodded in welcome after seeing who it was.

The women stood at the bottom of the garden, the now-larger oaks spreading out before them.

'Anything?' Daire asked, stopping to stand behind them.

Kim looked up startled, clearly not expecting the thunderous tone and then frowned when she took in his appearance. Shaking her head in answer, she looked unnerved by him but said nothing.

'Liv?' he asked, peering at the goddess with a look of concern.

'Nothing,' she replied, not looking at him and either oblivious or uncaring of his transformation. 'But I feel,' she continued, shivering uncharacteristically before shaking her head. She turned to him then with a trace of doubt in her voice.

'If I use my power here, I'll be noticed by those that would banish me,' she said, looking worriedly up at him. 'I am not permitted to be involved and especially not directly,' she added, causing Kim to frown at her in confusion.

Moving forward, Daire entered the forest at a slow jog.

'Watch my back,' he called, moving silently ahead.

Low growls sounded in answer to his words as the forest came alive around them, the wolves moving at last, having laid in wait for him.

Swallowing hard, Kim had not detected them around her and wondered at the strange relationship between the two.

'So many questions,' she thought, least of which was the true identity of the girl beside her.

A yelp of pain announced that the demon had been found and a howl rose up amid the growling as the wolves around him sprang into action.

The sound of fighting could be heard in the distance and Daire knew instantly where he needed to go.

'Always the glade,' he thought, wondering whether it was because of what had happened to him there, or whether he had been drawn there in the first place by some unseen force.

With a sudden burst of speed, the forest blurred past him as he traversed the trees like a shadowy wisp of blackness.

A shiver ran up his spine on hearing yelps of terror, knowing that those that issued them normally felt none.

'Anticipation of the fight is worse than the fight itself,' he told himself, trying desperately to calm his growing fear. His instinct told him that this was something different from what he had faced before, even the demon in him seemed more nervous than ever it had been.

Clearing the trees, he saw what was waiting for him and slowed his pace instinctively as his body reacted to the sight of the demon.

'Bloody hell!' he gasped, seeing the creature like death incarnate.

Only one name identified it and he knew upon first glance that it was stronger than he was.

Looking apprehensively at the still forms of the wolves around it, Daire held his breath as it turned its hooded head his way.

'Reaper,' the name screamed in his mind, identifying the thing from the knowledge of Spirit.

Looking at the dead wolves that were previously renowned for their resilience, he knew that this abominable creature could be none other.

The mass of wolves backed away, snarling their hatred at the one who had killed them so easily and looked now for the legend to make the next move.

The Reaper turned as he approached and appeared to glide towards him with a deathly grace.

Though demonic himself, Daire could feel that this creature was on a completely different level, and apart from its name, he had little else to go on.

Reaching for the power of Spirit, he sent it arcing into its deeply-cowled hood but with blinding speed, the reaper rolled under the attack and came forward more swiftly, its long-fingered hands extending towards him.

With tremendous force it clashed with his shield, turning it white in an instant. Reacting to the contact, the whitened sphere turned hostile and struck out at the thing from all across its surface.

An element came unbidden to his aid, hurling its great might against it. Fire engulfed the Reaper, becoming thick like lava, but the demon had defences of its own and the fire was cast back.

With relative ease it drove its hand through his defence, causing a crack to form as it clutched at him through the puncture.

White light lanced into its limb and up through the forearm into its torso, causing the demon to thrash wildly as it tried to retreat.

Holding it firm by the wrist, Daire sent the white magick further into its body, causing it to wrench its arm back repeatedly.

In defence, its free arm drove forward, smashing the shield into what looked like thousands of butterflies taking flight, only for them to fade almost instantly into the gathering darkness.

Standing a foot taller than Daire, the Reaper moved in too swift to see and was upon him in an instant.

Looking up into the deeply-hooded cowl, Daire's blood ran cold as the demon's stare held him.

'No!' his mind raged, fighting against the mind-numbing hold, and with a great mental effort, he steeled his mind against it.

He struck out, aiming a vicious punch into the darkness, but the fist was caught in a crushing grip before being twisted savagely to the side.

Crying out in agony, Daire jumped forward to roll out of the lock before his arm broke and received a slash across his midriff in the attempt.

From nowhere, a blast of energy struck at the demon, followed by a cacophony of explosions that erupted about its head, dazing it and causing it to release its prey.

With sweat glistening on her skin, Kim was breathless from her run and drew up short at the legend's side.

With her chest heaving from the exertion, she flashed him a look of annoyance for being left so far behind.

Disoriented for a moment, he struggled to one knee and raised his hand to lift the approaching Reaper into the air.

It hung there for a moment, suspended in mid-air before slowly slipping back to the earth.

In desperation, he repeated the move, sending his white light into it at the same time, just as an arc of lightning forked down from the sky, highlighting the demon in its raw energy and earthing itself through the creature to the ground.

'About bloody time!' he growled as his huge rock smashed against its back, sending the demon crashing to the ground.

Amazingly, it shrugged off the attack and was back on its feet almost instantly, appearing uninjured by the ordeal.

'I can't beat this thing,' he whispered, the truth of what that meant exploding in his mind.

As silently as before, the Reaper came for him, but a sudden wind struck it with force, slowing the creature for a moment only.

As before, the Reaper seemed to slip past the attack and came on again, as though passing through the element itself.

Drawing on the earth's inexhaustible energy, Daire sent its might directly at the demon, pouring all of his own magick into the attack as he did so. The light from Spirit and the darkness of the demon both struck the loathsome creature, driven now by the will of the man, in one blinding assault.

The blast hit the creature and stopped it, causing it to take but a single, agonising step back.

Appearing from the trees, Jack hurled his blue lightning at the creature, hitting it with a sickening force and driving it back further.

The God-King's Fall

Following suit, Kim sent her magick into the mix and for the third time, the Reaper stepped back.

Under the thrice-willed attack, the demon was grudgingly forced backwards until it twisted past the attacking trio and stepped forward yet again.

As with all things brought against it, the demon began to slip between the attacks, and moving slowly but surely, it came at him again.

'Can nothing defeat this thing?' Daire quailed and looked back at the goddess in desperation.

'Only physical force can kill it,' Olivia screamed, her eyes wild with indecision, wanting desperately to help but afraid of the consequences.

'But it's too strong!' he cried, panic in his voice.

Glancing back, he saw the demon descend upon him again, seeing its black robes billowing out like the wings of a bat.

In pure desperation and panicked need, Daire was forced to do something that he had sworn to himself never to do again.

Raising his outstretched hand, he summoned the legendary red sword of power, the blade seeming to thrust out from his palm.

The Reaper slowed at the sight, hesitant as to the power of the weapon and the damage that the Blood Sword could wreak upon it.

With sword in hand, the conflicting natures within him harmonised for the first time, his internal struggle cast aside as it focused his need and his will into one clear goal, the death of the Reaper!

Having delayed enough, the towering creature sprang forward to end the conflict once and for all but the blood-red blade sliced across its midriff, causing the demon to screech like nothing else on Earth, a cry of pain that echoed deafeningly in the large open area.

Sharing a look of hope, Jack and Kim looked on as the two demonic creatures came together again.

Lightning fast, the Reaper took the offensive, swooping back and forth like a wraith as it sought a way past the legend's defences.

Jack saw in his mind the battle of the brothers, seeing again the duel between the two godlike warriors as they danced across the sandy arena floor. Holding his breath, he saw that one of them had lost none of his skill in the passing ages and watched as though mesmerised by the blurring blade, seeing it sweep out defensively, like a lion tamer's whip.

With a sudden idea widening his eyes, Jack raised his arms into the air and sent small lights, no bigger than his hand, out into the night. Shooting forth, they began circling above the scene below as though to bear witness to the gigantic struggle. Now and then they would flare abruptly like floodlights at a football game, glaring at the cowled figure and dazzling it.

The demon flinched away mid-attack, the blinding lights clearly having an effect on it and forcing it to lower its head against the glare.

Seeing this, Kim summoned up the power of the land again and sent it up into the night sky, the light like that of the sun itself.

Shining down upon the glade, it chased all but the darkest shadows away, two of which now fought to the death below.

Jack gasped in shock at the blackened plant life, seeing it spread out like a sea of darkness from the ugly looking scar that hung in the air.

'Gilga's balls!' he whispered, nudging the mage at his side.

Kim scowled at him and turned back to the fight, unwilling to be distracted by the old man's antics.

As the fight wore on, the wolves sat lower in the grass and began twitching and jerking in anticipation, readying themselves to launch when the time was right.

Under the mage's sun, both demons looked to be cut from the same cloth, appearing black and dead in the world of the living. There was not much between the two in appearance, each looking equally demonic in their own way but the goddess knew what separated the two.

'Free will,' she thought, a whisper of a smile touching her lips.

He chose to be different, choosing to love his children and her as well, and her heart swelled in the knowing of it.

'My Daire,' she whispered, watching him move with his deadly grace.

The Reaper attacked again, its terrifying speed beyond what this world could measure, only to fall back in pain, its clutching hand split open from the contact of the deadly crimson blade.

Black blood oozed down the length of the legendary weapon after splitting the demon's hand almost in two, sliding between the index and middle fingers to the wrist.

Seeing her chance, Kim sent the light of her magickal sun at the Reaper, focusing it into a laser of intense heat. It struck the creature squarely, causing it to falter momentarily but as it had done before, it recovered again and somehow allowed the light to pass by it.

Taking advantage of the distraction, Daire took the offensive in a haze of red fury as the two clashed again. The assault seemed never-ending and the Reaper was driven back, having only the time to defend itself against the incredible attack.

Amid the torrent of colour, the screeching began again and Kim felt goosebumps rise upon her flesh. Excitement built in her and she tensed reflexively at the approaching conclusion.

The Reaper's scream grew louder before cutting off suddenly as the black form began to crumple to the ground with the Blood Sword protruding from its hood where the demon's eyes should be.

Standing alone with his hand still on the hilt, the legend stood panting, taking in huge lungfuls of air as he laboured in his breathing.

'Yes!' screamed Kim, throwing her fists into the air, laughing in relief at seeing the impossible.

Her laughter stopped abruptly when the sword was removed to smash down again and again upon the motionless form.

Jack looked at Olivia questioningly but she only had eyes for the victor in that moment.

'I think you've killed it, Daire,' he called before realising that the darkness had taken hold of him.

Placing a hand on the powerful black shoulder, Olivia calmed him, the sword stopping mid-stroke as though frozen in the motion.

Shaking her head, Kim stepped back in alarm and gasped at her sudden appearance.

'How did she get there so fast?' she cried, seeing her simply materialise beside the legend in the blink of an eye.

The wizard smiled tensely and mouthed his answer.

'Goddess,' he mimed, causing her eyes to widen.

'Which one?' she mouthed back, spreading her arms for the answer.

'Fae,' he replied, looking back at the goddess.

Jack's face paled, seeing both Olivia and his friend staring back at him silently.

'Awks,' Kim whispered before her eyes widened again in terror.

Dropping to his knees, black blood bubbling from his mouth, Daire pitched forward and looked unable to support himself any longer.

Catching him as he fell, Olivia laid him back gently to the ground, moaning in dread at the state of him.

'I can't...' he gurgled, coughing and spraying blood onto her chest.

Realising that his friend could no longer connect with the earth's magick, Jack drove his awareness down but reeled back clutching at his head.

Power like none other he had ever encountered filled his mind as the golden light of the goddess beat him to the punch. The ground thrummed with the energy she had called and the blackened earth began to revitalise immediately, turning a healthier shade in the sunlit night.

'You must reach for it, Daire,' Olivia screamed, cupping his face in her hands. 'I can't influence you, the daemon in you is too strong!' she cried, looking to the others for support.

Kim closed her eyes at her words, her fears of what he was now borne into reality.

Jack knelt beside him, taking hold of his hand and stifled the urge to shrink away from the unholy contact.

'Turn from the darkness and come back to the light!' he growled, seeing his hand like that of a child's within the black monstrosity. 'No!' he cried, seeing his oldest friend begin to convulse as his body was failing at its fight for life.

The fit passed and the black depthless body began to relax, sighing out its breath to the heartfelt scream of the goddess.

***

Kristina sat in darkness, perched on the chaise before her bedroom window. She stared out across the treetops of the forest with a sickly feeling in her stomach.

Refusing to be anywhere else but by her side, the children nestled into her at either side, waiting anxiously for their father's return.

They had heard the howling and the distant flash of magick and knew for sure that the fighting had begun.

She had expected the situation to be dealt with swiftly, picturing those who had gone to investigate, but the fight wore on and she felt the cold touch of dread creeping back into her.

'Whatever is out there will be dealt with, I'm sure, for how else could it go?' she thought, picturing the goddess in her mind.

Hearing the mages discussing what they thought was happening, she closed her eyes, wondering what new threat this creature posed and whether it was alone or the first of many.

The howling seemed not to bother them, causing her to relax a little, wondering at what could make such a dreadful noise.

'Not wolves, surely?' she thought, shivering at the memory of it.

She tilted her head a little at hearing Charlie's deep tones, though muffled now by the thickness of the walls.

'At least now we know where the wolves went,' he observed dryly, causing her eyes to widen in surprise.

'They are on our side?' she thought excitedly, desperately wanting to know the full story but then came the screech from something else entirely and she swallowed hard as her fear returned.

Wanting to hear the sounds of battle more clearly, she opened the window a crack in the hope of hearing a little better but on sitting back down, the window abruptly shut, causing all three of them to start in alarm.

'Okay,' she said softly, gesturing for calm. 'We shall keep the window closed,' she soothed, rolling her eyes up at the house.

Suddenly Lucian's head shot back, his body arching as though in pain.

Panicked, Kristina leant over him and fluttered her hands over his face nervously.

'Lucian! What is it?' she screamed, seeing his eyes roll back in their sockets.

'*From one dark shadow, there comes he. Where the Reaper stands, now fights three,*' Lucian intoned, his voice distorting with some unknown power that sounded too deep for a child of his stature to make.

'*The Reaper comes at the birth of midnight. Oaks last blood will unleash his first sight,*' the boy's voice echoed with the power of prophecy as John appeared in the doorway, frantically scribbling down the words.

'*Fight if you will, with light to see. Magick will not avail thee, only the blood of the tree. Wolves come and wolves cry. Watch and witness, lest you die.*'

At that very moment, a low howl echoed eerily as if in answer to the words, and the druid looked up from his work with blood draining from his face.

Francesca began rocking back and forth with eyes that stared vacantly ahead before they widened suddenly as her brother's words sounded again.

'*Men run scared, seeing their plight. Daemons clash, too quick for sight.*'

'*Goddess bears witness, her heart on her sleeve. Her love is lost, too painful to believe.*'

'*The needs of the many outweigh those of the few. Touch not with your essence or payment will be due.*'

'*The hoard is near, with hearts of hate. Hold to your promise to seal the gate.*'

'*After the worlds clash, the worst will come. All her great work will be undone.*'

The words were flowing now and John was struggling to keep up as he wrote the words down as quickly as he could.

Kristina, at her wit's end, screamed and shook her son fearfully, trying to wake him from the never-ending intonation.

Lucian stopped abruptly, breathing in deeply as his eyes blinked and refocused again as though waking from a deep sleep.

'You stupid woman!' John spat, waving his notepad furiously in her direction. 'Do you know how rare true prophecy is?' he shouted, his face flushing in his anger.

The screeching from the forest stopped her wrathful response and her mouth was held open as it sounded again.

In silence, they all looked out of the window and it was some time before the same screeching was heard again.

Francesca whimpered and Lucian buried his head into his mother's side, crying pitifully.

'Daddy's fighting it!' he cried, his voice muffled by her thick flannel dressing gown.

'You can see them?' she asked, looking down at him worriedly as she felt his nod of response.

'What can you see?' Francesca demanded, pulling on his shoulder until he whined and shrugged her off. 'Tell me!' she cried, pulling at him again in an attempt to make him speak.

'Daddy's hurt but now he has a big red sword,' he screamed, shaking violently at the images he saw.

A bright light suddenly shone through the window, lighting up the entire room with what looked like daylight. Squinting through the glare, Kristina heard the mages again.

'Mage fire!' Kevyn exclaimed, excitement clear in his tone. 'We should go,' he stressed, but Charlie's authoritative tone cut him off with a note of finality.

'We stay to safeguard the children,' he replied, causing the other to grumble uncomprehendingly.

Without warning, Lucian jumped up and began flailing about, swinging his invisible sword before him.

'Take that!' he cried, attacking the invisible enemy with a skill that surprised his mother.

Kristina held a finger up to silence her daughter before she could interrupt the vision, feeling happier now that he seemed not to be in pain.

As he struck with his imaginary weapon, she heard the screeching again and it was clear to her that what he saw was in real-time.

Louder and louder the demon's cry came before it was cut off abruptly and there was silence again.

Lucian stood panting, smiling up in victory.

'Daddy's killed it!' he announced, laughing and jumping around with joy. 'Oh, wait a minute!' he said, hacking again at the invisible monster, over and over again.

'Is it dead?' Kristina shrilled, causing him to stop and look at her stupidly before shaking his head with a scowl.

'Yes, Mammy! I told you already! Daddy's just chopping it up,' he replied, smiling at her manically.

A cold shiver ran up her spine as a dreadful thought entered her mind.

'Do you see it from Daddy's eyes or from somewhere else?' she asked, catching the druid's eye with concern.

Lucian looked at her with his father's frown upon his face.

'I saw it from all around, Mammy. From everywhere!' he replied excitedly, throwing her arms out wide.

Closing her eyes, she sighed in relief, not knowing why this was better, but somehow it was.

'Anything is better than that,' she thought finally, fearing what his father had done to him.

Lucian's face slowly creased in pain, bearing witness to that which no child should and a scream tore from him, chilling his mother to her bones. He threw his bead back with a howl of heartbreak, causing Kristina to grip the bedpost for support as she heard the same howl of despair coming from the forest.

**

All was quiet in the glade, the suddenness of what had come to pass shocking them into silence.

Daire lay still and the goddess, for all her might, could do nothing to change it.

She was unable to penetrate his demonic flesh. She had known this to be the case from that moment by the river in her own world but still, she could not accept that she could do nothing at all.

'Live! Live for them,' she screamed suddenly, shocking those that sat beside her. 'Please!' she cried, grief wracking her slender frame, but he was dead and could no longer hear her plea.

At last, she sat back on her haunches before kneeling in the renewed lush green grass. She stared at him, waiting for him to move.

His eyes looked up at her, unseeing in death and looking as black now as the rest of him.

A low mournful howl was taken up, the cries from those that mourned him.

Kim turned at the sound and felt chilled by the sight of hundreds of wolves padding towards them, baring their teeth in silent snarls.

As one, they took up the pitiful song again, crying at their loss of the one they had loved.

Jack leant forward to look down at his friend, unable to believe what he was seeing.

'Daire?' he called softly, staring down as the demon began to fade.

He gasped then at the damage that had been wrought upon his body, hidden until now by the demonic darkness.

'Oh, Daire,' he sobbed. Seeing the ripped flesh of his friend's body he began to weep, thinking of his children.

Dark red blood almost completely covered his legendary friend, splattering up his neck to the chin, like some grotesque crimson body paint.

The ground on which he lay was slick and puddled with the legend's lifeblood and they all knew that this was the cost of what it was to do battle with the Reaper.

'Go! Leave this place,' the goddess commanded suddenly, barely able to contain her grief as she stared towards the dimensional tear. 'I will safeguard this place, for them,' she continued and Jack knew that she meant the fallen man's children.

Her lip began trembling suddenly and then she moaned at seeing the scar begin to fade.

'It's over,' she sobbed, seeing it finally disappear.

She let the tears fall as her face creased in the pain of her heartache. Throwing her head back suddenly, she screamed out her anguish, joining in with the chorus of the wolves.

Her cry was guttural, sounding demonic itself as her feeling of loss threatened to undo her. Looking around wildly, she searched for something to vent at and began snarling madly at the only two in her vicinity.

Backing away from her in dread, both wizard and mage could feel the wildness in her and felt that in her grief, she was more a danger to them than even the Reaper had been.

The sky started to lighten in the east but not one of the house's inhabitants took notice of it, lost as they were within their own thoughts.

Sitting on the sofa, Kristina's head began to nod from exhaustion, fighting the weariness after finally settling the children.

The same tiredness had finally beaten the children, seeing them drift off to sleep as they cried in her arms.

A sudden sense of movement brought her awake with a start, causing her heart to pound as she saw the mages move silently out into the garden.

Getting up, she moved as silently as she could and awoke the druid in the process, who had nodded off while studying the prophecies he had written down.

Moving to the kitchen window, Kristina stared out and saw Jack standing stony-faced, staring at the bleak-looking mages. She knew by the look on his face that her son had seen true and closed her eyes with a whimper of loss.

'He's gone!' she thought, finally feeling the impact of what that truly meant.

After her son had howled himself hoarse, he had cried inconsolably, refusing to answer any of her questions. It had been her daughter that had said the dreaded words, breaking Kristina's heart in the process.

'Daddy's dead,' she had announced in a heartfelt whisper, her eyes staring ahead but looking at nothing.

Jack turned at her approach and she saw the pain in his greying eyes.

'I know,' she whispered, her hand going to her mouth.

Unable to speak, he walked forward and took her in his arms, choking on the words that he had prepared for her. Weeping into her shoulder, he was unable to contain his emotion and secretly hated himself for it.

Charlie conferred with the mages in a series of hushed tones, Kim relaying much of what had happened as they moved off to the side.

Chloe appeared in the doorway with her hair an unruly mass of tangles after being left to sleep inside.

'Dark is dead,' John announced coldly, but then smiled apologetically for the bluntness of his tone. 'He was killed fighting a demon,' he continued, forcing a milder tone as he lifted his hand to reach for her.

Ecstatic by the news, the witch tried hard to conceal her elation by pretending to be slighted in her tone.

'Do you think he knew?' she asked unconcerned, ignoring his hand completely. 'What I mean is, do you think he knew that he was going to die?' she corrected herself offhandedly, a look of defiance entering her eyes. 'He must have thought so, why else make us swear our oaths,' she continued, smiling coldly up at him.

He scowled at her and curled his lip into a snarl, but more from her coldness towards him than the way she spoke.

'Does it matter? We've given them!' he hissed, keeping his voice low.

'Indeed,' she sneered scornfully, turning abruptly and walking into the house. 'Some things are more important than a broken promise,' she whispered, shoving the door closed behind her.

***

The sun peeked up over the rim of the mountain, lighting the treetops at the far side of the glade and looking like a blanket of gold that slowly made its way towards her.

The goddess was motionless, still kneeling with her hand placed tenderly within his. She was unable to take her eyes off him, feeling that to do so would be to admit to herself that he was finally gone. She silently wished to join him but knew that was a luxury forbidden to her, for those of her kind could not be taken from the light for long.

Vaguely aware of the diminishing line of shadow, she sat quietly as the light continued towards her. It came to her, this golden line of brilliance, bearing down upon her, on them! The heat that eventually touched her skin gave her little solace to the pain inside and she felt hate inside her for the thing that had killed him. Hate for those that angered him and hate for the fact that she would never again feel his arms around her. It was rising from within and she smiled in welcome, hearing again the prophetic words of the dragon.

'You will lose yourself,' Ddraig had said, warning her not to get involved, and he had been right, she thought, succumbing at last to her emotions.

She felt wrath for losing him, her one and only love, after only just finding him and she screamed her anguish at the world, unleashing her pain as the land about her shook in her agony.

'Heal him!' an urgent voice whispered, rising on the breeze and stopping her dead. 'Heal him!' it insisted, sounding more urgent this time.

Without hesitation, she drew up the magick of the land but cut the link as another thought struck her.

'If there is the slightest chance of bringing him back, he will never die again,' she thought, placing one hand over his heart and the other on his brow before sending her own essence into him.

She felt him now, could see into him as she had all through the ages and sobbed at finding no energy of his own.

The large gashes across his body closed almost instantly, but she pushed her power further, binding it to the very essence of what he had been, remoulding him and changing what he had been yet again. She merged her might with his in a desperate need to raise him, adding yet another aspect to his already overcrowded persona.

'He will not fall prey to death again!' she promised, changing the white of him to gold, and knowing that the demon in him had been the most dominant, she gave to him the one thing that would overshadow it.

In the spectral realm, his aura burst forth, brighter now than even the sun appeared in its brilliance.

Sitting back, she waited, knowing that what she had done was not what was intended.

'Are there no bounds to what you would do for him?' the deep voice boomed, anger now evident in its tone.

'None!' she snapped, stroking the brown hair from her dead love's eyes affectionately.

A shadow fell across her, causing her to look up at the wide set of antlers adorning the Horned God's head. Tall and masculine, he stood before her and shook his head in disapproval.

'The mother will not be pleased with this,' he grumbled, gesturing towards the body with exasperation. 'You have interfered with this world for the last time,' he said softly, though in a tone of total authority.

Her eyes snapped up to meet the golden-brown gaze of the god and blazed fiercely.

'I "interfere" because you do not act!' she snapped, looking down again, immediately regretting her reaction. 'Forgive me,' she whispered, giving the god his due.

The antlered-head nodded, the golden eyes looking sad as he replied.

'We understood your first transgressions against this world, though we did not condone them,' he replied, seating himself gracefully beside her. 'This was a world of subtle magick, easily controlled and even easier to contain. You, unwittingly though it was, introduced direct magick to those that would learn it, and learn it they did,' he admonished her, in a deep but calming tone of voice.

'I know,' she whispered, looking at him sadly. 'What am I to do? I cannot be without him,' she sobbed, staring searchingly into his eyes.

The Horned God was handsome, strong and depending on his form, very temperamental.

The Queen of Air was silently thankful to be speaking to the sage at this time and not the more reactive of his identities.

'As a father myself, I understand his need to protect them, especially after his loss those ages ago,' he said, smiling suddenly at the still form. 'You have been corrupted by him,' he pointed out, his great antlered head shaking back and forth as though bothered by something.

'Is love a corruption?' she countered, controlling her instinct to snap at him again.

'I speak not of love but of infatuation. You have sought this one for longer than is natural and the fact that it has turned into love is immaterial at this time,' he said, shaking his head again in annoyance as though to a bothersome fly.

Reaching up, Olivia pulled a strip of velvet skin away from the bottom of one antler, causing him to sigh in appreciation.

'Your nature is a good one,' he breathed with a knowing twinkle in his eyes. 'Your instinct was to help, as it is in all things!' he continued, giving her a cynical glance.

'If only we could always be so kind,' he said sadly, before closing his eyes.

Looking back to the body, she sobbed unexpectedly, her melancholy taking hold of her again.

'Since first seeing him, you have lived in the "now" and so he corrupts you. We belong outside of time and for you to live like them, makes you too dangerous,' he lectured, spreading his muscled arms wide.

She knew this, had known it from the very beginning.

'He is here… was here,' she corrected, her tears welling once again. 'I cannot help but be where he is, no matter my frame of mind,' she continued, shrugging unconsciously before closing her eyes at the memory it invoked. 'Why did you have me heal his body?' she sobbed, wiping away the tears with her hand.

'Heal!' he snapped, a rising note of frustration in his voice. 'You have gone beyond what I asked of you! Something that even *I* will have to answer for,' he said, arching an eyebrow at her in displeasure.

'In answer to your question, I did not wish for him to die here today. I only desired the daemon part of him to do so, so that the rift would be closed,' he answered, shaking his head a little. 'He would have risen half the daemon he was and therefore, not the beacon he had been to the underworld. I did not want him to die,' he answered, confirming to her that it was indeed Daire that had been the daemons draw. 'Though that is what the mother had planned for him. I fear that I have set many unplanned things in motion, by allowing you to change him thus,' he continued, speaking with a note of regret.

'He will live?' she asked, her eyes widening in hope as she glanced down at the motionless body.

'He lives now, Queen of Air!' he boomed, angered by her lack of insight.

She placed her hand to Daire's chest, a frown of doubt setting on her features.

The god looked at her patiently but said nothing as he waited for her to see the truth for herself.

Realising her foolishness, she closed her eyes and nodded her understanding.

'Time,' she answered, shaking her head in annoyance.

'You have fallen far, Liv,' he scolded her and then laughed aloud at her expression of shock. '*Unagi*,' he intoned, touching his temple with his fingers and letting his laughter peel out. 'I have watched him well I think,' he continued, sobering a little. 'When he awakes you must tell him to come to me,' the god ordered, authority back in his voice. 'Say only that I have a gift for him,' he added, looking sternly at her. 'In for a penny and now in for a pound,' he said, shrugging nonchalantly as he rose to his feet. 'There will be a price to pay before this is played out and I fear that you may not like how steep that payment is,' he warned, pointing down to the ground.

'Look!' he thundered, wild and ferocious in the morning light. 'Your god awakes!'

Looking down, Olivia held her breath, seeing the great love of her existence take in a deep breath of life and let it out again more slowly.

Sitting up, he looked around him dazedly before settling his gaze on her.

'I see you,' he whispered, seeing her now inside and out.

Smiling through her tears, she understood what he meant.

'I see you,' she whispered back, seeing past the darkness that had protected him and into his spirit for the very first time.

'Did I die?' he asked, shrugging with his face and causing her to laugh her joy into the world.

She grabbed his face spontaneously and kissed it repeatedly, smothering him in her love.

'I'll take that as a yes,' he laughed as soon as she had finished, only for her to kiss him again and hug him in her crushing embrace.

Olivia beamed at him, unable to say anything for the moment.

'I feel different,' he mused, frowning down at himself suspiciously. 'What have you gone and done, Liv?' he asked, frowning at her judgementally. 'I don't feel so... dark anymore,' he observed, feeling lighter of spirit than he had before.

'Look inward, you dolt,' she replied, interlacing her fingers with his and kissing him again.

Chuckling at her words, he closed his eyes and, after a moment, opened them again to stare at her in shock.

'Was it not you who was angered by me taking in the dragon's essence?' he chided, looking at her with a shake of his head. 'Little good it did me,' he continued, wondering at what the point of Ddraig's gift had been.

'We are truly one now, my Daire, for you have my essence in you. I have smothered all else with my divine grace,' she continued in her queenly tone, causing him to smile lopsidedly.

'I do believe that you are correct,' he replied in the same lofty tone and then cried out when she thumped him on the arm.

'I'm wounded,' he complained, rubbing his arm tenderly and marvelling at her precision in finding his soft spots.

'Poppycock!' she replied, rolling her eyes at his overreaction. 'I more than healed you,' she added, shaking her head in amusement.

Daire looked down involuntarily, peering at his chest and stomach in concern but found nothing of the wounds he knew he had sustained.

'So, I guess we'll find out what I am somewhere down the line?' he asked, pulling his annoying face again.

'I already know what you are,' she replied, punching him again.

Flexing his arms and stretching his body, he analysed himself more closely.

'The darkness is still in me,' he said soberly, looking into her hazel eyes with a look of depression.

'I know,' she whispered, all humour falling from her face. 'But it's not what it was,' she said softly, nodding for him to believe her. 'Where the daemon in you took precedence over your other aspects, now the godliness overshadows them all.'

Closing his eyes, he let the essence of humanity slip from him and found himself staring again at the same black depthless hands of before but now lacking the demonic visage.

'Well this is new!' he announced, looking at her again in confusion.

With a wistful smile on her face, the Queen of Air appeared before him, looking as she had when they had first met.

'See?' she replied, slipping her black arm through his. 'We are the same now,' she smiled, walking him towards the trees that came alive at their approach.

As they neared, the trees began to shake as they shed their leaves to land at their feet. Stopping before the blanket of leaves, she turned to him with a smile on her face.

'This is for you,' she said, untangling herself from him and gesturing him forward. 'They wish to pay homage to you,' she continued, stepping back to follow from behind but he held out his hand and pulled her to him.

'We are one now,' he said, kissing her on the nose. 'And we will walk as such,' he whispered, taking her by the hand and leading her into the falling leaves, cast down now in honour of him.

Chapter Nine

The mood in the house was tense with those inside separating into the groups of their choosing now that the power had seemingly shifted.

The fall of the legend had left them on a precipice, none of them knowing for sure quite how to continue. The high priestess clearly believed herself to be in a high-ranking position, especially with John at her side, but the mages were a law unto themselves and the aggressive glances from Kim gave her cause for concern.

The mages had remained outside, talking privately in what seemed like a heated debate, while Chloe and John were whispering likewise at the far end of the room.

The high priestess glanced repeatedly over her shoulder at Kristina, who sat on the sofa staring off into space.

Jack sat silently beside her, lost within his grief.

Startled from her misery, Kristina saw the priestess stamp her foot in anger and shrug off a restraining hand from the druid before marching over towards her.

Sitting down rather catlike upon the opposite sofa, she stared at her intently before she finally spoke.

'We need to talk,' she began, crossing her legs in an attempt to look relaxed.

'Do we?' Kristina replied, looking at her dispassionately.

'Though your circle was destroyed, you are still a witch by oath and held by the pact that you made,' Chloe said carefully, her cold blue eyes flashing with authority. 'As are the children!' she added, causing Kristina's face to flush.

'You gave your word,' she retorted, shaking her head in angered disgust. 'You swore to the goddess herself!' she continued, her wrath igniting from her heightened emotional state.

Chloe leaned further forward, nearly leaving the sofa completely, and spoke her reply through her teeth.

'Don't talk to me of the goddess! I know her will better than you!' she hissed, her face shaking in sudden fury.

Awakening from his wallowing, Jack turned his head to look at the witch with a dispassionate glare.

'What are you doing, Chloe?' he asked, his eyes wide with accusation. 'What are you doing?' he growled again, seeing her scornful expression turn on him and hating her for it.

'This is faction business, old man, and as such, none of your concern. As the priestess of my order, it is my right to retain assets that are due to me,' she sneered, glaring back as though daring him to continue.

'Where has the shivering, pathetic little girl gone?' he asked as the blood drained from his face. 'Where is the victim?' he taunted, incensed by her words.

She smiled at him but it did not reach her eyes.

'It's called biding one's time,' she replied sweetly but her face flushed hotly with embarrassment. 'I hold all witches to their covens be they damaged or not,' she continued, glaring back at Kristina with venom.

'The coven was destroyed and the circle is broken!' Kristina stormed, her voice rising in anger.

'Not so!' Chloe snapped, a triumphant look shining in her eyes. 'Your priestess lives!' Chloe said slyly, leaning forward as though to accentuate her words. 'Jacky lives. And though you have been removed from the coven, I hold you to your oath. One does not simply leave the witches' faction,' she continued warningly, the knuckles of her hands going white as she gripped the sofa tightly.

'I will kill you right here and now if you continue down this path,' Jack growled, his summoned magick dancing in his eyes.

'You may try, wizard,' she replied confidently, and smiled wickedly as he began to rise. 'I have connected to all my remaining covens and have all their might at my command. Try me!' she dared, rising to her feet to meet him. 'Do it!' she hissed, wiggling her fingers as her magick crackled between them.

Jack raised his hand and snapped his fingers loudly, unleashing his power in an instant flash of blue light.

The priestess fell, crippled in pain and writhing on the floor in agony.

'You mistake me for some common practitioner of the arcane, my lady,' he growled, towering over her majestically, the power in his voice echoing throughout the lower levels of the house. 'I am, however, somewhat more!' he confessed, shaking his head at her in disappointment.

A hint of laughter came whispering through the walls, causing Kristina to look around for the source before realising it was the house itself that showed its mirth. She had wondered why it had not acted before now, thinking that maybe the priestess had enchanted it somehow.

'Oh my god!' she gasped, realising at long last that it was *his* house and that it knew how powerful Jack was.

The house had simply stayed quiet, waiting for the conflict to unfold, waiting for the inevitable conclusion.

'Such intelligence,' she thought, having assumed the house was more single-minded. 'At least that's what *he* had led me to believe!' she thought darkly, wondering what else he had hidden from her.

Looking back to the wizard, she saw his image phase suddenly from the old man that she had grown to love, to that of a dark-haired man of middling years and guessed that this was his true form.

'I am the Blue Wizard!' he announced, glaring down with disdain etched into his features. 'And you have incurred my wrath, woman!' he fumed, twisting her in pain with a flick of his wrist.

Chloe screamed, attracting the attention of the mages and that of her druid, who instinctively raised his hands in her defence.

At a glance from the Blue Wizard, the druid found himself impotent, the energy leaving his hands and his power forbidden.

Michael stepped forward and pulled the druid back, throwing him heavily onto the sofa with a growl of impatience.

'Enough,' Charlie growled, glowering at John and then looking the wizard in the eye.

'What are your intentions?' David demanded, having cast the image of Jack aside as he held the mage's glare with his own.

'Release her,' Charlie replied, glancing at the witch and ignoring the ancient's question.

'You have not my age nor my power to order me, boy. Now answer the damned question!' David demanded, clearly in no mood for negotiation.

'My word is my bond, as it is with all mages,' Charlie replied, folding his arms peacefully before him. 'I am not the enemy of the Blue Wizard, nor have I ever been,' he added, bowing his head and acknowledging the mythical man with respect.

David relaxed slowly, his anger abating as he took in a deep calming breath.

'She *is* my enemy,' he replied, glaring down in disgust and then giving a look of warning to the druid. 'Raise your hands to me again, druid, and I will remove them from you,' he promised, shifting his appearance back into the old man.

'I don't doubt it,' Charlie said agreeably, taking a seat next to John and patting his knee warningly.

The hulking figure of Michael stood behind them, crossing his arms over his huge chest like some intimidating henchman.

Jack caught his eye as the big man nodded once, letting him know his mind, as did Kim and Kevyn both.

Breathing in deeply, Jack let his anger slide and seated himself back down beside Kristina.

'Blue Wizard?' she asked, staring as though he had two heads.

She had read of 'The Blue Wizard' of course, knowing him to be an ancient like Daire, born from the ruins of that old world, and though not as notorious as the Dark Wolf or his violent family, he was nevertheless respected and feared when the situation was called for. Named thus for the blue robes he wore, the ancient man was more known for his kindness than his butchery. She had come across him often, but only in the oldest of books and always it was the same. They spoke of him as a benign force that would appear to save the lost or to hide the innocent, protecting them from the wicked in those cruel times. Some people actually still prayed to him, calling upon the Blue Wizard to deliver them from whatever trouble they were in.

Not known for his destructive abilities, all in the room now knew that the power this ancient wielded was nothing short of godlike.

He had taken down the high priestess with a snap of his fingers when she was prepared and linked to her covens, and the druid had fared no better, she thought, looking at him with a shake of her head.

'Blue,' she mused, remembering the greeting that Cristian had used on first recognising him. 'What is it with you ancients and your three faces?' she asked, genuinely interested by the meaning behind it.

'Did Daire have another name besides the Dark Wolf?' Kevyn asked and immediately regretted it, flushing red as he looked at her in apology.

'I am so sorry,' he apologised, lowering his eyes to the floor.

Charlie glared up at him and shook his head at the thoughtless comment.

'Tactless fool,' he berated his mage and then looked at her apologetically.

'What a dick,' Michael whispered, looking at his friend from the corner of his eye and then up at the ceiling with a roll of his eyes.

Kristina waved off the comment and forced a smile.

'It's fine,' she whispered, her eyes watering more from the expressions of sympathy than her own feeling of loss.

'Would you mind releasing them please?' Charlie asked, looking at Jack and then pointedly towards Chloe, who was clearly still in pain upon the floor.

'And if she's foolish enough to attack?' Jack asked, arching an eyebrow at him questioningly.

'Then I will kill her myself,' the mage answered, bringing a slow smile to Kim's face.

'Fine!' the wizard replied and, with a huff of displeasure, he dispelled his bindings upon them.

John let out a huge breath of air, clearly held in by the magick also.

'What if I attack you?' he stormed, embarrassed at the ease in which he was put down.

'Then *I* will kill you!' Michael roared from behind him, clamping his hands down menacingly on his shoulders.

Kristina rose to her feet, claiming the chance to speak.

'I am no longer a witch and neither are my children,' she announced, putting her hands on her hips. 'I may not be born into magick like the rest of you but I will not be used or bullied for my shortcomings,' she continued, looking down at the recovering priestess. 'My children will be free as he wanted them to be. Now that the threat from the Bloods is over, so too is the law of choosing,' she announced, sitting back down rather awkwardly.

Silence greeted her words until Jack politely patted her knee and smiled at her supportively.

'Well said,' he whispered, winking at her warmly. 'Though I think we're all old enough to know that it won't end here,' he said, glancing down again with distaste. 'If she lied after swearing to the goddess, then she will lie again now. I see no way past this but the obvious,' he growled with a darkening look of determination steeling his face.

John began to speak but Michael slapped him on the shoulders again, his powerful hands silencing him abruptly.

'Time to think with your big head my friend, the little one will be your undoing,' he warned, causing Kevyn to smirk in response.

John calmed himself, breathing out slowly before opening his mouth again, but then paused, silenced this time by the high-pitched howls from outside.

The howling continued incessantly, echoing louder by the second as those that made them grew nearer. Heavy-footed impacts were heard all around the house, followed by a sound that resembled the laugh of a hyena.

Deep sniffing sounds came from the back door and at either end of the room as giant shadowy figures passed by the window.

'House?' Kristina called out nervously, fearing for their safety.

Instantly, Chloe was launched into the air to smack against the ceiling with a sickening force.

'Oh my god! Stop! That's not what I meant and you know it!' she cried, waving her arms about frantically.

Dropping to the floor, the witch fell somewhat more forcefully than expected, causing the wind to wheeze out of her as she landed.

Michael barked a laugh in surprise but bit it off sharply before shrugging apologetically to Charlie.

Kevyn walked briskly into the kitchen, hiding his smile with his hand before he too incurred his elder's wrath.

Not as considerate, Kim threw her head back and laughed hysterically, caught off guard by the sudden attack.

'Fear not, for the wolves are happy... but as to the reason...' Jack whispered, his voice trailing off.

Kristina looked shocked but her attention was taken by the heavy-footed footsteps that came running down the stairs.

Screaming their excitement, the children ran from the hallway, repeating the same name over and over again.

'Daddy! Daddy! Daddy!'

Joining his friend to peer through the large window above the kitchen sink, Michael saw wolves the size of ponies prancing everywhere and bounding over each other in their show of excitement.

At the edge of the garden, they saw leaves begin to fall and glanced at one another in confusion.

Not the odd discoloured leaf that fluttered slowly to the ground but a torrent of green that began to cover the ground like a carpet.

Standing by the rear window of the living room, Kristina saw two shadowed figures detach themselves from the shedding trees and flushed with relief at recognising the goddess and the one beside her.

Though black and as depthless as before, Daire no longer looked demonic. He appeared to be a little shorter and lacking his previous cruel edge.

Closing her eyes, she threw out her awareness, but the blinding golden light caused her to snap back into her body immediately.

Having felt the presence of the goddess when she had sent her awareness down the stairs, this was the same but somehow different, for now there were two blazing beings where only one was expected.

She shook her head, regaining her faculties as tears welled once more in her eyes. The knowledge that he was alive, more than alive, filled her with relief and she clapped her hands together excitedly.

'Oh, thank god!' she cried. Her fear of him was gone, replaced now with the love she had for the father of her children.

The instinctual fear of what had been within him faded, her resentment towards him now washing away by the blinding golden light.

The children ran to her, jumping up and down in their excitement.

'Luc said that Daddy's coming!' Francesca screamed at the top of her voice, her excitement making her breathless.

'He's in the garden,' Kristina replied as tears rolled down her cheeks.

'Daddy's bright,' Lucian remarked, visibly shivering in his eagerness.

'I know,' she whispered in a barely audible tone.

Opening the door, the mages fanned out to meet the two, causing the wolves nearest them to snarl in warning, taking the strategy to be of hostile intent.

'They've definitely switched sides,' Kevyn observed but did not take his eyes off the ancient man of legend.

The smile slipped from Daire's face as he approached, the blackness of him becoming more natural in the morning light.

'So it's true,' Charlie observed, looking at Olivia warily. 'You are a goddess,' he stated, bowing his head to her in respect.

'I am,' she replied, smiling warmly. 'But I would still like you to call me Olivia,' she said, becoming the young woman again as she spoke.

'As you wish,' he replied, again bowing his head.

'What is this?' Daire asked, looking at Kim because of the bond forged between them in the fight against the Reaper.

'Are you a demon?' she asked, her features tight and her stance that of readiness.

Daire pursed his lips while studying her and then smiled with a shrug of his shoulders.

'I was,' he answered, holding her eyes for a moment. 'Now I am less so,' he continued, realising that he was being vague.

'But for how long?' Charlie demanded, scowling across at him aggressively.

'It matters not, for you can do nothing about it regardless,' Daire replied, taking in the four of them with a sweep of his eyes.

'Before you do something foolish,' Olivia advised, stepping forward, 'you must know that I have put what is in me, in him,' she warned, positioning herself in front of him. 'You, therefore, would be fighting a god, a goddess and the wolves around you,' she said, her eyes growing angry at the threat they projected.

A silence ensued as each waited for the other to react.

'Let this foolishness go,' Olivia commanded, arching her eyebrow at all four of them. 'This is not a fight you can win,' she continued as Daire stepped around her.

'I commend your bravery and your sense of what you deem is right, but I am not your enemy,' he said, walking amongst them. 'Now, I wish to see my children,' he whispered, walking through them into the house.

***

Watching the exchange from the window, Kristina guessed correctly at the mages' concerns and breathed out nervously, thanking the goddess, Olivia that he was no longer the demon he had been.

'I must stop praying to her,' she admonished herself, finding now that the whole situation was simply too awkward.

Entering the room, Daire swept up his children and hugged them close.

'Miss me?' he asked, kissing them both repeatedly.

Francesca immediately began to cry and he looked at her worriedly before kissing her again reassuringly.

'I wasn't gone that long, baby girl,' he said, holding her close and felt that Lucian also, held him that little bit tighter.

'He somehow saw the whole thing,' Kristina informed him, shrugging her shoulders as to why that was. 'He also had some kind of prophetic trance thing going on, but there is something more immediate that you must sort out,' she continued, looking pointedly at Chloe who was now seated on the sofa.

John sat beside her, his long arm wrapped protectively around her, and though there were no words he could utter in her defence, he was beside her nonetheless.

Turning, Daire stared at them both and shook with no sign of the demon rising up, which caused Kristina to sigh in relief.

Reaching out, he touched the wall with the palm of his hand, causing it to ripple with a golden wave of light that spread out from the point of contact.

'I see,' he breathed after a moment, looking first to John. 'This witch is going to be the death of you, druid,' he warned, shaking his head in disapproval. 'You must learn not to write me off so quickly,' he continued, pursing his lips with indecision.

Chloe kept her head low and avoided his eyes at all costs, wishing desperately that she had not been so eager in setting her trap.

Shrugging at last, Daire turned to Olivia who had only now entered the room.

'Since she has broken her oath to her goddess, I think it only fitting that her goddess pass judgement upon her,' he remarked, gesturing Olivia forward with a sweep of his arm. 'A permanent solution if you will,' he advised, not wanting to have this situation repeat itself.

Stepping forward, Olivia looked down with eyes that burned into the dishonourable witch.

Staring sullenly up at her, Chloe frowned and wondered why this strange young woman was standing over her.

'A high priestess should know when she is in the presence of her goddess, don't you think?' she asked, her tone now that of the Queen.

Trembling from head to toe, Chloe's eyes darted around the room for confirmation as John gasped beside her, his arm tightening involuntarily around her shoulders.

'I relieve you of the burden of being a priestess,' the goddess announced, a cold smile flashing across her face. 'You have managed to corrupt what I had intended to be pure and coveted those that are under my protection. Never again will you be a priestess or blessed within a circle. I free you,' she finished, raising her hand over the witch's head.

A shimmer of golden light seemed to be drawn from Chloe, blurring out of her into the hand of the goddess.

Chloe cried pitifully and threw her hands together in prayer.

'Forgive me!' she wailed, falling in supplication at Olivia's feet. 'Please?' she cried, feeling her connection to the covens snap.

'You are not without your own power,' Olivia replied soothingly as she lowered her hand once more. 'But you are no longer a witch,' she finished, turning her back on the kneeling woman to walk back to Daire.

Looking at him with incredulity, Kristina was shocked at his show of restraint until, that was, he opened his mouth.

'House?' he called, gesturing towards the door with his pointed finger.

The house came alive instantly, lifting Chloe off the sofa as though by the scruff of the neck and leaving her there to dangle for a moment.

'Don't let the door hit you on the way out,' he advised, laughing mischievously.

Kristina closed her eyes and shook her head disapprovingly at his dark humour.

'So, not completely healed then,' she remarked, as Chloe left the room with John at her heels, literally.

Kristina sighed with relief when the front door closed, hearing it open and close just the once.

Daire smiled at her and spread his arms innocently.

'Come on! She deserved far worse,' he replied, looking at the goddess for support.

'You've come a long way,' Olivia replied patronisingly and rolled her eyes at Kristina who laughed in response.

'Well, I think I did brilliantly,' he remarked, picking up his children again and spinning them around in a circle to make them laugh. 'See? I will always come back to you,' he promised, kissing them again and again.

***

'You don't need the cloak any longer,' Olivia informed him, watching him as he got ready to meet the Horned God. 'You can travel the paths now without it,' she continued, tilting her head to the side.

Pulling it around his broad shoulders, he smiled in response.

'I love it,' he replied, eyeing himself in the mirror, 'because you gave it to me,' he added, kissing her lips and savouring the heat of it. 'What do you think this gift is then?' he asked, giving her 'the face', which caused her to shrug over-dramatically.

'Stop pulling that ridiculous face and I will stop shrugging,' she bargained, lifting her chin in challenge.

'I have zero issues with you shrugging,' he responded, raising his eyebrows and pulling the corners of his mouth down again.

Closing her eyes so as not to see, she breathed out and tried not to smile.

'I don't know what the gift is, but if I thought it a danger to you then I would not allow you to go,' she answered, unwilling to be goaded by him. 'Just don't agree to anything or make any deals,' she added and then paused, deep in thought, 'or allow yourself to be changed any further… in any way,' she finished, looking at him sternly.

Chapter Ten

The glade seemed to be teeming with life when he walked from the trees, and Daire sighed at the pleasure that swelled in him.

A mass of flocking birds swirled high into the sky, looking more like a swarm of bees as they danced through the air before diving low as though for the simple pleasure of it.

Butterflies flew delicately among the tall grass, causing the young god to smile at their beauty. He spotted his huge stone instantly, though sitting in an entirely different location after his fight with the Reaper. He felt drawn to it somehow, as though a bond had formed between them after all the things that had happened.

Walking over, he patted it affectionately as though greeting an old friend before springing atop it to await the one who had summoned him.

Thinking of nothing but aware of everything, he waited patiently as the time ticked by.

An hour passed before he felt a new presence moving cautiously towards him and upon opening his eyes, he saw that it was a bushy-tailed fox eyeing him warily.

Stopping a short distance away, the animal lifted its nose to sniff at the air, trying, the god knew, to pick up his scent.

'Hello,' Daire greeted, bowing his head to the little animal but it just stared back at him curiously and sniffed at him again.

Narrowing his eyes, he saw that the beautiful russet fur was matted on one side, appearing black in the midday sun.

'Have you been in the wars, my friend?' he asked, his brow furrowing with mild concern. 'Come,' he called, reaching out his hand.

The fox regarded him silently, its angular head cocking to the side.

'Do you want me to heal you?' he asked, nodding slightly at the creature's wound.

The fox appeared to smile suddenly, the corners of its mouth widening at his words.

Laughing at the ridiculousness of the situation, Daire slid off the stone lightly and expected the creature to bolt, but it stood its ground, the golden-brown eyes looking up at him knowingly.

'Is this what it is to be godly?' Daire thought, smiling down at the beautiful face as he knelt to inspect the wound.

Large puncture wounds lacerated the skin just beneath the fur and he realised instantly that the damage was not made naturally. Running his fingertips across the broken skin, he felt the small bits of metal buried within the wounds.

Making hushing sounds and talking soothingly, he pulled a piece free and rolled it between his fingers.

'Lead,' he whispered, his mood darkening. 'A bloody shotgun,' he growled, shaking his head slowly.

Placing his hand over the wound, he brought up the power of the land and sent it into the fox, knowing that the metal would poison the little animal.

'Not a good way to die, my friend,' he whispered, happy that he could help the creature.

Removing his hand from where the wound had been, he smoothed the now lush red fur back into place.

'Better?' he asked, scratching behind the large pointed ears.

As though in answer, the fox leapt up and ran around him several times, making yipping sounds of delight.

It ran away from him suddenly, only to return almost as fast to cannon into him. Rolling onto its back, the fox presented its belly to him with a friendly whine.

'Okay, Red,' he chuckled, rubbing its chest and stomach affectionately as its small paws crossed over his forearm.

A bark from the trees brought the fox up in an instant, its pointed muzzle sniffing at the air.

'Shh, Red. You are safe with me,' he said assuredly and rose to his feet to investigate.

Across the clearing, the head of a dog bobbed up and down in the long grass, baying again as it picked up a scent.

Spying its prey, the hound stopped dead and barked its discovery before running headlong towards the little fox.

'No,' whispered the god. The command in that single word was infinite and the hound could only obey, looking at him questioningly with a nervous wag of its tail.

The dog was of a similar colour to the fox, with its short fur glistening like burnished copper in the midday sun. It slowly sat down and began to pant with its long pink tongue lolling to one side.

'Blood, meet Red,' Daire said, introducing the animals to each other. 'You are no longer enemies,' he commanded, watching as the bloodhound moved forward again to tentatively touch its nose to that of the little red fox.

Smiling with pleasure, he watched as both hunter and prey began to play, jumping and pawing at each other rather comically. The fox pounced at the lumbering beast as it turned its rear in defensive strategy, causing Daire to laugh out loud at the tactic.

'You are not meant to hate each other,' he whispered, saddened suddenly by the way of this world.

An angry shout from the trees ended the playful shenanigans and both animals looked up in alarm.

The hound immediately turned, cocking its head at the tone of the voice.

'Ignore them,' Daire ordered, seeing two men enter the glade with their shotguns broken over their shoulders.

On seeing him standing there alone, the two approached more cautiously, repositioning the guns to rest over their forearms but leaving them broken and pointing at the ground.

'Who the hell are you? The king in the north?' the lead man said, taking in the long black cloak.

'Roleplaying, are you?' scoffed the second, causing the other to laugh in response.

Noting their distinctive ginger hair, Daire could clearly see they were brothers, but they had very different builds. The lead man was wiry and looked slightly older, with a cold look to his eyes, while the other had a large 'chunky' build that gave him a sense of strength.

'Speed and power,' he thought, seeing the two for what they were. 'Scum,' he decided, recognising the vile look.

'I wish sometimes that's all it was,' he replied, shrugging his shoulders with an easy smile.

The brothers laughed, edging a little closer, spreading out a bit as they did so.

'Please tell me you have a sword?' Chunky asked, laughing as he spoke.

'Look! There's our bloody fox,' slim barked, locking his shotgun in an instant.

'Stop,' Daire whispered, feeling his face drain of colour, but he was ignored and the trigger was pulled.

The first barrel exploded with a sound like thunder and the shot from inside hurtled forward with the deadly intent of its wielder.

Growling in rage, Daire sent the exploding bits of metal back at the man with a sweep of his arm, causing spots of blood to erupt on his face and shoulders.

Screaming in agony, Slim dropped the weapon and fell to his knees with his hands hovering over his ruined face.

'Lee!' Chunky shouted, rooted to the spot.

'Take your brother and leave!' Daire commanded, stalking forward wrathfully to point back to the way they came.

Locking his gun in place, Chunky lifted the barrels and aimed them straight at Daire's head.

'Or what, Jon Snow?' he growled, saliva dripping from his open mouth as his finger hovered over the trigger mechanism.

'Shoot the bastard!' Lee screamed, his one good eye glaring hatefully as the trigger was finally squeezed.

Nothing happened and the finger pulled again but the firing pin refused to move, the gun unwilling to fire.

'Shoot him!' Lee wailed, blood beginning to pool in his shaking hands. 'Kill him!' he screamed, turning to glare at his brother.

Chunky squeezed the trigger repeatedly, pulling on it again and again as he screamed in frustration.

The shotgun exploded suddenly, blowing away half of Chunky's head into a mass of bone and gristle.

Daire stood frozen, the shock of what had happened causing him to stare in astonishment.

'Did I do that?' he thought, trying to recount his thoughts the moment before.

'Sometimes...' a deep booming voice sounded from behind, causing Daire to turn as a giant of a man stepped by him.

Stooping down, the newcomer placed a large hand upon the crown of Lee's head and casually twisted his wrist. There was a loud crack as the neck was broken before the body slumped to the grass.

Taking in the giant's appearance, Daire stared in awe at the great head that now turned to look at him.

A large horizontal antler sprang from the head, with but one claw-like spike pointing skyward at its very tip. On the other side of the giant's head, the antler appeared to be broken off half-way up, causing it to point out to the side like a jagged bone.

Short light-brown fur covered his navel and nether regions and ran up his broad back to cover his shoulders like the hide of a deer.

A huge sword was strapped across his back, the hilt of which was shaped like a crescent moon. Stretching out of it came a long wide blade of silver that almost touched the ground as the giant stood to his full height.

'Sometimes, it is acceptable to kill those that require it,' he finished, standing before Daire like the god he was. 'Do not let yourself be changed too much by her will,' he advised, smiling down with unmatched confidence.

'I'm trying to control my inner demon,' Daire began but the Horned God waved off the comment, cutting him off before he could continue.

'Don't think! Do!' he boomed, pointing at Daire's heart. 'From there,' he said, his golden-brown eyes glaring into him. 'Stop fighting your nature, Dark, do what it is in your nature to do,' he continued, standing proudly before him.

Sighing, Daire shook his head disagreeably.

'But what if I bring out my darkness again?' he asked, spreading his arms in exasperation.

The Horned God looked at him as though he were an idiot as he placed his large-knuckled fists to his waist.

'You are a god now! There is no inner demon! There is only you,' he answered, pointing at his chest again. 'Stop overthinking, my friend,' he said, putting his massive arm around Daire's shoulders.

Looking up at the giant, Daire smiled uncertainly.

'We are friends then?' he asked, not sure what to make of this overbearing god of the forest.

'You saved me, did you not? Healed me and protected me to no gain of your own. Now that is a friend indeed,' he replied, laughing thunderously at Daire's expression.

Glancing around, Daire looked for the fox but the glade was silent except for the continued rumbling chuckle of this Horned God.

There were no bodies either, no blood and no hound.

'Wow,' Daire gasped, clearly impressed by the display of power. 'I actually liked the fox,' he grumbled, feeling sad at the loss of the little creature.

'And I like you too,' the god laughed before winking at him slyly. 'I shall come to you again in that form the next time I need a belly rub!'

The two gods, old and new, spoke for a long time, discussing what it was to be a god and their ways.

'Do you wonder why you could not control the brothers as you did the dog?' the Horned God asked, laying down flat upon the ground and tucking his hands behind his head.

Daire thought for a moment until finally understanding the truth of it.

'Free will!' he answered, thumping his head with the palm of his hand.

'Indeed,' the old god rumbled, smiling proudly at his would-be prodigy. 'Impressive, most impressive, but you are not that godly yet!' the giant continued in a deeper tone.

Daire laughed, throwing his head back as he did so, caught completely off guard by the adapted Vader line.

Frowning after a moment, he looked at the forest god suspiciously.

'Have you been watching me? That is something I would've said!' he asked, narrowing his eyes in suspicion.

'*Unagi!*' the giant rumbled, touching his middle finger only to his temple and giving more than one gesture at the same time.

Caught off guard, Daire laughed again and found himself liking this larger-than-life deity.

'One more thing!' the god said seriously, sitting up with a stern expression. 'Reach for the daemon that you so believe is within you,' he ordered, waving his hand for him to get on with it.

Daire shook his head, unwilling to bring forth what he now hated within himself.

'Not a chance,' he replied, shaking his head determinedly.

'It is the only way for you to believe and to truly understand,' the booming voice advised, waving his hand in the air again with a note of impatience.

Looking uncertain and holding the Horned God's eyes, he took a deep breath and waited.

'I will bring you back if you fall into darkness,' the god intoned robotically, saying each word in a monotone.

Shaking his head again, Daire was determined to remain as he was.

'Open your mind,' the god continued in a hoarse whisper, causing Daire to laugh again.

'Give me a break!' he replied, chuckling for a while before finally reaching within himself.

He sought the hate and the desire to kill and felt the darkness immediately, but it was no longer dominant, no longer barely contained. It was a small part of him now, as were all the conflicting natures within him, and it felt to him now that he was trying to remember a fading dream.

The gold of the goddess interlaced everything, binding all aspects of himself under its unrelenting will.

Clapping his hands together in applause, the god smiled at him broadly and nodded his approval.

'Very good, Dark,' he congratulated, closing his eyes in contentment.

Looking down at the prone giant, Daire began to smile questioningly.

'Why do you call me Dark?' he asked, intrigued.

The God-King's Fall

'You have three names, I chose one,' the god answered with a shrug.

Daire stiffened and looked perplexed by the seemingly flippant response.

'What? I have but one name, and it is Daire. Dark was a name given to me by the vampires. It is not my true name and I have no other,' he replied, his frown deepening.

'All things are governed by the power of three, we gods especially see this. I am Herne the warrior, the father and the sage. You are the same,' he replied without opening his eyes.

Daire shook his head, lost as to his meaning.

'I have no third name, and Herne? The hunter?' he asked, easily distracted by the mythical name.

The Horned God merely grunted, shrugging with his face as Daire had done so many times before.

Holding in his smile, Daire continued and felt unwilling to let the topic drop.

'That's it? No response?' he asked, spreading his arms a little.

The god rose onto his elbows, frowning up at him in annoyance.

'I have spoken and so shall it be. Would you like me to repeat myself? You have three names, the fact that you do not know the last matters not,' he replied, nodding his head slowly.

Pursing his lips in thought, Daire pondered Herne's words.

'Oh, here we go! He's pursing! Look! Before you go asking any more questions, I will tell you this much! As you were named the Dark Wolf, whether you like it or not is irrelevant. So are you known by another and so are thrice named as are we all. When you were named Dark, you were different, yes? Different to what you were and are now?' Herne asked, nodding for him.

Daire nodded his agreement anyway but said nothing.

'So shall it be again, if you live long enough to hear it. The name is yours whether you like it or not,' Herne said, looking seriously at his new friend.

'So, it is a name I already possess?' Daire asked, frowning in puzzlement.

'Just because you have not heard it, does not mean it is not there,' Herne replied, clearly growing impatient with the topic.

'Now for my gift,' he announced, changing the subject and rising to his feet. 'Come, walk with me, Dark,' he said, walking him deeper into the forest. 'It is time for you to gain a sad truth,' he said, slowing his pace. 'The daemons will come again and come soon,' he announced, causing Daire to stop with a lurch.

'What?' he gasped, but the giant continued on ahead and so he was forced to catch up.

'The daemons will come like moths to a flame and to defeat them you must call forth an army, mankind's army, or this world will fall,' Herne prophesied, walking through the trees but hitting none of the low-hanging branches.

Feeling the old god's power at work, he sensed them moving to a different location and went along with it regardless.

'When?' he asked, seeing the Reaper in his mind and feeling again the fear he had felt when fighting it. 'But I am a god now,' he thought, feeling his confidence return. 'If you are Herne, the hunter, that surely gives you four names?' he asked, causing the giant to turn in anger.

'That is what you choose to put your mind to?' he admonished, his brow furrowing with displeasure.

Seeing that he would need to explain this topic further to put an end to this conversation once and for all, Herne growled his answer in anger.

'Hunter warrior, it's the same manifestation. Youth, man and elder. Warrior, father and sage. Herne is my name! I have never walked among men as a man and so the naming will be different according to their interpretations, but three I am and no more! I have three names!' he growled, enraged now by the continued conversation.

Daire threw his head back and laughed, cutting off the irritated deity.

'Too easy Herne, way too easy,' he replied, continuing to chuckle to himself. 'Where have you taken us, anyway?' he asked, feeling the wind on his face from atop the high, rolling hills.

***

The atmosphere in the house was tense after Olivia had gathered them in the living room, something was wrong and they could feel it like a cold wind in winter.

The mages stood spread out along the walls with Charlie at their centre, looking ready for battle as they always appeared to be.

Chloe and John sat rather uncomfortably on a sofa, looking down and staring at no one. They were as surprised to be back as the others were at seeing them, for one moment they were walking into their hotel room and the next they found themselves entering this house again.

The goddess had assured them that the house would not move against them and thus far, she had been right.

Kristina and the children sat on the remaining sofa with her son's head buried in his iPad.

Jack casually sat on the arm next to him, causing the boy to look up now and then with annoyance.

Kristina sat rather pertly, her back straight and hands placed flat upon her lap, for she too felt the pent-up atmosphere, feeling a heaviness that seemed to weigh her down.

Francesca sat likewise, waiting patiently for her father's friend to speak.

Olivia stood before the fireplace, her queenly mantle draped about her like a protective armour.

'I have called you here to tell you what Daire is no doubt being told at this very moment. A rift will open again soon,' she said, gauging their reactions coolly.

'What draws them?' Charlie asked, breaking the momentary silence with his sharp, inquisitive mind.

Olivia smiled at the insightful mage and considered the question before answering.

'The Reaper left a weakness in the veil when it passed, the more powerful daemons have sensed it and make their way again, in force this time,' she replied, choosing her words carefully.

'What drew the Reaper?' he persisted, his eyes holding her own.

'He knows,' she realised before spreading her arms casually. 'What draws a moth to a flame?' she countered aloud, avoiding the question for the moment.

'What is the flame?' he asked, not letting the question go unanswered.

The silence grew, and Charlie knew that he was testing her patience.

'Initially, it was Daire,' she admitted, thinking it best to get it out in the open. 'As daemonic as he had become, his presence here was like a magnet to them. The Reaper was one of, or maybe *was*, the most powerful among them and, therefore, the first to crossover, but the others will come. Deadly and more powerful than anything you can imagine, they will come to conquer this realm,' she announced, glancing at Kristina's raised hand.

Lowering her hand rather awkwardly, Kristina's face flushed with embarrassment.

'Sorry, I don't know why I did that,' she said abruptly, giving Jack a stern look after hearing him laugh.

'I must not raise my hand in class,' Jack whispered, avoiding her glare as Michael's mouth began to twitch.

Taking a deep breath, Kristina finally asked her question.

'Daire has killed two of these demons already though, hasn't he? I mean, surely after his latest transformation he will be able to handle more of them?' she asked, smoothing her dress down at the knees self-consciously.

The goddess slowly shook her head and Kristina saw a flash of worry in her eyes.

'Daire is yet to come into his power... his true power,' she answered, her expression controlled. 'Yes, he is now a god, but new, with untested might. Each god is as unique as each daemon is and there are those in the underworld who have had an eternity to master their art. Time is irrelevant in the darkness and to be there is to have always been there. You cannot fathom this because in this realm you see the passing of time. Let it just be said that those that come will be at their full potential and he will not be,' she replied, looking around the room.

'Why is it different? I mean, why does it even exist at all?' John asked, leaning forward intently.

Olivia shook her head and was about to dismiss the question when she tilted her head to the side.

'Too long an answer, John,' she replied but then added offhandedly. 'There was a war long ago and they were cast into the underworld. A place where only the strongest survive… a place of many layers. This breach, this crossing, is from just one of many such levels,' she answered, looking around for any more questions.

'Why can't *you* help my daddy?' Francesca asked, her head lifting accusingly towards the goddess.

'I want to, Cesca. I really do. And I am, as much as I am able, but I'm forbidden from doing what I wish,' she replied, looking lost and alone at that moment. 'There is already a price I must pay for doing what I have done,' she continued, her eyes looking pleadingly at his daughter.

'Who do you have to pay?' Francesca asked, her eyes wide with concern.

Olivia's head dropped a moment, the line of questioning unsettling her. Not wishing to upset the child, she finally answered the question. 'I am not the goddess of this world,' she admitted, baring her soul to the little girl. 'And I must answer to the one that is,' she confessed, forcefully looking away.

'So, what are we to do?' Kim asked, folding her arms in frustration and seeking for a way to act, as was the battle mages' way.

Regaining her regality, Olivia turned and was glad of the interruption.

'You must summon all those that will come and force those that will not. John, you must summon the druids. All druids the world over. They must come, now!' she said, turning to Chloe with a pointed finger.

Light flared suddenly, causing the woman to gasp as her status was restored.

'For your transgressions against the one I love, I charge you to unite the covens and call them to battle. Do you accept?' the goddess challenged, raising her chin for her answer.

Dropping to her knees with tears flowing to her cheeks, the priestess sobbed her gratitude.

'I do my Queen, with all my heart,' she replied, looking up in praise.

The goddess turned to the mages and raised her eyebrows to Charlie.

'The mages will fight, it's what we do,' he announced, receiving approving looks from the others of his faction.

Finally, she turned to Jack, who looked back uncertainly at what his role might be. The mages would organise the defence, summoning all of mankind's might to the table and John had the druids, leaving no others for him to gather. On that thought, he closed his eyes as the colour drained from his face.

'I charge you, Blue Wizard, to call the vampires to war,' she intoned, looking away only after he had nodded his assent. 'This is a war that you cannot lose, a war for your right to exist. This will truly be the first war of the worlds,' she proclaimed, staring at them all in turn.

Chapter Eleven

The wizard that was sat staring into the flames of the large stone hearth, brooding on the past and the choices he had made.

The abnormally large fireplace was set within a wall of large stone blocks and housed a fire so wide, that it in itself was enough to light his large rounded chamber of the castle-like building in which it was set.

Sitting high on the mountainside, this fortified tower overlooked the towns and villages of the surrounding valleys, seeming to look down upon them rather than over them.

Continuing to stare into the flames, Colin's eyes looked unfocused as he relived all his actions since and before he had turned to the darkness.

By far the worst for him now was his denunciation of his son and it was that which stuck in his throat like an uncooked chicken bone.

'How old must one be to finally see the light?' he thought, closing his eyes as a solitary tear rolled down his cheek.

His intolerance of his sons had been complete in the end, annoyed beyond reason by their constant disagreements.

Being a near match to himself, his youngest son, he had found, was totally unmanageable and had opposite views on almost all topics.

Only his eldest had kept the peace, talking them down and even threatening them when it went too far, for he had the respect of all the brothers.

Carl, being only a little older, was the first to clash with Daire and the first to learn that his younger brother was not to be contested in the art of magick. Though never hateful towards each other, the two had always had what he had believed to be a healthy rivalry, but with Paul it had been different.

Being the second eldest and known throughout the land to be the deadliest in the art of war, their rivalry had been more dangerous and their growing dislike for one another other had turned deadly in the end.

Being the elder even after so many centuries, Paul had simply found it impossible to allow his younger brother to surpass him in any way.

Shaking his head, Colin closed his eyes and sighed miserably.

'Even I felt that sting,' he thought, finally admitting it to himself with a feeling of shame.

'Is that why I sided against you?' he asked aloud, the words echoing off the large stone walls.

'It is!' rasped a voice that sounded low and dangerous from behind him, which caused him to turn with white light arcing between his fingers.

'Put your power down, wizard, or I shall show you mine!' the sinister voice warned before cackling in delight at his readiness to act. 'You will need that instinct in the times to come, Collinus!' the voice cackled as its owner stepped from the shadows.

Standing before him was an old woman that appeared to be bent over and crippled with age.

Colin looked around wildly, wondering how she had entered his chambers without him hearing or sensing it.

'I should have sensed her upon the mountain, let alone here within my own halls,' he thought, knowing that she was more than what she appeared to be.

'Worry not child, for had I wished you dead, you surely would be,' she rasped, cackling again as she hobbled forward to seat herself where he had been.

'Who are you?' he asked, involuntarily stepping away from her to keep a distance between them.

Looking him in the eye, she patted the space next to her invitingly with a leering grin spreading on her face.

'Can you not guess?' she asked sweetly, tilting her head to the side.

Refusing her offer, Colin stayed where he was as his every sense told him to run.

'If you are who you appear to be, I would have seen or heard from you before now,' he replied, standing his ground.

She laughed loudly at that, a high-pitched shrill like that of the fabled evil Queen.

'I do not show myself to vile, corrupted creatures such as you were!' she hissed, rising slowly to stalk him.

Backing away, Colin brought his hands up before him and readied himself for whatever came next.

The firelight cast an ominous glow upon her frame and he could see that she was anything but fragile. What he had initially thought to be a shawl about her head was in fact, a deep-hooded cloak or maybe a robe.

'But you are a vampire no longer and there is a great need for us to converse,' she continued, straightening regally before him.

Colin let out a gasp of surprise at the astonishing height of her suddenly, causing him to flinch back as she towered over him.

What had first appeared to be a decrepit old crone, hunched over as she had been, was now a tall, slender form with the hood fallen forward to hide her face.

'Great Queen,' he whispered, looking up and wondering if she had come for him this night.

'Was that so difficult, Col?' a much younger voice asked as the goddess lowered herself to stand eye-to-eye with him.

Gasping in recognition, he saw a face from his distant past emerging from the darkness. A face of a woman that he loved to this day and always would.

'I am all women and all women am I. Do not be troubled by the face now before you,' the goddess soothed, touching his face with a tender hand. 'You have strayed far, Magickian,' she admonished before drawing her hand away.

'You must go to him, Col,' she whispered, calling him by the name that only she had used. 'He is going to fall and you need to be there,' she said, leaning in to kiss him on the lips.

He closed his eyes at the contact, feeling unable to do anything else.

'The daemons come to devour this world and it falls to you to drive them back,' she continued, pulling back at last and stepping away.

A sob escaped him on opening his eyes, seeing that his life-long love was gone, and feeling alone in the darkness the wizard that was, wept.

***

It was twilight when the two brothers pulled to a stop, the deep growl of the engine the only sound to hear on the darkening mountainside.

Drawing in a nervous breath of cold evening air, Cristian looked up at the castle-like structure that rose intimidatingly before them.

The diminishing light highlighted the old keep in dark shades of blue, giving the impressive tower a rather haunting aspect.

Paul smiled back at his brother, knowing only too well the reception he anticipated from within.

'He is not the same as he was, Cris,' he reassured him, reaching back to pat his thigh supportively. 'He sent me to find you, did he not?' he asked, turning to look up at the large structure. 'None of us are the same,' he added to himself, silently struggling with his recently recovered emotions.

Having been sent to investigate his brother's whereabouts after his father had not sensed him leave his last location, Paul had found him only after following his father's instructions.

'He's a sneaky sod,' Paul laughed sardonically, shaking his head in amusement. 'Did you know that he could track us through the swords?' he asked, turning back to look at his brother.

Cristian shrugged, showing his ignorance on the matter as he smiled himself.

'Daire must have figured it out,' he answered finally, picturing the blood-red sword in his mind. 'He's learned the charm of making too, for I saw his daughter wearing a ring which clearly had a power of its own,' he said innocently, smiling at his brother.

Paul scowled at the words, irritated by the impressed tone.

'You sound like a fan,' he replied sarcastically, twisting his wrist to throttle the engine of the custom-made Harley Davidson that was his pride and joy.

'Don't be a dick,' Cristian sighed tiredly, casting his eyes skyward in exasperation.

Paul revved on, grumbling under his breath at the continued references to his younger brother. He knew that he was being a dick but found it impossible to be any different where 'the legend' was concerned.

Cristian sighed and cuffed him about the head before narrowing his eyes at the sight up ahead.

Paul stiffened momentarily as a large black crow flew past his head, squawking madly before veering off to the side.

'Bah!' he exclaimed, ducking away from the menacing bird and stepping from the bike in one fluid motion.

Straightening himself, he saw the form of an old woman shuffling towards him, an unnatural light shining eerily in her eyes.

The Black Sword flashed into his hands, held before him by the double-handed hilt.

'Back away, hag!' he warned, lowering the tip to her eye level.

Looking up at him in anger, her bony finger stretched out in accusation.

'You would accost an old woman while she is about her duties?' she screeched, her eyes large and glaring.

'You are no old woman,' he replied, sidestepping cautiously as he hefted his blade between them.

'Oh, but I am, Blade Master,' she argued, rounding on him with incredible speed. 'The oldest of women!' she hissed, smiling maliciously at his look of concern.

Her wide eyes flicked to the right suddenly and grew serious as the Silver Sword was drawn.

Glancing to Cristian briefly, her reflective glasslike eyes shifted from one brother to the other in excitement.

'Two brothers of corruption, come to kill an old girl like me. Your father would be so proud,' she crowed, her mock expression of fear slipping into a leer.

'What do you want?' Cristian demanded, eyeing the hag warily.

'I want... you!' she spat, her head snapping back to Paul before lunging for him.

The black blade sliced down, cleaving a vicious arc towards her head with deadly precision.

Committed now that his brother had acted, Cristian attacked an instant later but twisted his blade at the last instant, flattening it so as not to kill.

Paul, however, did not, intending to smite the crone where she stood and consider later whether he should have or not.

Cackling in delight, the goddess slipped past them, the swords of power ripping from their grasp as she passed.

Paul looked at his brother with an expression of alarm and saw the same look mirroring back to him.

Spinning around, their fear increased at seeing the hag crouching low, the black and silver swords clutched expertly in her hands.

'You will need to be faster than that if you are to kill daemons!' she admonished them with a tut, moving the swords back and forth like disappointed fingers.

Sharing another glance, the brothers could think of nothing to say after being bested so easily and simply stared back at her with open-mouthed incredulity.

Shocked into silence, both knew that the swords should not have let her hold them, let alone wield them, knowing that the enchantment upon them allowed only those of the same blood to do such a thing.

Though the weapons wailed and vibrated in their effort to escape, harm her in any way they did not.

'Impressive,' she whispered, appraising the swords approvingly. 'He truly is a master craftsman,' she acknowledged before opening her hands.

The swords lifted immediately from her hands and flew forth into the hands of their rightful owners, glowing slightly at their return.

Smiling warmly at Cristian, the goddess then surprised him by dipping her head in his direction.

'For the turning of your blade,' she whispered, straightening into a taller and more regal-looking figure. 'You truly are my knight of honour,' she whispered, her face hidden now by the cowled hood about her head.

The imposing woman turned to Paul slowly and regarded him in silent contemplation as an unsettling quiet ensued, causing the swordsman to brace himself.

'You will need that killer instinct, Blade Master. Strike swift and strike true when midnight's time is upon you,' the hushed voice advised, cold and seemingly devoid of its previous warmth.

Paul looked at her quizzically, the meaning of her words clearly baffling him.

'Huh?' he murmured, glancing again to his brother.

'You must travel now with haste towards the one you consider your enemy and drive back those that would claim him,' she ordered, leaving little room for debate. 'Through one of my own, I have taken the corruption from you and the emotions you now feel are the direct result of this. You will have need of them if you are to succeed, for to defeat the daemons you must have less of their taint in you,' she informed, looking back again to the other.

Cristian's mouth fell open, realising that she was talking of Kristina and what she had done to him.

'Great Queen,' he whispered, dropping to one knee before her while Paul appeared dumbfounded, looking from his brother to the tall, cowled figure before them.

'Shit,' he whispered, realising at last that this must indeed be the Triple Goddess, better known as Morrigan or the Great Queen.

She was the goddess of fate and death and the crone was but one aspect of her nature. She was also the 'Maiden' who promised love and the 'Mother,' who brought forth life into this world.

'My goddess,' Paul gasped, also taking a knee before her. 'Forgive me,' he whispered, looking down to the ground.

Cupping his chin in her elegantly-shaped hand, Morrigan lifted his head so that he looked her in the eye.

'My angry son,' she admonished him seriously, her now visible features showing him her disapproval. 'Put away your anger and your pride, for he is your brother and I love you both,' she said as a wisp of blonde hair blew across her deep blue eyes.

Paul could not speak, tears of loss welling in his eyes at the seeing of her, but he slowly nodded before taking her hand and kissing it.

Turning again to Cristian, she bid him rise and embraced him tightly.

'My knight in shining armour,' she whispered, kissing him on the cheek. 'Drive back the horde and leave none alive,' she whispered, holding his face in her hands and staring at him intently. 'Only when they are defeated to a one will the gateway close,' she continued, kissing him on the other cheek.

The ancient men, boys once more, looked at her longingly with tears in their eyes.

'What demons?' Cristian sobbed, almost choking on the words.

'I am so proud of you all,' she whispered, ignoring his words.

'Promise me that the feuding is over,' she asked, looking again at Paul.

'I swear it,' he replied instantly and sobbed suddenly when she stepped back from them.

'Tell Carl that he is not forgotten,' she breathed, taking a further step back. 'My four beautiful boys,' she whispered as tears began to well in her eyes.

In desperation, Paul rose and began to follow, unwilling to let her leave him again, but her arm shot out to point behind them.

They turned instinctively to see a blue-robed figure approaching haphazardly from some trees, his arms flailing about him in an attempt to keep his balance.

The brothers could not bring themselves to look back again, for they knew in their hearts that she had gone and instead, shared the look of loss at her passing.

***

Looking down at the rolling hills of grassland, Daire saw a large lake spreading out below him that looked black in contrast to the grey shades of the approaching dawn.

He was not quite sure where the day had gone, for one second the sun had been high in the sky and the next it appeared as it was now, an hour or so before the dawn.

The God-King's Fall

The surface of the water unsettled him as large dark shadows seemed to move beneath its surface, swirling out from its centre towards the distant shoreline.

From high on the mountain top the lake had seemed so much smaller, but as he descended it had taken on mass and a sense of depthless mystery that caused him to feel uneasy.

Upon reaching the water's edge, a low mist had risen, as though a prelude to the dawn that rapidly approached. The water was calmer than he had expected and a deeper blue than he had perceived in the predawn light, looking like a sheet of black ice waiting to be broken.

'Llyn Y Fan Fach' the Horned God announced, his tone low and somewhat reverent.

Turning his proud head, the god looked out across the water with a dreamy cast to his golden eyes.

'Here you must wait,' he whispered, still staring off ahead. 'Time to see if you are indeed an oak!' he added, chuckling to himself.

Silently, Daire reached down to retrieve an oddly-shaped stone and pondered at how a small flat stone could have a hole going all the way through it, as though worn away from an age of running water.

'Hello, little one,' he greeted, seeing that a black leech had attached itself to his index finger. 'Curious little thing,' he thought, holding it up for the god to see but found that he was alone.

'Mysterious!' he whispered spookily, shaking his head in amusement. 'Time for you to find another food source, my little friend,' he sighed, pulling the leech free and placing it back into the water before climbing onto the rocks to his left.

He had heard of the legends regarding this lake and of the lady who reputedly dwelled within it. He found himself wondering suddenly if his father had actually had dealings with the lady of the lake when he had played his role as magickian to the king.

Keeping his distance in those old Arthurian days, Daire had chosen to remain silent and forgotten lest the war begin again. He had assumed that the sword given to Merlin was a fable, told by the magickian himself to manipulate the simple-minded in those gullible days.

'He always knew how to spin a good yarn,' Daire whispered and smiled despite himself, remembering his father's knack for storytelling. 'There's definitely something powerful here, though,' he thought, sensing a presence watching him even now from the disturbingly calm water.

'*Ysbryd Dŵr*' he called, summoning the spirit of water to his side in the ancient language.

The soft-lapping water intensified momentarily, the sound having a calming effect on his mind.

'*Brawd*,' Water answered, calling him brother in the same tongue. Daire smiled in response.

Taking a deep breath, he realised that he had missed conversing with the elements and vowed not to leave it so long before the next time.

'I may have need of you,' he whispered, feeling the element settle in around him.

The sound of the water had changed now, he noticed, as though the gently-lapping water now moved in reverse.

Pursing his lips in thought, Daire summoned the remaining elements to him for good measure.

'*Ddaear aer a thân yn dod ataf*,' he whispered, his voice suddenly resonating power.

'*Ein brawd ysbryd*,' came their immediate replies, filling him with reassurance and more than a little confidence.

Several glowing embers drifted to him on the air, looking like fireflies as they slowly began to circle him.

'Be watchful,' he warned, feeling the rock beneath him vibrate in response and the wind lift a little, igniting the embers to burn more brightly.

Turning his attention back to the water, Daire took in a deep lungful of air and blew it out slowly, instantly casting the morning mist from the water's surface.

Understanding his intent, the water element took all moisture from the air, causing the mist to dissipate almost immediately.

A sudden flash of silver disturbed the dark water before it disappeared into the depths.

'I seek the lady of the lake,' he called, sending his thoughts out also to be heard beneath the rippling water. 'Lady,' he whispered, letting the wind take his words and echo them back to him eerily.

With his awareness spread out across the entire area, he could feel the presence beginning to rise again. The water began to ripple into choppy splashes as though some sort of battle was being fought from within.

'Oh, bollox!' Daire whispered, realising that this was indeed the case and that the element had once again anticipated his need.

Finally, on breaking the surface, a silver-scaled head rose up slowly with two baleful black eyes fixing on him in anger.

Her very white teeth flashed brightly as the lady of the lake drew back her lips in a snarl.

'You dare to drag me here against my will?' she hissed, rising menacingly from out of the water.

Daire spread his arms wide and bowed in apology, hoping that she had not been too put-out by his summons.

'I am truly sorry, lady, a misunderstanding,' he replied, though mentally thanked the water for its aid.

He took in her beauty, seeing past the wrathful Titan and her murderous scowl. As the water left her body, he could see a warmth enter her cheeks as metallic silver hair began to flow down past her shoulders. Scaled flesh became more humanlike as she stalked towards him, and he began to wonder at what manner of creature she truly was.

She appeared unnaturally alluring to him, even in her heated state, and he had the sense that she was a force to be reckoned with when crossed.

Hoping that this was not such a time, he smiled awkwardly and shrugged his apology.

'I did not intend for you to be brought to me thus but to come of your own free will,' he continued, spreading his arms helplessly before bowing again respectfully.

The lady regarded him in silence, the heat in her face beginning to cool at the tone of his words.

'Who are you to control it so?' she asked, seeming to resent his will over the water.

'I did not control it, lady. It was the element itself that brought you to me,' he replied, pursing his lips in thought before narrowing his eyes. 'Would you like an introduction?' he asked, extending his hand to her slowly.

She seemed to ponder his offer with mild curiosity but he could see that she was excited by the prospect.

'I have had many men try to bind me to them before,' she said, holding his eyes with hers. 'They all failed,' she continued, trying to read his intentions.

'I am no man and belong to another,' he replied, drawing a scowl from her at his lack of interest. 'Though if I were not, I would indeed attempt to woo you,' he added swiftly, not wishing to cause her any more offence.

She smiled at that and took his hand as she stepped gracefully from the water, chuckling throatily at the turning of his eyes.

'A pleasing response,' she replied as the silver scales of her body suddenly became a dress of shimmering silk.

The metallic-looking hair darkened to a deep black, which made her green eyes stand out all the more in a dazzling contrast.

He took a deep breath and almost gasped at the sight of her beauty, which caused her to smile wide in appreciation.

'Are you so sure that you belong to another?' she asked teasingly, bumping her hip against his seductively.

'I am afraid so, lady,' he answered, taking a mental grip of himself and guessing that she was using her power on him.

'Not many can refuse me, not even the one who brought you to me,' she whispered, bowing her head to him in acknowledgement of his strength. 'You may call me Nimuë,' she continued, giving her name before raising her eyebrows for his.

'Daire,' he replied, answering her unasked question with another dip of his head.

'Daire?' she asked with a look of recognition before narrowing her emerald eyes in thought. 'Are you belonging to Merlin?' she asked, tilting her head to the side as she studied him.

Nodding slowly, he wondered what his father had told her of him and began to feel concerned at how close she was to one who was now his enemy.

She put a reassuring hand on his shoulder and gave it a gentle squeeze.

'It is how you end up that matters, the rest is just the journey,' she soothed and nodded as though she agreed with her statement.

'I doubt that the end will be any different from the rest of it,' he replied, failing to keep the bitterness from his tone.

Nimuë tilted her head again, seeing his anger and the pain hidden within it.

'Listen to my words, young god,' she whispered, leaning in close to share her secret. 'All will be forgiven before the end,' she continued, nodding sadly but keeping something back he thought, noting her slight hesitation.

'The end?' he asked, spooked by her cryptic words.

'Yours? His? Theirs? Ours?' she replied flippantly, dismissing his question with a wave of her hand. 'Now, you may introduce me,' she said, looking back to the water excitedly.

Feeling that he had to give a little to receive anything more, he closed his eyes and sought out the element of choice.

'I am here, brother,' the water soothed, washing through his mind as it always had.

'The lady of this lake wishes to commune with thee,' he sent, mildly curious as to the element's reaction.

With a gasp from Nimuë, he opened his eyes to see a look of rapture crossing her face. Her deep green eyes stared into his as she reacted to the words that were said to her. Now and then her eyes would widen or her mouth twitch at the conversation she was having in her mind. For some time the lady did this until, finally, she breathed out a long, satisfied sigh.

'You have given me the greatest gift of my life,' she whispered. Awed by the experience, she wrapped her arms around him and hugged him tightly.

Pulling back, she held him at arm's length and shook her head in wonder before growing serious again.

'I understand the reason you have been brought here, even if you do not,' she whispered, smiling at him warmly. 'Herne was wise to bring you to me,' she continued, squeezing his shoulders again before lowering her hand and bringing up her fist between their faces. Her emerald eyes held his own as she opened her hand, revealing a signet ring of gold and silver.

He blanched at first seeing it, thinking it the one now worn by his daughter, and felt instantly afraid at how it now came to be here in her possession.

'This is *Caledfwlch*,' she whispered reverently, staring down at the ring in her hand. 'It has had many names and has been many things,' she added, holding it up closer for him to inspect. 'I give it now to you, to wear until it can be worn no longer,' she said, offering him the ring without further comment.

Mystified by her words, he reached up and placed it on his little finger. It fitted perfectly, as he knew it would.

Impulsively, he lifted his fist into the air, causing the ring to flash suddenly, like the last star in the early morning light.

'This is a great gift I give to you, Daire,' she said, placing her hand on his chest. 'I am its keeper as you are now its wearer. Wear it well,' she said, stepping back from him. And without another word, she turned to the water's edge.

As though in afterthought, she turned as quick as a cobra and kissed him before he could react.

'Think of me when you are alone in the dark, and I will come for you,' she whispered fiercely before turning to dive from sight.

Daire just stood for a moment, staring once again at the calm surface of the water with goosebumps rippling across his flesh.

'Why did you have to say that?' he asked nervously, feeling stunned by her sudden prophecy.

Chapter Twelve

Catching sight of the three figures on the path ahead, David cast his shield about him at seeing the silver sword being drawn.

Moving cautiously forward, the frown upon his face deepened at seeing only two on the road where the three had been. Doubting that his younger eyesight had made the mistake, he drew up the might of the earth in readiness.

'There were definitely three!' he thought, preparing himself for whatever came next.

'Jack!' Cristian shouted, causing the wizard to pause momentarily.

'What the hell, Cris?' he shouted back, seeing now only one on the path and finally began to doubt himself.

'Paul, wait! It's Blue!' Cristian shouted, causing David to glance around nervously.

'I know,' the Blade Master whispered, speaking into David's ear from within his circle of protection.

'Gilga's balls!' the wizard blustered, breaking wind in fright at the unexpected turn.

Letting out a roar of laughter and releasing the built-up tension within him, Cristian guffawed, holding his hands to his ribs in the effort to control his mirth.

'This isn't funny!' David roared, raising his hands peacefully into the air.

Paul laughed wickedly and put his arm around the wizard's shoulders before walking him closer to his brother.

Shaking his head at the continuous change in his appearance, Cristian sighed, preferring the old man to the dark-haired man before him.

'Come now "David", it was a little funny,' he replied, wiping tears from his eyes.

David cursed, thinking that he would be treated differently if in the guise of Jack.

'I have not the time for this,' he stressed, glaring at Cristian as he shrugged off the escorting arm.

'Bah!' Paul huffed and began stalking away while grumbling under his breath, his mood darkening at the wizard's lack of humour.

'Why are you here?' Cristian asked as the thought only just dawned on him that the Blue Wizard, Jack or even David as he appeared now, would never come to the lair of the Egni without good reason.

'I was sent!' the wizard snapped, his face still flushing with embarrassment. 'There has been a breach at the house,' he announced, staring seriously at the silver warrior.

Feeling the pull of destiny at the announcement, Cristian realised that this must have been why the Great Queen had appeared to them just moments before.

'And?' he asked, a cold, sickly feeling erupting in his stomach.

Paul continued to stalk off, throwing his arms up in frustration.

'Not my concern!' he growled back, more out of habit than any real desire.

Waving off the comment with impatience, David turned back to Cristian with eyes that glistened from the untold tale.

'A demon somehow passed through into our dimension from hell itself! The bloody Reaper, of all things!' he answered, causing Paul to stop and turn. 'I have never before seen its like, not in my long life, for nothing I did could harm the damned thing. It just came on and on until I was forced to merely watch...' he said, trailing off towards the end.

Cristian closed his eyes and his face drained of colour, the dark circles of his eyes giving him a somewhat skeletal look.

'Daire and the Reaper fought, demon against demon, for that is what your brother had been, it seems,' he continued as tears welled in his eyes.

Cristian's breath caught in his chest and he felt unable to speak after the wizard's use of the past tense in regard to his brother.

'The Reaper was going to win and we all knew it until Daire pulled forth the Blood Sword. I thought it long destroyed or discarded... I never once thought that he carried it with him,'

The God-King's Fall

he said, wiping away his tears. 'I tried to help as best I could but what I did had little effect,' he continued, raising his hands in a manner of uselessness.

'Who won?' Cristian exploded, the words surging out of him from his wrath and frustration.

Taken aback by the emotional outburst, the wizard realised that he had been delaying the conclusion for too long.

'I find the telling of it much harder than I ever thought possible,' he whispered, taking a deep breath to compose himself.

Raising his arms into the air, the wizard sent balls of light high into the night sky.

'See for yourself,' he choked as a vision of the fight appeared above them.

They saw the Reaper in all its deadly mystery, darting in and out in a blur of motion, even though the vision appeared to be slowed quite considerably.

Paul stood transfixed by the scene, his features now a mask of stone but for the steady pulse of his jaw muscles.

Cristian was more animated, bringing his hands together hard at seeing the Reaper fall with the red blade through its eyes, but then sucked in air through his teeth when Daire faltered moments later.

He stared open-mouthed, seeing the black blood seeping into the ground and then the damage to his brother's body.

'No!' Paul cried, seeing his brother's face after so long but as a lifeless mask with the eyes unseeing in death.

Cristian moaned in grief at the finale, dropping to his knees at the sight of his brother's death.

He cried out in agony which seemed to be in time with a wail from a young woman who now crouched over the legend's broken body.

Cristian looked to Paul and saw him also upon his knees, bent over in silent despair with his face buried in his hands.

'I promised to put our differences aside! How can I do that now?' he cried, looking up in desperation for a moment.

Cristian shook his head, not having the words to console his weeping brother.

'Who's the girl?' he choked finally, turning again to the wizard as he began to cry freely, letting his emotions run free.

David blinked his tears away and looked at his friend soberly.

'The Queen of Air,' he replied, taking in a deep, shuddering breath.

'What you just witnessed was, I believe, the second death of Daire, or rather, the death of the demon within him,' he announced, standing awkwardly and waiting for his statement to sink in.

The Blade Master's head snapped up, his tear-streaked face a sudden mask of rage.

'What do you mean, second death?' he growled, his lips snarling back to bare his teeth. 'Wait a minute! The Great Goddess said that he was alive!' he roared, looking to his brother for confirmation.

'What devilry is this, wizard?' Cristian hissed in a dangerously low tone.

'Daire died in the glade as you just saw,' he replied, meeting the challenge head-on. 'However, somehow she brought him back and in doing so, changed him yet again. I think he might even be a god now, I sensed as much in him anyway,' he continued, shrugging a little.

'If I were you, I would leave this place before it is you who dies,' Paul advised, rising smoothly to his feet.

Lifting his chin stubbornly, David held the blond vampire's glare with one of his own.

'I needed to know whether you wished him to live or not, and you do, don't you?' he asked, nodding for him. 'So gather your army and meet me in that place, or he *will* die,' he continued, looking back to Cristian. 'I'm sorry Cris but you needed to see what we're up against,' he said, smiling sadly. 'The goddess has assured me that more will come and has called all the world to fight. As of this moment, we are at war with the demons of the underworld,' he declared fiercely before turning to leave.

'How long?' Cristian asked, hating the wizard at that moment and wanting nothing more than to throttle him.

Walking away, Jack called back from over his shoulder.

'The day is short and the darkness comes,' he called before pausing to turn once more. 'You may already be too late.'

***

The large double doors opened wide at their approach, the two men at either side bowing a little as the Egni Lords entered.

The lobby within was packed with battle-clad vampires, the metal in their clothing glinting dully in the subdued lighting.

Surveying the open area, Cristian saw his brother, Carl, standing nearby and nodded to him in greeting.

'The prodigal son returns,' Carl observed, smiling slightly at his eldest brother.

'Yeah, right,' Cristian replied, half-smiling as they clasped hands together.

Paul stalked past, his face scowling in anger as the crowd parted before him, unwilling to get caught up in one of the angry lord's moods.

'What's up with him?' Carl asked, rolling his eyes before frowning at the insult of being ignored.

'Wizards!' Cristian answered, scanning the faces of those nearby before frowning towards the far side of the room.

Sitting before the large hearth, he spied Warren glowering back at him over his shoulder and was immediately incensed by the look of aggression.

Storming over with his anger unchecked, Cristian approached him with white-faced fury.

'Have you got a problem, boy?' he challenged, glaring down at the seated man.

'Not with you, no,' the doorman replied, looking bitterly back into the fire, but his face twitched with the struggle of containing his emotions.

'What was that look, then?' Cristian challenged, his voice shaking with the effort of control.

Warren glanced up again, shock registering in his eyes.

'He's the one that made Geez!' he seethed, glaring back over his shoulder. 'He's the one that left us to be the Bloods' playthings!' he raged, scowling back again into the fire. 'And we can do nothing about it because he's your brother!' he whispered bitterly, shaking his head at the injustice of it all.

Cristian looked about, wondering to whom he was referring before slowly closing his eyes in shamed realisation.

'Of course it was him,' he sighed, seating himself heavily beside the man. 'I am truly sorry, War,' he whispered, shaking his head in apology.

Carl stood back awkwardly in the distance, trying to act as though he was oblivious to the situation, but failing in the attempt completely.

Catching his brother's eye, Cristian shook his head judgementally.

'You tit,' he mouthed, causing Carl to shrug and nod at the same time.

'I know,' he mouthed back, shrugging again before resuming his awkwardness. 'Sorry,' he mimed, looking up to make a study of the ceiling.

Turning back to the doorman, Cristian reached out to squeeze him on the shoulder.

'How did you know? I thought it was only Geez who had seen him?' he asked, searching the fighter's face.

'Geez is upstairs with your father to plead our case. We want nothing to do with this war. No offence, but it's nothing to do with us,' he replied, unwilling to meet the Egni Lord's eyes.

After a moment's silence, Cristian shrugged and leaned back in his chair.

'So long as you know that you'll be alone, and I do mean, alone. That, and if you cause any trouble, any trouble at all, then you will be dealt with as the Bloods have been,' he warned, unable to hide the disappointment from his voice.

'Rumour has it that it was that Dark character that wiped them out and not you. Maybe he'll like that we've named ourselves with him in mind and leave us be!' Warren retorted, irritated by the judgemental tone.

'You remember that when he comes for you,' Cristian sneered, rising to his feet. 'You remember that when you come grovelling back!' he hissed, walking away.

Carl raised his eyebrows questioningly, seeing his brother stalking back towards him.

'Sorry,' he said again, looking as guilty as sin itself. 'Don't tell Dad!' he added, causing Cristian to smile despite himself.

'You donkey,' he replied, taking him by the arm and leaning in close. 'Stay away from them! I don't want them dying at our hands. That would be wrong on so many levels,' he said, breathing out tiredly.

Carl spread his arms in innocence, intent on defending himself from any further wrongdoings.

'I tried to smile at them but they were having none of it,' he complained with a look of 'what else can I do?' on his face.

Laughing quietly, Cristian punched him on the arm and then cuffed the back of his head.

'What's he done this time?' Paul asked, appearing out of the crowd beside them.

'Oh, nothing really, he just decided to create a new faction, teach them nothing and leave them to breed,' he answered, grimacing in Carl's direction.

Paul closed his eyes and whispered the only words that came to mind.

'You tit,' he remarked just as the door to the stairwell opened and the hulking figure of Geez came striding into view.

Halfway to the fire, he paused mid-step at seeing Cristian. Their eyes met for an instant and the black giant nodded in greeting before continuing.

A moment later, Colin entered and scanned the room before finally walking over to his sons.

Without a word, he took Cristian into his embrace and held him there tightly, kissing him on the cheek.

'I'm glad that you're home,' he whispered before greeting his remaining sons in a similar fashion.

'We leave at once!' he announced and the entire room stood to attention. 'Let us pray that we are not too late,' he added, looking worriedly at his eldest. 'To war!' he growled, inciting the crowd into a roar of approval.

Chapter Thirteen

Olivia saw that the one who had called her was sitting on the large stone in the clearing and seemed to be enjoying herself as she waited for her to come.

'Here goes,' she thought, walking from the trees to enter the glade.

She had felt the summons while laying on Daire's bed in the attic after she had sent out her awareness in search of him.

Feeling instantly afraid, she knew that this 'meeting' was way overdue. The goddess of this world was not like her, preferring instead to work her ways subtly and guide mankind without their belief or their knowledge. Being possibly the oldest of her kind, this goddess was rarely known to take corporeal form and to do so now meant only one thing, Olivia had gone too far again.

Materialising some distance away, Olivia had decided to walk the rest of the way on foot, preparing herself mentally for what she thought would come.

'Merry meet, Olivia,' the goddess greeted, using the old way of welcoming and smiling as though with genuine warmth.

Olivia smiled too, bowing her head respectfully to the true goddess of this world.

'Merry meet, Morrìgan,' she replied, using one of the goddess' true names.

Smiling at their familiarity, Morrìgan patted the stone at her side, gesturing for the Fae Queen to join her.

Olivia walked forward, taking in the beauty of the goddess as she did so, seeing the long golden hair that was cut into a fringe just above her eyes, with the rest hanging straight well below her shoulders.

She saw a simple gown of green clinging provocatively to the curves of her body and the deep blue eyes that watched her intently as she approached.

The God-King's Fall

Once seated, they linked arms and stared out across the clearing like childhood friends, taking in the beauty of the world around them.

Tilting her head at seeing some sort of movement, Olivia finally noticed that it was the trees themselves that were the cause, as though they were consciously moving away from what was to come, causing the clearing to get bigger.

'They are in retreat,' Morrìgan informed her, as though in answer to her sister's thought, and then smiled sadly that it had finally come to this. 'They know what is to come,' she continued, turning to look at Olivia for her reaction.

Smiling nervously, the Fae Queen stared back with a flush of colour in her cheeks.

'As do we all,' she replied, sighing apprehensively at the coming battle.

'Do we?' the goddess asked, looking back with more than a little sympathy, which caused Olivia to frown back in puzzlement.

'I thought you had called me here to chastise me,' she replied, moving past the awkward moment.

Morrìgan nodded, her eyes narrowing into a scowl.

'All in good time,' she replied, looking back to the trees. 'You have caused irreparable damage to my world with your continued meddling, trusting not the gods of this world to keep their house in order,' she said, shaking her head sternly. 'Do you not think that we would have stopped the war that you so feared would occur?' she asked, frustration edging her words. 'We act discreetly, changing the flow of things at just the right time. You invited darkness here, where it was only a shadow before,' she admonished again, frowning now with irritation.

Olivia swallowed hard, feeling unable to reply for the moment.

'Why is it, do you think, that the daemon essence gets weaker rather than stronger as it is passed down from one generation to another and not as those cursed creatures had intended?' Morrìgan asked, nodding at the look of comprehension on the Fae Queen's face. 'Why do you think it is that when one slips past my web and becomes what they had intended, that they develop a flaw and perish over the simplest of things, like forgetting to use the earth's magick, for example?' Morrigan asked, staring coldly now at the dawning light in Olivia's eyes.

'Lucian!' gasped Olivia, shocked to her foundations on what she was hearing.

'He is but one of many and though it pains me to hurt one so young, it is a necessary step in the eradication of the darkness. A darkness that you set loose in *my* world,' Morrigan seethed, getting angrier the more she spoke. 'But for all my long-striving efforts, you keep insisting on changing the game and have now created a god! In *my* world!' she thundered, causing Olivia to flinch in surprise.

'The child is innocent, please spare him…' Olivia begged, remembering her promise to put his children first.

Morrigan's eyes widened at that and then narrowed with hidden intent.

'His boy will be safe and so too his daughter, but their line will get weaker from this point on,' the Mother Goddess replied, causing the Fae Queen to breathe again.

Waiting for the required amount of time to pass, Morrigan added her condition. 'But only if you play your part before you leave my world,' she continued, holding her eyes coldly.

Olivia launched herself from the rock and backed away nervously, seeing the goddess age before her eyes. Old and bent, the hag appeared, scooting to the edge before following her descent.

'You have forced my hand, Queen of Air, and I have already taken the necessary steps to remove you from this world,' she crowed, following Olivia back across the clearing. 'Did you think it was those filthy blood drinkers that destroyed your precious covens? I destroyed them, and with it your undeserving link to this world. *My world!*' she spat, following Olivia doggedly to the tree line.

'What do you want from me?' Olivia cried, backing away step by step, knowing in her heart and mind that she was no match for this goddess in her own world.

'There is a price to pay for your undying infatuation! A price that will now cost you dearly! You are to remove him from this world and yourself along with him!' she crowed, leering at her maliciously. 'Why is it, do you think, that the daemons still come?' Morrìgan asked, looking up at the retreating trees.

Olivia shook her head, unable to voice what she dreaded in her heart.

'They come because of him! Because of the daemonic essence that still resides in him!' Morrìgan answered for her and nodded when the Fae Queen shook her head. 'He has become what they had intended! He is like a beacon to them, a link to this world like you and your blessed covens! All want a foothold here in my world!' she seethed, enlightening her further.

Olivia shook her head, knowing that this dreadful crone of death was now playing for keeps.

'What the elements did to him for themselves to stay was what he unwittingly did for the daemons, and in enhancing the daemon taint in himself, he inadvertently bound the daemons here also,' Morrìgan cried, shaking her head in anger but then unexpectedly paused in her pursuit.

'But I have overshadowed the daemon in him, making him a god,' Olivia cried, knowing that he was no longer what he was.

Morrìgan nodded slowly, her eyes fixing on the distant trees again.

'Yes, and no,' she whispered, closing her eyes. 'You have fallen in more ways than one,' she announced, shaking her head sadly. 'In falling in love with him, you remain in the "now", unwilling as you are to leave him. In doing so, you have fallen from grace and are unable to see the things that you would otherwise have seen. I fear for you, sister, now more than ever,' she said, letting out a long, tired sigh.

Olivia already knew this, had known it even before the Horned God himself had told her so.

'You have indeed overshadowed his darkness, but you have not changed what is within, not one iota, only caged it with your will. You have made him a god, yes, but for which side?' she asked, looking deeply into Olivia's eyes.

'You must free him from your will before this is over. The underworld will continue to be connected to him with or without your cage, so you must free him to become what he is now meant to be. I have taken steps to see that the fight in him is lessened but it falls to you to undo what you did. You must him free!'

'Okay!' Olivia snapped and immediately regretted it. 'I am sorry, Morrigan. It's just that I have seen into him and it was...' she stopped, choking on the words.

'My sweet sister, you have so much love inside and it breaks my heart to see it curse you so,' the crone soothed, reaching up to stroke Olivia's hair. 'But there is only one way to mend the rift completely. Our dear brother should have left well enough alone and allowed your "Daire" to die heroically after defeating the Reaper,' she whispered, continuing before Olivia could respond.

'You both have a role to play in setting this right and like it or not, you will abide by my will on the way it is to be played out,' she said, her tone cold again.

'The dragons seem to think that there is a way to save him,' Olivia sobbed, looking lost and all alone.

'Have they told you how?' the crone screeched, peering up at her with one large eye.

'Only that they are playing the long game. Ddraig would say no more than that,' she replied, shrugging her shoulders and sobbing at the emotion it caused in her.

Morrigan nodded, her eyes narrowing with a calculating look.

'Dragons cannot be trusted! They would have been cast into the underworld themselves if not for their gift of leaving it. Nothing can cage them and more's the pity! They may help us, but are just as likely to side with the daemons. Remember this, they serve no one and their "long game" may be a very long time indeed. We cannot rely on them,' she replied decidedly, unwilling to negotiate the matter any further.

Olivia nodded, having already reached this conclusion herself.

'Am I allowed to assist him in the fight?' she asked, lowering her head pleadingly to look into her sister's eyes.

Morrigan shook her head, her stern expression returning.

'Not directly. However, you may influence what others do in aid of this world. The only direct action you may take is to free him of your will. Without the dragon's foresight, mine will have to do and you will abide by my wishes on this! You have a debt to pay if you want his children to survive,' she warned, looking at the Fae Queen until she nodded her understanding.

'What of their father?' Olivia cried, needing to know the goddess' intentions.

The hag stood silently for a moment, simply staring into the wide, desperate eyes of her sister.

'For the father, nothing,' she replied, turning suddenly to stare into the distance.

'Nothing!' Olivia thought, shaking her head and backing away again.

'The time is upon us,' Morrigan whispered, taking Olivia by the hand before she could withdraw it.

'No!' Olivia cried, desperately struggling against the grip, but Morrigan held firm and brought her authority to bear.

'No more direct involvement!' she crowed, dragging the screaming goddess away. 'The board is set and the pieces placed but it is for them to make the first move,' she cackled as a crow cawed in the gathering darkness, mixing in with the laughter of the crone.

***

Kristina looked up from her book with a confused expression upon her face. Glancing about, she felt unsure as to what had disturbed her.

She saw Francesca sitting open-mouthed, watching her favourite YouTube channel on her iPad. Lucian, who sat next to her, looked to be daydreaming as he stared off into space.

About to return to her reading, she saw her son's back arch and knew from experience what was about to happen.

Distracted by his movement, Francesca frantically reached for her iPad.

Rushing forward with her book falling from her lap, Kristina took her son in her arms and cradled him to her.

'Lucian!' she cried, summoning up the healing magick of the earth, in case it was needed. 'Please baby, it's okay. You're okay,' she soothed, dreading the prophetic speech that was sure to come.

'Light and dark are about to collide. Men and women should run and hide.'

'Struggle on, good lady, though you hear the daemons roar. It will only be time to leave when the wolves are at your door.'

'Armies of the world, gather your might. The darkness comes to end your sight.'

'Queen of Air, don't hide your fear. The gate is open and midnight is here.'

'Oak's last touch will close the gate. Love's last kiss will seal his fate.'

Kristina froze at yet another reference to the wolves and was about to break the spell when his body slumped down in exhaustion.

Without hesitation, she lifted her head and shouted aloud.

'House, protect us!' she called and breathed a sigh of relief when it instantly responded to her words by locking down immediately.

She had a sense of the house taking in a deep breath as the walls began to vibrate around them.

'Safe,' a sinister voice whispered, frightening her to the core.

A golden shield formed around the house, replacing that which was previously white.

'Daddy upgraded the house!' Francesca squealed in delight, clapping her hands together in nervous excitement.

'Thank you!' she called up to the ceiling before smiling at her mother, innocent of the impending danger they were in.

'How much more can we take?' Kristina thought desperately, feeling a sudden bout of panic that threatened to unhinge her.

Looking outside, she saw the golden light fade and remembered the same godly glow from Daire's hand after returning from the fight with the Reaper.

'They're coming!' Lucian whispered, looking fearfully at his mother to protect him. 'They are here,' he corrected, starting to visibly shiver.

Kristina sobbed at the need in his eyes and felt somewhat inadequate to the task ahead of her. Mentally shrugging off her dread, she knew that she had to step up now in their hour of need.

'It's okay Luc, it's okay. Daddy will kill it again,' she said, wishing desperately for his father to return. She froze at the look on her child's face.

Shaking his head, Lucian sat back and peered up in dread.

'There are so many,' he replied, biting his lower lip in an attempt to be brave.

'Something's out there!' Francesca screamed, her voice rising high as she pointed out into the darkness.

Looking closer, Kristina saw large silent shapes prowling past the French doors and all across her garden.

'It's the wolves!' she announced, sighing with relief before a thought struck her. 'They are retreating without even attempting to fight!' she realised, wishing that they were not alone and that at least one member of the group was with them.

A wolf pressed its nose up against the windowpane, causing Francesca to smile nervously at it before taking a step back.

'The house must consider them friendly to allow them so close,' Kristina thought, just as Francesca giggled and blew the beast a kiss.

'It winked at me!' she gasped, clasping her hands to her chest in a swoon-like manner.

Kristina looked at her as though she were mad and then turned back to the window, but the huge wolf had already moved on.

A deafening peal of thunder overhead shook the house abruptly, sending everyone cowering down in fright as the sky turned instantly red, casting a dreadful crimson glow over everything in sight.

Before looking up, Kristina knew that it was the moon that had changed and then saw that it was several times bigger than it had been just moments before.

'Oh my god!' she gasped, seeing this to be the worst kind of omen and wishing again that they were not alone in this fight. 'The Blood Moon,' she whispered, goosebumps rippling over her skin.

A low growl came out of the darkness from many places at once, a sound that quickly turned to whines from those stuck outside the golden protection.

Without knowing how, Lucian held up his hands and the shield extended to encompass all the wolves in the garden.

'How did you do that?' Francesca asked, clearly impressed by his show of power.

'*Unagi*,' the boy replied, causing his mother's blood to ice in her veins.

Packed together like sheep for the slaughter, the wolves' whining grew louder as something dreadful approached from the trees.

A roar unlike anything they had heard before came from within the forest before turning into screeches of anguish as the forest came alive in their defence.

Nothing could be seen from where they stood, but the sounds of what must have been hundreds of creatures could be heard fighting in the darkness.

'Cesca!' Lucian barked, snapping her terrified eyes to him. 'Kiss the symbol on your ring... Now!' he shouted when she did not respond fast enough.

Reflexively she raised her hand and kissed the ring on her index finger, closing her eyes as she did so.

Kristina watched in mute fascination, seeing that the fear in her eyes had gone when she finally opened them.

'Okay, I'm ready,' Francesca gasped, running into the kitchen to stand by the sink for a better view of the forest.

'Stand and cover the front window and if you see anything, let me know,' Lucian commanded, taking control of the situation as though born to it.

Kristina did not move, unable to comprehend this sudden change in him.

'Now, woman!' he snapped, causing her to flinch at the tone.

'Oh my god,' she gasped again, recognising the presence in that last command before rushing forward mechanically to take up her position by the window.

Scowling into the darkness, Lucian raised his arms into the air and closed his eyes in concentration. The sound of stone on stone sounded, grating even above the fearful sounds of forest battle, and the ground itself began to tremble from the impact of what was clearly approaching.

The trees rocked and waved in the distance, causing Francesca to squint her eyes at something that popped up above the trees for an instant.

Without warning, several lion-like creatures burst from the trees, huge and dark as the light of the moon cast a red sheen to their slick black skin. Burning red eyes studied the wolves evilly as they spread out before the barrier, their instincts telling them to hold at the danger ahead.

The growling of the wolves intensified, causing Kristina to shiver at the bestial sound.

The closest demon approached the shield and raked its claws across it experimentally before an explosion of golden light ripped the creature's front leg off at the shoulder, sending it hurtling several feet back into the air.

The creature hissed and spat as it scrambled to get away, but it was dragged back by golden tendrils of light that wrapped about its hind legs, causing the lion to roar in its agony.

Slowly dragged back towards the now-glowing shield, the lion's remaining claws raked up the grass as it fought against it. The second contact with the shield saw an end to the demon, seeing it explode into tiny golden embers that floated slowly back to the ground.

The remaining lions stalked back and forth in front of the shield, constantly looking back into the forest at what was quickly approaching and very nearly upon them.

Seeing this, Francesca held her hands out in a grasping motion and with a quick tug, she pulled a second demon to its death.

The explosion was blinding, the creature hitting the barrier head-on and causing even more glowing embers to float to the earth.

'Did you see that, Luc? I pulled it right into the shield!' she cried, clapping her hands together manically.

Scowling back at her, Lucian raised his hand to lift three lions into the air at once as fire instantly engulfed them.

'Try to kill them yourself, Cesca, in case the shield weakens,' he advised, seeing that the fire only hurt the lions and did not kill them as he had intended.

Changing tact, his hands tightened into fists and Francesca grimaced at the loud cracking noises of shattering bone that caused the lions to go limp in the air. As an over-measure, he opened his hands again and splayed his fingers wide, causing the lions to burst apart into black, fleshy chunks.

'That should do it!' he growled sadistically, looking at his sister with a wolfish grin.

'Ew,' Francesca cried and grimaced as though she were about to be sick.

'Three, one,' Lucian hooted, looking victoriously over to her. Competition on!

Francesca reached out to catch up the remaining two lions and on cupping her hands together, she made as though to mould them into an invisible ball.

Lifting them off their feet, she drew up the earth's energy and intensified it into a sphere of blinding white light.

The lions roared, biting and clawing at each other in their attempts to get free, but the ball of light burned brighter, appearing at last to look like the sun.

The roars of pain finally settled and eventually quietened as the last of the lions died by her hand.

'Three, all!' she fumed, staring competitively back at him with a determined look on her face, not willing to be outdone by her little brother.

As she let the magick go, an enormous figure crashed through the trees, shaking the very ground with its entrance as it stood towering above them. A huge rocky foot came crashing down, crushing the still smoking demons underneath it.

From the doorway, Kristina let out a gasp of fear as more of the stone giants took up positions around the house.

'Five, one,' Lucian replied, smiling triumphantly.

'Three, all!' she retorted, her face flushing with righteous anger. 'They were already dead!' she screamed, stalking towards him angrily.

'If they were dead then why did my golems kill them again? Five, one,' he replied, smiling at her annoyance.

'Mammy! Lucian's cheating again!' she stormed, looking for her to discipline him as though this was not out of character for him.

Eyes fixed on the towering mountainous rock figures that stood now with their backs to the house, Kristina ignored her as shock threatened to freeze her mind.

Fighting down the urge to simply lock her and the children away, she knew in her heart that she would damn them if she did. She remembered when her son must have made these mountainous things and knew that she would never forget the sounds of the grinding stones in the distance.

Taking a deep, composing breath, she shook the memory away before glaring at each of them in turn.

'Next time I'm going to play and then we'll see who wins!' she challenged, deciding to make a game of it.

A knock at the front door caused Kristina to spin on her heel and grip the doorframe for support at almost falling over in the turn.

Peering into the hallway, Kristina looked at the large front door in fear.

'House?' she whispered as her heart hammered in her chest.

The house growled low for a few seconds, and she thought it was a reaction to what was outside until she finally realised that it seemed to be aimed at her.

Picking up on the irritation, Kristina finally understood that the shield would have killed any who meant them any harm.

'Okay! I was just asking!' she whispered back, moving forward slowly to open the door.

As if in answer to her words the golden shield pulsed more brightly, causing her to roll her eyes as she opened the door.

Peeping out through the crack, Kristina flushed in response to the unexpected sight before her, for standing just outside the doorway were two enormous men, both heavily muscled and very naked.

Clasping their hands to cover their modesty, the larger of the two stared at her blankly while the other smiled as though without a care in the world.

'Sorry to bother you, but we were wondering if we could have a cup of tea or something?' asked the shorter of the two, his unusually bright golden eyes sparkling with mischief.

'I beg your pardon?' she asked, bringing her hand to her mouth in surprise while wondering who these men could possibly be.

'I told you she wouldn't go for it, Vince!' the larger man grumbled, his face flushing at their self-initiated predicament.

'Well, if you don't ask, you don't get, Gav!' Vince replied, looking at his friend with over-emphasised sadness.

Though shorter than the mountainous Gavin, Vince still stood nearly two feet taller than Kristina and possibly twice as wide. Turning back to her, he continued his look of woe by pouting with his bottom lip.

Francesca peeked around the door, having crept up on her mother when her back was turned and giggled at the sight of their barely concealed private parts.

'Aw, see! I'm changing back!' Gavin cried, stepping back to the path in embarrassment.

Unfazed by the little girl, Vince smiled down at her warmly and winked at her covertly in a show of friendship.

'Ask your mum to make me a cup of tea, will you?' he asked, switching back to his sad look.

With a sharp intake of breath, Kristina suddenly realised that these men were somehow the wolves from outside and felt her face flush a deeper shade of red at seeing them in this way.

'Oh my god,' she gasped, the truth finally dawning on her as she took a moment to really look at them.

Though abnormally large, she noticed that their height was due to their elongated bodies and not that of their legs, which appeared quite short by comparison. Built for power, with their large barrel chests, she noticed that they expanded massively at their intakes of breath.

Staring at their unusually bright eyes, she noted that Vince's were a golden brown, whereas Gavin's were many different shades of blue.

'Oh my god!' she said again, looking from one to the other and back again.

An awkward silence settled on the scene as they looked at one another without speaking.

'Mammy! Make them a cup of tea!' Francesca cried, scolding her into action.

'Oh, yes, of course,' her mother stammered, stepping back to let the huge men in. 'Have you any clothes?' she asked, her eyes innocently wide.

'Obviously not,' Gavin grumbled, frowning down at her as he passed.

Vince laughed and rolled his eyes in his friend's direction.

'Ignore him,' he whispered, leaning in on his way through. 'He's just embarrassed by his little twig there,' he smirked before walking on with his hands clasped before him.

Sitting on one of the sofas, the wolves sipped their tea and sighed contentedly at the creature comforts in life.

Dressed in some of Daire's old clothes, they felt somewhat more at ease in front of the children and began to relax a little, especially Gavin.

It had taken Kristina some time to find clothes that would fit, having had the giants rip many of the tops that had been presented to them.

'So… werewolves…' Kristina began awkwardly, breaking the uneasy silence between them. 'Why are you here of all places?' she asked, saying the first thing that came to mind.

Vince cleared his throat, seemingly happy to be engaged in conversation.

'There are not many places we can go,' he replied, shrugging his huge shoulders sadly. 'We appear too different to blend in with the humans and so aligned ourselves with the wizards, but after the attack, we realised certain things and decided to leave them to their own devices,' he replied, speaking with a look of honesty in his eyes.

Kristina raised her eyebrows questioningly, almost laughing at the quickness of his summery.

'Certain things?' she prompted, sipping her own tea and looking at them over the mug's rim.

'They put their shields up and left us to die!' Gavin growled, his blue eyes glowing suddenly in anger.

'That's not very nice,' Lucian observed, frowning up at the towering man who shrank back awkwardly from the unwanted attention, grumbling his agreement.

'But then old "LegenDaire" turned up and started kicking some arse, I mean… bums,' Vince continued, correcting himself in front of the children. 'We were blown away at the sight of him, having thought him a long time dead, and can't say how overjoyed we were to see him there. All demonised-up as he was, we knew it was him! Didn't we, Gav?' he asked, shouldering the large man so that he spilt his tea.

With a look of panic in his eyes, Gavin put his hand under the mug and paled at having spilt some on the sofa.

'Whoa!' he boomed, shaking his head at Kristina in a way that suggested it was not his fault.

'It's fine,' she chuckled, seeing him relax a little, not before he wiped at the stain with the back of his hand, glaring at his friend with a look that could kill.

Ignoring him, Vince carried on as though nothing had happened.

'We have a long history with him that goes all the way back to before the war,' he said, finishing his cup in one big gulp.

'Really? What history?' Francesca asked, leaning forward in her excitement.

'Why do you think he was called the Dark Wolf?' he challenged, winking mysteriously at the unrecorded secret. 'But that is a story for another time,' he said, standing up a little too fast and startling Francesca.

Smiling apologetically at the look in the little girl's eyes, he looked then to her mother.

'You have another guest heading this way, and we should go scouting anyway,' he added, looking down at his still-prone friend.

Gavin moaned, clearly quite comfortable where he was, before scooting forward in his seat and rising with a groan, blocking out much of the light as he did so.

A loud ripping noise announced the ruin of yet another piece of clothing and Vince sighed very audibly at yet another pair of joggers torn by his enormous friend.

***

Before the hand could rap upon the door it swung open aggressively, causing John to jump back in fright as the two massive wolves stepped out menacingly to stand at either side of the entrance.

'State your business!' Vince growled, giving the druid a look that could have curdled milk.

'I am here to see Kristina,' John replied promptly, looking from one wolf to the other in undisguised fear.

Desperately averting his eyes, the druid tried to look at anything other than the two men. Armed with the knowledge of how temperamental wolves could be, he forcefully kept his gaze at eye level.

'What for?' Gavin growled, leaning lower to leer at him aggressively.

John's mouth opened but the words failed him as both faces turned suddenly bestial, the 'crop tops' they were wearing ripping from them in shreds as their bodies began to transform.

'They are just teasing you, John, please come in,' Kristina said, coming to stand between the vicious-looking creatures.

Dropping to all fours, the wolves yipped and laughed as they slunk passed him, eyeing him fiercely the entire time.

The smaller wolf turned suddenly and stuck its nose up between the druid's legs, sniffling loudly before elevating him through the open doorway with its giant maw.

'Horned God!' John cried, lifting off his feet and then stumbling through the doorway.

More than a little shaken by the incident, John gathered himself together on the sofa with the colour still high in his cheeks.

Kristina, red-faced herself, struggled to contain her amusement at the two roguish wolves and found herself glad to have met them.

'I'm sorry John, they are very naughty,' she said, seating herself opposite him with her barely-contained amusement.

The children stood at the kitchen sink, staring out of the window in the hope that the demons would return, intent on continuing the competition.

'What are those statues you have outside?' John asked, changing the subject masterfully and causing Kristina to frown.

'The massive stone statues all around the house?' he elaborated, waving his arm in a circle above his head.

'Oh, the golems!' she realised, looking towards the kitchen with concern. 'Lucian's golems,' she continued in a lower tone with a shrug of her shoulders. 'We've been attacked already by some black lions, the house killed a couple and they killed the rest,' she said, gesturing towards the kitchen. 'It's a game to them now as to who kills the most,' she sighed, her eyes wide with the shock of it all.

'How are you holding up?' he asked, concerned by the manic look in her eyes and clearly seeing past her false bravado.

Shrugging her shoulders again, she simply nodded and felt unable to speak as her eyes brimmed with tears.

Moving to her, he took her in his arms and cradled her to him gently.

'It's okay to let it out, Kris. This is beyond comprehension and it's understandable to feel panicked by it all,' he soothed, patting her back comfortingly.

She nodded, wiping at her tears.

'They think it's a bloody game, John!' she cried, shaking her head in disbelief. 'I've encouraged it of course, so that they don't feel as I do,' she continued, looking up at him with fear in her eyes.

The druid nodded in sympathy, seeing that she was clearly out of her depth.

'You've done well,' he whispered, keeping his voice soft. 'Better than you know,' he added, smiling warmly at her.

Straightening, Kristina blew her nose in a handkerchief and began laughing off her need for a good cry.

'Why are you alone?' she asked at last, still dabbing at her eyes.

'The army will be here soon,' he answered, pulling out his notebook. 'I came ahead to discuss my findings regarding the prophecies,' he said, flipping through the pages. 'I believe that your son was foretelling the arrival of a demon god...' he said, turning over yet another page.

'He's had another one,' she interrupted, causing his head to snap up at her expectantly.

'Please say you wrote it down,' he begged, looking at her pleadingly and grimacing when she shook her head.

Smiling at last, she picked up the iPad and waved it at him.

'Cesca recorded it,' she replied, unlocking the device and passing it to him.

'Good girl!' John growled passionately, pressing the play button immediately.

After listening to the prophecy, John became animated which caused Kristina to start in alarm.

'There! There it is again!' he exploded, almost leaping up in his excitement, his long fingers fumbled through the pages of his notepad. 'Midnight! I think that reference is to do with a god of the underworld. I have read through some of the books of prophecy and the name "Midnight", shows up more than I would like,' he continued, leaning back and rubbing at his temples. 'I have not a clue as to what the "oak" references are, though, damned frustrating!' he sighed, continuing his massaging.

'What does it say about this "Midnight"?' she asked, glancing nervously towards the kitchen again.

John stopped what he was doing and leaned forward, sighing in frustration at the limits of his understanding.

'Born in the darkness, born from the fear. The world shall tremble, when Midnight is here.'

'Lost to the shadows, the oak will perish. Love is the key and theirs to cherish.'

'God in the darkness, god of their hate. The blades dark touch, will seal his fate.'

'So, which will kill Midnight, love or the sword?' she asked, frowning at the druid.

John sighed, shrugging his shoulders.

'I wrote the oak one down because Lucian spoke of it in his prophecy, but I think it's about something else. I just don't know,' he confessed, shaking his head in misery.

Kristina sat up straighter and stared off into space for a moment.

'What?' he asked, closing the book and reaching out to her, but she shook her head at his reassuring hand.

Waiting patiently until she was ready, he had the feeling that what she was about to say would change everything.

'In the old tongue, *Daire* means *oak*,' she whispered, hugging herself tightly and lowering her head.

John's mind was a whirl of questions as he quickly flicked through the pages and with pen in hand, he corrected the wording in his book.

Finishing his task, John rested his head back and closed his eyes.

'So much to take in… it sounds as though only Dark can kill Midnight, but at what cost?' he asked, sharing her concern.

'Dark blade's touch will seal his fate,' Kristina intoned, looking at the druid expectantly.

'Exactly! Dark's blade! So, Dark kills Midnight, right? Sounds good to me,' he replied, clapping his hands together. 'But first, we all have to survive long enough to see it,' he said, rubbing at his temples again and wishing that he had more time.

'There was another prophecy I read that turned my blood cold,' he whispered, keeping his eyes closed.

'When the demons are down and the tree is no more, Midnight will knock on three goddesses' door. He comes not to talk or to parlay in any way, his intent only is to take her last day.'

Kristina felt chilled by the words and stared at him until he opened his eyes.

'Are the oak and the tree referring to the same thing?' she asked, speaking the words in a small tone of voice.

'I can only assume so,' he whispered, knowing that these words would not ease her anxiety. 'The three goddesses' door?' he asked, hoping that she could shed at least a little light on the subject.

Kristina looked up suddenly as her children began to argue again, their tones turning more heated by the second.

'No, they're not!' Francesca screamed as her mother entered the room.

'What's the matter with the two of you? We may be fighting for our lives at any minute and you two are fighting amongst yourselves!' she admonished them, placing her hands upon her hips.

Francesca looked back with her fists clenched at her sides.

'Tell him then! Golems are neutral!!' she shouted, her face flushing red with anger.

Frowning at her in disbelief, Kristina shook her head incredulously.

'What on earth are you talking about, Cesca?' she asked, looking from one to the other.

'I made them, so they fight for me,' Lucian stated coolly, looking for his mother to side with him.

'They are neutral!' Francesca screamed, her face shaking in fury. 'The points only count if you kill them yourself!!'

Chapter Fourteen

The silver ring was beautifully crafted, Daire thought, looking at the interwoven silver knots that ran down each side and the looping triquetra symbol that was placed between.

Remembering when he had made his own ring, he found it mind-blowing that they were nearly identical in appearance.

He saw that they were the same in almost every way except for the central design, and began wondering which of the rings had ultimately influenced the other.

His old ring that was now his daughter's had multiple enchantments hammered into its metalwork but, above all else, he had infused the ring with the intention of creating the perfect mind. One mind or many, its function was to focus one's mind to the task at hand, unifying the conflicts within into a singular, unhindered desire.

The Blood Sword had a similar enchantment placed upon it, which had been his sole reason for creating the ring in the first place after putting the sword of power away.

The 'charm of making', his father had called it, the ability to imbue magick into his crafting so that it could work independently on your behalf.

The trick Daire had found in making it all work, was to craft the item from scratch and to put the intention of its abilities into every stroke of his hand. Willing the intent of what the talisman would do, he had then carved sigils into its depths at each stage of crafting.

It had taken him many years to perfect the art, learning new ways of strengthening the residing magick so that it no longer waned after extended use.

Holding up his hand, he turned the ring around with his thumb and could sense the great unknown power locked tightly within.

'What do you do?' he whispered, staring at the looping design of its face.

'I thought it would have been a sword,' a deep voice mused, sounding disgruntled as it spoke from behind him.

Turning, Daire looked up at the Horned God with a questioning smile.

'What do you mean?' he asked, rising to his feet.

Herne regarded him dubiously for a moment before narrowing his eyes.

'You do not know the gift she has bestowed upon you?' Herne asked with amusement, unable to hide his mocking tone.

Frowning up at the towering giant, Daire held up his hand for him to see more clearly.

'A ring?' he asked in a goofy voice, sarcasm dripping from his tongue.

The god threw back his majestic head and roared in laughter, his great shoulders jerking with genuine amusement.

'I will miss conversing with you, Dark,' he admitted, wiping tears from his eyes. 'That there...' he said in an ominous tone and cutting Daire off before he could reply, '... is Excalibur!'

Of course, he had heard of the legendary sword.

'Who had not?' Daire thought while staring down at the ring in disbelief. 'She called it by another name,' he replied, turning it around again with his thumb until it rotated full-circle.

'It has many names, as have we all, but it matters not which she used, that is what was the sword of the king,' the god assured him, spreading his arms wide for emphasis. 'Never one to stay with its wearer long, mind you, so don't go getting attached to it, my friend,' he continued, smiling sadly at the younger god.

'So, I guess that makes me king,' Daire replied, raising his head regally. 'One land. One king,' he announced, raising his arms into the air with a classic Rocky pose.

Herne erupted again, causing the land to tremble under their feet.

'A God-King, perish the thought,' he chuckled, but his expression darkened momentarily at the suggestion. 'This has been given to you to see an end to the daemon presence and that is all,' he warned, frowning down at him suddenly.

Daire grimaced with a look of disgust at what was being implied.

'I don't seek power, though everyone seems hell-bent on thrusting it upon me. I want only the strength to defend my children,' he retorted with a frown of annoyance.

The Horned God dipped his head at the rebuke and sighed in sorrow.

'There has never been one to elevate themselves so quickly as you have done, my friend. That said, I do see you, Dark, and say to you now, that if you do indeed perish, I will watch over your children in your stead as recompense for my doubt,' he replied, bowing his head again in apology.

Unable to speak for the moment, Daire nodded at the heartfelt sentiment and extended his hand in friendship.

***

Standing at the edge of the forest and within the shadow of the trees, Daire looked at the faces of his children peering out of the kitchen window.

Seeming to stare right at him, he stared back longingly and wished with all of his heart that he could hold them one last time.

He had intended to spend the night with them before he finally went into battle but knew now that it was not meant to be.

Feeling thankful that they at least looked unafraid, he smiled in gratitude for this small mercy as tears glistened in his eyes.

'I will die before you do,' he swore, longing to take them in his arms and never let them go.

Looking up at the red moon, he knew that this could no longer be, for the gate had been opened and the time was upon him before he was ready.

'As is always the way of such things,' he thought sadly, thinking that you could never really be ready for such events as this.

Pulling him out of his thoughts, two wolves padded up to him with glowing red eyes, lit now by the light above.

Whining in anticipation of what was to come, they seemed to nod at him in determination.

'You cannot help me in this fight, my friends,' he whispered, wiping at his fallen tears with the back of his hand. 'Will you stay here and protect them?' he asked, looking once more towards his children.

They were arguing now and he heard his daughter's enraged scream at something his son had said.

Smiling at the pair, he burned their images into his mind as more tears came unbidden to his eyes.

'I love you so much,' he whispered, his tears blurring his vision as their mother came into view.

Her features were stern as she placed her hands upon her hips in her familiar way.

'Please protect them,' he sobbed, willing her to step up and be counted against what would surely come if he failed this night.

Hearing the slow grating sound of stone, he lifted his head to see the towering forms of the golems looming over him and noted that all their heads were fixed on him.

'My clever boy,' he sighed, feeling a swell of pride suddenly. 'My brave little wolf,' he whispered, turning again to the house with a steely expression.

'Let nothing through,' he ordered, putting his will into the house. 'Protect them with every ounce of your being,' he added, holding the ring of power up before him.

'Until I lay in ruin,' came the deep reply before the shield brightened assuredly, illuminating him in its golden light.

***

Kristina's head snapped up at the sudden flare of light and she saw him in that instance.

Smiling suddenly, she was about to point him out when she saw him shake his head and raise his hand in farewell, causing her to sob suddenly for the reason he could not stay.

Her hand came up in return but the shield faded and he was swallowed again by the darkness.

'Goodbye,' she whispered and tried unsuccessfully to hide her tears.

***

Walking through the trees, Daire could feel them following and shook his head before turning to wait.

'Come on, I know you're there!' he called, his voice sounding thick in the dense forest.

Ever so slowly, two wolves detached themselves from the trees and began groaning loudly at being found out so soon.

'I need you to stay,' he said, pointing back towards the house. 'I want them safe, first and foremost,' he continued, his voice breaking as he lowered his arm.

One of the wolves came forward and raised itself onto its hind legs before it shortened in height to become more humanlike.

'We want to fight beside you,' Vince replied, stopping before him. 'We want to fight with you, as we used to,' he went on, looking sheepishly to the floor.

Daire felt touched by the admission and walked over to embrace the monstrous creature.

'I know you do, and I would like nothing more than to have you with me, but what I am asking of you is more important. I'm entrusting you with the safety of my children, you and no other. Will you do that for me, my old friend?' he asked, feeling his facial features twitch with anxiety.

Vince was silent a moment and was seriously struggling with the notion of not following him into battle, but at last he nodded, though still stared at the floor like a scolded schoolboy.

'I trust this to none but the wolves,' Daire continued, causing the wolf to look up. 'I need them to be safe, now and always,' he added, pleading for him to comply.

'None shall pass us,' Vince promised, pride suddenly shining in his golden-brown eyes as he held out his hand to his god.

'Though they be stronger and will take us with ease, we will die before the demons pass by us,' he swore, puffing out his chest bravely.

Stiffening at the contact of the handshake, a golden hue radiated into him as it did to all the wolves, highlighting them briefly as they hid in the darkness.

'Now you are stronger than them and need rely on no one from this point on,' Daire announced, nodding his head with a fierce determination in his eyes.

'What have you done?' Vince gasped, flexing his arms experimentally before smiling at Gavin who smiled back sinisterly while still in his wolf form.

'I have given you the light while it is mine to give,' Daire answered, giving his ancient friend a reassuring smile. 'You have been dealt the shorthand for far too long and it's about time that changed,' he continued, bowing low before them.

The trees sensed him pass and silently shed their leaves as once they had, honouring him again for what was to come.

Demon carcasses lay everywhere, battered into ash as far as the eye could see, causing him to think of his son again and the power that he wielded.

The tall, reaching trees were not unscathed by the conflict, he realised, seeing that some had actually been felled by the battle.

'Where are you, Liv?' he whispered, feeling a sudden fear that almost crippled him. 'I need you,' he begged, feeling like a condemned man on his way to the noose.

He could sense what awaited him in the glade, could feel the hateful power emanating from the place where all things of note seemed to take place.

'Fear is the mind-killer,' he whispered, but there was no denying the dread he felt and no possible way to overcome what awaited him.

'I go, so that they may live,' he growled, gritting his teeth and steeling himself as best he could.

The trees abruptly ended a mile or so from where they had once been, leaving a vast open area of flat blackened earth that was lit now by an alien moon from another dimension.

His breath caught in his throat at finally seeing what waited and not even his sense of them could have prepared him for what he saw.

A shiver of fear almost dropped him to his knees as he looked at those who should never have been allowed.

As silent as the grave in this red, demonic darkness, they had massed together on the back half of the battlefield, seemingly waiting for him to come.

Huge bat-like creatures with formidable black wings circled silently above, buffeting the ground with the cold night's air.

The horror he felt almost crippled him at the sight of what could only be the Reaper, seeing it stand tall and renewed in the midst of them all.

'It can't be!' he gasped, hoping for a moment that it was a different creature altogether, but as the cowled head turned, he knew that it was indeed the very same creature.

The ring of power burned bright suddenly, causing him to raise his free hand to shield against its glare.

'*Caledfwlch!*' he screamed, throwing his hand up high as the light flared into the darkness.

The white brilliance lit the field and blinded those closest to its touch, driving them back beyond its far-reaching light.

Sudden pain lanced through him, a crippling agony that took him by surprise and drove the breath from him.

Taking a faltering step back, his hand still pointed up to the heavens as though held there by the ring itself. All definition of his hand was lost within the cold light and he knew that something was wrong when the pain began to increase.

The power of the talisman kept building, the light of it becoming brighter and brighter, but it seemed unable to unleash at the last moment.

'Work, damn you!' Daire cried, almost overwhelmed by the power of the ring.

Seeing his pain, the deathly silent army erupted into spontaneous roars of hate and as one they launched themselves into their attack.

'Olivia!' Daire bellowed, feeling as though he was being stripped away, layer by agonising layer.

Throwing out his good hand, he brought what might he had to bear but found that even his magick was now denied him, the pain from the ring appearing to hamper his will.

'I am sorry, brother,' a voice whispered to him, a note of deep regret sounding in the words. 'This was not my intention,' the voice continued, sounding full of shame and utter remorse.

Daire simply stood there, with the army of darkness bearing down upon him and began to cry at what had been done to him again.

'Am I destined to always be betrayed?' he cried, his eyes filling with bitter tears.

'I am truly sorry,' the Horned God whispered remorsefully, the guilt he felt evident in his tone.

As if in answer to his cry, the wind suddenly tore into the advancing army as fire spontaneously erupted through their ranks with a fury never before seen.

'We are with you, brother!' the elements raged, hammering into the horde with brutal efficiency.

Many of the advancing demons were cut down in seconds but many more seemed resistant to the attacks and continued their headlong rush across the red-cast field.

Suddenly, a great chasm ruptured through the blackened earth, creating a divide between them as the earth itself rose in his defence.

'Fight!' a voice screamed, though in his mind or out loud he could not tell.

'I am betrayed,' he whispered, falling to his knees, the fight in him dying with the remainder of his will.

'Fight!' the voice screamed again, a voice he suddenly recognised through his agony. 'My Daire, you must fight!' Olivia screamed, causing him to force his head up to look for her.

Through the haze of pain, he sought her face one last time before the darkness was finally upon him.

'I wish you were with me,' he cried, seeing a demonic lion sprint ahead of the rest.

'Would you leave them to fight alone?' her voice challenged, though sounding more distant this time. 'Will you not fight for them?' she cried, her scream fading into the thunderous charge of the horde.

The image of his children sprang into his mind and he saw again their looks of excitement as they stared out of the window.

'Fight!' she screamed, sounding so far away now that he thought he might have imagined it.

The lion leapt high into the air, its black claws extending maliciously for the kill.

Anger flared in him then, his wrath igniting from the very core of his being. The agonising chains of restraint lifted from him, the power of his rage releasing him from what the ring was doing.

He felt free suddenly, uncaged, and the dark power within him began to flow like ice in his veins, fusing suddenly with the golden light of the goddess.

He saw the demon baring down upon him as though in slow motion, its wide jaws extending wide in anticipation.

Silver light burst from him suddenly, seeming to resonate right out of his pores as the lion finally reached him.

On contact, the blinding silvery light caused the creature to disintegrate and to brake against him like water on rocks.

Lifting his arms out wide, Daire threw his unchained might at the rest of them, driving them back from the combined might of gold and darkness.

The demons fell before him, crumbling to ash as the Bloods had at their destruction.

Caught by the similarity, he could not help but wonder if that would happen to him when it was his time to fall.

Adapting to the change in him, the ring brought on a fresh wave of pain that caused him to cry out in anguish.

He felt himself separating, the different aspects of himself ripping free, and he suddenly knew what the ring was trying to do to him.

One of the huge bats swooped down on him with the talons of an owl extending out for the kill.

With a crushing gesture, Daire clenched his fist and the demon dropped like a stone to twitch uncontrollably upon the dead earth.

Staggering with pain, he dropped again to his knees as a wave of dizziness threatened to unbalance him.

The demons were still again and seemed unwilling for the moment to test themselves against him. Lining up at the edge of the fissure, all their lusty eyes were fixed firmly upon him.

A blast of sudden wind hit them from behind, those closest to the edge tumbling into the chasm as the remaining mass withdrew in growls of dismay.

With a gasp of shock, Daire looked at the dimensional tear and saw it stretch open as a lone cloaked demon stood tall from within, its burning fiery eyes fixed on him coldly from beneath its deeply-hooded cowl.

All the gathered demons cowered back from this other with a look of dread, its position among them clear as it raised its arms high.

The demon's eyes burned like lava as large leathery wings spread out behind it. Black as pitch and as depthless as the hell that spawned it, this demon sent its terrible power into this world.

'No!' Daire cried, feeling the wind die and the fire fade as the chasm too began to close.

He realised that the power of this new demon was too much for the elements to handle and knew now that it was only a matter of time before he was undone.

Closing his eyes, he sent out his senses in search of the elements but it was as though they had never been.

'So, this is it,' he whispered, looking at the massing demons gathering once more before him.

'Too many and too strong,' he thought, taking in their mass and the might of this new demon.

Suddenly, the air became alive with static before hundreds of arcing bolts of lightning crackled from the trees, striking the slowly approaching army from the side.

Glancing to his left, Daire could see robed figures step from the trees and realised with relief that he was no longer alone in this fight.

From his right, more energy lanced forth, sending many more from the underworld into whatever afterlife awaited them.

New pain coursed through him, the ring of power seemingly about to explode from the energy trapped within it.

Crippled in agony, he tried to pry the ring free and cast it from him but his attempts were futile, his efforts clearly wasted.

Looking back, he saw Charlie's look of concern but had not the time to acknowledge him as the Reaper rose up before him.

Raising his good hand, he sent out a bolt of silvery lightning but the Reaper sidestepped swiftly and took the blow in the shoulder, spinning it into the mass of approaching demons.

'It wants to hurt my children!' Daire raged and then threw his arms wide, unleashing his very being into his next attack.

The bright ball of light that looked to be held in his hand, blended suddenly into the rest of him, and he shone like a star as he took the offensive.

***

Moving through the forest, the mages had heard the sounds of conflict along with the silvery light they saw flooding through the trees.

'Damn!' Charlie cursed, running headlong through the undergrowth, heedless now of the stealth he had intended.

Upon entering the open expanse of land, he saw the source of the light and shared a look with Michael.

The legend stood alone, a star of silvery-white light held in his hand and the bodies of demons, or what was left of them, laying all about him.

Without hesitation, the mages sent their power into the enemy, creating a wall of devastation before the legendary warrior.

Training all their lives for a battle such as this, the magick of the battle mages was far beyond what the other disciplines could achieve. The demons died before them, unable to withstand the destructiveness of their magick and Charlie's excitement grew at their early success.

A shout of alarm from Kim brought his attention back to the legend, seeing him begin to shine like the star he held in his hand.

'Reaper!' Kim shouted, pointing the creature out as it stalked forward.

Charlie gasped, seeing the towering demon for the very first time just as Daire faltered again, the bright ball of light pulsing erratically and out of control in his hand.

Fighting against the pain, Daire saw the demon approach, its hideous hands reaching out for him with the magick from both the wizards and the mages arcing around it.

Suddenly, the dark horde clashed against the mages, ending all of their cohesion with a terrible gnash of teeth.

The ground shook as demonic fire erupted everywhere, casting the legend's defenders screaming to the earth.

A fresh wave of pain seared up through Daire, causing him to fall back and writhe in agony. He felt as though he was being stripped again, feeling everything that had been thrust upon him pull free suddenly and leave him as he had been all through the ages. Though unable to fight against it, he recognised and understood what was happening to him, having gone through it before with the elements. He knew that the pain he felt was that of change. It was as though he was on fire again, burning into something different.

'Get up!' her voice screamed, but she was cut off again almost immediately.

'Where are you?' he cried, searching desperately for her face.

Looking down at the ring, he raised it to his face and snarled in anger.

'Finish it!' he screamed, venting his frustration at the object. 'The lady would not have gifted it to cause me harm,' he knew, fighting his way to his knees.

Shaking his head in an attempt to get his bearings, he saw that he was surrounded by mages as they fought in his defence.

Feeling a rush of respect for the hardy warriors, he fought for his inner peace that now seemed so elusive to him.

Had he his old ring, he would not have had a problem he thought, remembering the enchantment that he himself had placed upon it.

Looking down in anger, the thought struck him to cut the talisman from him, to draw forth his red sword and remove it, finger and all.

As though sensing his intent, a fresh wave of pain sent him to his back as he silently screamed out his agony.

He felt a tearing sensation as the golden light of the goddess and the demonic darkness were finally stripped from him, feeling also the dragon's wildness and the serenity of Spirit all leave him at that moment.

Panting in relief as the pain finally subsided, he was as he had been before the elements had changed him. He was a man again, himself, without the corruptions that had altered him.

A deep rumble of thunder sounded and the air felt charged suddenly with its terrible power.

Looking between the mages, Daire saw again the feared hooded demon with its burning eyes fixed directly upon him.

Clear-headed at last, he saw that it appeared to be contained within the gaping maw of the gateway and that for some unknown reason, it was stuck there.

'What are you waiting for?' he screamed, glaring back in defiance. 'Who are you?' he roared, hating the creature and all it represented.

Looking at the ring once more, his eyes widened momentarily with a clarity he had previously been denied.

'It's trying to correct me!' he realised suddenly, understanding that it not only looked like his old ring but had the same design enchanted within it, only on a much grander scale.

Caladfwlch was trying to unify him, not just mentally as his ring had done but in every way, rebuilding him from the inside out.

With his vision unfocused, he sought the magick of the ring and saw its power struggling to break free, the star-like light hampered by that of a godly gold.

Rage renewed within him but it was a man's anger now that the demonic influence had been loosed.

'Gold is the god's colour,' he knew this, for it was also his own, or had been until the ring's might had taken it from him.

'Damn you to hell!' he screamed, feeling the sting of betrayal for the very last time. 'You will come to rue this day!' he growled, speaking to those who bound him.

The ring was indeed the same as the one his daughter now wore, its power was in unifying its wearer in a way that his ring never could. Not only to be of one mind in the moment of need but to simply be one in all aspects.

He was unnatural to this world as he had been and had lost his right to be here, no longer truly belonging to this dimension after his corruption.

The ring was attempting to fix that, to correct him and bring him back into harmony, against the wishes of the one who ruled here. To this end, the ring had stripped him down before it could start over, correcting him so that he could at last be in total control of himself.

He saw for the first time that his golden aura... her golden aura... was his no longer and that it had changed now into that of starlight.

'Like that of the ring!' he thought, realising that this starlight was not issuing from the ring at all, but was what his aura should have been all along.

Clenching his teeth in rage, he cupped his hand over the ring and with all of his considerable force of will, he poured his heart, soul and might against that which had secretly held him.

***

Behind the demon horde at the far end of the clearing, the druid and witch factions gathered within the shadow of the trees.

Coming up behind the dark army, they saw the steady stream of demons entering this world from the tear beyond, from the gateway that linked this world to that of the underworld.

Appearing like a giant rip, the doorway looked as though an invisible fabric had been torn apart and the black void of space gaped ominously behind it.

White-faced with fear, John took Chloe's hand and brought it to his lips.

'Until next we meet, fair lady,' he whispered, looking deep into her eyes.

The high priestess looked up at him, her deep blue eyes mirroring the fear she witnessed in his but she was unable to find the words she needed to respond.

'We must act now,' he continued in a tight voice, seeing the plight of their comrades on the other side of the field.

He could see that the demons were stronger than those they fought and that the magick used against them was clearly insufficient.

He smiled despite himself, seeing great skill employed by the mages and their instinctive reactions to the threats around them.

'My turn,' he whispered, taking a deep breath before raising his arms high into the air.

The blackened earth heaved and pulsated as the druidic order put their knowledge to the test.

Chloe gasped in surprise as the land began to rise, thinking that it looked like a newly-forming volcano as it covered the gateway with its mass.

On the clapping of his large hands, the earth compacted and then compressed with a sound like crunching glass as it sealed the tear within it.

'That should hold them,' he said hopefully before holding his breath in fear.

The demons already across turned at the noise and threw their might against them.

Chloe sat down and linked with the priestesses around her, drawing from the power of a hundred or more circles that had survived the night of the vampires.

A shield of white laced with veins of gold rose between them, just as the advancing demons began to attack.

'Goddess help us!'

***

The betraying containment of gold shattered suddenly, the godly binding breaking as he drove his wrath against it.

Caladfwlch's power unleashed immediately, giving him its might as it completed its untethered design upon him.

Starlight burst from him with such force that it sent the mages and demons alike sprawling to the ground, turning many from the underworld to ash in the process.

Recovering quickly from the unexpected blast, the battle mages came together quickly, forming themselves into small, tight circles around him.

Where the demons fell, they shattered like black glass upon the scorched earth, the light of the awakening god too much for them to handle.

Rising out of their ashy remains, the Reaper stood tall before darting past the tightly-grouped mages in a blur of motion. Stopping before the starlight, the haunting demon launched itself at it but screeched as the intense light burned it back.

A rhythmic whooshing noise sounded overhead as air was suddenly blasted down upon them, closely followed by a deafening sound of violence as the heavy ordinances caused devastation upon the army of demons.

'Helicopters!' Daire thought, his eyes seeking the one who had called them.

Charlie caught his eye as more commands were given into the radio at his lips.

'Mankind's defence indeed,' Daire thought excitedly, seeing more of the aircraft lining up all around the forest.

Faint booms sounded, one after another, at first thought to be thunder but for the repetitiveness of the sound.

Realising his mistake, Daire saw the destruction caused on the battlefield, the explosive shells decimating the unprepared demons.

Charlie looked back to him and nodded gravely with a wink of his eye.

'Tanks!' he mouthed, showing a toothy grin of satisfaction.

'They're going to win this without me!' Daire thought, blinking through the haze of his transformation.

A feeling of warmth swelled suddenly within him as the golden light settled back into place, before abruptly changing into starlight as it finally became his own.

With growing excitement, he knew that this was the first of his influences being returned to him.

With this godly grounding in place, he felt the familiar essence of the elements settling within him, bringing a calmness of mind and a knowledge of what was to come.

Merging into the silvery light, the spirit element caused him to grow even brighter and he had a fleeting wish that the ring would stop there, leaving him without those that were to follow.

Shocked back into the moment by a momentous explosion, he saw that it was the gateway and thought for a moment that it had been destroyed by one of the many missiles flying through the air.

The ground around him shook like an earthquake, sending himself and all who fought with him flat on their backs.

Standing in the darkness, the hooded demon stood again just inside the gateway with its fiery eyes burning into his own. Huge wings like that of a dragon flapped behind it as the demon stood there with a look of frustration.

'It's a god!' he whispered, realising at last what this one must be. 'He can't cross over, or he would have by now!' Daire shouted, struggling to point out the creature with his outstretched arm.

Looking over at his words and then following the line of his direction, Charlie frowned back at him in confusion.

'Who?' the mage growled, shaking his head in confusion.

'The god of the underworld!' Daire cried, gesturing frantically back to the gateway with his head as a numbness settled upon him.

Raising its hands, the demonic god sent out its might for the second time, striking now at the world of man and the technology that had denied him his early victory.

Daire could only watch as the helicopters spun out of control, and wanted to turn away when they finally exploded on impact with the ground.

Fiery mushroom-clouds formed above the wreckages, billowing up like the cowled figure that suddenly rose before him.

'Midnight,' the Reaper hissed, as though confirming the name of this unholy god.

'I will kill him,' Daire swore, choking out the words in defiance.

Gripping him by the chin, the Reaper wagged a long forefinger in front of his face as though warning an unruly child to be silent.

Lifting him off his feet by his neck, the towering black form swooped past the desperately fighting mages and back across the battlefield.

Kim's scream of alarm faded behind him as the snarls of hate drowned her out, and he knew then with dread in his heart, where he was being taken.

With the legend taken and mankind's defences laying in ruin upon the battlefield, the war was lost and nothing and no one could change that. The night belonged to the demons!

**

Kristina flinched, causing the children to startle with her as they sat in fear beside her.

The flash of light that had caused her reaction had been closer by far than that of the others, and the accompanying sounds a moment later did nothing to ease her growing fears.

Knowing in her heart that it would not be long before they had to fight again, Kristina felt her whole body beginning to tremble.

Sitting upon the chaise in her bedroom, the three watched the light show that lit up the sky in the distance.

Recognising the flickering flash from the wizard's lightning, she knew that the battle had begun, and guessed that Daire was right in the middle of it.

A steady stream of what looked like moonlight had been the first sign that something was happening, shining brightly through the trees as though from some fallen star.

The ghostly rays from whatever it was had come blasting through the gaps in the trees, lighting up the garden with a cold, colourless light that chased away the sickly red of the moon.

Kristina did not know how she knew exactly, just knew without a doubt that the light was somehow from Daire, sensing him in its touch as surely as she had anything in her life.

Keeping this knowledge to herself, she hugged her children closer and prayed silently for his safe return.

Seeing him in the darkness for that brief moment, she had felt a pang of sorrow for him and a regret that gnawed at her still.

She understood at last that all he ever wanted was to protect his children, and her too, she supposed. She had seen his fear and had wept for him, wishing with all her heart that he would come back as he always had, the conquering hero.

Looking down at her daughter, she saw that her eyes were wide and fearful, her small hands pulled up tightly to her chest with the knuckles of her clenched fists pressing white under the skin.

Hugging her a little tighter, Kristina stroked her arm affectionately and then leant down to kiss the side of her head comfortingly. Smiling at the thought of her brother getting jealous, she turned to him and was about to do the same to him until she caught the look in his brooding dark eyes.

With his hands clasped before him, Lucian had his index fingers pressed over his pursing lips, pointing up to his nose as he frowned in concentration.

Feeling her gaze upon him, he scowled up at her with a look of annoyance.

'I'm fine,' he snapped, turning back to the window to continue his brooding.

She stared at him for a moment, recognising the look and tone of his father and began to fear that he was no longer her little boy.

'Daire?' she called, whispering out the name that caused his head to turn questioningly.

Seeing the look of concern on her face, the brooding expression faded to leave only her son's face behind.

'I love you, Mammy,' Lucian said naturally, cuddling into her as he always had.

The light show in the distance was getting brighter but there was a new sound now, a deep thrumming whoosh that got steadily louder, causing all three of them to look at one another in alarm.

The God-King's Fall

'Look Mammy, lights!' Lucian shouted, jumping to his feet and pointing out into the night. 'Helicopters!' he shouted, pressing his face up against the glass.

Spread out in some sort of tactical formation, several large helicopters flew too low and too fast to be anything other than the military aircraft they were.

With his eyes widening in rapture, another squadron flew directly overhead.

'Oh my god! This is bloody crazy!' Kristina cried, pulling her son back and gaining a scowl from her daughter.

Coming to a stop a little distance away, missiles streaked across the treetops, turning the children's excitement to fear in a heartbeat. Adding to this, Kristina heard a deep thunderous boom that was quickly followed by another, sounding as though it came from somewhere down in the valley.

The deafening sound of projectiles ripping through the air caused them all to cower down, 'the sound of it is like nothing you'd hear in the movies,' Kristina thought, hearing them tear through the sky with an unholy efficiency.

The eventual impacts shook the ground with an earth-shattering ferocity, causing the red night to flash suddenly with moments of gold and copper as the shells found their marks.

Fighter jets streaked across the sky, adding their might to what was happening below and sounding for all the world like deafening peals of thunder as they roared overhead.

Heavy gunfire began and seemed not to stop as the hovering copters sparked into life.

Pulling the children away from the window, Kristina covered their eyes as the glass vibrated violently and seemed about to break.

'Good god!' she cried, clutching her children close as they backed away together. 'This is an all-out war!' she wailed, turning them to the stairs.

The house lit up suddenly with a blinding flash of light and a moment later it shook to its foundations as a deafening explosion of sound vibrated through them.

Breaking loose from her mother's grip, Francesca ran back to the window, her eyes panicked but with a need to see more.

Screaming for her to return, Kristina ran back to grab her by the wrist and drag her back from the war outside her window.

Unable to stop herself, she gasped on glancing out herself as huge chunks of earth fell slowly back to the ground, causing her to stop and watch in shocked fascination.

'No!' she cried, bringing her hand to her mouth, seeing the helicopters rotate out of control and the speeding fighter jets veer off sharply into the nearby mountainside.

The huge explosions cast their golden light again amid the reddened darkness and she felt what it must be like to look into the underworld.

'How can he survive this?' she thought, thinking that their father had perhaps already met his fate. 'How can any of us survive this?' her mind quailed, seeing the destruction just outside her window.

A roar sounded, rising even above the din of battle, a sound that sent fresh shivers of fear rippling through her, for it was a roar of victory but uttered not from the mouths of her kind.

A low howl moaned up to her from outside, and she felt a sinking sensation in the pit of her stomach.

'Oh, no,' she sobbed, dreading the reason behind it. Lucian began to shake violently as he backed up into her.

'They're coming!' he whispered, clutching at her dress from behind and causing his sister to lift her father's ring to her lips.

Seeing her do this, Lucian turned to face his mother with a look that was no longer his own.

'Now, we fight!' he growled, speaking the words through gritted teeth. 'House! Fail me not in our hour of need,' he called before striding purposefully from the room.

The children took up their positions again at the kitchen window, with their mother shaking behind them as adrenaline coursed through her veins.

Low growls came from just below the windowsill and were soon taken up by all the wolves outside.

Kristina instinctively reached for the door to let them in, but a vicious snarl of warning stopped her dead in her tracks.

'Stay outside then!' she snapped, shocked by their commitment to protecting them.

Lucian clapped his hands together and the golems crouched low, readying themselves for what was to come.

Francesca cracked her knuckles, mimicking the way her father used to and then stared out calmly, the ring focusing her mind to the task at hand.

Calling up the power of the earth, Kristina found that it was already there, summoned by the enormous will of her children and maybe one other, she thought, as she looked at her son.

'Visualise and commit! Don't think about it!' Lucian ordered in his father's deep, commanding tone before nodding to his mother as though letting her know she was up to the task.

'Okay,' she answered reflexively, hearing him say it so many times in the past before, and cursing herself for responding at all. 'He is not Daire!' she told herself, anger suddenly driving away her fear.

That was all the time they had as large skeletal creatures broke suddenly from the trees, with movements too swift for human muscle to achieve.

Kristina saw long, skinny pale limbs and hairless heads that must have given rise to the skeleton warriors of myth and was taken by surprise by the speed of the assault.

On impact with her home's defence, they roared with an unexpected bass to their voices before the shield cut them off, ending their existence.

She stared open-mouthed as the golden shield sparked from the mass of contacts, instantly reminded of flies being zapped in the village chip shop the summer before.

Wave upon wave of the creatures ran headlong at the shield, attacking now from many angles at once, causing Kristina to finally realise what they were attempting.

'They are trying to weaken the shield!' she shrieked, having seen a similar tactic used in a movie she had seen.

Kissing the ring out of habit, Francesca made crushing motions with her hands, opening and closing them in rapid succession.

'Four, five, six, seven,' she counted, every time a skeleton was crushed into a bone-breaking ball.

Seeing that the competition was back on, Lucian swept his arm wide, cutting the creatures in half at the waist.

'They're not dead!' Francesca shouted, pointing toward the still crawling torsos. 'You're still only on three!' she scoffed, her eyes wide in victory at the lead she was taking.

'Fight!' Kristina screamed, clapping her hands together and then thrusting them out to unleash her attack.

Beyond the shield wall, hundreds of mini-explosions erupted all along the tree line, blasting the skeletons apart and causing their charge to falter.

Closing her eyes and feeding the magick beneath her into her craft, Kristina sent the explosions into their ranks with continued destruction.

Inspired by her mother's art, Francesca closed her eyes to create something new and equally as deadly.

Among the explosions of light, magickal horses began to appear, directing the explosions into the oncoming horde. The ghostly white creatures charged at the oncoming demons, chasing them down and destroying them with the shining single horns placed majestically upon their heads.

'Unicorns!' Kristina gasped, unable to resist the urge to clap her hands together excitedly.

'That one is called Uni!' Francesca informed her, pointing out the smallest among them.

In frustration at falling so far behind in the kill-count, Lucian hammered his fists down hard upon the draining board, causing the metal sheeting to flex and buckle under his impacts.

The skeletons that remained were hammered unceremoniously into the ground, shattering the bony demons into splintering, bloody shards.

Within the shield wall, the wolves paced back and forth in frustration, seeming beyond eager to join in on the fight.

Kristina could see that they were angry and guessed that they were acting against their own desires.

'Daire,' she thought, assuming that they held back at his instruction.

Having met two of them earlier and seeing how unruly these creatures could be, she wondered at their history with the legendary man and felt curious at the amount of loyalty they clearly had for him.

Peering out into the red haze of darkness, she sighed in relief when all was quiet once more.

It looked as though a low mist had formed but she knew from experience that it was the wispy ash that hung thick in the air, adding to her feeling of foreboding.

Thrusting her hands out, Francesca sent her unicorns further into the forest, their mystical spectral light illuminating the darkness between the trees.

Many more of the demons' decimated remains could be seen stretching out of sight, the forest taking much of the sting out of that first wave.

Not to be outdone, Lucian looked up to his golems and snapped his fingers, causing the sockets of their eyes to shine forth, covering the entire area with almost daylight clarity.

Francesca's head turned to him, her face flushing in annoyance.

'Didn't kill many though did they?' she remarked, looking disgustedly up at the gigantic figures.

'Six giant bats,' he replied, smiling back at her smugly before turning his attention back to the garden.

'I still killed more than you!' she replied, incensed by his condescending smile and further spurred on to win the next bout.

Before Lucian could respond, a high-pitched screeching pierced the night and they saw huge black shapes come flapping into view.

Without hesitation, Lucian ran for the stairs desiring to elevate his position for the next wave of attack.

'Come on!' Kristina screamed, dragging Francesca by the arm.

***

The battle was lost with only small pockets of resistance remaining on the battlefield.

Forced now to combine their powers, the wizards, druids and witches all battled together for the future of their world and their kind.

Surrounded by the demonic forces of the underworld, Daire could see how outnumbered they were as shame flooded through him at being so impudent, he felt he was the reason for this final defeat.

Still held by the scruff of the neck, the torn gateway loomed up before him as the shadowy figures at either side bristled at their approach.

Huge three-headed dogs, larger than a bear, rose slowly, glistening in the red light of the moon and baring their teeth in warning.

These appointed guardians of the dimensional tear stared at him with strangely weary eyes, looking almost confused as they looked to the one who held him.

The Reaper stood silently as though taunting his prey with what awaited him, then stretched out its arm to show the demonic dogs its prize.

The ring of power had completed its work but still he could not move and guessed that there was more to come before he would finally be free.

Closing his eyes in defeat, he knew his time had run out and felt unable to take his eyes from the flapping black void of the underworld.

The darkness and wildness of both demon and dragon were the last to return, both absorbing into him with little or no resistance.

Looking within himself, the gold of the goddess had been transformed into the cold glow of starlight and he felt his power there, though was unable to touch it.

There was no more conflict in him, just a quiet calm of being one with himself and one with what had been done to him.

'Why am I still like this?' the thought wailed in his mind as he wondered what else needed to be done.

The Reaper turned suddenly, showing him the end in one last and final torment.

He looked back to the field of destruction and witnessed the suffering, seeing the dark shadow of death clinging to faces he felt he should have known.

'Will there ever be an end to what should never have been?' he thought, regret heavy in his heart for his part in this sad end.

He heard roars of rage mixing with the screams of defiance, seeing the dwindling army of mankind fighting to the last.

'How noble our race can be,' he thought as tears of pride and regret ran down his blood-smeared face in tandem. 'I've brought them to this,' he choked, cloaked now in his self-damnation. 'How could we win this?' he thought to himself, witnessing the great acts of valour that would never now be told.

Black smoke swirled in the air, rising from the dead and from the ground of what had been his glade, now scorched and unrecognisable as the lush green of before faded into a memory.

'Would there be any to witness this valiant end?' he wondered, watching the scene as though in slow motion.

He saw Michael fighting a huge winged demon, a chopping motion of his hand sent the hapless creature crashing back to the earth.

He saw the druids' valiant stand, arcing the earth magick into the hateful horde and noticed John with his hair now white, heroically giving his life's energy to the final fight.

Tears came to his eyes at seeing Kim swallowed within a mass of black talons, brought down by the sheer force of numbers.

Charlie and Kevyn stood back-to-back with the rest of their faction laying still at their feet and a look in their faces that spoke a thousand words.

The glint of silver sparked suddenly atop the low mountain rise, catching his eye as he narrowed his eyes to call the image closer. As he watched, a line of dazzling silver crested the horizon, reflecting the light of the sun that was rising at their backs.

A horn sounded, a low and beautiful sound that rose higher like the hope swelling suddenly within him.

Emotion flooded up through his chest and flushed his face with instant recognition.

'The Fae!' he sobbed, his emotion too strong for him to get the words out properly.

Try as he might to send his awareness out, he could sense only the darkness and godly gold that seemed to surround him.

Screams too loud for humans to make suddenly sounded from the forest, causing him to turn his head back towards the battle.

From within the trees, an army charged forward with a speed that none but the Egni could achieve, now that the Bloods had been burned from the land.

All held swords of glowing red and he sobbed at what he thought was the meaning of it.

Red was his colour, the blood-red tone bestowed upon him by his father, and for them to be carrying that colour now meant only one thing. They were here to fight for him, with him, as it should always have been.

Thousands of vampires entered the field, driving the startled demons back from the battle-worn heroes, and from within the midst of red, three swords of gold, silver and black broke away to cut a deadly path towards him.

He heard his brother, Carl, scream in rage at the sight him so defeated and he closed his eyes, for it was too hard to witness.

He could feel their desperation and could even smell it in the air as though the emotion itself had a scent.

Opening his eyes again, he felt like he was being toyed with, feeling that he was given hope only for it to be ripped from him at the last moment.

He saw devastating white lightning shoot out from just behind the trio, clearing a path before his brothers' charge.

There was no stopping the power of the attack, the might of it turning all it touched into ash in an instant.

Seeking out the black-haired man, their eyes locked on to each other from across the battlefield.

'Dad?' he sobbed, knowing that the time he had was now borrowed and allowed only by the whim of the Reaper.

'Break their hold on you, my son!' Colin's iron mind replied to him sharply. 'There is a web upon you!' his mind screamed, while also sending a bolt through the chest of a giant black lion.

The demon crumpled without a sound, whatever life had existed ripped away in the instant.

Blinding light from atop the mountain caused him to squint suddenly, shielding his eyes at the sudden glare as the merciful sun finally showed its face.

A low moan erupted but not from any creature here present, it was a sound of one celestial body being dominated by another as the demon moon faded from existence.

Waiting for the sun to be at their backs, the silver-clad elven knights finally began their descent. The silvery horses on which they sat galloped down the grassy mountainside with a grace previously unseen, seeming to flow down the green hills like liquid mercury.

Something flashed upon the heads of the horses and all could see the single horns pointing up as though to heaven.

Unicorns as far as the eye could see were covering the distance with incredible speed, and as they came so too came death, for they were not as delicate as the mythical artistry had portrayed, these creatures were immense and just to look at them chilled the blood.

'A web?' Daire whispered, sensing no such power about him, just the blackness and his godly gold.

'Midnight is powerful indeed if he can hold me in this way from beyond the veil,' he thought, wondering why the demonic god had not acted against these new threats.

Search as he might, he could see no dark threads woven about him, only the blackness and his golden aura.

Suddenly, his eyes glared fiercely and his face began to tremble with the knowledge of what he had now become.

'I am no longer gold!' he seethed, causing the Reaper to nod silently in his direction.

Driving his will into the gold, he saw at last the light of the God's bindings upon him and noted its perfect precision, smothering him and keeping him weak.

At first, they had prevented the ring from renewing him and now they put their will on him to keep him from fighting.

Focusing on the intricate web, he saw the almost undetectable threads of gold. The tangle of strands was beautiful to behold, bound as they were with their godly art.

He saw that there were two shades of gold, interwoven and enhancing a third slightly brighter strand that lay bound tightly around him.

With all his heart, might and spirit he attacked the treacherous bindings, breaking first one strand and then the second. Finally, he sent his unrelenting will into the remaining thread, the main and, without a doubt, most powerful of the three.

For a long time, it held, with an immense resilience that he could not help but admire.

Finally, it snapped, causing the binding to fade from existence. With the web destroyed, he felt what he should have on the completion of *Caladfwlch's* work upon him.

He was now a demonic, elemental god with the wild blood of dragons pumping through his veins, but what governed him above all these was the free will of a man.

Rising slowly to his feet, the Reaper, he noted, was now gone and nowhere to be seen.

'Shame,' he thought, wondering what game this creature was playing.

Curiously, he watched the riders of light turn in his direction, their shining silver swords lowered to attack. Realising that they were bearing down upon him, he instinctively raised his hand to turn the attack aside and wondered at the reason they would turn their sights on him.

Sweeping his arm out before him, he batted them aside and winced as the unicorns screamed, for harming them was not his intent.

The Fae charge drove past and straight into the army of darkness, cutting a deadly, desperate swath through the demon horde and dividing it in two.

Colin cursed at having been halted by the charge of the elven riders, diving back as the monstrous unicorns thundered past.

In anger and frustration, he swiped his might out in a wide arc, sending his lightning out in a deadly half-circle of crackling light.

The demons dissolved before him, the raw power of the Egni Master's magick beyond anything they could take. He paused a moment from the expense of so much energy.

The gap that was created filled almost immediately as more of the creatures instantly took their place.

Seeing his father's exhaustion, Cristian threw up yet another shield which turned white almost immediately against the onrushing mass.

'Draw from the earth,' he shouted from over his shoulder as he hefted his silver sword in his hand.

Frowning at the suggestion, Colin knew that the old magick was forbidden to him, lost from his lust for immortality.

'Do it!' Cristian screamed, struggling to hold the barrier in place as his brothers lent him their strength.

Not merely the dangerous misshapen creatures of nightmare, the demons had their own dark magick that had proved too much for the might of mankind.

Arcing red lightning along with a sickly black smoke was sent out, breaking the shield with relative ease.

Taking a deep breath, Colin drove his awareness down, searching for the elusive green power that had been denied him for so long.

With eyes flaring open, a wild, ecstatic look washed across his face.

'I feel it,' he gasped, immediately drawing up what had previously been lost to him. 'I feel it!' he roared ecstatically, the natural magick washing through him and drawing tears from his eyes.

Keeping the link open, he sent his lightning out again to devastating effect, ripping the demons apart more easily than ever before.

Looking back, Cristian could see the rest of their faction break through the wall of darkness, their red swords now dripping black with underworld blood.

The large form of Geez staggered into view, his laboured breathing causing his slick dark-skinned chest to heave from exertion.

'We've just been killing skeletons!' he announced, bending over to catch his breath. 'I'm knackered!' he gasped, sucking in air while looking up at the sky.

'Hold the shield for Christ's sake, I'm bolloxed,' Lee gasped, dropping to his knees and lowering to all fours.

Cristian smiled, not caring to ask how or even why they were here, they were here and that is what mattered.

'Where's Warren?' he asked, gripping the black man's shoulder, but it was Lee who answered with a look of the unknown.

'I don't know,' he gasped, leaving the implications to speak for themselves. 'We lost track of him and the others ages ago,' he continued, sucking in great lungfuls of air.

Cristian nodded with a cold expression, having no further time to dwell on the matter.

Turning to his father and brothers he raised his head, asking with the gesture if they were ready to push on.

'I'm ready,' Colin answered, his dark eyes dancing with the untamed power of the earth, but at that very moment, a giant demonic bat smashed into the renewed shield from above, shattering it completely into leaf-sized pieces that faded into the sunrise.

***

Standing before the gateway, the demons on the other side halted, unwilling, it seemed, to cross while the god was there.

Daire was oblivious to them, however, his focus now on the dwindling army of darkness after the tide had finally turned.

With a shrug, he looked within himself and was unsure if he felt better or worse after the darker aspects had merged into place. He felt more emotional, to be sure, feeling hate again, along with his want to kill, but it was weaker than it had been and more like a desire than a real need.

With inhuman speed, he stepped to the side, narrowly avoiding a sword's tip thrust to his back. He turned then to look at the threat with loathing in his eyes.

'Diarmuid,' he whispered, stepping back as another vicious swing nearly took off his head. 'You have come to me at the worst possible time,' he continued, speaking the words in the deep tones of thunder.

'Time to finish what we started, peasant! I care not for the inopportune timing!' the demigod spat, spinning the sword into a different position.

Nodding slowly, the legend extended his arm as the long crimson blade grew out from his hand.

'You should have acted earlier,' Daire replied, smiling with ill-disguised delight.

The God-King's Fall

Looking at the Fury Sword held in his enemy's hand, knowledge came to him of its power and design. The blade was death to those it touched, gifted to the demigod by his father, Donn, the God of Death in one of the many dimensions, and a weapon used all too often as far as the new god was concerned.

Unwilling to test its enchantment upon himself, Daire put his might into his own weapon to even out the odds with a terrible creation of his own.

The Blood Sword darkened but still showed red as the blade began twisting at the tip, continuing its turn up towards the hilt.

'Tell your father that I come for him next,' the new god said, before sweeping the slowly twisting blade with speed at the demigod's head.

It was all Diarmuid could do to hold off the assault, unable to think and only react to the speed of the devastating attack.

Screaming in frustration, the warrior turned and ran to clear some distance before turning again to face his deadly foe.

'Would you like me to show you my back again?' Daire asked, laughing humourlessly before narrowing his eyes. 'Is this why you are here, to kill me with your fury?' he asked, pursing his lips in thought.

Without answering, the warrior jumped forward with an upward sweep of his sword and then spun on his heel expertly to drive the blade down, but the god was no longer there, having stepped to the side with an attack of his own.

A low, mournful groan issued from the blood-red blade, as though the sword itself had felt pleasure from the contact.

'Well, that was satisfying,' Daire confessed, lifting the sword for the other to see.

The demigod's blood appeared to be absorbed into its still twisting blade and began flowing up into the sword's fuller.

Nausea swept through the warrior and he staggered back with an accusing look in his eyes.

'Come now, I'd be dead already if the situation was reversed. How many have died by your hand from such a little cut?' Daire chided, remembering what Olivia had said upon their first encounter.

Her face flashed before his eyes and he felt a flush of warmth swell from inside him, his enhanced emotions giving him pause for a moment.

'Olivia,' he whispered, smiling at the image in his mind.

Taking advantage of his delay, Diarmuid launched another series of attacks, hurling his smaller Blade of Fury and following up with a cross-cut of his sword.

Ignoring the god's shield completely, the blade came on and passed through the air where his head had been only moments before.

Taken off guard momentarily, Daire ducked instinctively and felt the blade pass overhead as it barely missed him.

The attack continued as the blade darted again and almost made contact several times but for the unseen reflexes of the legend.

Slipping past yet another thrust of the deadly sword, Daire spun on his heel to elbow his enemy from his feet.

'Now you die!' the god raged, stepping over his adversary to finish it, but at that very moment, a blast of heat erupted from behind him as something colossal passed through the gateway.

A colossal flaming bird, larger than even a dragon, exploded from the void with a deafening cry of rage that pierced above all the other sounds as it soared higher into the morning sky.

Frowning as the phoenix departed, Daire wondered momentarily why it had not joined the battle and then shook his head to be back in the moment.

Stepping forward, he drove his rotating blade down, puncturing his enemy's stomach with such force as to pin him to the corrupted black earth.

Immediately, the blade began to moan again in what could only be described as ecstasy and began to vibrate maliciously as it drank in his enemy's essence.

'No!' Diarmuid screamed, trying desperately to pluck the hateful sword free, crying as it fed on him greedily.

'Yes!' Daire hissed, taking pride in his creation and watching intently as his enemy was absorbed. 'Whatever is left of you will return to your father, but you will be but a shadow of what you once were. Your power, what little there was, will now reside in my weapon, aiding me against worthier foes,' he explained, looking down at his enemy with absolute hate. 'Tell Donn that I come for him next for introducing you to this world and that I will do unto him what I have done unto you,' he continued, seeing the life ebb from the warrior's eyes.

Oblivious to all else, the god stared down at the dead warrior and then smiled coldly at his sated weapon.

Chapter Fifteen

The golden shield, now streaked with white, burned the demonic bats into sparkling embers like a firework display above the Disney castle.

It was clear to them all that these demons wanted the shield down and that they would pay any price to achieve this end.

No price was too high to get to those within, and they sacrificed themselves in the attempt to get through to them.

To this end, these flying monstrosities began bombarding the golden barrier with anything they could get a grip on, from huge boulders to small trees, and then themselves when nothing else was at hand.

The huge golems did their creator proud, catching many of the creatures mid-flight before crushing them within their unyielding palms and casting them aside.

As each attacking wave ended, their rocky heads would turn up to the heavens and their blazing eyes would sweep the sky like the searchlights during the 'blitz' of the Second World War.

Fighting all through the night, the children were exhausted and Kristina too felt the dizziness of fatigue hanging about her like a blanket that dulled her reactions.

Silently, she began to pray for the night to end, desperately hoping that the demons would withdraw with the approaching light as they did in the movies.

Sighing in relief at the early signs of dawn, she hugged her children and kissed them repeatedly but a low growl of warning caused her to halt her affections as the wolves alerted her to yet another attack.

'Will this never end?' she cried, hearing an ominous shriek like that of an eagle.

Pressing her face against the glass, she looked up to see what had made the sound and then threw herself back, grabbing for her children as she did so.

'Run!' she screamed, a new terror gripping hold of her as she dragged her children down the stairs.

The phoenix hit, punching a hole through the shield before continuing down into the house.

Thrown from their feet, they tumbled down to the hallway as the rest of her home followed.

With a tremendous explosion of noise, the demon crashed through the roof and ignited the entire first floor with its searing golden flame.

The debris from the upper level came crashing down the stairs, causing the mortar of the destroyed walls to cloud around them with its thick black dust.

Not stopping for a second, the three scrambled into the kitchen to flee from their home that had protected them for so long.

Once outside, they could see the fading remains of the golden shield, floating down around them, a beautiful and somewhat disturbing sight.

'No!' Kristina cried, feeling the loss of her house that had been her protector and safe haven.

The children screamed also, seeing the top half of the structure completely ablaze, the roof having been utterly destroyed upon impact.

'My god!' Kristina gasped, seeing something move within the rubble and her arms encircled her children protectively as she pulled them away.

As they backed away, the head of the phoenix lifted from out of the chaos, causing a part of the roof to slide off and crash to the ground with furious bouts of flame. More masonry slipped off the demon's torso as it heaved against the weight upon its back, appearing injured as it struggled to get upright.

Kristina found the size of the demon incredible, noting that it took up the entire first floor with its fiery mass.

It began screeching again, more angrily this time and shook its massive head as it tried to wriggle free.

The truth of what was happening dawned on Kristina suddenly, seeing finally that the creature was not injured at all but held by the dying grip of her ruined home.

'Fly, you fools!' the house cried, hissing out the words in a sorrowful tone as it restrained the demonic bird, seeming to hold onto the creature with its last ounce of strength.

Needing no further incentive, Kristina ran for the trees and dragged her children along with her, but Lucian resisted momentarily to point back in anger.

At his command, one of the stone giants lumbered over to the burning wreckage and reached inside to cut off the piercing screech with a savage twist of the neck.

***

Francesca felt dizzy, her exhaustion now complete as she fled through the forest. Tripping over herself, she fell into the undergrowth only to rise again robotically to look up into the eyes of a nightmare, its red eyes boring into her own and burning her soul with their hate.

The black lion had laid in wait at seeing them flee from the building and had hidden itself well with its unknown magick, patiently waiting for a chance to strike.

Scrambling backwards, Francesca cried out in terror as the lion pounced, its huge clawed pads landing at either side of her head.

The snarling pointed teeth dripped black saliva onto her face, causing her to scream all the louder at her inescapable predicament.

'No!' Kristina screamed, the shock of the attack freezing her in fear. 'Please?' she begged, dreading what was to come.

Lucian, however, had no such compulsion and threw up his arms to lift the creature.

Its claws raked at the air mere inches from Francesca's face, forcing her to turn her head to the side and shut her eyes tight.

Twisting in the air, the demon tried desperately to find purchase on the low-hanging branches, intent on escaping from the magickal hold.

'React!' Lucian bellowed, glaring at them both before dragging his sister clear.

On contact with the branches, the forest came alive at the demon's touch, whipping its limbs down around the struggling beast.

Huge bloodied wolves came bounding through the undergrowth, growling and snarling at each other for missing the threat.

'Back!' Lucian commanded, the annoyance at their mistake evident in his tone.

Turning at the tone, they looked at him curiously for a moment and then sniffed at the air as they cocked their heads in confused recognition.

The lion roared its fury at the boy and then hissed at him with its gaping black maw.

He hushed at the creature as if in answer and gestured with his hand to keep its mouth shut.

Immediately, the lion did exactly that, leaving it only to growl deeply through its chest.

'You truly are your father's son,' a voice said, causing Lucian to turn in recognition.

The wizard gasped, seeing the man's glowering expression where the boy's should have been.

'Blue!' Lucian greeted, the frown deepening suddenly across his young face. 'You took your bloody time, wizard!' he growled, admonishing him with a shake of his head.

David's eyes widened and he looked at the boy's mother in alarm. She looked lost, he realised, seeing her look back at him blankly.

Ignoring the boy's tone, he nodded seriously before striding forward.

'Stand back!' he ordered, struggling to regain his composure as he sent his fire at the demon.

It burned in silence, its hateful glare never leaving that of his own until it finally succumbed, burning at last into thick black dust.

Stooping down, David held his arms open to Francesca but she flinched away and stumbled behind her mother.

'What's wrong, Cesca? You look exhausted little one, come, I'll carry you,' he said, his brow furrowing in concern.

Silence greeted his words and he looked at her mother with an expression of confusion.

'She doesn't know you, Blue!' she stated, putting heavy emphasis on his name while reaching back to comfort her daughter.

The wizard's frown deepened with misunderstanding before reaching up to scratch his head in thought.

'Ahh,' he sighed, seeing that he was not recognised as he was and was only known to the child as the old man, Jack.

Taking a knee, he whispered into Kristina's midriff.

'It's me, Jack,' he coaxed, keeping his voice soft and reassuring. 'I've just grown younger,' he added, waiting patiently for her reply.

Very slowly, her tired eyes peeped out from behind her mother and she eyed him suspiciously as she studied him further.

'See? It's me! I've just grown younger, that's all, so that I'm stronger in the fight,' he continued, roughing up his hair with his hand. 'Like what you did for John, remember?' he asked, smiling at her tenderly.

She nodded tentatively and peeked out a little more.

'See? It is me. Don't I look better?' he asked, reaching out to wipe her tears away.

Shaking her head immediately, she looked at him up and down critically.

'I prefer you as Jack,' she whispered, stepping forward doubtfully.

'As do I, princess, as do I,' he admitted with a sad smile spreading on his face. 'But it's still me underneath,' he added, taking her into his arms.

***

The smoke rose high into the air, billowing out from above the distant trees and far beyond where the battle had taken place.

Like a pillar of stone, the god watched it and felt unable to tear his eyes away, knowing in his heart from what the smoke was rising.

'My babies!' his mind wailed, realising that his protection for them had at last failed. 'Until I lay in ruin,' he whispered, remembering the promise made by his house.

On hearing the explosion in the distance, Daire was immediately ripped back into the 'now' and felt all of the emotions that came with it.

He had been set apart since the ring's completion of him and had felt far removed from the feelings he now felt.

'If that's what it is to be a god, then I will have no part in it!' he swore, cursing life itself for not going to them sooner. 'I could have saved them!' he cried, but the thought had not occurred to him until it was too late.

He stared at the trees, dreading the confirmation to come and sent out his awareness in his desperation.

'Please!' he whispered, looking for signs of life within the forest.

The battle raged on before him with the screams of the dying sounding on both sides, but he cared not in that impossible moment.

Tears of loss filled his eyes and he screamed his anguish at seeing the wolves.

'They would never leave them if they lived,' he knew, unable to contain his grief.

Casting his weapon to the ground, he crouched down and wrapped his arms about his head in despair, crying for the lives of his children.

His mind was awash with what could have been, imagining that they had indeed survived and that all was well. He dreamed that they had escaped the fire and were found by his friend and that the wolves only preceded the children, clearing the forest of the demon filth before them.

'I definitely made them strong enough,' he knew, multiplying their abilities tenfold and more. 'Demons!' he raged, turning his anger to wrath. 'If they don't live, then no one shall!' he seethed, the blind response bursting forth from him.

Rising smoothly to his feet, he grew darker by the moment, his hate gripping hold from within and without.

'This world has betrayed me!' he cried, listing the deeds against him in his mind. His father's attack, his brother's betrayal, Olivia putting her will upon him and now leaving him to die! The witches! The Horned God and his web of deceit! Kristina! The open door and the trip to the forest! The coven! 'If not for her, none of this would have happened!' he raged, the rising hate twisting his face into an ugly expression.

The only ones who had remained true and who would have always been so were now dead! His reasons for living and for being his best were now dead! 'Dead!' he raged, welcoming the volcanic eruption inside.

***

The charge at the shield caused a large crack to form right up its front as a single-horned demon resembling a rhino backed up for yet another strike, lowering its head as it did so.

With a blinding flash, a bolt of searing light took it in the eye socket, dropping it immediately and causing its legs to writhe as though beginning its next attack.

Jumping forward and lost completely within his fear-induced rage, Carl cleaved his golden sword through several demons at once and then spun on the spot to deliver a second devastating attack.

More demons went down from his wide-sweeping blade, catching several of them at once and sending them to dissolve in the air before they would have landed on the ground.

Sliding on the slick, bloodied mud, Carl lost his footing and slipped to his back, the boot of his right foot flying off in the process.

Black and silver blades rose immediately in his defence, cutting and slashing at those seeking to take advantage of the mishap.

'Get up, you clown!' Cristian growled, severing the neck of what looked like an ork and spewing its rank green blood upon his fallen brother.

Out of nowhere, the dark form of the Reaper appeared and lashed out at the defending swordsmen.

Paul's sword darted forward but was batted away almost leisurely before he was gripped at the throat by the demon's other hand.

'Damn!' Cristian cursed and sent his lightning at the creature's midsection, driving it back with its victim still attached.

The Reaper went down, falling over Carl as he struggled to rise, sending all three into the gory green of the ork's blood.

The Reaper's long-fingered hand lashed out at Paul but he managed to roll free, straight into the mass of hate-filled demons.

Climbing to his knees, Carl stabbed up with his sword viciously, causing the Reaper to howl unexpectedly as it lifted off the ground.

Silver steel instantly blurred towards it in a mesmerising whirl of motion, hammering the black-robed creature backwards until it too was lost within the throng.

Blinding white light sizzled past Cristian's head, clearing a path to either side of him as his father stepped forward with an expression of rage.

Driving his power into the wall of demons before him, the 'wizard that was' cast the demons from where his son had disappeared.

Seeing the desired flash of white from within the hulking masses, the ancient high wizard spread his arms wide and sent out his magick to either side of where the shield had been.

Dark forms died as they were forced into a single file, the white light and the silver sword making short work of them in their confusion.

Finally regaining his feet, Carl coughed and sucked in a little of the sticky ork juice, causing him to gag as it trickled down his throat. Passing the point of no return, he did the only thing he could do and swallowed. Gagging again, he glared at the wall of demons before dropping his shield.

'Die!' he roared and launched himself forward, going back to work on the demons as though they had eaten his children.

Slashing his golden sword wide with both hands, the demons fell before him and as they did so, he looked for the boot that had deserted him.

Knowing that there was very little time to get to his brother, Cristian spun his blade and drove his enemies back from where his brother had been.

The demons died before the silver blur, dismembered with a cold precision that knew no pity or remorse.

It was not long before Cristian stood again at his brother's shield, for most of the demons had died at the Blade Master's hands.

Paul was in continuous motion, his perfected skill now a dance of death to those that sought his own.

The Night Sword had now become two, splitting apart into twin blades of destruction as the Reaper came for him again.

At the sight of the cowled figure, all the other demons had shrunk back in terror, and a ring had been formed for the deadliest fight to begin.

Cristian noted the fear in the other demons' eyes and realised that it was a thing apart, even from them, understanding that though it moved among them, it was clearly something else.

Unable to move from within the safety of his father's white might, the tall silver-clad warrior was forced to stop and watch as the Reaper darted forward with outstretched fingers that seemed to flex in anticipation of the kill.

The twin blades moaned at the creature's approach as though they desired the contact to come and the life they were soon to take, but instead of the expected retreat, the Blade Master stepped in to unleash the power of the black blade in a dazzling display of skill.

Having crafted each magickal sword to the respective son's personal specification, Colin had imbued each with one chosen ability of the wielder's choice, and though the swords had various enchantments placed within them, this dominantly chosen powerboat had been placed above them all.

The Night Sword had been designed to open things up, allowing nothing to stand against its touch. No shield or flesh could withstand the black blade's touch and the dreaded Reaper was no exception to that rule.

Screeching in agony at the third being to ever truly hurt it, the demonic thing backed away, but the howling blades had tasted its blood and eagerly desired more.

Taking first the demon's hands and then its elbows, the black blades continued their surgical dissection in such a way as to cause Cristian to remember Gilgamesh and what the red sword had done to him.

The Reaper's wail rose high into the air, drowning out the colossal din around them and causing all of the surrounding demons to falter.

Again, the blades cut flesh, decimating the creature that seemed to be feared above all others until, at last, the Reaper lay broken and smote upon the battlefield.

Turning to his elder brother with his blond hair now hanging loose, Paul nodded in acknowledgement of his deed.

'I killed me the Reaper!' he growled, widening his grin as he spun the blades at his sides.

'And took your damned time about it!' Cristian grumbled, shaking his head at his brother's smug expression.

Gripping him by the shoulder, he shook him gently as though to see if he was real.

'Let's finish it!' he growled, staring fiercely into his brother's pale green eyes.

With his trademark scowl setting back in place, Paul nodded his determination as he cast his eyes to the fleeing dark army.

***

The demons lay defeated, routed now by the Fae on one side and mankind on the other.

Though many of the demons still lived, the Reaper's demise had taken the sting out of them and they fought now for one thing only, to return to the darkness from whence they came.

Standing still amid the chaos, Daire stood staring across the battlefield towards the wolves. He wondered why they had not joined in on the fighting, knowing absolutely that they would want to, for it was in their nature to do such things.

'How do you live when they do not?' he thought darkly, knowing that the gift he had given them was more than sufficient to keep them safe.

Steeling his mind, he saw the demons fleeing his way and waited for them to come. He relished in the thought of what he was going to do to them, knowing that they would be running back again in a moment or two.

'Come to me,' he whispered and began to walk forward with impatience.

A gentle hand touched his shoulder, the contact catching him off guard and causing him to stop.

'My Daire,' Olivia whispered, slowly turning him to face her.

'Liv,' he gasped, searching her face. 'Where have you been?' he cried, unable to keep the hurt from his voice. 'You come now when it is too late!' he sobbed, feeling the heat leave him suddenly.

Stepping in, she kissed him desperately, wrapping her arms around him.

'I am so sorry,' she whispered, holding him to her. 'I was forbidden to act and only come to you now at the close,' she explained, stepping back so that she could look at him. 'Look,' she continued, pointing a finger at the end of the battle, the defeated demons still swarming towards them.

'It's over,' he replied in a broken voice, thinking only of the loss of his children.

Nodding her agreement, her eyes filled with tears suddenly.

'I know,' she sobbed, kissing him again. 'I love you,' she said, rubbing her nose against his.

'Love… is no longer enough,' he whispered, his tears of loss freezing white upon his face.

'I know this also,' she sobbed, stroking her hand across his cheek. 'Put your hate away, my Daire,' she whimpered, opening her hand as though to take it from him.

He looked at her, knowing only too well what she was asking of him.

'I have no desire to,' he admitted, shaking his head in refusal. 'This world will know the loss of my children and the gods themselves will weep at the retribution I will visit upon them, as I cry now,' he swore as fresh tears fell from his eyes. 'Even if I could agree to your request, the pain of losing them will unhinge me in the end,' he admitted sadly, surprising her with a soft kiss of his own.

The sounds of snarling and the gnashing of teeth came from the gateway suddenly, causing Daire to turn with a look of hate.

'Will they not stay away?' he asked, frowning up at the rift with an urge to enter and destroy all those within.

'They will,' she answered, turning his face to kiss him again before resting her forehead against his.

A sense of movement from within the trees caused him to turn, but her hand pressed hard against his face to keep his eyes on her.

'Do you trust me?' she asked, sobbing out the words as she affectionately stroked his cheek with her thumb.

'Yes,' he answered, holding her eyes with a look of defeat.

'Close your eyes,' she whispered, holding his face firmly in the palms of her hands.

For a moment only, he resisted her, but then seemed to sag as he closed his eyes compliantly.

Holding back her tears, she kissed him again, long and passionately.

'I love you, my Daire, and shall never love another for the rest of my existence,' she whispered before stepping back to drive the misshapen red sword all the way through him.

With eyes flaring open, he instinctively cast her away from him before reaching for the weapon that had impaled him.

Bringing her hands to her mouth, she seemed to look in shock at what she had done and slowly shook her head in disbelief.

He stood there looking down at the hilt and then back to her in disbelief.

'Liv?' he gasped, curling his hand around the weapon's hilt as he locked his eyes onto hers.

He saw her head shaking in misery and saw something else in her that seemed to be rising rapidly from within.

The gateway pulled at him suddenly, dragging him back several feet to the precipice of the void as it instantly reacted to the spilling of his blood.

Throwing out his arms to stop himself, he gripped at the very fabric of the world to stop him at its edge.

Glaring at her in disbelief, blood suddenly bubbled from his mouth as he shook his head at this unforeseen act of betrayal.

'What have you done?' he gasped, coughing up more blood as he searched her face for the answer.

In the distance, Elimon turned to disengage from the slaughter and reined in his mount with a look of despair.

'My Queen?' he called, leading an unridden unicorn for her to ride. 'Goddess?' he called again when she seemed not to have heard.

Still aghast and with her hands held to her mouth, a look of madness entered Olivia's eyes as she stared fiercely at what she had done.

'I love you,' she cried and then frowned as though she was unsure of the words.

'Olivia,' Daire choked, clenching his blood-stained teeth against the pain in his chest and the insistent pull of the underworld.

He could not comprehend why she, of all people, would turn on him at this juncture and felt the need to know after she had risked herself so many times in the past.

'What have you done?' he asked again, beginning to feel panicked by the increasing pull from behind. 'Why?' he screamed when she did not answer, the need to know burning within him. 'Why?' he growled, glaring now at the mounted knight.

'I do not know, my friend,' Elimon replied, tears of shame welling in his eyes. 'I am sorry,' he mouthed fearfully, looking at his Queen with a shake of his head.

Turning back to Olivia, Daire watched as her expression began to relax a little, seeing a coldness there that he had not seen before.

'Why?' he repeated, feeling the pull become stronger, and knowing that he could not break its hold unaided.

The goddess shook her head as though to clear it and looked at him as though seeing him for the very first time. With wide shocked eyes, she began screaming at his plight and pulled at her hair in a crazed kind of anguish.

'No!' she screamed, fighting some internal conflict before her features softened once again. 'Their lives before yours!' she sobbed, her features creasing at her remembered promise.

'None come before him!' she growled suddenly as though in answer to her own words and began striking herself as though punishing herself for what she had done. 'Weak pathetic fool! You don't deserve him!' she raged to herself, reaching out to him at last. 'We could have protected them from her!' she cried, striking herself again when her hand drew back.

'Your time in my world is at an end, Queen to the Fae! Now more than ever!' an ancient voice croaked as Olivia was dragged back by her hair.

'No! He's mine! Let me save him!' she cried, struggling with all her might to break the unyielding hold.

Rising from behind her, the old crone and goddess of this world yanked her head back viciously, before putting a long-nailed finger under her trembling chin.

'I put my will upon you fairy Queen, for here in my world, I am the stronger!' Morrigan crowed, looking down at her with utter contempt.

The eyes that glared back were a match for her own, as the venomous reply was hatefully spat.

'I will come and kill all you love! I will render this world to ashes if you take him from me! I will seek the end of you and all of your...' the mad torrent of promised vengeance ended abruptly, as the now silent Queen crumpled to the earth.

Dropping her to the floor like an undesired burden, the hag turned to the rider and motioned him to her.

'Time to leave, elven warrior, come and take your prize before leaving this place, for you are now banished from my world,' she said, eyeing the tall knight dangerously.

Jumping from his mount, Elimon gathered up his Queen and stood staring at the old goddess with fear in his eyes.

'Please goddess, can you do nothing for her? I beg you, do not cast her out like this!' he cried, looking down at the darkening hair of his queen.

Looking up without emotion, Morrigan cackled at the dread in his eyes.

'All things come to an end, Elimon, as all things are to begin. One can never live in the sunlight forever, for the darkness is but a memory away,' she replied, waving him away with an impatient gesture of her hand.

Riding away with his goddess in his arms, Elimon led his force from the field of battle and never once could bring himself to look upon the betrayed man.

Daire followed their progress in silence, watching her leave him to the most terrifying fate.

'What has become of my Olivia?' he thought, the one he loved and who had clearly felt the same for him.

'I am destined to be betrayed,' he thought in self-pity, feeling the bitter sting of tears in his eyes.

Still not knowing why she had done what she had, he saw her eyes open weakly to stare back in desperation.

'Nothing!' he screamed, seeing her head shake at the word and fight against the control that was placed upon her.

Unwilling to take his glaring eyes from her, he wanted her image to be the last thing he saw.

'Nothing!' he sobbed, as she slowly began to rise.

'No!' she moaned, knowing that between them it was either all or nothing and remembered what his promise had been if she were ever to betray him.

'Liv!' he screamed, seeing her struggle in the knight's arms, desperate it seemed to get back to him.

'I will find you!' she cried, fearful of his promise to disappear from her existence. 'I will find you and you will be mine! Mine!' she screamed, her voice fading along with her image.

The sadness within him was total and this latest betrayal his final straw.

'Time to die,' he whispered, seeing that the remnants of the horde were almost upon him.

'Why?' he gasped, looking to the old woman who now straightened up before him to become something different.

'You are the flame,' she replied simply and then shook her head sadly. 'Through you, the daemons are linked to this world and so you must fall, so that many may live,' she informed, taking little pleasure from the statement.

Daire barked out a laugh but there was little humour in it.

'You mean, the needs of the many outweigh the needs of the few?' he asked bitterly, thinking suddenly of his friend and the game they used to play. 'There was another way,' he added suddenly, but the goddess was gone, leaving him to his fate.

Feeling more alone than at any other time in his life, he looked down at his chest and the pommel of his sword, feeling the twisting of the blade almost complete now.

'How did it ever come to this?' he asked, looking finally to the trees one last time and seeing then what had been denied him.

Running from the forest with his wolves spread out before her was his beloved daughter, her hair in the sunlight unmistakable even from this distance and though he could not hear her words, he knew the name that was screamed from her lips.

At her side, the Blue Wizard stood with his colourful lightning arcing out at some hidden threat.

'My friend,' he whispered, sending out his words on the air.

The wizard reeled back as though struck by his call and shook his head before finally catching his eye.

Seeing the mortal danger his friend was in, David froze for a moment, staring back in open-mouthed horror.

'Don't let her see me die!' Daire thought, willing the words to his friend as his grasp began to fail.

Without hesitation, David caught the child up in his arms, but she had sensed the exchange and began to reach her arms out desperately to her father.

Looking back at his dying friend, David's face creased with pain at his failing of this final task and shook his head in apology with tears flowing from his eyes.

'I'm sorry, Daire,' he sobbed, holding his friend's child close as she screamed for her release.

The day had one more gift to give as Kristina came running from the trees. On seeing her daughter so distraught, she knew before looking that her father was lost.

Lucian began screaming at the sight of his father and threw back his head to howl his dismay before thrusting out his hands in defence.

The retreating demons exploded instantly, ripping apart into disgusting brick-sized chucks, reminding Kristina somehow of Lego, and in her shock, she wondered if that had indeed been what her son had envisioned.

She saw David sweeping up Lucian as he passed, trying to save them both the torture of what was surely to be.

Feeling the wind pick up as he passed, she heard the words that were sent along with it.

'I love you and will always be with you,' his whispered words breezed, following the children back into the trees.

Unable to move, Kristina stood rooted to the spot and looked past the devastation to the man who had, at one time, been everything to her.

'It's on you now,' he cried, a sound so lost that she could do nothing but cry.

'No!' Colin cried, looking beyond the retreating elven riders to the now visible gateway and his son who stood at its centre, arms spread out like the Christ's crucifixion.

Cristian ran ahead and slashed his sword at anything that came near.

'Hold on!' he bellowed, almost blurring across the field with his brothers at his heels.

With a cold realisation, Colin knew that they had arrived too late and began to cry at seeing the fear in his son's eyes.

'Daire,' he whispered, calling the attention of his youngest.

Their eyes met and held for a moment as they began their silent communication.

'Protect your grandchildren,' he heard, sensing the plea as their minds connected.

'Oh, Daire, I will,' he sobbed, reaching out his hand as though to touch him but knowing in his misery that he could not.

'Run!' Cristian heard his father cry, spurring him on even faster, for he was almost there and was going to save him, he believed, feeling a flush of exhilaration.

All was going to be as it was, his family reunited after all the ages of hate, he dreamed, holding his legendary brother's desperate stare and feeling himself willed on by the other.

Suddenly, Daire slipped and Cristian saw him shake his head in fear.

'Hold on!' he growled, leaping into a dive as his brother's hold failed.

The God-King's Fall

One hand let go, leaving Daire to dangle in the air as though he were hanging over a depthless black pit. He hung there for a moment, suspended over the vacuumous dark chasm as his grip began to fail.

Gritting his teeth in determination, Cristian threw out his arm to reach for his brother, but at that very moment he fell and caught a last agonising glimpse of his brother's despairing face, as the darkness pulled him away from him.

Looking down, he flinched in revulsion at the misshapen, twisted thing he now grasped in his hand, for what had once been the handguard of the red sword of power, now appeared to have flattened and spread outward, moving, it seemed, of its own volition.

He cast it from him instinctively, seeing that the Blood Sword of legend was now something grotesque as it followed his brother into the underworld.

The gateway loomed up before him but it appeared as though he were looking down into it somehow, and in his despair, he thought that maybe he was.

Stunned by his failure, an insane resolve possessed him. He would follow his brother into the underworld, here and now. He would lay down his life if need be, to recover his fallen brother, but as he launched himself forward, he was held from behind by those that wished him to live.

Locking their hands on him, his brothers hauled him back and pinned him down against his will.

'No!' he cried, fighting against them.

'He's gone!' Paul growled, though in a voice that shook with uncharacteristic emotion. 'He's dead. I won't let you join him!' he raged, placing a knee across his back to hold him down.

The gateway began to fade, the rip between dimensions healing now that the link had been severed.

Screaming at the sight, Cristian fought desperately to gain entry one last time but the gateway disappeared and only the blackened earth was a testament to it ever having been.

In the aftermath, the silence was total and was only broken when a pitiful howling sounded from within the trees.

The battle was over, the war truly won and the legendary Dark Wolf was now nothing more than a memory.

EPILOGUE

Black smoke blew slowly across the battlefield, the flames from the explosions having died out long before. Here and there, people could be seen walking among the dead to search for signs of life, crying finally at what they found.

Almost crippled with exhaustion, the mages came across the body of Kevyn. Looking unmarked and half-buried beneath a large black lion, he could have been alive but for the blackness of his eyes.

On seeing the state of his friend, Michael gave out a cry of anguish and rushed forward to fall to his knees, but the face stared up blankly, the normally brown eyes now black as the dilated pupils expanded in death.

Leaving him to mourn his friend, Charlie walked on and struggled to contain his agony as he silently wandered this field of desolation.

In the distance, looking battered and bruised, he saw Kim stumbling about aimlessly, stopping when she felt his eyes upon her.

Though having had their differences on more than one occasion, he smiled and shook his head at the wily mage, wondering how on earth she had managed to survive.

She nodded to him, and though they had succeeded in driving the darkness back, she had the look of defeat about her as she turned to wander on.

Knowing how she felt, he moved on and spotted the high priestess sitting with her back to him, cradling something in her arms.

Moving up behind her, he saw that she sat there rocking back and forth, whispering soothingly to the ancient-looking man in her arms. Her hands stroked tenderly through the white hair and though unrecognisable to Charlie, he knew this to be the druid.

Crouching down, he placed a hand on her shoulder, causing her to start in surprise as her head snapped up.

'He saved me, again!' she cried, the shock of what had happened showing madly in her eyes. 'He's such a brave man,' she said knowingly, clearly unhinged by her ordeal as she began rocking him again in her arms. 'My poor John,' she whispered soothingly, kissing him upon the forehead delicately and humming as though sending him to sleep.

At the contact, the old grey eyes flickered open, his laboured breathing rattling in his chest with the effort of this simple act.

Charlie smiled at the lovesick druid and shook his head at the once-charismatic man.

'I told you that she would be the end of you, Druid,' he said, shaking his head again. 'But not this day, my friend,' he promised, crouching down beside him. 'Maybe a little good could come out of this after all,' the mage thought sadly, sending his awareness in search of his snowflake.

***

The room was dark, lit only by the light of the thirteen candles that reflected warmly off the golden furnishings set about the room.

Witches chanted in the summoning of a god, a ritual that had been practised throughout the long ages.

'Horns of the forest, we beseech thee,' the priestess intoned, tilting her head back after closing her eyes.

'Horns of the forest,' the women repeated, holding their candles up high as though in worship. 'Bless our circle!' they finished.

Waiting with bated breaths, the room dropped in temperature as a darkness descended upon them suddenly, causing the priestess's breath to fog from her nose.

A soft tutting noise sounded as two white eyes appeared to regard them coldly.

'I can't express how happy I am that you called on me again,' a voice purred as the eyes narrowed in malice.

Looking about frantically, her dread causing goosebumps to spread over her skin, the priestess began to shake in her terror.

'You were warned,' the cold voice chided, sounding as icy as the eyes that bore into them.

'Oh, Queen of Air, we did not summon you! Please forgive us,' Jacky pleaded, throwing herself to the floor, her fear now total as she begged for mercy.

'Did not summon me?' the goddess asked mockingly, tutting again in mock disappointment. 'How embarrassing!' she added, before stepping into the flickering light.

At the sight of her, the priestess screamed, for instead of the flowing hair of the Queen of Air, there now appeared the horned blackened head of the Queen of Shadow.

'You really should be more specific in your wording,' the goddess advised, lowering her head with an evil grin to look from under her eyebrows.

'Please, forgive us!' Jacky cried, clasping her hands together in prayer as she grovelled at her feet.

'I think not!' the dark Queen hissed as the flames snuffed out.

Here ends
Book Two of Magick –
The God-King's Fall

Printed in Great Britain
by Amazon